PRAISE FOR DONNA GRANT'S BEST-SELLING ROMANCE NOVELS

"Grant's ability to quickly convey complicated backstory makes this jam-packed love story accessible even to new or periodic readers." - *Publisher's Weekly*

"Donna Grant has given the paranormal genre a burst of fresh air…" – *San Francisco Book Review*

"The premise is dramatic and heartbreaking; the characters are colorful and engaging; the romance is spirited and seductive." – *The Reading Cafe*

"The central romance, fueled by a hostage drama, plays out in glorious detail against a backdrop of multiple ongoing issues in the "Dark Kings" books. This seemingly penultimate installment creates a nice segue to a climactic end." – *Library Journal*

"…intense romance amid the growing war between the Dragons and the Dark Fae is scorching hot." – *Booklist*

Dragon Night ~ Dragonfire ~ Dragon Claimed
Ignite ~ Fever ~ Dragon Lost ~ Flame ~ Inferno
A Dragon's Tale (Whisky and Wishes: *A Holiday Novella*,
Heart of Gold: *A Valentine's Novella*, & Of Fire and Flame)
My Fiery Valentine ~ The Dragon King Coloring Book
Dragon King Special Edition Character Coloring Book: Rhi

DARK WARRIORS SERIES

Midnight's Master ~ Midnight's Lover ~ Midnight's Seduction
Midnight's Warrior ~ Midnight's Kiss ~ Midnight's Captive
Midnight's Temptation ~ Midnight's Promise
Midnight's Surrender ~ A Warrior for Christmas

CHIASSON SERIES

Wild Fever ~ Wild Dream ~ Wild Need
Wild Flame ~ Wild Rapture

LARUE SERIES

Moon Kissed ~ Moon Thrall ~ Moon Struck ~ Moon Bound

WICKED TREASURES

Seized by Passion ~ Enticed by Ecstasy ~ Captured by Desire
Books 1-3: Wicked Treasures Box Set

HISTORICAL PARANORMAL

THE KINDRED SERIES

Everkin ~ Eversong ~ Everwylde ~ Everbound
Evernight ~ Everspell

KINDRED: THE FATED SERIES

Rage ~ Ruin ~ Reign

DARK SWORD SERIES

Dangerous Highlander ~ Forbidden Highlander
Wicked Highlander ~ Untamed Highlander
Shadow Highlander ~ Darkest Highlander

ROGUES OF SCOTLAND SERIES

The Craving ~ The Hunger ~ The Tempted ~ The Seduced
Books 1-4: Rogues of Scotland Box Set

THE SHIELDS SERIES

A Dark Guardian ~ A Kind of Magic ~ A Dark Seduction
A Forbidden Temptation ~ A Warrior's Heart
Mystic Trinity (a series connecting novel)

DRUIDS GLEN SERIES

Highland Mist ~ Highland Nights ~ Highland Dawn
Highland Fires ~ Highland Magic
Mystic Trinity (a series connecting novel)

SISTERS OF MAGIC TRILOGY

Shadow Magic ~ Echoes of Magic ~ Dangerous Magic
Books 1-3: Sisters of Magic Box Set

THE ROYAL CHRONICLES NOVELLA SERIES

Prince of Desire ~ Prince of Seduction
Prince of Love ~ Prince of Passion
Books 1-4: The Royal Chronicles Box Set
Mystic Trinity (a series connecting novel)

DARK BEGINNINGS: A FIRST IN SERIES BOXSET

Chiasson Series, Book 1: Wild Fever
LaRue Series, Book 1: Moon Kissed
The Royal Chronicles Series, Book 1: Prince of Desire

MILITARY ROMANCE / ROMANTIC SUSPENSE

SONS OF TEXAS SERIES

The Hero ~ The Protector ~ The Legend
The Defender ~ The Guardian

<u>**COWBOY / CONTEMPORARY**</u>

HEART OF TEXAS SERIES
The Christmas Cowboy Hero ~ Cowboy, Cross My Heart
My Favorite Cowboy ~ A Cowboy Like You
Looking for a Cowboy ~ A Cowboy Kind of Love

<u>**STAND ALONE BOOKS**</u>
That Cowboy of Mine
Home for a Cowboy Christmas
Mutual Desire
Forever Mine
Savage Moon

**Check out Donna Grant's Online Store at
www.DonnaGrant.com/shop
for autographed books, character
themed goodies, and more!**

SHOULDER THE SKYE
© 2023 by DL Grant, LLC
Cover Design © 20223 by Charity Hendry Designs
Formatting © 20232 by Charity Hendry Designs
ISBN 13: 978-1-958353-06-6
Available in ebook, print, and audio.
All rights reserved.

Sneak Peek at **HEART OF GLASS**
© 2023 by DL Grant, LLC
Cover Design © 20223 by Charity Hendry Designs

Glimpse of **DRAGON ARISEN**
© 2023 by DL Grant, LLC
Cover Design © 20223 by Charity Hendry Designs

www.DonnaGrant.com
www.MotherofDragonsBooks.com

SHOULDER THE SKYE

SKYE DRUIDS

two

NEW YORK TIMES & *USA TODAY* BESTSELLING AUTHOR

DONNA GRANT

DEAR READER

If you ever feel in need of help, remember there are resources available all day, every day.

<u>The National Suicide Prevention Lifeline</u>

The National Suicide Prevention Lifeline provides free and confidential emotional support to people in suicidal crisis or emotional distress.

Telephone: **1-800-273-8255**

Text or call: **988**

For Deaf & Hard of Hearing: **1-800-799-4889**

Online chat: **suicidepreventionlifeline.org**

You are not alone.

Trigger Warning: This book contains references to suicide.

CHAPTER ONE

Isle of Skye

It was a joke.

Or a nightmare.

That was the only conclusion Elias could come up with as he stared at the two couples before him. His sister's light blue eyes held a note of misery. Beside Elodie was Scott, the man who had helped her when he hadn't been there. Scott's face was as impassive as his assessment was cool, his arms crossed over his chest as he met Elias's gaze.

Next to Scott was Rhona, the leader of the Skye Druids. Concern lined her face, but her green eyes held a fierceness that only someone of her position could have. On Rhona's other side was the imposing figure of Balladyn. He wasn't just Rhona's lover and Warden of the isle, he had also once been a legendary Light Fae turned Dark before becoming *King* of the Dark. Now, he was a Reaper.

"Tell me it isn't true," Elodie begged Elias. "Tell me George is wrong about you being a murderer."

Georgina Miller, also known as *George*. Just hearing the name made Elias want to punch something. Hard. He fisted his hands in an effort to control the surge of anger that bubbled up within him. Balladyn's red eyes lowered to Elias's hands before the Reaper quirked a black brow.

The fury that clogged Elias's throat was so thick that it took him two tries before he could answer. "Of course, George is wrong. How could you even think that I was the one killing Druids?"

"George said—" Scott began.

"I doona give a flying fuck what she says!" Elias shouted. He closed his eyes and sucked in a breath, hating that he'd lost control. The outburst brought back memories of his youth and the father he wished he could forget. Elias didn't open his eyes until he had his anger tightly leashed once more. Then he looked at each of the four before him. "George is wrong."

Elodie smiled, though it looked forced. "I knew it wasn't you."

"I'm no' saying George is never wrong, but she's a seer," Scott said.

Rhona held up a hand to quiet everyone. "I've yet to talk to George myself. I'll listen to what she has to say, but I'll also do my own investigating. Seers are a rarity in the Druid community, but that doesn't mean they aren't infallible or see the entire picture."

While it wasn't an acquittal, it was all Elias would get for the moment. He felt Balladyn's penetrating gaze and looked into his red eyes. The Reaper could use glamour to hide the eye and hair coloring that signaled him as a Dark Fae, but he didn't. And Elias respected him for that. He'd had few run-ins with the Light and even fewer with the Dark. He tended to steer clear of the Fae as a whole, which was harder than it sounded since they could blend in and walk among humans so easily.

"It's going to be okay."

Elias looked down at his sister, who had moved closer to him. She squeezed his arm as their gazes met. He'd returned to Skye for her, but in the end, she hadn't needed him. Their family was so fucked up that he didn't like to think about it, but it seemed that things were finally beginning to turn around for them.

Elodie had her magic once more, and she knew the truth of how she had saved their mother, sister, and both of them from their father. Her actions—and the resulting panic attack—however, had ended in their mum erasing Elodie's memories and binding her magic while also taking the blame for Edward MacLean's death. Elias had left Skye soon after so he wouldn't inadvertently say something that reversed his mother's magic and brought all the heartache back to Elodie.

But that meant leaving his sisters and his home behind for fifteen years—long years he had spent trying to outrun the past.

Now, Elias was back on Skye, Elodie's memories had returned, and their mother, Emily, was set to be released from prison soon. The only one blessedly ignorant of everything was Edie. She was the only MacLean who had a normal life, and he was grateful for that. She had remained on Skye, gotten married, and now had two beautiful children. If anything proved that he and his mum had done the right thing the day his father died, it was seeing Edie and her family flourish.

Scott came up behind Elodie and nodded at Elias. "You're right. George hasna given us any proof of you being a killer. I shouldna have accused you. I'm sorry."

"Doona worry about it. You trust her. I would've done the same in your shoes." It was a lie. Elias had learned long ago not to accept someone's word—no matter how much he trusted them. He always verified things for himself.

"Then I guess we'll see you at home later?" Elodie asked, her gaze searching his.

Elias glanced at Rhona and Balladyn. The couple had more to say to him, which was fine since he wanted to get it out of the way. He nodded at his sister, and she shot him a wide smile before she and Scott filed out of Rhona's cottage.

When the door shut behind them, Elias turned his head to Rhona. For as long as anyone could remember, Corann had led the Skye Druids. There were no pictures of him, but if you asked the eldest of the community, they would say that he'd looked ancient, even when they were young. But his actual age was anyone's guess.

Corann had died defeating the Others—a group of Light and Dark Fae and *mie* and *drough* Druids from this realm and another—and had chosen Rhona as his replacement. Even in his time away, Elias had kept tabs on the happenings on Skye. He knew the respect Rhona had earned before stepping into Corann's role. But her actions with the Reapers and her connection to the magic through Balladyn set her apart from anyone on Skye—or on the planet.

Rhona might still be finding her way, but she had the wisdom of someone much older than her young years.

Obviously, Corann had seen that, as well. She was a good choice as leader—especially in such turbulent times.

Because not only Druids were being murdered. There was a malevolent force on Skye. Someone was controlling the mist that had attacked Elias, though whether it was the same person killing the Druids had yet to be revealed. Then there were the Druid Others, based on the original group who had tried to take over their world.

Elias blinked and found Balladyn standing before him. The Reaper quirked a black brow again and held something out to him. Elias looked down to find a tumbler filled with amber liquid.

"Thought you could use this," the Reaper said in his Irish accent.

"Thanks." Elias lifted the glass and inhaled the scent of whisky. He brought it to his lips and savored the flavor as it touched his tongue and slid smoothly down his throat. Dreagan whisky, made by the Dragon Kings, an immortal group of ancient beings who could shapeshift into humans. He'd met one recently, and it had been as awe-inspiring as he'd thought it would be.

Rhona turned and walked to the sofa. Sitting, she motioned Elias to the chair. "Have a seat."

Elias knew it wasn't exactly an order. He could leave. He hadn't lived on Skye in years but he *was* from the isle. That meant he would always be considered a Skye Druid. He made his way to the chair and lowered himself into it. Balladyn moved to the opposite side of the room, crossing his arms over his chest and leaning a shoulder against the wall, the Reaper's red gaze never leaving him. Elias listened to the rain pinging against the windows as he anticipated the inevitable questions. He didn't have to wait long.

"Why would George accuse you of the murders?" Rhona asked as she tucked a strand of red hair behind her ear.

Elias shrugged and finished the whisky. "I doona have a clue."

"Have you ever met her?" Balladyn queried.

Elias shook his head, suddenly feeling weary to his bones. "Never. But I know of her."

That got Rhona's attention. "How?"

"You can discover a lot by asking the right people."

There was a hint of a smile on Balladyn's lips. "And that's what you did?"

"Aye. It isna some great gift. It's just taking the time to study an area and the people within it. It doesna take long before you begin finding those who like to talk." Elias turned the empty tumbler around in his fingers. "There are always those who say more than they should."

Rhona nodded. "True. What did you find out about George?"

Elias thought about that for a moment. He didn't know Rhona or Balladyn. He didn't know George either. Most people in his position would attempt to make George out to be corrupt or guilty in an effort to get others on their side. It might work for a short while, but it rarely lasted in the long run.

Despite his anger at George for her accusation, Elias decided to be candid. "She works hard to find Druids in Edinburgh and bring them into her organization. She's well-liked."

"Not by you, though," Rhona pointed out.

Balladyn grunted. "And given the anger in your voice, it goes much further than her recent accusation."

Elias ran a hand down his face. He sat the tumbler on the table beside him and leaned forward to rest his forearms on his thighs. "Nay, I doona like her."

"Why?" Rhona pressed.

Elias looked at the floor for a heartbeat before meeting Rhona's gaze. "Call it a hunch."

"I'm going to need more than that."

"I've traveled all over the world, met a lot of people, and I've seen many just like her." Elias paused, trying to put his thoughts into words. "I doona have specifics, exactly."

Balladyn pushed away from the wall and dropped his arms to his sides. "Something's bothering you. What is it?"

"She's never wrong. In everything she's seen through her visions, she's never wrong."

Rhona's brows drew together in a frown. "That's not normal. I don't care how powerful a seer is, no one gets everything right."

"Precisely. She's wrong about me," Elias stated. This time, he let his fury come through. "I willna say I've no' killed, but it was always in self-defense."

Balladyn stalked closer with his eyes narrowed. "Oh?"

Fuck. Elias had said too much. He shouldn't have let his anger get the best of him. But to be called a murderer? To be blamed for the killings he was actively trying to solve? It was too much.

"Elias," Rhona pressed.

He looked from her to Balladyn. There was no way he would get out of here without telling them something. Besides, they'd find out soon enough anyway. Probably from him. "I've been tracking the murders."

"What? How?" Rhona asked as she scooted to the edge of the couch cushion, curiosity and interest propelling her. "There are murders everywhere, every day. How do you know someone is a Druid?"

Elias slowly sat back. "It's the *type* of killings."

"The mist that attacked here," Balladyn said. "Is that happening in other places?"

Elias shook his head. "No' exactly. But there *are* things like that. Things out of place. Unexplained murders and such. No' to mention the notes that say *bàs ort,* death to you."

"Where?" Rhona asked in a soft voice.

Elias released a breath. "Everywhere we look."

"We?" Balladyn asked.

Elias shrugged, hoping to deflect. "A slip of the tongue."

"I doubt that." Rhona's green gaze held his, daring him to lie. "An operation this big would take others."

Well, fuck. Elias wished he could take back the words, but he couldn't. He flattened his lips and nodded.

"How many of you are there?" Rhona pressed.

Elias shoved to his feet. "I've said more than I should've already."

"It looks suspicious when a group wants to remain a secret," Balladyn stated.

Elias slid his gaze to him. "The Reapers remained secret for how long?"

"That isn't the same."

"Is it no'?" Elias argued.

Rhona rose and stepped between them, her eyes on Elias. "You've made your point. We may not know each other well, but my goal is to protect the Druids on Skye."

"And mine is to protect *all* Druids. I respect your position, and I ask that you give me the same courtesy," Elias replied.

Tension radiated from Balladyn. "She's not been accused of murder."

"Stop," Rhona told Balladyn. Her long, red hair swung behind her as she turned back to Elias. "One way or another, we're getting to the bottom of this. Work with me. And just so you know, I'm going to ask the same of George."

Elias wasn't surprised. It was the same move Corann would've made. No doubt the old Druid would've been proud of Rhona. It was a smart decision. Unfortunately, it wasn't one he agreed with. "I can no' work with George."

"Rhona's not asking that of you. She is asking you to work with *her*," Balladyn corrected.

Elias studied the Druid leader for a long minute. "In the short time I've been back home, I've seen the lengths you'll go to in order to protect the Druid community. Corann made a good choice with you."

"Wait, Elias," Rhona called.

But he ignored her as he strode from the house. Elias half-expected Balladyn to teleport him back inside, but no one stopped him as he walked through the rain and got into the rental car. He waited until he was a few miles from the cottage before pulling over and putting the vehicle in park.

"Fucking hell!" he yelled as he slammed his hands against the steering wheel.

Elias gripped the leather so tightly that his knuckles turned white. There was a reason George had pointed the finger at him. And he was going to find out what that was.

CHAPTER TWO

Bronwyn hated when she had to make a trip into town. She parked and shut off the old SUV's engine but didn't get out, she just watched the rain pelting the windshield until it completely distorted the outside world.

She felt like the glass. Bombarded. Flooded. Engulfed. She stared at the building before her—the only place within miles to get grocery items. It also doubled as a post office. The co-op stocked a little of everything.

Bronwyn drew in a deep breath and steeled herself. Maybe she'd get lucky, and not many people would be inside. The longer she waited, the more she tried to talk herself into coming back another time.

"For fuck's sake. I'm an adult," she mumbled and shoved open the vehicle door.

It creaked loudly, metal rubbing against metal. As soon as she stepped out, the rain drenched her. Bronwyn pulled up her raincoat's hood and slammed the door closed. She walked toward the store, her wellies splashing in the puddles.

A small bell chimed when she entered the co-op. Almost immediately, her gaze landed on four people toward the back. They didn't look her way, but they didn't need to for her to recognize them. Her fight or flight response wavered as she contemplated leaving until the sound of the cash register drawer closing drew her attention. Bronwyn's gaze met the pale green eyes of the cashier, Kirsi.

They had never been enemies, but Bronwyn wouldn't call her a friend either. Kirsi thanked the customers who had just paid, but her eyes never left Bronwyn. There was no way Bronwyn would leave now. She shoved back the hood of her coat, lifted her chin, and grabbed a basket as she started down the aisle.

Pulling out her mobile phone, she opened it to the list. Coming into town for necessities always made for the worst days for Bronwyn. Today, she was determined to buy enough that she wouldn't have to return for at least a month. It made her contemplate getting deliveries again, but that meant spending more, and she was stretching money as far as she could at the moment as it was.

The only way to make things better would be to disappear altogether. Unfortunately, that wasn't an option. Well, it *was*, but she couldn't do that quite yet. So, that left her in her current predicament: the despised errand day.

It wasn't as if she particularly liked food. Honestly, she'd be fine not eating if that were an option. Sadly, it wasn't. Food kept her alive. Nothing more. Nothing less. She didn't understand people who called themselves *foodies*. What even was that? And she certainly didn't understand those who loved to cook.

Bronwyn gathered the items she needed and moved to the next aisle, inwardly berating herself for not paying closer attention. She'd ended up in the aisle with the group she'd seen when she first entered, and there was no escape now either because Sarah, the leader of the pack, had caught sight of her.

"Well, well, well," Sarah said as she put back the can she'd been looking at. "What do we have here?"

"A drowned rat," Lizzie said with a snooty laugh.

Sarah grinned, her malicious intent clear. "A drowned rat, indeed. Bronwyn, you look worse for wear. I mean, that hair. Really?"

Bronwyn felt her wet hair sticking to the sides of her damp face. She fought the urge to reach up and shove it away. Sarah was a bully and had been since they were children. Sadly, she hadn't grown out of it in the years since—nor had the others who ran around with her.

Bronwyn generally ignored their snippy comments. Usually, people left her alone for the most part because they were afraid of her. While Bronwyn hated that people crossed the street to get away from her, she could do without Sarah. Maybe it was time to put a little fear in her old frenemy.

The bell over the door dinged as someone entered the building. Bronwyn kept her gaze on Sarah as she closed the distance between them. The trepidation that flashed on Sarah's face almost made Bronwyn smile—that was always the case when someone stood up to a bully.

"You have something to say about my hair?" Bronwyn asked in a soft voice.

Sarah swallowed nervously and tried to back up, but the shelves and her friends blocked her way. "It's…it's wet."

"Very perceptive." Bronwyn looked her over slowly. "Perhaps I should say something about you. I know just the words."

"No need."

The fear that rolled off Sarah was palpable. Bronwyn held Sarah's gaze as she muttered something unintelligible and walked away. Bronwyn blew out a breath, only to discover other customers staring at her. As soon as she met their gazes, they hurriedly looked away, partly in fear and partly in disgust.

All but one person.

The man stood in the next aisle, watching her over the short shelves. He shoved his wet, dark blond hair away from his face, though a thick lock fell back over his forehead. His bright blue eyes held her entranced, utterly enthralled. It felt as if he saw through all her defenses and straight to her soul—laying all her secrets bare.

He didn't stare at her with contempt or quickly lower his gaze, hoping she didn't notice him. No, he *looked* at her. Unable to help herself, she studied him, noting the handsome face and square jaw dusted with a shadow of a beard that made him even more appealing. His eyes crinkled at the corners, and she realized that his lips had curved into a smile. That was when she noticed his mouth. Surely, a man shouldn't have such full lips—lips that made her think of his mouth against hers and slow, wet kisses.

Deep, scorching, *hungry* kisses.

Her heart pounded, her breaths came faster, harsher, and her blood heated. This was desire. Sizzling, brazen, beautiful desire.

It had been so long since she had experienced it. The dull memories of the past couldn't compare to the spine-tingling intensity that found her now. She pulled her attention from his mouth and found herself caught by his gaze again. It was a mistake, but even as she realized it, she couldn't stop herself from drowning in the incredible blue shade.

Time paused. The world ceased. It was only her.

And him.

The spell broke when someone bumped into him, causing him to look away. That allowed Bronwyn the opportunity to pull herself together. She hurried to finish her shopping in record time, refusing to let herself look for him, no matter how much she wanted to.

She was so intent on her list and ignoring the man who had made her forget, well, everything, that she forgot who else was in the store.

"I can't believe you let her in here, Kirsi."

"She shouldn't be on Skye at all."

"There's no place for her around decent folks."

Bronwyn instantly drew up short at the sound of the voices. Anger and embarrassment replaced the desire, causing her to shake. She felt the other customers' eyes on her, their gazes accusing, probing. Sarah and her minions made sure to speak loudly enough for everyone in the small shop to hear.

There had been a time when Bronwyn would've gladly shown them exactly what they had to be afraid of, but she didn't give in to that now. It would only make things worse. The only thing she could do was prove to everyone that their words didn't wound her. She'd wait until she got home to cry.

Bronwyn got the last item on her list and made her way to the counter. Kirsi finished ringing up Sarah, and Bronwyn set her basket down, holding Kirsi's gaze and waiting to see what she would do. When the woman began ringing up the items, Sarah huffed.

"You can't be serious, Kirsi," Sarah all but shouted. "Send her out."

Bronwyn didn't give Kirsi a chance to answer. She turned to Sarah and said in an even tone, "If you have a problem with me, we can settle it outside. Now."

"I wouldn't lower myself to that," Sarah stated nastily as if picking shite off her shoe.

Bronwyn stood calmly, even when she felt something dark and nefarious coil within her. It would be so easy to strike out and retaliate for such ghastly behavior. Somehow, she kept herself in check. "Then I suggest you leave so the others can shop in peace. And if you can't, then go to Rhona about your issue with me."

After several tense moments, Sarah stormed out with her crew. Bronwyn turned back to Kirsi and handed her some money, then grabbed the bags and left, all with the store so silent you could hear a pin drop.

She didn't put up the hood of her rain jacket as she made her way to the vehicle. Adrenaline raced through her, making her tremble as she hastily glanced around to see if Sarah or any of her gang waited for her. It was such a silly thought. Something school kids would do. But, sometimes, people didn't grow up. And Sarah certainly fit into that category.

Bronwyn shoved the bag into the boot of the SUV and closed the hatch, taking a moment to look around. The rain had yet to let up as it pelted her and ran between her jacket and jumper. She didn't see anyone. No doubt what'd happened would get back to Rhona. Which meant Bronwyn could expect a visit from the Druid leader.

"Just great," she mumbled.

Sarah was right. Bronwyn didn't belong on Skye. Though, did she really belong anywhere? The only place she felt safe was at her house, so that was where she would stay until she took care of her current problem. Hopefully, that would be soon. Until then, she would wait.

Bronwyn walked around to the driver's side and unlocked the vehicle. She was prepared for the slight sticking of the door, but it was just another agitation in an already shite day. Inside, she buckled the seat belt and started the engine. Glancing up, her gaze landed on the co-op's window, and the entire debacle replayed in her mind. Her eyes burned with unshed tears. The Druids of Skye had caused her enough pain. She wouldn't give them the satisfaction of showing them how much they could cut her to the quick.

Bronwyn put the SUV in reverse and backed out of the space. The wipers shuddered across the glass, managing to clear away most of the water. She put the vehicle in drive and looked up in time to see the sexy man exiting the building. Even from a distance, she saw his blue eyes directed at her.

It caused her stomach to flip unexpectedly as she recalled how it had felt to be caught in his gaze. It had been so long since anyone had looked at her with anything but hatred, fear, or revulsion. She'd wanted to linger and bask in his attention. But that wouldn't have been fair to whoever the man was. Something about him seemed familiar, but it was probably only her imagination. No doubt he was a tourist. She'd never see him again. Therefore, there was no use lingering over him.

Or the feelings he roused.

CHAPTER THREE

Elias watched the woman drive away. He'd gone after her to…
well, he wasn't sure what he'd wanted to do. It wasn't as if he
could do what he desired—kiss her. Even now, his balls tightened
as he recalled the instant their eyes met. It'd felt as if lightning
had struck him.

A frown suddenly formed as he thought about how badly she
had been treated in the store. He waited until the woman with
the most beautiful hazel eyes he'd ever seen drove out of sight,
then returned to the co-op. By the time he reached the register,
only one other person was shopping, the elderly gentleman
seeming preoccupied with picking out the perfect toilet paper.

"Can I help you with anything?" the woman behind the
counter asked.

She had a pretty smile. Her pale brown locks were tinted
with red, and he bet she would appear more of a redhead in the
sunlight.

Elias scratched the side of his nose as he leaned over the counter so he wouldn't be overheard. "The woman that just drove off—"

"Bronwyn," the cashier said with a nod, her smile gone, her eyes guarded. "What about her?"

"Why was she treated so?"

The cashier glanced down nervously. "Just local stuff."

"How do you know I'm no' local?"

"If you were, you'd know about her," she said, her lips easing into another smile.

"Verra true," he said with a nod, easing his lips into another grin. "Forgive my nosiness. It's been some time since I've witnessed adults acting so…"

"Childish?" she offered. "Aye. I'd like to say it's not a common thing with Sarah and her followers, but it is. You'd think they would've outgrown it. It's been some time since we were in school."

He straightened. "I understand the type. Have a good day."

"You, too."

Elias walked out into the rain. Out of habit, he scanned the area, looking for anything or anyone that appeared out of place. He climbed into his rental car since his vehicle was lying at the bottom of the Minch. The Atlantic channel's depth and rapid current had made it impossible to retrieve it. Not that he'd wanted to. The mist that had slammed into him with the intention of ending his life had ensured not much remained of his SUV.

Water dripped from his hair, running down his neck and beneath his clothes to his skin, sending chills racing over him. Elias shivered and cranked up the heat after starting the engine.

He pulled out of the carpark and drove the winding roads to the small cottage tucked in a quiet cove. The property belonged to Edie and her husband, Trevor, who had several rental houses on the island. Thankfully, one had been available for him to use.

Elias didn't see the beauty that was Skye as he drove. The island was still awe-inspiring, even with the gray clouds hanging low and the rain falling. But it had lost its luster for him a long time ago. He understood why Druids were drawn to the isle and didn't even blame the tourists who flocked here to witness its breathtaking charm.

But he saw none of the appeal. He might have been born here, but Skye held nothing but bad memories. He wouldn't be here now if it weren't for Elodie's return. Yet he had to admit, it *was* nice being with his sisters again. He hardly knew either of them anymore, and he might get the chance to rebuild the bond they'd once shared. Besides, he wanted to know his niece and nephew.

He carried many secrets and had no intention of telling either Elodie or Edie any of them. It was better that way. He would stay on Skye to clear his name, gather as much information as possible regarding the murdered Druids and who might be controlling the mist, and get his mother settled. Emily's release from prison was something the two of them had planned for some time. He wouldn't miss that.

It was almost impossible to believe that his family would be together once more.

Elias pulled off the road and drove down the narrow lane that led to the cottage. He liked its seclusion as much as the water view. Stones crunched beneath his tires as he pulled into the parking area. He grabbed the milk and climbed out of the car. The small porch offered protection from the rain as he unlocked the door. He stepped inside the cottage, greeted by warmth from the furnace. He shrugged out of his coat and hung it on the pegs before heading to the kitchen.

There, he came to an abrupt halt at the sight of the woman seated at the small table with two cups of tea before her. Deep blue eyes regarded him gravely. She wore a black fleece sweatshirt, dark denim jeans, and black ankle boots. Her straight, chin-length, black hair was slightly damp.

Elias softly set the milk on the table. "Sabryn."

"Elias," she replied, her American accent evident in that one word.

"What the bloody hell are you doing here?"

She rolled her eyes and scooted the chair beside her out with her foot. "Sit and drink your tea while it's still hot."

He ignored her and put the milk into the fridge before grabbing the chair and pulling it out farther, then sinking into it. Elias stared at Sabryn for a silent minute. "What are you doing here?" he repeated. "I told you I had things in hand."

"You told me that before George named you as the killer."

Elias looked at the ceiling and blew out a breath. He'd hoped to keep that bit of information to himself for a while longer. "How did you find out?"

"Really?" she asked with another roll of her eyes.

He grunted. "Sabertooth."

Elias could navigate the internet better than most, but Sabertooth was what some might call a hacker. He dug up information that others would never find—or had thought to bury. While none of them had ever met Saber or even knew his real name, he was, for all intents and purposes, part of their team —just from behind a screen.

That group being the Knights, started by Sabryn in her journey to find her aunt's killer. Sabertooth had been the last to join their small band, rounding them out to five. But they worked well together.

"Yes, Saber." Sabryn's blue eyes glittered with anger. "Imagine my surprise—and ire—when I discovered that one of my guys was in trouble and didn't bother to tell any of us."

"I didna want to bring you into it."

"Tough shit," she replied curtly.

Elias lifted the mug of tea to his lips and took a drink. He let the warmth run down his throat to pool in his belly. "There's too much focus on me. If you and the lads are here, it willna take Rhona or Balladyn long to piece things together."

"Or your family."

Aye, them, too. But he didn't want to talk about them now. "I can handle this."

"I don't doubt that for a second. But you shouldn't have to. That's what being a Knight means, dumbass. We look out for each other—personal or business. You know that."

Elias blew out a breath. "Rhona and Balladyn are already asking questions. I might have let something slip."

"Maybe we tell them."

"I doona know if that's a good idea."

She quirked a brow as she slumped in the chair and stretched out her long legs. "Oh? Why's that?" she asked as she daintily lifted the cup and drank.

"Skye Druids are..." He paused, searching for the right words.

"Arrogant? Proud? Vain? Snobbish?"

Elias couldn't help the snort that followed. "Aye. All of that and more. They—"

"You mean *we*," she corrected. "I don't care how long you've been gone, Elias. You *are* a Skye Druid."

"Fine. *We* have more magic than most," he bit out.

Sabryn grinned, her eyes twinkling. "Most. Not all."

He looked away as he fought to rein in his temper.

"You're not telling me anything we've not already discussed about the Druids here. Every report we've gotten about Rhona said she's fair. I'm not saying we tell everyone who we are, but I don't see a reason *not* to tell her. She and that tall Reaper will know you're keeping a secret. And that, my friend, makes you look guilty. Besides, there's a bigger issue."

Elias sighed, fighting to keep his frustration in check. "Bigger? What could be bigger than George coming here and informing my sister and Rhona that I'm the one killing the Druids?"

"George went to the police."

It was a good thing Elias was sitting because his legs wouldn't have held him. All the air rushed from his lungs as if he'd been punched. "*What?*"

"I'll give her credit. George did her homework. She went straight to one DI Theo Frasier."

Elias leaned forward and pinched the bridge of his nose with his thumb and forefinger. "Theo's a Druid. He'd be the only one to listen to her."

"Exactly."

Elias thought through the problem. Then he raised his head and met Sabryn's gaze. "She can no' prove anything."

"Saber got into the police cameras. He sent me the recording of George's visit with Frasier. She claims there's an eyewitness who puts you in Edinburgh at the time of the last killing."

"Of course, I was there!" Elias rubbed his palms on his damp jeans to calm down. "We were all in Edinburgh tracking the killer."

"Frasier doesn't care about other places in the world. He cares about Skye."

"I didna get here until after the murders."

Sabryn held his gaze and nodded. "You and I both know if Frasier digs deep enough, he'll find something."

"I was never charged at Cardiff. It was self-defense."

"I was there. I know that. But you know how this looks."

Yes, unfortunately, he did. "Fuck!"

"Do you understand now why we came?"

His head snapped to her. "Finn and Carlyle are here, too?"

"As if you could keep them away," she replied with a grin.

Elias had to admit it was nice knowing the Knights had his back, but he didn't want them dragged into whatever mess he suddenly found himself in.

"What's the one thing we've found?" Sabryn asked, breaking into his thoughts.

He shrugged. "There's been a lot. What are you referring to?"

"This is about you, Elias. Something didn't want you on Skye, and it went to great lengths to ensure you stayed away."

His stomach knotted painfully. "But I survived the mist's attack."

"It's no coincidence that George showed up with the accusation now. You've not just returned home, you've also reunited with your sisters. Not to mention, your mother is about to be released. If you put all those pieces together, someone doesn't like the idea of the MacLean family being back together again."

Elias shook his head, not wanting to put the pieces together. "My family has been through enough."

"I don't disagree, but this means we're getting close to something. All of our hard work has paid off."

"I know the risks of what we do, and I gladly accepted them. My family didna. Elodie. Edie, and her kids. My mum. No, I doona like this."

Sabryn sat up and leaned forward, holding his gaze with her deep blue eyes. "The Knights have your back. We also have your family's. That's why I think you should bring Rhona and Balladyn in and tell them about us."

Elias watched as she got to her feet and finished her tea. She then went to the sink and washed the cup before setting it on the towel to dry.

"Oh. One more thing." Sabryn pulled something out of her back pocket and laid it on the table.

Elias stared at the three sets of wires and the tiny, rounded ends. "Bloody hell. Those are cameras?"

"They were installed in here. Seems your sister and brother-in-law like to spy on their renters."

Elias frowned at her. "You'll be on those cameras."

"Please," she replied with a flat look. "Saber disengaged them before I entered."

Elias didn't bother to ask how she had found him or entered the cottage. Sabryn was nothing if not resourceful—even without the Knights. "Thanks."

"Someone is after you, Elias. That means they've taken on *all* the Knights. We'll find who it is."

He nodded when he saw the determination in her eyes. Some of the tension that had tightened his muscles loosened. "It's good to have you here."

"I know," she said with a wink before walking out.

CHAPTER FOUR

Bronwyn tightened the blanket around her as she sat at the table in the kitchen and tried to finish her current design project, but it was difficult when she couldn't stop shivering. She took a drink of her coffee, only to gag at the cold liquid that met her lips.

She unfolded her legs and slipped her fuzzy-sock-covered feet into Ugg boots. The shoes were a splurge she really shouldn't have made, but they helped to keep her feet warm in the old, drafty house. She would love to turn up the heat, but she couldn't afford it.

Bronwyn glanced out the doorway and down the long corridor. If she turned her head just right, she could see the soft glow beneath the parlor's closed doors, where a fire waited. She would be working in there now if she had remembered to charge her computer before leaving for town. She could sit on the floor and complete the designs so she could reach the outlet, but she paid the price with a stiff back and neck for days after. So, she opted to freeze instead.

She brewed fresh coffee, listening to it percolate slowly. She didn't particularly like the taste of the brew, having to doctor it with plenty of milk and sugar, but the caffeine would help her stay awake long enough to beat her deadline and earn a little extra for doing it. Money was money, and she never seemed to have enough.

Once she had the coffee, she wrapped her hands around the mug to warm them in her fingerless gloves and then returned to the table. The creaks and groans of the old house were enough to make even the bravest soul believe in ghosts and otherworldly things. Bronwyn had grown up with them, never thinking twice about it. She still didn't—at least, not often. Sometimes, her imagination ran away with her, though. If she knew one thing, it was that she was safe here.

From anyone trying to get to her from outside.

And from anything that might be in the house.

Bronwyn checked the laptop battery and grinned when she saw it was full. She unplugged her computer and gathered everything in her arms before heading out of the kitchen. She paused beside the grand staircase that led to the upper floors. Her thoughts lingered for a moment, and then she hurried to the parlor.

The room was spacious, and she had moved furniture around to accommodate her needs since she was living and working out of this one room. The warmth that met her as she entered made her sigh in relief. Bronwyn made sure the door shut behind her and then settled herself in her favorite chair near the roaring fire.

She tugged the blanket over her legs and placed the computer on her lap, setting the mug of coffee next to her on the small table. After adjusting her headphones, she hit play.

Tonight's playlist was the soundtrack to *King Arthur: Legend of the Sword*, one of her favorites.

When the music began, she kicked off the boots, crossed her legs in the chair, and adjusted the blanket around her once more. It was after two in the morning when she finished the project and sent it off. She added more wood to the fire and then crawled beneath the warm covers, still in her sweats and socks, falling asleep quickly while thinking about the extra money she'd just made and how long it would last.

It felt like barely a second had lapsed when her alarm went off, pulling her from an intriguing dream of a man with penetrating, bright blue eyes. Bronwyn groaned at being dragged from the nice fantasy and reached for her phone to stop the alarm. When she looked over, she saw the fire had gone out. She threw off the blankets, and the chill that seemed to seep through every stone immediately assaulted her. She went to the hearth and shifted through the coals to find a few that still glowed, working tirelessly until she had the fire going again.

"Same morning, different day," she mumbled as she made her bed.

After a quick shower to help her warm up, she changed and went into the conservatory to tend to her vegetable garden. Then she bundled herself and braved the windy morning to feed the chickens and gather their eggs. At least it wasn't raining. In no time, she was back inside to fix her usual breakfast of eggs, toast, and tea.

She eyed the end of the loaf of bread and grimaced at the thought of carving out time to make more. It would be so much simpler to buy it, but when every cent counted, she did what she had to do, and it was cheaper to make her own.

Once she'd cleaned up the kitchen, she made another cup of tea before stopping at the stairs and putting a hand on the newel. She called to her magic and let it flow from her palm into the stained wood, no longer shining with a high polish. The gleam had long since faded, but it still looked beautiful to her. Though only her memories had the house as it had once been, in its glory.

"You'll be returned to your rightful splendor one day soon," she whispered.

Bronwyn lowered her hand and looked up the stairs. A part of her wanted to venture up, but she knew nothing would come of it. With a sigh, she returned to the parlor. She settled herself in the chair and checked her bank account to see if she had been paid. Relief surged through her when she saw that it would post that day.

She drank her second cup of tea as she checked her email. There was one from a prospective client that she answered immediately. Word was finally spreading about her work. She was working on two other jobs at the moment and had a possible third if she and the new customer could work out the terms. Since she didn't know if work would continue coming in, she couldn't be choosy about what she accepted. Maybe one day, but she was just happy to be paid for her designs.

Bronwyn had joined a few social media groups dedicated to cover designs for authors and had created dozens of premades in various genres to show off what she could do. But her first love was romance, and she devoured books in every sub-genre. When authors asked for cover designers, she made sure to put herself out there. No one had chosen her. Yet.

The morning passed quickly. She was nearly finished with her next design when her stomach growled. Bronwyn would rather keep working because she was in the groove, but a glance at the clock showed it was nearly two in the afternoon.

She set aside her computer to charge as she made her way to the kitchen. She had a dull headache but ignored it as she made a sandwich with the last of the bread. Bronwyn didn't bother to sit as she ate. She stood at the window and looked out back toward the loch. The sky was clear, and the sun sparkled on the water. The loch had once been a beacon she couldn't resist, but that was a long time ago.

Once, she might have gone down to the water to enjoy the day, no matter what time of year it was, but those days were long gone. She turned her back on the loch and finished her meal. Memories had a hold of her, though. Thoughts of her father, her mother, of a time when happiness had filled every corner and crevice of the house.

She was chained to the home, but she was thankful for that. Honestly, she wasn't sure where she would be if she didn't have it. The structure had been in the Stewart family for six generations, and it would stay that way—one way or another. Thinking about the house had her thoughts turning to her dad.

The same ache of loneliness and guilt assaulted her. Her face creased as she fought the onslaught of regret for how she had left her father alone, harsh words passing between them. She had pushed him away for so long, but he had been there for her when she needed him.

Her throat closed, clogged with emotion as she thought of his absence. He wasn't with her or in his beloved house, because of her. She owed it to him to fix her mistakes, which was exactly what she had put into motion. She had expected things to come to a head already, but it would happen eventually.

Bronwyn looked at the ceiling, her thoughts shifting upstairs for a moment, but she quickly diverted them. She dusted off her hands and returned to the parlor. She saw an email alert when she opened her computer. The books she had bought for small business information as well as one for cover design, had finally arrived at the post office. Which meant she had to go back into town—the very thing she loathed.

She looked at the fire. She hated to waste it, but she couldn't leave it unattended. And she couldn't use even a little of her magic to keep it shielded while she was gone. With no choice, she extinguished the fire completely, then put on her coat and boots and left the house, locking it.

The ride to the post office was uneventful. She kept her head up when she walked into the co-op, trying not to think about the day before. Kirsi was once more behind the counter, and her pale green eyes met Bronwyn's briefly as she approached.

"I'm here to pick up a package," she said, aware of the other customer in the store.

Kirsi nodded without looking at her. "Sure. Let me get it."

Bronwyn shifted uncomfortably as the woman went into the post office side of the business and disappeared through a doorway. Thankfully, she returned quickly with the box.

"Thanks," Bronwyn said as she took it and turned to leave.

"I'm sorry."

She halted and looked over her shoulder at Kirsi. The cashier was a few years younger than her. Pretty and popular, Kirsi had never wanted for friends. Bronwyn was trying to figure out why she was apologizing. The box seemed intact.

"About yesterday." Kirsi swallowed nervously. "With Sarah."

Bronwyn was taken aback. She shrugged, not wanting to talk about it. "It is what it is."

"You're not the only one on Skye."

The community that always touted being there for everyone had stopped speaking to her after her father's funeral—or, rather, after she'd altered her life irrevocably.

Maybe Kirsi was being nice, but Bronwyn didn't trust that. They hadn't been more than passing acquaintances before. They certainly weren't friends now. Bronwyn wondered how everyone would react if they knew all the details. Would they continue judging her so harshly?

Maybe they would condemn her more severely.

"I'm still sorry," Kirsi said in a soft voice.

Bronwyn nodded and walked away, heading outside. She blinked against the bright sunlight and was nearly to her vehicle when someone stepped in front of her. Her stomach dropped like a rock when she found herself staring into familiar cold brown eyes. Dead eyes. Sydney Russell.

His too-perfect face split into a smile. "Hello, Bron."

"Don't call me that." She despised when he shortened her name.

He chuckled and moved closer as if there weren't deep hatred between them. It took everything she had to hold her ground. All she wanted to do was back away and run to the safety of her home.

"Still the same old Bronwyn," he said in a soft voice, the one he'd used to woo her. One she used to love. He tsked as his gaze raked over her. "I bet you thought I wouldna find you."

"I haven't been hiding."

The wind ruffled his dark hair. "You look good."

He tried to touch her face, but she batted his hand away. "Don't touch me."

"You used to like my touch, babe."

She nearly gagged at the hated *babe*. "I don't want any part of you anymore. You know that."

He chuckled and turned his head slightly to the side, never taking his eyes off her. "Did you hear that, gang?"

The sound of laughter joined his. Bronwyn's stomach roiled violently. She should've known he wouldn't be alone. Sydney always had an entourage. They stoked his already inflated ego. How had she ever found that attractive?

Then again, she had been looking for trouble. And she'd found it in spades with Sydney.

"Leave," she ordered him.

Sydney's smile died as he leaned close enough that their noses nearly touched. "Babe, you know no one tells me what to do. What *you* will do is tell me where I can find Beth."

"My cousin is somewhere you'll never find her." Bronwyn was proud of how clear and steady her voice sounded when she was quaking inside.

Sydney's nostrils flared, and his eyes narrowed dangerously. "I've been looking for Beth. I know you know where she is."

"Do you really think I'd have that kind of information? I knew you'd come here searching. I have nothing for you."

"Oh, you do," he said after a moment, his gaze intense. "You'll tell me, Bron. Mark my words. You will tell me," he threatened, his voice promising danger.

She didn't look away.

She didn't fidget.

She didn't flinch.

Bronwyn stood her ground against Sydney but ran to a bush and vomited the minute he walked away and out of sight. She'd known this day would come. Had prepared for it. But she hadn't expected to be caught away from the house. Now that Sydney was on Skye, she would have to be extra careful.

Bronwyn wiped her mouth and hurried to her vehicle, climbing inside. Her days of feeling even a modicum of safety were over. But she had prepared for what was to come. Sydney had won against her once.

He wouldn't be victorious a second time.

CHAPTER FIVE

Elias's gaze had been riveted on Bronwyn from the moment she walked out of the building with a package under her arm. He'd spotted the group of five before she did. When the tall, slender man had stepped into her path, Elias had reached for his door handle to get out. Only Sabryn's hand on his arm kept him inside the vehicle.

"Well," Sabryn said. "I'll give it to her. She's got style."

Elias swallowed and forced his body to relax against the driver's seat. The male and his friends were gone now, but given the exchange, things were far from over between him and Bronwyn.

"Did you see how she didn't back down from that asshole?" Sabryn asked.

Elias released the door handle one finger at a time. "Aye."

"There's some history between those two—and not the good kind."

Elias took a deep breath and then slowly released it. "Why did you stop me from helping her?"

"Because you don't need to bring more attention to yourself. Besides, I had a feeling she didn't need it."

"Didna need it?" he barked, his head swinging to the side so he could gape at Sabryn. "She went behind the bushes and got sick. I'd say she needed it."

Sabryn crossed one leg over the other and silently regarded him. "You've got a penis, so I'll forgive you for that outburst. Obviously, you've never had to endure the things a woman has. For all the shouts of equality in the world, there is still a vast expanse between what men and women go through, and I won't even touch on skin color and other factors. The truth, Elias, is that men have always assumed they can intimidate. Sometimes, it's trivial things like staring at our boobs instead of looking into our eyes. Annoying, yes, but it immediately puts women on the defensive—not to mention angers us. Men get away with it because, well, they're men. Then there are the not-so-minor instances of leaning over us to make us feel inferior. The threats and power they use that seem forever at their disposal."

Elias frowned as he realized the thin man *had* leaned over Bronwyn, looming. But she hadn't backed away. She had held eye contact, everything in her bearing daring the arse to do something.

"That chick has some balls," Sabryn continued. "She never let him see how terrified she was. That's someone who has been through some shit and come out the other side. She has scars you'll never see—and maybe some you can."

He glanced at Sabryn, wondering if she compared herself to Bronwyn. Because Sabryn also had a complicated past.

She caught his gaze. "She needed to do that on her own. She could've run. She didn't. She stayed and faced him because she had to."

"You saw all that by watching her for only a few seconds?"

"Don't sound so shocked. You have your gifts. I have mine. And, yes, to answer your question, I did. Not so much by her walk but her attitude when she saw the prick." Sabryn smoothed her hand over the front of her cream angora sweater. "I'd advise you to keep your head on finding the murderer and clearing your name, but I recognize that look on your face. I only have one request."

He raised his brows, waiting.

"Doona let the lass take up too much of your time," Sabryn said with a perfect Scottish accent.

He chuckled. She had a knack for accents and picked them up quickly. "Heard."

"Good." Her deep blue gaze swung back to the cars around him. "I and the boys are going to do a little checking around while you're with your family."

"Be careful."

She rolled her eyes as she clicked her tongue. "Do you know me at all? *Careful* is my middle name."

"That's shite, and you know it," he called as she climbed out of his vehicle.

Sabryn bent to look at him. "Tallyho."

"Verra funny."

She waved her fingers at him and shut the door. Elias started the engine as she walked away. She was out of sight within moments. He backed out and started the drive to Edie's. He was supposed to have lunch with his sisters. It wouldn't be the first

time they had eaten together since his return to Skye, but that
didn't mean things weren't still a little awkward. He had been
away for nearly two decades, rarely speaking to Edie and having
almost no contact with Elodie. They were strangers for all intents
and purposes. Memories of their childhood and their blood bond
could only take them so far.

But he wanted to mend the rift he had caused by leaving. At
least Elodie knew the truth of things. That made things easier.

When he arrived, Elodie met him at the door. He embraced
his youngest sister. Her bright smile and vibrant face eased some
of his worries that she wouldn't be able to carry the weight of the
past, but she was stronger than he gave her credit for. It helped
that she wasn't dealing with this alone. Scott's love and support
helped.

"You're late," Elodie said as she led him into the house.

"That's a single man for you," Edie called from the kitchen.

Elias chuckled as he inhaled the delightful aromas. "I
promised wine," he said and held up the bottle, entering the
ultra-modern room. "I had to stop and get some."

"Then you're forgiven." Elodie took the white and set about
opening it.

Elias rubbed his hands together as he walked to the island.
"What do you need me to do?"

"It's all done. Just finishing up the sauce," Edie said.

Elodie shot him a playful look. "And that's why he's tardy."

"No' fair," he shot back, enjoying the banter. It made things
feel almost as if they were teenagers again.

Edie motioned to the wine Elodie had poured. "Seriously,
take your drinks and have a seat. The food is ready."

Elias did as his sister requested. When he turned to the table, he only saw three place settings. "Is Trevor no' joining us?"

"He had a work lunch he couldn't get out of," Edie replied as she concentrated on the food almost a little too hard.

Elias looked at Elodie, who shrugged and wrinkled her nose, telling him she had no answer to his silent question. He opted not to discuss it further. Mostly because Elias knew very little about his sister's marriage, other than they seemed happy. He didn't want to stir up problems where there were none. From everything he'd seen, they had a great life.

Edie was a terrific cook, and the meal of baked salmon and asparagus was delicious. They talked about the past, reminiscing on their antics and the things they had gotten into as children— though Elodie was careful not to speak of their father. Elias followed suit, but Edie, not knowing the truth of the horrible man their da had been, had no such qualms. She brought him up several times.

With the bottle of wine empty and only a little left in their glasses, Elias waited for a lull in the conversation before pulling the small cameras from his back pocket and laying them on the table in front of Edie, who sat across from him.

She eyed them. "What's that?"

"Your cameras," he replied.

She took a drink of her wine before shaking her head, confusion in her eyes. "What cameras?"

"The ones in the cottage I'm renting."

"We don't install monitoring equipment inside our rentals. The tenants have a right to their privacy. We do install some outside, though."

Elias noted the way Edie's lips tightened and her voice rose, indicating she was upset. "I'm sorry to say, but these were inside."

"Maybe Trevor forgot to tell you, Edie," Elodie offered.

Their sister grabbed the small cameras and rose from the table to put them on the island. "I'm sure that's it. I'm sorry, Elias."

"Doona be. I'm sure it was an oversight." It was a lie, but he felt compelled to ease the tension he saw in Edie.

It was obvious she hadn't known about the cameras, which meant that Trevor was responsible for placing them. And any landlord who installed hidden surveillance throughout a residence wasn't anyone Elias wanted to know.

Elodie cleared her throat nervously and caught his gaze. "How is the house?"

"It's great." He glanced at the island to see Edie staring at the devices as if she could make them speak. "I love the location."

"You mean you love that no one's around," Elodie teased.

He nodded. "Absolutely. The road is back far enough that I doona hear most of the traffic. It's quiet. I didna realize how much I've missed that."

"Meaning you've not had it?" Elodie asked expectantly.

Elias shrugged. "Nay, I've no'."

"Are you thinking of coming back to Skye for good?" Edie asked as she returned to the table.

She wouldn't meet his gaze now, and Elias wished he had waited until Trevor was with his sister. He'd have very much liked to see his brother-in-law's expression at the sight of the cameras.

Elias finished his wine, giving himself time to come up with an answer. "I'll be here for a wee bit, aye. That'll give me time to spend with both of you. Then, I'll get Mum when she's released. She wants to live here again, and I know you and Trevor need the rental back, so I'll look for a house for her. No doubt I'll stay with her for a month or two to make sure she's settled."

"You?" Edie asked tightly.

Elias slowly leaned back in his chair as he tried to figure out what he'd said that upset Edie.

Apparently, he wasn't the only one confused because Elodie asked, "What's wrong?"

Edie's smile was forced as she shook her head. "Nothing. Sorry. My mind is scattered today."

When she began picking up the plates, he and Elodie joined her. Elias shot Elodie a searching look. She shrugged, obviously as confused as he was. It wasn't until he was putting away their leftovers that he remembered what else he'd wanted to ask his sisters.

"Do either of you know a Bronwyn?"

Elodie shook her head. "Can't say as I do."

"Which Bronwyn?" Edie asked as she rinsed a plate before putting it in the dishwasher. "I can think of at least four."

"She's around Elodie's age. There was an episode at the co-op, some woman telling her she didn't belong on Skye and shouldna even be able to shop at the store."

Edie nodded as she said, "Ah. Bronwyn Stewart."

At least he had her full name now. "Something about her seems familiar."

"I remember her," Elodie said. "The family is well-off. The Stewarts have lived in the Carwood Manor for generations. Does she have dark hair?"

Elias nodded. "And hazel eyes."

"I know why she looks familiar to you," Elodie said with a wide grin. "You helped her up at school when she fell in the rain. She's a few years younger than me. If I remember right, she's pretty."

"Aye, she's bonnie," he replied.

Elodie's eyes widened. "Has someone taken an interest?"

"Stay away from her," Edie stated in the firm voice Elias had heard her use on her children. "She's *drough*."

Elodie's head jerked to Edie. "What? Are you sure?"

"That's why people treat her with such disdain," Edie answered and dried her hands.

"Rhona has kept to Corann's decree that *droughs* can live on Skye as long as they doona harm anyone," Elias said. He had known Druids who'd gone to the dark side, giving their souls to the Devil, but Bronwyn hadn't had that look about her.

Or maybe he hadn't seen it.

"Druids are Druids: *mie* or *drough*. If Rhona said they can live on Skye, and if Bronwyn has done nothing to warrant anyone treating her badly, then she should be left alone," Elodie stated.

Edie braced a hand on the counter and faced them. "I disagree. I don't want anyone like that around my children."

"There are bad people everywhere," Elias replied.

Elodie nodded solemnly. "I can attest to that. I'm sure people will be upset that Mum is coming back here, but she served her time. They'd better leave her alone."

Elias would make sure of it, especially since his mother was innocent.

"You know how small this isle is. People will come up with

their own stories and talk. Everything about Da will get brought back up again. We can't let that happen," Edie said.

"The same consideration should be given to anyone, regardless of their past—until they do something to warrant anger," Elodie argued.

Edie snorted. "Said by someone who doesn't have children. You can't possibly understand what a parent goes through."

"Druids have classified each other as *mie* and *drough* for too long. Black and white. Things are no' so cut and dried. I've seen plenty of *mies* do horrible things. And I've seen *droughs* do amazing acts of kindness. There is no us versus them. Humanity lives in a world of gray." Elias looked at each of his sisters. "We need to remember that."

CHAPTER SIX

"We should find Rhona," Nikolai said.

Esther shook her head as they sat at a table in the pub. Her gaze moved outside the window, taking in the cars and people. "I want to have a look around Skye first."

"You've no' told me what you're looking for."

She slid her gaze to her mate's baby blue eyes and spotted the concern. With a smile she didn't quite feel, she reached over and smoothed a stray auburn lock into the rest of his hair. "I don't know yet, sweetheart."

"And that's what worries me." His lips compressed into a line. "You shouldna be here without your brother. You're—"

"Half of a team," she said with a nod, trying not to let impatience fill her voice. "I'm very aware of that."

Nikolai took her hand in his. "You're the TruthSeeker. So, seek the truth. If you find something, I'll alert those at Dreagan, and someone will get Henry back to Earth. The JusticeBringer should no' have left without you. You're a bloody team."

Esther tried not to be irritated with her brother. She didn't know why Henry had felt drawn to leave this realm for Zora, but she'd known it was the wrong time for him to go even then. Though she hadn't been able to stop him—no one could stop Henry when he had his mind set on something.

She finished her coffee. "You're right. Let's see what we can find."

"After we see Rhona."

"No," Esther stated as she got to her feet. "Not yet."

Nikolai sighed as he stood. "Our arrival will only stay secret for so long."

"Something's off, Nik. It's here, on Skye, and it needs to be sorted. Quickly. Or…"

His brows drew together as he came around the table to her side. "Or?"

She put a hand on her chest and rubbed. "I don't know. The feeling inside me is urgent, demanding I sort things out."

"Then we'll sort them," he replied. "And I'm going to get Henry's arse here now."

Nikolai's protectiveness was just one of the many reasons she loved him. "Not yet."

"You've got a day."

She smiled at the finality in his voice. "I'll let you know when you can send for my brother."

"Och, woman. You used to listen to me."

That made her laugh as she kissed him. "Keep thinking that, my handsome Dragon King."

Bronwyn gave up trying to work after returning to the house. Her encounter with Sydney had shaken her more than she wanted to admit. She had looked through her new books, but her mind was too busy going over every word and look Sydney had given her. It wasn't until she realized she had read the same paragraph for thirty minutes that she finally gave up.

She shivered, partly from the weather and partly from what Sydney had said. Bronwyn paced in front of the hearth, trying to soak in as much heat as possible. She hadn't been able to get warm since she'd seen Sydney. She'd known he would come to Skye and had expected him weeks ago.

"What kept him away?" she asked aloud.

She grimaced when she thought of him now. What had she ever found appealing? But she knew the answer didn't lie with Sydney. It was with her. Unfortunately, she'd waited too long to figure that out. If only she could go back in time to right the wrongs and fix the mistakes.

"Fuck, fuck, fuck," she murmured as she rubbed the middle of her forehead.

The anger in Sydney's eyes had frightened her. It appeared he was prepared to do anything to find Beth, and Bronwyn was ready to do whatever it took to keep him from her cousin. Even if that meant welcoming the darkness within herself that she had ignored up until now. It was the least Bronwyn could do to make up for the things she had done.

"It won't make up for everything, but it's what I can do."

And something had to be done.

Bronwyn wished she could ask for help. The very thing her father had told her she needed to do more. But she'd done exactly that. Her father's death had been the horrible consequence. She wouldn't seek assistance from anyone again, no matter how frightened she was. She couldn't carry the weight of anyone else's death on her conscience. This was her mess, and she would clean it up.

She sank wearily onto the chair and stared out the window. Of all the ways she'd thought her life might go, her current trajectory had never even been in the realm of possibilities. One bad decision after another had led to her current predicament. She knew that what she planned now was yet another dreadful choice, but there was no other option. She'd had weeks to come up with something else.

It wasn't as if there was a manual for Druid spells. There wasn't an encyclopedia or databank of Druid events and their decisions—good or bad. All she had was her life experience and magic to draw from and fall back on.

The silence of the house reaffirmed that she was alone and the fight Sydney would bring to her door would be one of life and death. Bronwyn had known that from the moment she'd found Beth, and it hadn't stopped her then. It wouldn't now.

"We can do this," she said to the house.

She had to. There was no other option.

Her time with Sydney had let her know how to prepare, and she'd done that the only way she could. She'd become *drough*. Good or bad, right or wrong, she would carry the results of her choices from this life into the next. Everything was in order. She'd seen to her will within days of her father's death.

The question was, how long would Sydney wait before he came for her? He could arrive at any moment. Though, he was a sadist. The more pain someone was in, the more pleasure he got out of it. It would be just like him to wait days or weeks before attacking.

Bronwyn might have been startled by his confrontation earlier, but she wouldn't let that happen again. She had allowed herself to fall into a lull, clinging to tenuous pieces of hope that Sydney would give up on Beth. She should've known that he would never release his hold on her cousin. Beth had something he wanted, and Sydney would burn the world to find her.

But he wasn't expecting what Bronwyn had in store for him. That was her only advantage, and she would use it ruthlessly.

There was no more wondering when Sydney would come back into her life, no more agonizing over how the encounter would play out. It was done. Over. Now came the next part, which would be the trickiest as well as the hardest.

She jumped at the sound of the knocker on the front door. Bronwyn's head swung toward the front of the house, her heart in her throat. She slowly got to her feet. Sydney had come sooner than expected. Ice filled her veins. She glanced at the ceiling as her mind rushed through her plans. Her feet were as heavy as lead when she walked across the parlor, opened the door, and slipped through before closing it. Bronwyn paused and closed her eyes as she put her palm against the door for a moment.

Her magic moved from her into the door and then the rest of the house. Then she lowered her arm to her side and opened her eyes. She made her way through the large foyer and to the front door. Bronwyn took a deep breath and released it through her mouth, gripping the handle and turning the knob. The door swung open noiselessly, the cold air slamming into her. She found herself looking into dark eyes.

"Good afternoon," the man said and held up a badge. "I'm

Detective Inspector Theo Frasier. I was wondering if I could have a word."

She glanced at the badge and briefly spotted a photo and some writing before her attention returned to the dark-haired man. Her relief was so great that it wasn't Sydney on her doorstep that it took a moment for his face to come into focus. "About?"

Frasier put his credentials away and brought a closed fist to his mouth, where he cleared his throat. "I doona know if you remember me," he began.

"I know who you are." Just as he knew very well who she was.

He was a few years her senior, and while not all the Druids knew each other, Theo had dated one of her friends in school. He'd had a serious nature even back then. He was pragmatic, shrewd, and reasonable. Theo had always been fascinated with the justice system and catching criminals. It was more of a daunting task when you were a Druid on Skye, trying to take down other Druids. It seemed he'd found his calling.

Theo nodded and held her gaze. "May I come in? This willna take but a moment."

Bronwyn stepped outside and closed the door behind her. She crossed her arms over her chest for warmth. "If this is about me buying groceries, I have every right to be there."

"What?" he asked, his brows drawing together in confusion. Then he shook his head. "Nay. I'm going to all the Druids and asking if they've seen the mist. It isna like regular mist it—"

"Moves," she said over him. Bronwyn nodded. "I've seen it."

Theo's eyes widened as he pulled out a pad of paper and a pen, waiting for her to talk. "When? Where?"

"Anyone who is outside at night has likely seen it. Whether they admit to it is another matter. I saw it about a week and a half ago." She pointed to the left, in the direction of the road. "Over that way. It was low, hugging the ground. Before that, I witnessed it moving in the sky. Rather high up."

He wrote furiously in his small notebook. "Do you know who's controlling it?"

She'd been wondering if someone would ask her that. "It isn't me, if that's what you're thinking."

Theo paused and lifted his dark gaze to study her with cool detachment. "I didna insinuate it was."

"I'm sure every *drough* on Skye is being blamed."

"You know what it means to be a Skye Druid," he said as he lowered his arms to his sides. "We can no' use magic for evil or to help evil, lest we lose our magic."

She nodded, not hiding her irritation. "Then it must be a *drough*. But it isn't me. Before you ask, no, I don't have anyone to vouch for me. I live alone, as you well know."

A spark of irritation flashed before it faded. "People are dead, Bronwyn."

"I know. I read about it. If I knew something, I'd tell you, if for no other reason than to ensure I'm left alone. Just because I'm now a *drough* doesn't mean I go around killing people—or know who is. Plenty of *droughs* in the world never take a life."

He blew out a strained breath and pocketed his notebook and pen. "I'm just doing my job."

"I appreciate that."

Theo shifted his feet as his gaze sharpened. "About the altercation at the co-op."

Ah. Just as she'd expected. Bronwyn didn't say anything. She just waited.

"You should know that Sarah made a complaint. She said you threatened her."

"Perhaps I'll start wasting police time and complain every time someone harasses *me* when I'm going about my day. Shall I explain how she tried to humiliate me in front of everyone? How she demanded that I not be allowed to shop there or even live on Skye?"

Theo had the good grace to look abashed. "She said as much to me. I reminded her that per the decree, *droughs* can live on Skye at our leader's discretion."

"And what did Sarah say to that?"

"She plans to petition Rhona to change things."

Bronwyn had expected that would happen eventually. Still, it hurt more than she cared to admit. "I see."

"Rhona is fair," Theo urged. "Talk to her."

Bronwyn reached behind her and took hold of the doorknob. "Is that all?"

"Aye." But he didn't leave. Theo studied her for a moment. "Please, go see Rhona."

"Good day," she said and walked into the house, locking the door behind her.

When Bronwyn peered out the window, Theo remained on the stoop for another few moments before walking to his vehicle and finally leaving. Bronwyn blew out a breath she hadn't known she'd been holding and hurried into the parlor and the warmth it offered.

She opened her laptop and tried to work, but she ended up staring blankly at the screen as her mind repeatedly jumped from the recent confrontation with Sarah, the man who'd stared at her in the co-op, the clash with Sydney, and Theo's visit. When she finally looked up, the room was dark.

Bronwyn rose and turned on the lights. It had been hours since she'd last eaten, if her growling stomach was any indication. Since she still hadn't made any bread, she had to settle for eating peanut butter off a spoon. It wasn't the best meal, but it at least offered protein.

She walked out the back door to see the moon reflecting off the loch. Some might call it a beautiful sight, but it just looked eerie and wrong to her. Yet she couldn't stop looking at it. Maybe because it had been a night much like this one—the frigid air mixed with a clear sky—that her mother had walked into the water to take her life.

It didn't matter what excuse had been given. Bronwyn couldn't forgive her mum for giving up and leaving instead of fighting. Nor could she forgive herself for not being able to help.

Bronwyn turned to go back inside the house when something caught her attention out of the corner of her eye. She swung around in time to see a large cloud of mist slinking low through the trees on the other side of the loch, moving in what could only be described as a slithering motion over the water and straight toward her.

She wanted to run, but Bronwyn stood her ground, even when the mist swirled around her, first in one direction and then the other—never touching her—before darting into the air and disappearing.

CHAPTER SEVEN

SKYE DRUIDS

Dumbfounded, Elias stared through the binoculars at the sight of the mist as it wound around Bronwyn in what he could only describe as…sensual. Yet it was the rigid way she stood that really caught his attention. She didn't appear pleased to see the mist, much less have it near her.

It was the only reason he didn't think she was controlling it. It would exhilarate someone who wielded that kind of power to have the mist around them. Bronwyn remained still long after the mist shot up into the sky. Then, she went back to eating her peanut butter off the spoon before turning on her heel and walking into the house.

Elias lowered his binoculars and sighed. After learning who Bronwyn was, it was simply a matter of subtly asking the right people some questions. Most had nothing bad to say other than she was a *drough* now. That stigma held a lot of implications—none of them good.

Getting a feel for how the locals viewed someone he was

looking into was always his first step. His second was to search the internet. He found out enough that he didn't bother Sabertooth. Yet.

What he knew so far was that she was an only child and heir to the Stewart estate, which consisted of the manor built in 1783 and the twenty-two acres of land. Her mother, Arabella, drowned when Bronwyn was just seventeen, and the way Bronwyn had stared at the loch, Elias suspected that was where it had happened. Her father, Robert, died unexpectedly a few months ago during a trip to Inverness. The reports said that Robert died of a heart attack, and it was some time after Bronwyn returned his body for burial on Skye that she became *drough*. That was enough to make Elias wonder about Robert Stewart's death.

He sat on the cold ground and propped one foot on the earth, resting an arm on his knee and slowly moving his gaze over the estate. It was overgrown and in need of maintenance. The three-story manor had a few dead plants around, but it *was* winter.

He'd been watching the house for hours and had seen no movement that indicated anyone was inside. He'd begun to think Bronwyn stayed elsewhere when a light on the main floor clicked on. She had walked outside to look at the loch a short time after.

It gave him time to study her through the lenses of his binoculars, though he could describe every detail of her face from seeing her at the co-op. Oval face, stubborn chin, and full, luscious lips. Rich, dark brown hair she parted on the side with the thick, straight length falling to just brush the tops of her shoulders. It had been tousled that day as if she had run her fingers through it repeatedly.

Brows of deep brown curved elegantly over hazel eyes a

mixture of pale green, gold, and copper. Those orbs had sucked him in, holding him transfixed as nothing ever had before. She was strikingly beautiful. He'd been able to think of little else since their encounter. Thanks to Elodie, he knew why Bronwyn had looked familiar.

Tonight, he saw the woman in her element, at her haven, though she wore somberness tightly around her like a cloak. It was almost as if she steeled herself for something. Elias's thoughts immediately went to the thin man who had stopped Bronwyn earlier. Was he somehow involved?

The more Elias learned about Bronwyn, the more he realized she was a mixture of metaphors. She was courage and fire. She was reserved and independent. She was bold and undaunted.

But she was also uncertain and restless.

He wanted to know everything about her. Not only because he was utterly captivated by her but also because he recognized the isolation he'd once dealt with after leaving Skye. His mother was still alive, but he had lost both parents in a single day. He understood how that changed a person forever, especially when the circumstances were alarming and disturbing.

Elias had been lucky and found the Knights—or rather they had found him. Otherwise, he wasn't sure where he would've ended up. Perhaps he would've become *drough* himself. What he knew was that a Druid didn't decide to become a *drough* lightly. There was no going back from it. Something or someone had pushed Bronwyn to that point.

And he intended to discover what or who.

He knew Sabryn and the others wouldn't be happy about it, but they'd understand. The Knights weren't just about tracking down Druid murderers, they were also about helping Druids who didn't think they had anyone else to turn to.

Elias had no idea how he would juggle this with everything else. The mist had tried to kill him and Elodie. No one had seen it for days—until tonight. He didn't know what that meant, but he needed to tell everyone. If the mist was back, more killings would likely follow.

He wanted to know why it had targeted him and Elodie but not Edie. Or maybe it hadn't gotten to Edie yet. His stomach clenched at the thought of his niece and nephew getting caught up in all of this. He needed to discover who controlled the mist and learn what they were after. That was the only way to stop it.

As for George and her allegations, that would hopefully be over soon. Though he knew it wouldn't be. The police took things like that seriously. They would investigate him, which would bring up his past—something he'd hoped would stay buried. But George had other plans. It was just someone else targeting him when he didn't know why.

Elias rose and took one more look at Carwood Manor. The night was quiet and still, but he couldn't shake the feeling that he wasn't the only one watching Bronwyn. He'd have to delve into that later. Right now, he had to alert the others about the mist.

"Un-fucking-believable," Rhona stated as she paced.

Balladyn sat in the chair and watched her. She had been fuming since Frasier's visit a few hours ago. Balladyn was also agitated, but if he let it show, it would only increase Rhona's ire.

The Druids on Skye looked to her. She needed to be unruffled and impartial, but first, she had to get the influx of emotions out of the way.

"Who the bloody hell does she think she is?" Rhona demanded.

He opened his mouth to answer, but she kept talking.

"George has canceled on us three times. Three!" Rhona shouted, her green eyes flashing as she locked on him before whirling to pace in the opposite direction, her long, red tresses fanning out behind her. "And now she goes to Theo and tells him that she has proof about Elias?" Rhona shook her head angrily. "I don't like her, honey. She comes into our territory and continues moving our meetings. I get the feeling she has no intention of talking to me."

"She doesn't want to meet here. It's your home. You have the advantage," Balladyn said.

Rhona snorted loudly. "Too bloody bad. I don't care if that makes her uncomfortable. I'd do the same if I were in Edinburgh and making a claim against one of her people."

"She's not you."

"Damn right, she isn't. The nerve of her going to Theo instead of letting me investigate. She hasn't even told me anything herself. I'm hearing it from others." Rhona threw up her hands and let them slap against her legs.

Balladyn rose and stood in her way to make her halt. He gently grabbed her shoulders, forcing her to look into his eyes. "She could be doing all of this because she feels intimidated. The Skye Druids are known all over the world as the strongest of all Druids. You lead them, love. Think about that."

"Stop being rational. It dims my righteous anger."

He grinned.

Don't forget about yourself," she said with a ghost of a smile.

"Aye. There's me, as a Reaper and the Warden of Skye. And then there's us. Our combined magic."

Rhona blew out a deep breath. "I suppose I see your point."

"There's also the fact that she may very well have evidence that Elias is a killer."

"I don't believe that," Rhona said with a shake of her head. "Something's not right about any of this."

Balladyn gave her a soft kiss. "While I agree with you, you need to stay impartial until you gather all the evidence. I know you're thinking about how Elias was nearly killed by the mist. To play Devil's advocate, I'll remind you that he came out of that with only minor scrapes."

"And I'll tell *you* that we've done no investigating ourselves. We have only her word. Elias hasn't told us any details."

"Is that because he's guilty or because he has something he wants to keep secret? It could be both," Balladyn cautioned.

She rolled her eyes. "I concede that he's hiding something about the people he's working with. If Elias is tracking the murders, that would put him in the locations where there have been Druid deaths."

"Precisely my point."

"Do you think he's a murderer?"

Balladyn rubbed his hands up and down her arms before pulling her close. "He admitted that he's killed in self-defense."

"Both of us have, as well. You've been alive for thousands of years. You have to sense something."

Balladyn drew in a breath and released it. "I don't think he's guilty, but there are too many things stacked against him. That gives me pause."

"Things George instigated." Rhona leaned back to look at him, anger sparking in her eyes again. "I'm tired of her dodging me."

"Then don't give her a choice."

A slow smile spread over Rhona's face. "Do you have something special in mind?"

"I could bring her here."

"As tempting as that is, I'm certain that would put her on the defensive."

His lips twisted as he thought about that. "It depends on if you still wish to work with her."

"I want the truth. Whatever it might be."

"Then perhaps I shouldn't bring her to you," he admitted.

Rhona ran her hands up his arms to his shoulders and then wound them around his neck. "I'll tell her she has one more chance to arrange a meeting or we'll do it for her."

"I think that's fair." Balladyn released her so Rhona could send a text to George. There was an immediate response. "Well?" he asked.

Rhona smirked and tossed her mobile onto the sofa. "Tomorrow, two p.m. at Bog Myrtle Café."

"She wants to be in public."

"Is she afraid of what we'll say?"

"Perhaps how we'll react to whatever she says."

Rhona rested her cheek against his chest, her arms around him. "At least there've been no deaths or sign of the mist."

No sooner had the words left her lips than her mobile rang.

Balladyn glared at the device on the cushions as Rhona answered it.

"Hang on," she told the caller and held it out between them. "I've put you on speaker so Balladyn can hear you, Elias."

The Druid cut out for a moment, then he said, "I wanted you to know that I saw the mist tonight."

"Where?" Balladyn and Rhona asked in unison.

There was a brief pause before Elias said, "At Carwood Manor. I didna see where it came from, but it went directly for Bronwyn and circled around her a few times before going straight up into the air."

"Bronwyn?" Rhona asked, her brows drawn together.

"I doona think she's the one controlling it," Elias hurried to say.

Balladyn caught Rhona's gaze as he asked, "Why do you think that?"

"She didn't want it near her, but she didn't bat it away either. It almost looked as if it was investigating her."

"Did it do anything to you?" Rhona asked.

"Nay."

Balladyn noted that he didn't elaborate. "Did you ask Bronwyn about it?"

There was a brief pause. "I wasna with her. I was…watching her."

"Excuse me?" Rhona asked, her voice hard with outrage.

Elias sighed through the phone. "I know how that sounds but let me explain."

"We're waiting," Balladyn replied.

"I saw a confrontation between some women and Bronwyn at the co-op the other day. They didna want her there or even living on Skye. It made me curious about her, and then Edie told me about her being *drough*. The next day, I saw Bronwyn have an altercation with a man. I didna hear the conversation, but the tension between them was obvious. So was the male's threatening attitude. She never backed down, though."

Rhona pressed her lips together as she considered Elias's words. "That's when you decided to check on her?"

Elias blew out a breath. "Look, I know I didna tell you what you wanted to know before, but I will now. Personally, I doona like the idea of it, but Sabryn suggested I tell you everything."

"Who's Sabryn?" Balladyn asked.

"The leader of the Knights," Elias answered. "There are four of us. Well, five if you consider our cyber specialist. As I said, we've been tracking the murders. They're all over the world, but they're more concentrated in Scotland. We've amassed a great deal of data, but we've no' been able to pin down exactly who is behind it. I can give you proof of the murderers we have helped the authorities catch. And, well, we find Druids. We help them when they doona have anywhere else to turn."

Rhona quirked a brow at Balladyn, who shrugged in reply. She then asked Elias, "So, you want to…what? Help Bronwyn? Even though she's *drough*?"

"I doona think she'd take help even if I offered. What I can tell you is that I wasna the only one watching her."

CHAPTER EIGHT

Edie leaned her head back as steam rose from the tub. The water had turned rose gold from a bath bomb, and she sank deeper after taking a drink of her wine.

Even with her music playing, she heard the kids down the hall arguing over something. Every once in a while, she caught her husband shouting at the television for some stupid sports show he watched downstairs. Her baths were her quiet time. Her alone time. Her *me time*.

And she needed it.

How often had she brought up her parents at lunch with her brother and sister? Edie had intentionally spoken of their father to see if one of them would share the secret they thought they held—one she knew.

Not once did Elias or Elodie speak of it. They intended to hold that confidence among themselves. She didn't like being left out. She had been the only one either of them had spoken to in nearly two decades, and now, it was like they were best friends again.

Why did her siblings want to keep this secret from her? And what else weren't they sharing? What other confidences did they have? Did they think she couldn't handle things? That she was too wrapped up in her family? Or perhaps they just wanted to have that bond again.

It was too much like their childhood, where Edie had always felt left out. The middle child. Unless a person was one, they didn't understand.

Then Elias had the gall to bring up Bronwyn Stewart. A *drough* was a *drough*. They made their decisions, and there were consequences to such choices. Frankly, Edie didn't think any Druids but *mies* should be allowed on Skye, but she wasn't in charge.

"Maybe I should be," she murmured.

She slapped her hand on the water. Trevor claimed that she had been short-tempered lately. It was true that she snapped at him and the kids repeatedly, which was why she had come up for her bath early tonight.

Her husband knew everything about her—except for how her father had really died. Trevor accepted her magic and social standing as a Druid, but he always became uncomfortable when he learned how someone used their magic to harm another. She hadn't been sure how he would take what had transpired in her family, and then, after a year of dating, it had been difficult to bring it up and explain. So, she never did.

Now, when she wanted to talk to him about what her brother and sister were doing, she couldn't. Because he would want to know why she had kept it from him all this time. She didn't have a good answer for that. Which left her stewing in her anger now.

Maybe she'd call her mother and talk about it. No, she couldn't do that. Jail conversations were recorded. She didn't want to get her sister in trouble. That meant Edie would have to wait until her mum was released from prison.

Just thinking about that sent her spiraling again. Edie had always assumed her mother would live with them for a bit. Then she and Trevor would find Emily a house on Skye. There hadn't been specific conversations with her about it, but hearing how Elias planned to take care of all of that was just one more blow Edie hadn't seen coming.

She had been the only one to go and see Emily regularly. The only one Elias regularly contacted. And the only one Elodie would see. Now, she was irrelevant. And it hurt.

Painfully.

Then there were the cameras Elias had taken from the rental. Trevor swore he didn't know anything about them, but someone had put them there. She trusted her husband. That meant Elias was trying to stir shite. But why?

"Mum!" her daughter called and pounded on the door. "Teddy took my book!"

Edie squeezed her eyes closed. "Trevor!"

Her husband raised the volume as her daughter pounded on the door again.

She sighed and stood, water sloshing over the tub.

There was no sleep for Bronwyn, not after the mist had appeared. She still didn't understand why it had moved around her or what it wanted. It hadn't hurt her, but that didn't mean it wouldn't if it returned. She really hoped it didn't return—once was plenty.

She finished her morning chores and tried to get motivated to make bread but just couldn't manage it. Bronwyn gave up and tackled something she could get to work—her designs. She was surprised to find a request from a romance author for a book cover. She read the email twice just to be sure. Bronwyn had been waiting for this. She had the questionnaire ready to go for just such a client.

There was a smile on her face as she replied with her rates and specifics on how many changes could be made. Then she asked about the author's timeline. She'd do the cover whenever. She didn't care if she had to stay up for three days straight to meet the deadline as long as she could design a cover. Maybe even see her design in a bookstore. The thought made her so giddy it took her twice as long to compose the email and send it off.

Though she knew it was stupid to wait for a reply since the author might be on the other side of the world and sleeping, Bronwyn kept refreshing her emails, hoping a message would pop up. After thirty-six minutes, she forced herself to stop and move on to other things. Perusing Facebook didn't help much. Finally, she pulled up her current project for a nail salon in America that was changing their logo. The owner had known exactly what she wanted, which made Bronwyn's job much easier.

It took her another hour and a half to finish the design. Still, she didn't send it off. She liked to let things percolate for a bit first, just to be sure she was happy with everything. Even as she told herself not to, she checked emails—still no answer from the author.

Bronwyn slammed the laptop closed and headed for the kitchen. She got everything out and began making the bread. If she got the cover job, she would set aside a small portion for a bread maker. She made decent money on her designs, but one cover could replace three other jobs. Besides, covers were where she really wanted to focus her work.

She had been making her own bread for over a year, which meant she had the routine down pat. Now, she had two loaves rising. One was plain, and the other rye because she liked to have options. If there was one thing she enjoyed eating, it was bread. She might not eat well, but she never skimped on her carbs.

Though she hated the kitchen, she'd get an itch every once in a while to make things she could munch on later—like today. The potential of designing a cover was something to celebrate, after all.

After coming across something on social media, she decided to make ice lollies. The Americans called them popsicles, which just sounded funny to her. This time, she pulled out the frozen bananas she'd saved that had been about to go bad at the store and used them to make a banana coconut ice lollie. The only thing she didn't have was the chocolate chips to freeze on top. Still, this flavor was one of her favorites. Mixing up everything and setting the molds in the freezer didn't take long.

Unfortunately, it was time for lunch when she finished. The bread still had hours to rise before it could go into the oven, so Bronwyn opted to scramble an egg and eat it with some crackers. She barely got the last few bites down.

A quick clean of the kitchen, and then she was at her computer again. Excitement jumped through her when she saw that she had new emails. She bit her lip nervously to see one was from the author. Bronwyn scanned the email and then let out a little squeal when she saw they had agreed to the terms. And the turn-in date for the cover was more than reasonable. Bronwyn sent off the questionnaire and an invoice for half the price upfront. It would be a very good month.

"I'm manifesting more money," she told herself.

Maybe those meditations were working. If she could make enough to keep up with the repairs on the house and have enough for herself, she'd call it a win. She had a list of things she wanted to buy. Top of the list was a new mattress.

That was if things went in her favor when dealing with Sydney.

But she refused to let any of that bring her down from her high. Bronwyn soon lost herself in work for her next client. A few hours later, she received a notification that the author had paid the invoice. The smile didn't leave her face for the rest of the afternoon. Not even when it began to rain, and she had to haul in more firewood to keep the chill at bay.

She didn't even grumble about having to eat dinner. The bread was fresh and still warm when she made her sandwich. It even tasted good. She lost herself in enjoying the fruits of her labor and thus was taken aback when someone pounded loudly on her door.

Bronwyn didn't need to look to know it was Sydney. Anger and tension charged the air. She set her half-eaten food on the plate and walked out of the kitchen. It had been such a good day that she almost told Sydney to come back another time. But there was no getting around this.

Her stomach clenched when she realized she might never get to design the cover. If things didn't go her way, she hoped the author could have her money returned. Perhaps Bronwyn should do that now before she answered the door. Just in case.

She made her way through the long hallway, her gaze locked on the entryway. She paused long enough to look up the stairs when she reached them. Then she made her way to the door and opened it. On the stoop, water dripping from him, stood the man she hated fiercely, the one she intended to mete out her own brand of justice on. His dark eyes held such hatred that she was surprised she didn't go up in flames.

The battle would be intense.

"I know she's in there," Sydney shouted over the rain.

Bronwyn stared at him, waiting. She knew what was coming.

He tried to shoulder his way inside but was thrown backward. He landed on his arse, his head snapping back with such force that she heard it hit the gravel. He slowly sat up. "You'll pay for that, bitch."

CHAPTER NINE

Pure madness made Elias return to the manor. He didn't even leave when it began to rain. Something evil surrounded Carwood Manor, and he was determined to find out if it was Bronwyn or something else. At least that was what he told himself when he ignored calls from his sisters, the Knights, and even DI Frasier, who wanted him to come in and give a statement—or so the voicemail said.

Elias had watched the manor for hours. The feeling of something vile and malevolent intensified with the approaching night. By the time dusk came, Elias knew something would happen. He scanned the sky for the mist, but that wasn't what surrounded the house.

The moment he spotted the tall, thin man who had accosted Bronwyn before, Elias knew why his instincts had brought him to the estate. He debated calling the Knights, but they'd never get here in time. The more people involved, the more attention it would likely bring to him, which was something he wanted to avoid. So, he decided to take care of things himself.

He kept hidden in the trees a fair distance from the manor. Thin Man and his friends circled the house several times as if testing it. When the rain came, the bastard smiled. It wasn't long after that Thin Man knocked on the door. The way the other members of the gang readied themselves had Elias moving from the safety of the tree line to come up behind one of the men. No one knew he was there. He could sneak up on them and take them out one at a time. He'd rather ensure they could never harm anyone again, but dead bodies when he was already being investigated for murder wouldn't look good.

Elias crept up behind the man and wrapped his arms around his neck. The rain dampened the sound of the guy's struggles, and his comrades were too focused on the manor to notice that anything was amiss. The chokehold worked within moments. Elias laid the man on the ground and crept toward his next target —a woman.

When he glanced at the manor, he saw Bronwyn and Thin Man talking. The guy went to enter the house and collided with an invisible force that had him sprawled on the ground. Thin Man shouted something Elias couldn't hear over the rain and got to his feet. But the woman with Thin Man must have expected it because she raised her hands. He watched as the rain moved under her command. The droplets turned into tiny pellets that coalesced and swirled together before heading straight for Bronwyn.

Elias took off toward the woman, but the rain broke through whatever Bronwyn used to guard the house and grabbed hold of her. He watched as it yanked her from the safety of the home and slammed her into the front of her SUV, causing the metal to groan from the impact and the vehicle to rock.

Once Bronwyn was outside, Thin Man and two others went for her. Elias concentrated on the woman. He slid on the gravel, using momentum to swipe at her feet. She landed hard on her back. When he rose, she lay unmoving. Elias then spun around to look at Bronwyn. To his shock, she didn't use magic to defend herself. What *drough* didn't use the power they had sold their soul for?

Two of the men held her as Thin Man shouted something. Bronwyn shook her head, her expression defiant. Elias moved toward Thin Man, but one of his thugs spotted him and rushed Elias. Elias called to his magic. It sprang into his hands as he moved them up and out before pushing them forward and sending a blast of magic at the man.

The attacker jerked back, hitting his head on the bumper of the SUV and crumpling to the ground. Thin Man and the second goon turned to him. Without someone to hold her, Bronwyn sagged. She tried to hang on to the bull bar, but her hands slipped on the chrome.

Elias's attention shifted to the two men as they fanned out. Water dripped into his eyes and down his neck into his clothes. It wasn't the first time he'd been outnumbered, and it likely wouldn't be the last with his line of work.

The fury coming off Thin Man was palpable. He glanced at his friend, motioning toward Elias with his jaw. The second man came at Elias at the same time Thin Man made a run for the house while Bronwyn pulled herself along the ground toward the door. Elias didn't know what was inside the manor that Thin Man wanted so desperately, but he wasn't going to let him in.

Elias shot out his magic, causing it to tangle Thin Man's feet, tripping him. Thin Man pitched forward and slammed his head on the gravel with such force that it bounced once. Thin Man tried to lift his head, then went still.

The second man's fist, surrounded by magic, made contact with Elias's abdomen. The impact was so intense that Elias dropped to his knees, gasping for air, while pain radiated outward. His attacker grabbed him by the hair and yanked his head back before aiming his hand at Elias's neck. Elias got his arms up in time to block the blow. Then he elbowed the area above the man's knee. It caused the goon to lose his balance, and Elias tackled him, sending them both rolling on the ground.

Elias tasted blood when the guy hit him in the jaw, but he never stopped landing his own punches anywhere and everywhere he could until the man finally stopped moving. Elias's breaths came in great gasps as he shoved the attacker off him and rolled to his hands and knees. He felt for a pulse. Once he was satisfied the goon was still alive, he pushed to his feet and ran the short distance to Bronwyn. As soon as he touched her, she started fighting him.

"Bronwyn, I'm here to help!" he shouted over the rain.

Finally, she lifted her head to look at him before sagging against him. He tried to turn her to the trees to take her to the vehicle he'd hidden.

"Nay! I need to get in the house. The house!" she shouted, her entire body shivering, her clothes plastered to her body.

It was closer, and he was beginning to feel every punch that had pummeled his body. Bronwyn couldn't keep her feet and was bleeding from a head wound. Maybe the manor would be safer until he could call the Knights to help.

"All right, all right," he conceded.

She gripped his arm tightly as he adjusted his grip to keep her upright. "You can come inside."

He hurried to get them over the threshold. As soon as he did, he kicked the door shut behind him. He paused, considering where to take her.

"The newel. Now. I need to touch the newel," she insisted.

The urgency in her voice propelled him forward before he could think twice. She kept slipping out of his grip. He winced at the pain in his rib as blood dripped from her head onto his arm, but he got her to the newel.

She placed her hand on it, then cursed under her breath. Bronwyn shot him a quick glance before touching her hand to her wound, coating her palm in blood before returning her hand to the post.

"Blood magic," he murmured, shocked and abhorred as he stared at her hand on the wooden nob.

Suddenly, he was thrown off balance. Somehow, he managed to stay on his feet, but Elias belatedly realized that Bronwyn had fallen unconscious. It took him two tries to lift her into his arms because of his pain. Then he turned in a circle, once again trying to figure out where to take her. He didn't think he'd get them up the stairs without causing more damage. In the end, he went to where he saw light.

The door to the parlor was slightly ajar, making it easier for him to enter. When he did, he came to a halt at the sight of a sofa bed and a rack of clothes off to the side where three pairs of shoes were neatly stacked. Surely, this wasn't where she slept. But everything pointed to that.

Elias brought her to the rug before the fire. He lowered to

one knee, gritting his teeth at the agony, and laid her out. Her clothes were soaked. If he didn't want her to catch a cold, he needed to get her out of them as well as tend to her wound. He grabbed the throw blanket folded over the chair's arm and put it near her as he tugged off her boots. He set them next to the fire to dry. Then he removed her shirt and sweatpants, opting to leave her in her underwear. Elias wrapped her in the blanket to keep her warm. Then, he stood.

He weaved as the room spun. He had to grab the chair to keep on his feet, but once his head cleared, he strode out of the room. Elias locked the front door, just in case. He jerked off his wet coat, hanging it on a peg. Then he went in search of supplies. He found a small first-aid kit. He brought that, along with a bowl of hot water and a towel to the parlor, where he set about cleaning the blood from her.

The injury was near her hairline. Once he'd removed the blood from her face and neck, he could see the wound clearly. It was about an inch long, but he didn't think it needed stitches. He cleaned it and then used a butterfly bandage to hold the skin together.

Next, he checked her for other injuries. Her hands were cut up from the gravel, but the wounds were superficial. The laceration on her right knee was far worse. He cleaned and bandaged it before he checked her feet. He didn't like the look of the swollen left ankle.

Elias pulled back the covers on the sofa bed and moved her onto it before tucking the blankets around her. He glanced at the fire to see it nearly out. There was a small pile of wood nearby that she obviously used. What he didn't understand was why she didn't use magic to keep the fire going instead of logs. It was a simple spell, one of the first children learned.

It was just as confusing why she hadn't used her magic against Thin Man. Elias would have to learn the answers to those questions later. He chanted the spell to keep the fire burning until he or Bronwyn put it out.

Only then did he remove his boots and set them on the other side of the fire. It was time to call the Knights. Elias reached into his wet back pocket, only to find it empty. He realized he must have put his phone in his coat, but when he looked, he didn't find it there either. Had it fallen out in the scuffle? That was the only explanation. He returned to the parlor and found a laptop and mobile. Just as he expected, he couldn't unlock the phone to make a call.

"Bloody hell," he murmured.

His head pounded, not to mention his ribs. He didn't think any were broken, but that knowledge didn't help the pain. Elias needed something to dull the aches. He found some aspirin in the first-aid kit and took them.

"Well, it looks like I'll be here for a wee bit," he said with a sigh.

He stripped out of his wet clothes and gathered up the ones he'd removed from Bronwyn. After doing his best to scrub the blood from her shirt, he hung the garments to dry in the utility room. He found a downstairs bathroom and washed away the worst of the dirt and blood from himself. By the time he returned to the parlor, he was shaking from the cold.

It was difficult not to notice how bare the manor was of pictures or anything of value. He saw the outline of past frames against the wood in places, but there was no silver or any pieces of art usually found in such great homes.

And there was no heat.

He huddled in the chair near the fire beneath a throw blanket, his eyes on Bronwyn. "Looks like you have secrets aplenty."

Especially her use of blood magic.

CHAPTER TEN

"I don't like this," Sabryn stated as she turned from the window. She looked across the hotel room at the two men staring back at her. "Where is Elias?"

Carlyle Oliver, groomed since birth to inherit his father's title and estates in England and raised with more money than anyone knew what to do with, shrugged after wiping his mouth from finishing breakfast. He wore his auburn waves long and with just enough product to keep the locks from falling into his face. His turquoise eyes held as much concern as hers. "He didn't answer any of my calls or texts yesterday evening."

Her gaze slid to the seat where Finn O'Connor sat, the complete opposite of Carlyle. Finn got his education on the streets of Dublin, learning to survive by any means necessary. Where Carlyle preferred the finest clothes, Finn didn't wear anything but jeans and simple shirts. With brown hair so deep it was nearly black and deep brown eyes, he was the dark to Carlyle's light.

But both men had saved her ass. They were family, just as Elias was. An American, a Brit, a Scot, and an Irishman. They likely wouldn't have met except for the one thing that'd brought them all together—the deaths of fellow Druids.

"He's not talkin' to me either," Finn replied in a heavy Irish accent. "That's not like him. He's in trouble."

Carlyle flattened his lips as he set aside his cup of tea. "I agree. Elias knows what's at stake right now. He wouldn't go off-grid without telling one of us."

Sabryn thought back to her last conversation with Elias. "I think I know where we'll find him."

Elias's body was stiff as he woke and stretched. He grimaced at the painful kink in his neck. He was getting far too old to be sleeping in such a way. If he kept it up, he'd wake one day and be bent at an angle forever.

At least the fire was still lit, which kept the room relatively warm. He glanced at the bed to find Bronwyn still asleep. He'd checked her several times during the night, and he didn't like that she hadn't woken yet.

He stood and wrapped the blanket around himself. As he walked through the parlor, he opened the curtains to look outside. The sun was out, and while clouds that hung low and heavy in the sky approached, it wasn't raining yet. A glance showed that Thin Man and his gang had left sometime in the night. They might have gone for now, but they'd return. He was sure of that. It made him question his decision to leave them alive. But he wasn't a killer.

Not unless he didn't have a choice.

Last night, he'd had a choice. Whether his decision had been the right one remained to be seen. He looked at Bronwyn over his shoulder. Only her head was above the covers. Her dark locks had dried, but her skin was too pale. He worried she had sustained injuries he hadn't been aware of last night.

Elias was curious about so much with her. Like why was she alone in the huge house? Who was Thin Man, and what did he want? But more than anything, Elias wanted to know why she was *drough*, and why she had resorted to blood magic.

The Isle of Skye might be beautiful, but it could be harsh for the Druids who called it home. While their magic should band them together, it usually did the opposite. He'd learned that fear usually drove those tendencies in people, which caused them to alienate some. That left others like Bronwyn, those who should have a network available to them, to their own devices. From the little he'd seen of Bronwyn since his return, it was obvious she depended on no one but herself.

Was that by choice or because she had no other options?

He willed her to wake, to open her mesmerizing hazel eyes so he could sort through the myriad of colors once more. The part of him compelled to assist others had been very loud since the episode in the co-op. He wanted to help her. It wasn't the most convenient time, but he didn't care. In his years with the Knights, he'd learned to see troubles, and there was definitely an issue here that involved Bronwyn.

Elias sighed, no closer to finding a way to talk to her than he had been before. His gaze lingered for another moment before he left the parlor to check his clothes. They were still damp. He showered, which helped to work some of the stiffness out of his neck, but there was no getting around the large bruise on his torso—or the likely cracked rib.

He walked naked back to his clothes and tugged on his pants, the feel of the clammy denim causing a chill to rush over him. He grabbed his shirt and socks and brought them to the parlor to hang near the fire, hoping they would dry quicker.

Elias then checked Bronwyn again. The swelling in her ankle had gone down. There was that, at least. He gave her a little shake.

"Bronwyn? It's time to wake, lass," he urged.

But she didn't move.

He tried twice more before giving up. He felt her forehead, but thankfully, there wasn't a fever. His stomach rumbled. He needed to contact the Knights, but it was still early. He had time for a quick bite before he went looking for his mobile.

Elias scrounged in the kitchen and grinned in delight when he found the freshly baked bread. He toasted a couple of slices and coated them with strawberry jam. As he ate, he meandered through the downstairs and noticed the home's cleanliness. No one else was in the house, and Bronwyn didn't seem the kind who wanted people inside. That meant she took care of everything herself. He couldn't imagine how much it took to keep a house this size in order. His bare feet on the wood slats didn't make a sound as he stopped at the staircase.

It was wide and opulent with spots on the dark wood that still held a hint of polish near the deep blue runner with its gold swirl design. The first set went straight up to a landing with a table. Two more sets switched back on either side, going to the second story. Elias glanced at the closed parlor door before starting up the stairs. He wanted to know why Bronwyn slept downstairs. Was it because it was warmer? Or was there something more?

He put his foot on the first step. The walls were bare, showing additional proof in the light of day that riches had once adorned them. When he reached the second floor, he looked down the hallway, first one way and then the other. He finished off his second piece of toast and began walking the corridors. Every door was closed. It was significantly chillier up here than even in the kitchen. He tried a few doors and found them unlocked. He looked inside to find bedrooms with sheet-covered furniture.

He discovered another set of stairs that led to the third floor, with more closed doors. One person didn't need all those rooms. It made sense that Bronwyn would keep them closed. But to sleep in the parlor when there were plenty of more comfortable options? He didn't understand that.

Elias made his way back down the stairs, pausing at the last step and the newel that held the remnants of her blood from last night. *Mies* might become *droughs* for the extra power it gave them, but it took a brave—or reckless—few to delve into blood magic. When mastered, it was potent and violent. A Druid could rarely control it for any length of time since the end result was never kind. It was why so few ever attempted it.

Yet Bronwyn had.

"Why blood magic on the house but nothing to defend yourself?" he murmured, his confusion about her growing.

Could her use of blood magic have drawn the mist? Perhaps she had inadvertently called it up. One thing was for certain—he had to find the answer. Lives depended on it. The Druids who dared blood magic never came back from it. He didn't know how long Bronwyn had left, which meant he would need to work quickly to uncover everything he could.

He turned away from the stained newel and retraced his steps to the kitchen. As water heated for tea, he rummaged through the cupboards and found a tray. There, he set out a plate, jam, utensils, a glass of water, and two cups. Once the water boiled, he steeped the tea. That was when he saw the honey. He added that and the small carton of milk to the tray. When the tea had brewed, he carried the tray into the parlor.

It made him think of the times his mother had done the same for him when he'd been sick as a child. It might have taken years, but his family was getting sorted again. If nothing else, he was pleased about that. They could carry on with their lives as they always should have. As for him? He wasn't throwing in the towel quite yet. He'd been fighting for others for far too long not to do the same for himself.

Elias set the tray on a small table. When he turned to the sofa bed, he found hazel eyes watching him. The green was so pale there was almost no color. The gold and copper stood out the most in the morning light. Once more, he was transfixed.

Utterly spellbound.

In a blink, he was transported back to a long-ago day when a young lass with a thick braid down to her waist had tripped and fallen. He'd walked away from his friends to help her. Bronwyn had stared at him then as she did now—curiously and with a hint of trepidation.

How had he forgotten that moment?

Or her?

But just days after that, his life had imploded violently. He'd barely held it together. His every thought had centered around his mum, sisters, and himself. Everything else had been pushed aside and forgotten.

Until he'd come home to Skye and found himself looking into those beautiful eyes once more.

Elias didn't believe in coincidences. There was a reason their paths had crossed again.

He could stare at her forever, lost in the ocean of colors in hazel depths that captured him effortlessly. They were strangers, yet they weren't. She had nearly died last night, and that thought saddened and angered him. It also brought him back to the present.

"How are you feeling?" he asked.

"Like shite," she murmured and swallowed.

Her gaze lowered, remaining there for a moment. Elias remembered that his shirt was still drying. He shook himself when he saw her lick her lips. He brought her water and helped her to sit up so she could drink a little. "I have aspirin if you have need of it. I imagine you've a whopper of a headache."

"Aye," she said after drinking her fill. She sank against the pillows, her expression pained.

After he'd brought the pills and helped her sit a second time, he stepped back. "There's tea and toast if you're up for it."

"Who are you?"

He shouldn't be hurt that she didn't remember him. He had forgotten her, after all. But he remembered everything now. "I'm Elias MacLean."

Even after he'd announced his name, she didn't show any

indication that she remembered. For some reason, that bothered him.

She lifted the covers and looked down at herself. "You undressed me?"

"You were soaked through. You needed to get warm, and you couldna do that wet. No' to mention I needed to tend to your injuries."

"Right." Another swallow and a flash of unease. "I'm Bronwyn."

He held her gaze and smiled. "It's been quite a few years since I've been on Skye, but I know you. I confess, I didna recognize you at first. Your hair was much longer the last time I saw you."

She looked away nervously. "Now I know why you looked familiar. You seem to have a habit of helping people."

"You could say that."

They fell into an awkward silence. Elias grabbed the tray. When he turned back to her, she had pushed herself into a better sitting position, keeping the blanket tucked beneath her arms. He set the tray across her lap and took a cup of tea.

"Thank you," she said. "For, well, everything."

He sank into the chair. "I'm glad I was here to lend a hand."

Silence grew when she focused on the tray, adjusting everything nervously. He watched as she filled a teaspoon with honey before tipping it so the thick sweetener dribbled slowly into the liquid. Elias grinned when he realized she was making designs with the honey. She only stirred the tea when there was nothing left on the spoon.

"I suppose you want to know who those people were," she said without looking at him.

Elias tipped his head. "I would, aye."

Her gaze snapped to his, the look in her eyes stern and unyielding. "I'd also like to know what you were doing on my estate."

He fought back a smile at her courage. "Fair enough. I saw the man confront you the other day. Things looked…strained."

"And you took it upon yourself to spy on me? Or maybe you work with him, and by helping me, you knew it would get you inside." Her anger grew with every word.

Elias stretched his legs out in front of him and crossed his ankles. Then he took a drink of his tea, all without looking away from her as he decided how to answer her and defuse the indignation she had every right to feel. "If I were with those people, which I'm no', then the latter would be true. I was watching the manor, but no' on anyone's orders. I was here on my own."

"Why?"

He contemplated whether to tell her everything. Then he decided that was the only way he would get the same in return. "You're right. I help people. I have for years. Sometimes, I'm hired to do it. Other times, I stumble upon the opportunity. After your clash with the group, I suspected they might try something."

"Did I give you any indication that I couldn't take care of myself?"

He blinked and paused. Shite. "Nay, lass. I'm used to spotting trouble, is all."

"And I suppose the fact that I'm a *drough* now never crossed your mind?" she bit out.

Her anger was barely leashed. Someone who held in that

much emotion did it for a reason. Elias had learned that point himself. There were times the past still intruded, dredging up excruciating memories and a tsunami of fury. He had faced it with the help of the Knights. Who did Bronwyn have?

"It isna my place to judge. I shouldna have been spying. I apologize for that. I should've come straight to you, and I would have. I didna have time when the group showed up. I did what needed to be done."

She held his gaze without replying.

Elias didn't want to leave her. He didn't know why he felt such a strong need to be by her side, but there was no denying it. He needed to make up for mucking things up so epically as he had. "I'm verra sorry to hear about your father."

"Thank you," she said softly, her eyes lowering.

"I hope you accept my apology for snooping around," he said, watching her intently. "I was here because I was worried about what those goons would do. It had nothing to do with your change of magic."

Her hazel gaze slid to him before she chewed and swallowed a bite of toast. "How long have you been watching me?"

Elias hesitated. He'd made headway, and he just might lose all the ground he'd made up. "Two nights."

"So…you…?"

"Saw the mist fly around you?" he asked, his brows raised. "Aye."

She stopped chewing for a heartbeat, and a frown quickly flashed over her face. "I've seen it before, but it was the first time it came near me like that. I didn't like it." She shivered. "At all."

"Do you know who controls it?"

"Just because I'm *drough* doesn't mean I'm privy to such

things," she snapped. Then she briefly closed her eyes and sighed. "If I did, I'd let Rhona know. I appreciate your help last night, but it's best if you leave now. This isn't your fight."

Elias kept his expression blank as pain shot through him as he shifted and set aside his cup. He'd made his decision, and nothing could change his mind. He would eventually convince Bronwyn to let him help her. Until then, he'd give her what she wished. "You couldna walk last night. You were unconscious for hours." He motioned to the fire with his head. "I'll stay until my clothes are dry and I know you can get about without help."

She eyed him for a long moment. "You haven't asked about it."

"About what?" But he knew exactly what she referred to. He'd been waiting on her.

"The blood magic."

CHAPTER ELEVEN

Bronwyn might be able to think clearly if Elias put on a shirt. She couldn't stop staring at his upper body. The light dusting of hair, the broad shoulders, the muscular arms, the thick chest, the washboard stomach. And the V of muscles that disappeared into the waistband of his jeans.

Though she also saw the massive bruise on his right side.

The sight of that amazing chest, combined with the pounding of her head, made it nearly impossible to keep her thoughts focused on their discussion. Her stomach roiled. She needed to fill it. The toast stuck in her mouth, but she managed to keep a couple of tiny bites down.

Bronwyn was surprised that Elias had agreed to leave. She'd been sure that he would try to poke around and ask a million questions she didn't intend to answer. She took another nibble of toast before sipping the tea. Then, she made the mistake of bending her right knee. Her skin stretched, and the kneecap throbbed. She hissed in a breath. Elias was at her side in an instant.

He set aside the tray and started to lift the blankets. She slapped her hand over his and met his gaze. Blue eyes, clear and bright like a sunny day, met hers. She noted the band of navy that encircled his irises and the flecks of silver mixed with the blue.

"The cut on your knee was severe," he told her. "I just want to see if you're bleeding again."

Bronwyn felt a bead of blood run down the side of her knee. She was so used to doing everything herself that she wasn't sure how to allow someone to tend to her. It was a show of weakness that she couldn't afford. But with her head and the pain in her side that had taken her breath when she sat up, she wasn't sure she could do anything at the moment.

"There's nothing wrong with accepting help," Elias told her in a soft voice.

A gravelly, sexy voice.

That, along with his stunning eyes, was a combination she didn't stand a chance against. Her gaze dropped to his chest again. He was so near she could feel his warmth. Desire unfurled low in her belly, pushing aside her pain. She had the urge to move her hand up his arm to his shoulder and then over his chest.

It had been so long since she had touched someone—or had anyone touch her. He could shove her hand aside and do what he wanted, but he didn't. He waited for her. All the while holding her eyes. Her nipples hardened, reminding her that all that stood between them was blankets and her underwear. He had stripped her out of her clothes last night. She had missed out on feeling his hands, but if she'd been awake, she never would've let him come near her.

Would it really be so bad to accept this small touch? To allow someone to help her? To admit that she wanted to feel his skin against hers, however briefly?

The past few months had been the loneliest of Bronwyn's life. If the night before was any indication of what was to come, she should take what compassion was offered. And it was kindness. It might have been decades since she had seen Elias MacLean, but he was still the same gentle, caring lad who had come to her defense all those years ago. But he was all grown now.

Into a ruggedly handsome man who made her wish she'd made different choices.

She removed her hand from his. He nodded and shifted the covers just enough to expose her right leg from the thigh down. She spotted the gauze taped to her knee that was now colored red.

Elias carefully lifted the tape. His touch was light, tender. She had tensed, waiting for the pain, but there was none. She saw the jagged cut that ran from the bottom of her knee upwards at a diagonal toward the inside of her thigh. It throbbed in time with her head now.

He dropped the gauze and slid his gaze to hers. "You have two options. I can bandage this now and you can dress. Or I can help you to the bathroom if you wish to shower. Then I'll see to the wound."

"The latter option, please." She felt grimy, and she wanted to wash away her encounter with Sydney.

"Do you want to finish the toast?"

Bronwyn shook her head and tried to sit up more. She gritted her teeth at the pain that cut through her. The room began to spin. Suddenly, Elias was there.

"Easy. Easy," he whispered, his voice close to her ear. "Hold on to me. That's it. Give yourself a moment to let the pain pass."

The dizziness had passed. But in its place was heat that had nothing to do with her injuries.

"Better?" he asked.

Bronwyn nodded, afraid to use her voice.

Elias helped swing her legs over the side of the bed before wrapping an arm around her. It was a mistake to allow herself to be tucked against him as she was, but she didn't have the will to move away.

"Now, let's get you on your feet."

My God, his voice was so seductive he could probably get her to do anything he wanted. She locked her gaze on the fire, trying to tune out the fact that his bare skin was now against hers.

The warmth of his flesh called to her. She wound her arm around him, careful to keep away from his bruise. It felt so good that she leaned toward him, then she jerked her head up.

"It's okay. Lean on me," he urged.

But she knew it was better if she didn't.

His eyes, his voice, and his body were doing too many strange things to her. She had to get her head right again. It didn't matter how sexy-as-fuck he was. Elias didn't need to be mixed up in the shite storm that was her life.

She was so focused on that thought that when she took her

first step on her left ankle, she bent over in pain. Which in turned shot pain from her knee to her head and ribs. If Elias hadn't been holding her, she would have fallen.

"Take your time," he told her softly.

Bronwyn had gone only a few inches, and her body was covered in sweat from the agony of her injuries. She was glad she hadn't eaten more. As it was, her stomach was rebelling.

Elias steered her around the end of the sofa bed but paused. "You're going to need this," he said as he grabbed the blanket from his chair and wrapped it around her. "It might be easier if I carry you."

Nay! She was having a difficult enough time standing pressed against him. She wouldn't be able to handle being in his arms. "I'll be fine."

"Do you want energy to walk or shower?" he asked simply. "Because I'll be happy to stand in the shower and keep you on your feet."

Bloody hell. He had a point. Still, she hesitated. "I'll shower alone."

"That's what I thought."

His voice held a smile. She didn't look at him, even though she wanted to. The next thing she knew, he had shifted to the side and bent, placing one arm behind her back and the other under her knees. He lifted her effortlessly and with minimal pain. That allowed her to wrap the blanket around herself so only her lower legs and feet were exposed.

But as soon as they left the parlor, her feet chilled to the point they hurt. Elias's strides were long, and his steps didn't jar her too much. Soon enough, they were in the bathroom. He set her on the closed toilet lid and straightened. That was when she saw that he was barefoot.

"Aren't you cold?" she asked.

He chuckled as he turned on the shower. "Aye, it's chilly. How hot do you want the water?"

"Near to scalding." When he shot her a look, Bronwyn shrugged. "It's how I warm up."

"Fair enough," he murmured. It wasn't long before steam began filling the room. Elias walked to the door and paused with his hand on the handle. "I'll be right outside. Call if you need me. And doona overdo it. The heat might feel good, but too much isna good with your injuries."

"I'll be fine." When he didn't leave, she shot him a look. "I heard you."

The door closed softly behind him. Bronwyn blew out a breath, then regretted it at the sharp pain that lanced her rib cage. She let the blanket fall away and used the counter to steady herself as she got to her feet. She removed the bandage and grimaced at the droplets of blood from her knee that were now on her favorite blanket. She glanced at herself in the mirror and grimaced again.

She looked horrible. Her face was pale, her hair was a tangled mess, and she had dried blood along her hairline. She leaned toward the mirror and inspected the cut and bandage on her forehead. That explained the headache.

Bronwyn unhooked her bra and let it fall from her arms. Then she pushed her panties down her hips in slow movements to prevent more pain. It felt like forever before she was beneath the water. Once there, she sighed as the spray moved over her body, easing her aches and washing away the blood and grime from the battle the night before.

Battle. She snorted and shook her head. It wasn't much of a fight. Her spells on the house needed to be upgraded to prevent more than just people from entering. She didn't want to be caught like that again. Nothing should've gotten through her wards. Nothing. Yet the rain had. That meant Sydney had a water dancer with him.

It was only because of Elias that she was alive. Oh, Sydney wouldn't have killed her. No. He would've tortured her for however long it took for her to break and spill where Beth was hiding. Bronwyn was all too acquainted with the lengths Sydney would go to in order to get what he wanted. She had helped him at one time. But that was before she'd discovered just what kind of man he was.

Bronwyn washed her hair and body, which took twice as long with her injuries. By the time she turned off the water, she was barely able to stand. She sat on the toilet and dried off, only to realize that she hadn't brought any clothes.

There was a soft knock, then Elias's voice came through the door. "I'm sorry for digging through your stuff, but I have clothes for you. I wasn't sure what you might want, though. I grabbed the first things I could find."

She had never been so thankful to have someone dig through her things than she was right then. She wrapped the towel around her body. "Thanks. You can come in."

The door opened a crack to show his face. His gaze caught hers before his body emerged, fully clothed now. He looked her over quickly and set the pile of clothes on the sink counter. "You good?"

She was far from good, but she could get dressed on her own. "Aye."

"I'll go get the first-aid kit." He flashed a grin and left.

Why was she disappointed that he was no longer shirtless? Bronwyn rolled her eyes at herself then leaned over to grab the bra and panties. Next were the fuzzy purple socks with black cats. They were her favorites that she had gotten last Halloween. Only then did she tackle the sweatshirt and sweatpants.

She used the towel to cover her knee to keep the blood from getting on her pants. Once everything was in place, she told him he could come back in. Elias must have been near the door because it opened almost immediately. He said nothing as he sat on his haunches before her and pulled up her right pant leg. He dabbed the cut with the towel, then set about cleaning the wound before reaching for the bandages.

"I doona think you broke the kneecap, but it's bruised for sure. That combined with the cut will make walking fun." Elias glanced up as he taped the bandage over her knee. "I was worried you might have sprained your ankle last night, but that swelling is gone. How does it feel?"

"Sore but manageable."

"Any other injuries?"

She kept her breathing light and shallow. "Ribs."

"Ah," he said and flattened his lips. "With the way you hit your SUV's grill, I'm no' surprised."

"You have a rather spectacular bruise yourself."

He chuckled. "I'm fairly certain I have at least one cracked rib."

"And you carried me?"

"You weigh nothing."

"That isn't the point."

He ignored her as he rose to his knees and checked the butterfly bandage at her hairline. "It's exactly the point. If it had been too painful, I wouldna have done it. That looks good. Now," he said as he sat back on his haunches again, "anything else hurt?"

Did he mean besides her ego? "I'm good, thanks."

CHAPTER TWELVE

Elias was waiting when Bronwyn exited the bathroom. He had left her to brush her teeth and hair. She held herself stiffly, alerting him to her discomfort. He almost offered to carry her back to the parlor but suspected she would refuse.

"As you can see, I'm getting around myself. You can leave now."

He had agreed to just that. He didn't want to walk out of the house for several reasons, but he decided not to use any of them as excuses. His need to aid Bronwyn was too great to ignore, and in order to do that, he needed her to trust him. The only way to gain that was to keep his word.

He met her gaze and saw the argument waiting on her lips. "Aye. Let me get my shoes."

Surprise flickered across her face.

Elias walked past her toward the parlor room, glancing at the newel as he did. She had brought up the blood magic, and he hadn't pursued it. Now, he wished he had. Timing was everything, though, and he'd had to pick and choose what he pushed her on. Making sure her injuries were seen to had been more important. Next time—and there *would* be a next time—he would get the answers he sought.

He grabbed his boots and sat in the chair to put them on when the unmistakable sound of a vehicle rolling over gravel made him jerk his head up.

"Who did you call?" Bronwyn demanded from just inside the door. It clicked softly closed behind her, accentuating her question.

Elias stood, his gaze on the windows. "No one. I lost my mobile during the skirmish, and I didna want to leave the house last night in case I couldna get back in." He chanced a look at her to see Bronwyn's eyes wide, her fear tangible.

"The…bodies," she whispered, stricken.

He frowned as he walked to her. "What bodies?"

"Sydney and his people who came for me."

So that was the bastard's name. "Rest easy, lass. I didna kill them."

Her brows snapped together in shock. "You didn't?"

"Nay, I didna."

"Oh." She sagged against the door. "Then they'll return."

Which was one of the reasons he wanted to stay. "I take it you're no' expecting anyone?"

"No one comes here."

He walked to one of the windows and peered out. The minute he spotted the Range Rover in British racing green, he grinned. Then he remembered Bronwyn. He turned to her, trying to figure out what to say so she would allow the Knights inside. "It's my friends. They must have tried to get in touch with me. When they couldna, they likely traced my mobile here. They're good people."

"I'm just supposed to take your word for that? I don't even know *you.*"

"We can help—if you let us."

She shook her head and stepped away, but he saw how she held onto the wall and limped, favoring her right knee. "You promised to go. I need you to do that and take your friends with you."

A knock sounded on the door.

Elias noted the determined glint in her eyes. Bronwyn wouldn't change her mind, but that didn't mean he'd give up protecting her. Danger came at her from all sides, and she either didn't know or didn't care. He remembered the young girl from years ago who had been tripped. The sadness, anger, and embarrassment she couldn't hide when he helped her to her feet.

Bronwyn was older now, and those emotions were carefully hidden, but not so well that he didn't recognize them. Everyone had abandoned her. He wouldn't do that.

The knock turned into banging.

"You might want to get that," he told her. "I'll grab my shoes."

Elias's strides ate up the distance to the fireplace. He shoved his feet into the boots and was already on his way back to the front when he heard the door open.

"I'm looking for our friend. Elias?" he heard Sabryn ask.

He exited the parlor and stepped into the wide hallway. "I'm here," he called as he walked into the foyer.

Bronwyn didn't open the door any wider. In fact, she had

hardly opened it at all. She looked back at him as he grabbed his coat.

"I'll be around," he told her.

She lowered her gaze, her fingers gripping the door handle so tightly her knuckles turned white. "It's better if you forget all about me."

Elias didn't say that was an impossible feat. He shifted so he could see out the small crack to his friends. Sabryn's deep blue eyes met his. She was tall for a woman, but Finn was even taller. Instead of a smiling face, he saw the worry reflected in his friend's dark eyes.

"You'll want to rethink leaving, mate," Carlyle said from behind Sabryn.

"We'd like to talk for a moment." Sabryn eyed the door. "May we come inside, please?"

Bronwyn shook her head when Elias looked her way. He slid his gaze back to his friends. "I'm afraid no'."

"It's important," Sabryn insisted.

Bronwyn opened the door all the way, allowing him to see his friends clearly.

"I take that to mean we're not invited," Finn stated.

Elias wrinkled his nose. "Things are…complicated."

"Why haven't you answered our calls and texts?" Sabryn demanded.

The irritation and fear mixed in her voice put Elias on alert. "What is it? What's going on? Is it my family? Are they safe?"

"Your family is fine," Carlyle replied.

Elias frowned and focused on Sabryn. When she quirked a brow, he sighed. They weren't going to tell him anything until he answered their question. "Remember the bastard from the other day?"

"The one who confronted her?" Sabryn asked, nodding in Bronwyn's direction.

"Aye. He came last night with some friends. They attacked her."

Finn leaned to the side to better look at Bronwyn. "That's why she's so pale then?"

Elias ignored him. "There were five of them. I knocked each of them out before getting Bronwyn into the house."

"Why didn't you leave? You could've come to us," Carlyle interjected.

Elias glanced at Bronwyn to see her watching him. She feared what he would tell his friends. "That wasna an option. Bronwyn has protected the house."

"I'm aware," Sabryn said tightly. "I've already tried to shove my way inside. Did you leave last night?"

Elias shook his head as he crossed his arms over his chest. "She was banged up pretty badly. I barely got her inside before she fell unconscious. It was then that I went to call you, but my mobile must have slipped out of my pocket during the fight."

Finn held up Elias's phone, waving it. "We found it."

"So?" Elias asked Sabryn. "What's the problem?"

"Are you sure you didn't leave?"

Elias's frown deepened. "Aye, I'm sure. I was concerned about Bronwyn, and I wasna sure how long the assailants would be out. I decided to stay until she woke, and I knew she didna need a hospital."

"And you're positive all five were alive?"

A pit opened in Elias's stomach. "As you can see, none of them are here. They woke and left."

"They might have left, mate, but not all of them are alive," Carlyle said.

Elias tried to swallow as he digested the news. "What?"

"One of them was found dead this morning," Sabryn replied.

"If one of them died, it was by accident," he told them. "Maybe they dumped the body when they realized that."

His friends' silence made it difficult for Elias to breathe.

"They found the body at your place," Sabryn told him.

The blood rushed in Elias's ears, drowning out everyone's words. He saw their mouths moving, but he heard nothing. He took a step back, trying to find something to grab and stay upright. This couldn't be happening. He hadn't killed anyone, and he certainly hadn't left to dump a body at his place.

The world pitched around him, and it felt as though something were sucking at his feet, pulling him down. He blindly reached out for something, anything, when soft fingers met his. He clutched at them, grateful for the anchor. The room began to slow its wild spinning.

He searched his mind, going back over each encounter he'd had with the five individuals the night before. He was ninety-nine-point-nine percent certain they had been alive.

"It wasna me," he said, unsure if he said it to the others or himself. "I wouldna. No' when I've already been blamed."

The fingers in his tightened, drawing his gaze. He turned his head and found himself looking into hazel eyes. The green was darker now, making the copper stand out even more. He saw sorrow and understanding in her beautiful depths. That helped calm him, easing more of his panic.

He took a deep breath and looked at the Knights. "It wasna me."

"We know," Finn stated.

Carlyle nodded.

"You've been set up," Sabryn said. "It's why I don't think you should leave here. Not just yet."

Elias shook his head. "I gave Bronwyn my word. There are places I can go."

"Not like here," Finn said and looked up, taking in the size of the manor.

Sabryn's gaze turned to Bronwyn. "Elias is a good man who is being framed. We need to find out who is responsible and why they're focusing on him. We'll pay."

"Nay," he said.

But Bronwyn asked, "How much?"

Sabryn grinned. "A businesswoman. I like you already. How does a hundred pounds a day sound?"

"Deal," Bronwyn said. Then she looked at him. "They're right. No one will look for you here. Even if they do, they can't force their way in."

"Does that mean we can come in?" Sabryn inquired.

Bronwyn stared at her for a long moment before saying, "You three are welcome in my home."

Elias then watched as Sabryn, Carlyle, and Finn walked inside.

"Bloody hell, it's cold," Finn said and rubbed his hands together.

Carlyle shot him a peeved look. "Do you have any idea how much it costs to heat a home this size? The repairs alone cost a bloody fortune. Don't get me started on the heating."

"I'm sure you're going to tell me in great detail," Finn said with a roll of his eyes.

Sabryn looked Elias over. "You're injured."

"Busted rib or two. I've had worse." He cleared his throat and turned to Bronwyn. "Let me introduce my friends. This is Sabryn. She's American. The dark-haired Irishman to the left is Finn O'Connor. The cultured Brit is Carlyle Oliver. Guys, this is Bronwyn Stewart."

Carlyle bowed his head to her and smiled. "It's a pleasure. My grandfather used to speak of Carwood Manor and its beauty. I've longed to see it."

"It's nothing like it used to be," Bronwyn said.

Carlyle looked around him. "Nothing can diminish the great bones of such a residence."

Finn rubbed his hands together. "Right. Let's get down to business, shall we? Who has it out for our lad?"

CHAPTER THIRTEEN

Kerry stood before the mirror in her room and turned her head from side to side as she studied her hair. After years of having dull, lifeless locks, she had changed it with her magic. And she couldn't get enough of looking at it.

She had left the gray strands that mixed with her brown, though. After all, she had earned every year she had been alive. She wore the lighter streaks like a badge of honor. She also hadn't changed the length. She had gotten used to having it above her shoulders. However, instead of limp strands, she now had full hair that always did exactly what she wanted.

Kerry gently touched the bottom of her hair and smiled at her reflection before turning away. So much had changed about her life in such a short period. For once, she could honestly say she was happy. It was hard not to be when the Ancients had chosen her. Just thinking about the spirits of all the Druids who had come before made her smile. She couldn't wait to tell everyone that the Ancients had singled her out. That they now spoke only to her—in one voice.

And that they had granted her extra power.

They had a plan to right everything that had gone wrong with the Druids, and she would be the one to lead all Druids—even those on Skye—into a new day. She didn't know when that day would come, but she hoped it was soon.

Rhona and that filthy Reaper, Balladyn, had put her in the Druid prison deep within the Red Cuillins, thus taking her magic while she was locked within. But it had been Rhona who'd removed her as a deputy. *That* slight would be repaid tenfold.

Kerry grabbed a scone from a tin and stood at the kitchen window overlooking the land and people she had given her entire life to. The Druids in her quadrant of Skye were her family since she had no children, but the way they had treated her since she'd returned from the Red Hills was like having her heart cut out with a spoon. The pain was excruciating, agonizing. It wouldn't be too much longer before they came to her door once more for advice and direction.

She stuffed the last bite of scone into her mouth and wiped the crumbs from her lips. The Ancients had given her the mist to command. She knew the Druids they wanted removed, and she had quickly set out to do just that. Unfortunately, the Ancients had ordered her to hold off on using the mist for a short time. They wanted to lull the Druids on Skye into thinking things were back to normal, but Kerry hadn't been able to help herself the other night. She had bade the mist to come to her, and it had answered like a faithful companion.

It galled her that she hadn't been able to remove the one person the Ancients wanted gone. Elias MacLean might have gotten away once, but he wouldn't the next time she turned her attention to him.

But that wasn't who'd had her attention the other night. One on Skye had been shunned by everyone and decided to walk her own path: Bronwyn Stewart. She wasn't on the Ancients' list, and that was good. Kerry had simply wanted to see how Bronwyn reacted to the mist. And just as she had expected, the *drough* had accepted it.

There were others on Skye Kerry couldn't wait to bring into the fold. She had been concentrating on them, but every once in a while, she thought about the names on the list—ones that would be marked off one by one. Among those was none other than Elodie MacLean and her lover, Scott Ryan. Kerry wouldn't have put Elodie and Elias on the top of that list, but the Ancients obviously knew something she didn't.

Curiously, Edie wasn't listed. Neither were Edie's children. All the offspring with magic were to be spared the slaughter. They could be swayed, turned to be exactly what Kerry wanted.

"*You mean what I want,*" the Ancient said, her feminine voice smooth and commanding.

Kerry bowed her head to the voice that filled her mind. "Of course. What the Ancients want."

"*The Druids have run amok for too long. You've forgotten who you are at your core. The magic of our kind is fading. Rapidly. If things continue, Druids will cease to exist, leaving the realm in the hands of other magical beings.*"

Kerry's lips pulled back in a sneer. "The Fae and Dragon Kings."

"*The Fae are weak. The Dragon Kings' focus is split. Your concern should be for Death and her Reapers.*"

Reapers, who were Fae, but Kerry didn't argue the point. "Then let me proceed with your plan now. I'll dethrone Rhona and remove Balladyn once and for all."

"Not yet," the voice replied. *"Other things are happening."*

Kerry didn't like being left out. "Like what? Shouldn't the focus be on ensuring the Fae are never welcomed on Skye again?"

"I will determine what's important!" the Ancients stated curtly.

Kerry shut her eyes, cowering at the anger directed at her. "I only want to serve. I'm eager to see things through."

"You're eager for power and to dole out retribution." The Ancients paused. *"The time is coming."*

"And the list of those who have been chosen to die? When can I send the mist back out?"

"Soon."

Scott stood with Elodie in the kitchen of her cottage. His best friend, Filip, was off to the side. The three of them had been silent as DI Theo Frasier laid out the facts about the newest murder—and the suspect.

"You're wrong," Elodie finally said.

Frasier, for his part, didn't look pleased to be there. "I follow the evidence, Elodie. My feelings about anyone can no' matter."

"That's shite," Filip said with a snort as he crossed his arms over his chest.

Scott glanced at Filip, meeting his pale gray eyes. Then he returned his attention to Frasier. First, George had announced that Elias was the murderer. Now, Frasier was saying the same, only about a new body that had been found at the rental where Elias stayed.

Frasier rubbed his forehead and shifted his feet. "Look, Elodie, you said yourself that you have no' seen your brother in years. Nor have you spoken to him. You doona know what he's been up to."

"I know he isn't a killer," she stated flatly.

Scott could feel Elodie shaking with anger beside him. He put his arm around her and spoke to Frasier. "Something isna right. Surely, you see that. You said it appeared the man hadna been slain at Elias's. Why would Elias kill someone somewhere and bring the body back to his place to be found?"

Frasier shrugged. "People do strange things."

"Not my brother," Elodie replied.

"Regardless, I need to talk to him."

"You mean arrest him."

Frasier put one hand in the pocket of his pants. "I have questions I need answered."

"About this murder? Or the ones George has accused him of?" Filip asked.

Scott couldn't remember the last time he had been this confused. He had been a part of the Druid Others in Edinburgh led by George for years. Filip's brother, Kevin, who had been Scott's closest friend, had been one of the Druids murdered. Upon his death, Scott and Filip bonded, leaning on each other in their grief, and Filip became the brother Scott never had.

They had trusted George completely—had no reason not to. Then George sent them to locate Elodie and convince her to join their organization—a group, and ones like it, that Rhona and Balladyn were actively trying to disband.

Their origins came from the original Others that were made up of a *mie* and a *drough* from this realm, a Light and a Dark Fae, and a *mie* and a *drough* from another realm, a place humans themselves were descended from. The Others had formed to take over Earth, and the only way to do that was to get rid of the Dragon Kings. They'd nearly succeeded, too, but the Dragon Kings were too formidable to be conquered in such a way.

The original Others had disbanded, and most of the members had been killed. A Light Fae escaped and went to his people to begin the Fae Others, which the Reapers had recently stamped out. The Druids from Earth had then quickly spread the information about what a group of Druids combining their magic could do. It wasn't long before clusters of Druid Others began popping up around the globe.

Scott had once thought any group of Others was simply protecting itself from harm that could come to its members. It made sense when so many Druids were being murdered. Then he'd come to the Isle of Skye and learned the brutal truth about his organization. The Others, no matter if they were Fae or Druids, sought to assume power any way they could.

Filip made the decision to remain on Skye, where he had been born, and Scott chose to join him. It wasn't just Skye that had stolen Scott's heart, Elodie had, as well. George took their defections personally. Oh, she *said* she understood, but Scott didn't believe her. He still wasn't sure if George naming Elias as the Druid murderer was because of his and Filip's decision or not. But ever since George had come to Skye, things had continued to pile up against Elias.

The latest was one that left everyone reeling.

As Scott waited for Frasier to answer Filip's question, his gaze moved to Elodie. The MacLean family had suffered so much. Then just as things were about to sort themselves out, this happened.

"I'm still looking into George's allegation against Elias," Frasier replied. He held up a hand when Elodie went to speak. "You have to admit that your brother has secrets."

"We all do," Scott pointed out.

Frasier's lips twisted ruefully. "Be that as it may, it looks bad that we can no' find him. And this after I asked him to come to the station so I could ask about George's accusations."

Elodie threw up her hands and sighed loudly. "They're just that. Accusations. She has no evidence that he did anything to anyone here. Elias wasn't even *on* Skye when the Druids were murdered."

"But they stopped when he arrived," Frasier pointed out.

Filip dropped his arms. "They began when Scott and I came. Why are you no' looking into us?"

"Who says I'm no'?" Frasier ran a hand down his face. "Please, if you see Elias, send him my way. It'll go much better for him if he doesn't run." He paused and sighed. Then, with a shake of his head, he turned on his heel and walked out.

No one moved until Frasier was gone. Then, Elodie covered her face with her hands. Scott turned her, pulling her against him as he met Filip's gaze.

"What is happening?" Elodie asked, her face pressed against his neck.

Scott rubbed his hand over her back. "We're going to find out."

"You're damn right, we are," Filip said.

Elodie lifted her head. "What if…what if Elias *is* a killer?"

Scott smoothed her blond hair from her face and looked into her light blue eyes. "Then we'll find that out, too."

"I thought my family was past everything." She glanced down, swallowing. "Frasier's right, though. I don't know Elias. I don't even know Edie, not like siblings should. Elias is secretive about his life."

Scott shook his head. "I saw what he did to get to you. I saw his love for you, and for his family. And I doona think he's the one responsible for the deaths."

"Then where is he?" she asked in a soft voice.

Filip ran a hand through his black hair. "We need to retrace his steps from the last place he was seen and check with those who saw him."

"That would be Edie and me," Elodie said. "We had lunch together."

Scott kissed Elodie's forehead. "You told me Elias had plans to remain on Skye. I think he's still here." He looked at Scott. "Let's try to find his rental car."

"On it," Filip said and hurried from the room.

CHAPTER FOURTEEN

There were people in the house—several people, in fact. Bronwyn did not like that. But when they'd offered money, she'd jumped at the opportunity before she thought things through.

She stood among the four strangers, feeling left out in her own home. It wasn't their fault. Bronwyn had never fit in with groups. Not with Druids, not at the fancy private school her parents had sent her to, and not at the local school. It was like she had been marked to spend her life on the outside looking in from the moment of her birth.

As Elias and his friends talked amongst themselves, she rubbed her thumb over the tips of her fingers, the very ones she had used to grab Elias. It was so unlike her. Yet the despair and torment that had filled his eyes had been impossible to look away from. Or disregard.

She was well acquainted with the bleakness of desolation, the cruelty of hopelessness. Seeing those things in someone else had been like a kick in the stomach. The avalanche of emotions had nearly crushed the strong, virile man who had singlehandedly taken down Sydney and his gang.

And Bronwyn had reached for him instinctively, intuitively. The moment her fingers brushed his, he had taken hold of her as if she were the only thing keeping him standing. No one—not a single person in all her life—had ever made her feel as if she made a difference. Right then, at that very moment, she knew that she had. And she was glad that she had offered him a lifeline.

Then he'd looked at her. Just like at the co-op, she'd become lost in his eyes. He didn't hide the apprehension and uncertainty he suffered, he didn't try to conceal his panic or dread. He allowed her to see all of it as if they were friends. Maybe that was why she'd agreed to let him remain and had given his friends access to the manor. Though she was beginning to regret that.

Bronwyn made the mistake of trying to take a deep breath. Stabbing pain cut through her, cutting off her air. She gasped softly, not wanting to draw attention to herself. It felt like a hundred jackhammers were inside her head. As long as she didn't bend her knee, that pain wasn't too bad. Her ankle was beginning to throb some, but her ribs were causing the most discomfort at the moment.

No matter how she moved or stood, she couldn't stop the agony. The more she had to take shallow breaths, the more she felt the need to take a deep one, and each time she tried, she found herself unable to breathe.

Black dots began to edge her vision. She needed to sit. She tried to take a step toward the parlor and the warmth it offered, but her knee wouldn't hold her. She felt it give. Fear clawed through her as she reached for anything to keep her balance.

More darkness crept into her vision as she felt herself falling. Bronwyn thought she heard someone call her name as the darkness took her.

Elias caught Bronwyn an instant before she hit the floor. The momentum carried them both down. He cradled her head in his hand as his knuckles hit the faded rug in the corridor. That was when he felt the heat coming off her.

"Bloody hell," Finn said. "That was a good catch, E."

Elias looked at his friends. "She has a fever."

Carlyle squatted on the other side of Bronwyn and felt her head. "She's burning up."

"I saw her sway. I was about to suggest she sit down," Sabryn said as she and Finn moved closer.

Elias sat up, cradling Bronwyn against him. "She needs a hospital."

"We'll take her," Carlyle said.

But Elias hesitated as he recalled the night before. "I tried to get her to leave last night, but she wouldna. I doona think she can."

"We've seen her in town," Sabryn pointed out.

He turned his head to her. "I doona think she can leave for any length of time."

Sabryn's lips compressed briefly. "What aren't you telling us?"

"She used blood magic last night."

"Fekking hell," Finn murmured in shock as he ran both hands through his thick, dark waves.

Carlyle caught Elias's gaze. "None of that matters right now. She does. What are her injuries?"

Elias listed them, going over his ministrations. "She didna have a fever before."

"We have to decide. Take her to a hospital or treat her here." Sabryn shrugged. "And we have to understand that whatever choice we make might be the wrong one."

Finn grunted something beneath his breath. Then he said to the group, "It took a lot for her to let us inside, and she barely spoke to us after. I'm not sure we take her anywhere."

"I'd like to be the sane one here and point out that none of us is a healer," Carlyle stated.

Elias looked at Bronwyn in his arms. He remembered her urgency the night before, demanding he bring her to the house. It had taken all her will to stay conscious so she could use her blood. He wished he had pushed harder to learn what spell she had used now. Maybe it would have allowed him to make a better decision regarding her life.

"Elias?" Sabryn called.

He blew out a breath.

"We could contact Rhona," Finn offered.

Elias opened his mouth to agree when Sabryn said, "She'll realize we know Bronwyn. Even if you aren't here, she'll make the connection and either look for you or send Frasier to find you."

"Sorry, mate," Carlyle said with a twist of his lips. "Every decision has consequences."

Elias didn't want to be responsible for such a monumental decision. But he was, and he was thankful that he was here to make it. Happy that Bronwyn wasn't alone as she would've been had he left. He looked at each of his friends. "What can we do?"

Carlyle raised his brows, then turned his head and looked up at Finn.

The Irishman shot him a confused look. "What?"

"You're a bleeder," Carlyle said.

At one time, nearly every Druid had a special ability. When several Druids could do the same thing, it had been given a name. Wind talkers could communicate with the wind, and some could even wield it. There were fire walkers, water dancers, tree whisperers, and so many others. There were also healers, those who could mend injuries, though they could rarely heal themselves. Time benders could pause time for a few seconds. Bleeders took feelings from others. A rare few could alter someone's feelings.

"Aye," Finn replied. "I take emotions. I can't help someone who's sick."

That was when Elias realized what Carlyle was getting at. "Doona take Bronwyn's pain. Remember what you did with Sabryn last year? When she was hurt?"

"That's right," Sabryn said, nodding. "You scanned my body and figured out which bone was broken."

Finn swallowed nervously. "Aye, but that wasn't a life-or-death situation."

"You did it. That's what you need to focus on," Elias urged. "Please."

"I hate all of you," Finn murmured but moved to Bronwyn's head.

Carlyle scooted down to give him room. Elias watched as Finn spread his palms over Bronwyn and closed his eyes. When everyone went quiet, Elias noted the shallowness of Bronwyn's breathing.

"Fek," Finn said softly. "She's in a tremendous amount of pain. I don't know how she stood there for as long as she did."

"Where?" Elias urged. "Is it her head? Is that what's causing the fever?"

Carlyle put his hand on Elias's arm to calm him. "Give Finn a chance to look at everything."

He was right, of course, but Elias couldn't help but feel that time was of the essence. Had he missed something last night when he examined Bronwyn? He wasn't a doctor, but all the Knights had tended to each other's injuries over the years. They all had picked up a lot of knowledge during that time.

Finn's hands were over Bronwyn's chest now. Sweat began beading his forehead, but he said nothing. Then Finn's lips flattened before he moved down Bronwyn's legs, pausing at her injured right knee and left ankle. Then he returned to her chest.

He was pale when he opened his eyes to look at Elias. Finn's hands shook when he rose them to wipe his face. "It's her ribs. Two are broken. And a sliver of one punctured her lung."

"Hospital it is, then," Carlyle said as he got to his feet.

Sabryn turned and started for the door. "I'll get the car."

"Wait," Elias called. Everyone stopped and looked his way. He swallowed, his mind racing at the impossibility of what he was about to suggest. "We can heal her."

Finn moved to lean against the wall for support. "We're not healers, E."

"Nay, but maybe we doona need to be." Elias glanced at Bronwyn. "When Elodie was injured, I was there when she was healed. I heard the chant the MacLeod Druid used."

"Bloody hell," Carlyle said, shock causing his voice to lower.

"The MacLeod Druids? You actually heard it and are just now telling us?"

Finn's brows shot up on his forehead as he let out a low whistle. "That's ancient magic that has been lost to many of us."

"But do you remember all of it?" Sabryn asked. "One wrong word, and it won't work."

"I'm aware. I can't explain it, but I think this is what Bronwyn would want," Elias told them.

The three looked at each other. Carlyle nodded. Finn shrugged. Sabryn sighed.

Then she said, "We give it one chance. If it doesn't work, we're off to seek medical help."

"Agreed," Elias said.

Finn looked around. "Do we do it here? It's fekking freezing. Why isn't the heat on?"

"Take a look around, Finn. Things have been sold off," Carlyle snapped. "Most likely to pay the inheritance tax from her father's death."

"Where's her room?" Sabryn asked, stopping Carlyle or Finn from saying more.

Elias attempted to get to his knees, but his rib injury made it impossible. Carlyle bent and gently gathered Bronwyn in his arms. Elias pushed to his feet and motioned for the three to follow him. He strode into the parlor, grateful for the heat that met them.

"Over there," he said, pointing to the sofa bed.

"No wonder she jumped at the money offered," Finn said when he saw the area Bronwyn had made into a bedroom.

Carlyle laid her on the bed and stepped back. The four of them situated themselves around the sofa bed, arms stretched wide to be able to reach. Their magic rushed from one to the other, gathering and rising as they called to it.

Then, everyone looked at him.

Elias took a deep breath and closed his eyes. He had memorized the chant, thinking it might come in handy in the future. He'd never expected it to be so soon. He spoke the words clearly. By the second iteration, Carlyle joined in. Not long after, Sabryn added her voice, and then Finn. They repeated the chant eight more times.

Elias paused, and the others went silent. He felt Bronwyn's forehead. A smile broke over his face when he realized her fever was gone. Finn stepped forward and once more scanned her body. He pitched to the side when he was done, weak from using so much of his magic. Carlyle had to grab hold of him and help him to the chair.

But the Irishman looked at Elias and nodded. "She's healed."

"That's a bloody powerful chant," Carlyle said, his gaze on Bronwyn.

Sabryn blew out a breath, her fatigue showing. "I honestly didn't expect that to work."

"That's the difference between the chants we know now and the ancient ones we've lost," Finn said.

Elias tucked the blanket around Bronwyn and then faced Finn. "Are you sure everything is healed? Do we need to keep going?"

"Not sure if I could," Finn admitted. "But, aye. She's healed. I double-checked the rib and lungs. All's good. There's nothing there to cause her pain."

Sabryn shoved her fingers into her black hair and moved it away from her face. "Is it too early for a drink?"

"Food. That's what I need," Finn replied.

"There isna much here," Elias told them as he motioned them out of the room. He wanted to give Bronwyn time to rest.

Carlyle grabbed his keys from his pocket. "I'll get some things for us."

A moment later, the sound of a motor reached him as Carlyle drove away. Elias took the others to the library. He was so exhausted from using his magic that it took him two tries to get a fire going to heat the room. When Elias next looked at Finn, the Irishman was stretched on the sheet-covered sofa, fast asleep.

"So," Sabryn said as she faced Elias. "Blood magic, huh?"

He sighed and nodded.

"That's going to be an issue."

He ran a hand over his jaw. "I know."

CHAPTER FIFTEEN

Bronwyn snuggled contentedly beneath the heavy blankets as she slowly came awake. She blinked open her eyes to see the dancing flames of a fire. A log popped, sending sparks shooting up into the chimney. She felt rested. Restored and warm. She couldn't remember the last time she had been any of those things.

She sat up and looked toward one of the windows. The curtains were closed, but one had a slit wide enough for her to see that it was dark outside. Had she woken that early?

Confusion filled her as she swung her legs over the side of the bed. Something pulled on her right knee. She yanked up the leg of her sweats and saw the bandage. Memories poured into her then. The last thing she remembered was not being able to breathe.

Slowly, she tugged one side of the dressing off to find the jagged cut healed with only puckered, pink skin to prove that she had been injured. Bronwyn removed the bandage completely and tugged her sweats down. Then she took a deep breath. No pain followed. Next, she circled her left foot first one way and then the other. Again, no pain.

Bronwyn sat for a moment, letting all of that sink in. That was when she realized the house felt different—almost as if it rested, breathed easier. She listened for anyone, but the fire and closed door made it difficult to hear.

She got to her feet and went to her Ugg boots by the fire. They were warm and toasty as she slipped her feet inside. Bronwyn smoothed her hands over her hair and rubbed the sleep from her eyes. Then she slipped out of the parlor and quietly shut the door behind her.

She stood, listening once more. The house was undeniably calmer. Her boots didn't make a sound on the rug that ran the length of the wide corridor. She paused beside the newel and put her hand on it. There was no need for blood this time because the house wasn't under attack.

Her gaze lifted to the room she hadn't ventured into in weeks. She would need to go soon, but it reminded her why she was alone and had chosen the path of a *drough*. Still, she needed to visit the space.

After a deep breath, Bronwyn turned her head toward the kitchen, where the smell of something delicious reached her. Her stomach growled in response. She dropped her arm to her side and walked along the runner, each step cautious and guarded.

As a child, she had run amok through the manor's many rooms. That was back when her mother had been alive, and her parents had hosted elaborate events where every speck of wood had been polished to a high shine. The women who entered had glittered with jewels and stunned in bespoke gowns. The men had been dressed to the nines in evening attire. Bronwyn had hidden on the stairs, watching and dreaming of joining the parties someday.

She wondered if the house remembered those happier times when laughter had run free and risen often. Not once had the manor let her down, though. It had stood guard over her, around her, shielding her from the hurtful world outside. The dwelling had sheltered her when she cried her river of tears, mourning all that had been lost, that she would never regain.

It hadn't pulled away from her, even when she turned to blood magic. It was almost as if it understood. The manor couldn't speak to her, but they were connected in a way that only someone with magic could truly understand. It had been that way for as long as Bronwyn could remember, but things had strengthened when she returned.

Some claimed that a house was just a building, but she knew differently. A home was something you accepted and brought into your life to shield and safeguard. The energy of its inhabitants could be felt in every nook and cranny of the space, and a home protected its family valiantly.

The fact that the manor had accepted her as a *drough* spoke of how deeply tied she was to it—and it to the Stewart line.

Which was why she was pleased to sense its current contentment. It might be short-lived, but she hoped the house soaked in as much peace as it could. It deserved so much more than Bronwyn could give it.

She heard the laughter as she neared the kitchen. She paused outside the door and simply listened. The four within had an easy camaraderie she envied. She had never been that free with anyone. She'd longed for siblings or close friends to share things with, but it had never worked out for her.

Bronwyn recognized Finn's voice as he told a story about Carlyle and some posh woman. She couldn't hear everything, but the room erupted in laughter a few moments later. She wanted so badly to go inside and be a part of the group, to be accepted. Then she remembered who she was. *What* she was.

And what she had done.

If she had been apart before, she had solidified that by becoming *drough*. She was about to return to the parlor and hide away when she recalled that this was her home. She had never shied away from any place in it. She wouldn't now, no matter how uneasy she was about entering the kitchen with the others.

Bronwyn squared her shoulders and pushed open the swinging door. Her gaze landed on Carlyle, who stood at the stove, cooking. Finn was at the counter, holding a bowl in his arms as he stirred something within it. Sabryn sat at the table in the middle of the room, smelling a sprig of rosemary. Bronwyn hadn't realized she had searched each face for Elias until her gaze finally landed on him. He casually leaned back against the counter with a glass in hand and a wide smile as Finn spoke.

That smile remained as his expression softened, and he straightened. "Bronwyn."

Everyone went quiet as all eyes turned to her. She nearly buckled under the scrutiny, but she remained on her feet and entered the kitchen—a room that seemed to have come alive with its occupants. A plethora of foods lay on the counters, several pots rested on the stove, and plates had been set on the table. No wonder the house was happy. The very air around her hummed with cheerfulness.

Bronwyn realized that her healed wounds were a result of the people before her. "It seems a thank you is in order for healing me."

Finn nodded at Elias. "Direct that at him. It was Elias who saved you."

"It was all of us," Elias explained without taking his gaze from her. His blue eyes burned brighter. "I remembered a healing chant I heard one of the MacLeod Druids use on my sister."

MacLeod Druids? That stunned her. It seemed there was a lot about Elias she didn't know. She owed him her life—twice now. It might have irked her that he'd been spying on her, but she was alive and away from Sydney because of him. "I appreciate it. Truly. My thanks to all of you."

Carlyle caught her gaze and grinned. "Hope you don't mind us making use of this amazing kitchen."

"Not at all. I'm glad to see it's being put to use." And, oddly, she meant it. Maybe it was because the house was so blissful. That had to be the reason.

Finn set aside the bowl and found another place setting. He then pulled out a chair next to Sabryn. "Come, sit. I hope you're hungry. Carlyle only knows how to cook for an army."

Bronwyn walked to the chair and lowered herself. "I am very hungry."

"You should be. You slept the day away, and you didna eat much this morning," Elias told her.

Bronwyn looked up as he set a glass of water before her. Had his eyes gotten bluer? She hastily looked away and brought the water to her lips, drinking deeply. The minute she swallowed, she realized how thirsty she had been.

"They like to fuss," Sabryn said with a grin. "I've learned to let them do it. It makes them happy."

Bronwyn set the empty glass down, which Elias quickly refilled. She met Sabryn's gaze. "I see that."

"It's hospitality," Carlyle said as he focused on his cooking. Then he glanced at her over his shoulder with a teasing grin. "And a little fussing."

The smile that pulled at Bronwyn's lips was so foreign that she reached up to feel her mouth. No wonder the atmosphere in the house was relaxed. It was hard not to be with the four of them near. Their bonds were thick, their trust evident. Their friendship deep.

The conversation picked back up, and while Bronwyn wasn't part of it, she didn't feel excluded. Mainly because each of them took turns looking at her as they spoke, bringing her into the different stories they told about one another. By the time Carlyle set the food on the table, Bronwyn knew that he went out of his way with comical measures to ignore his father's near-constant urging to take a wife and have an heir, that Finn had the worst taste in women, which ultimately always led to some kind of dating disaster, that Elias had a book-buying habit, and that Sabryn had some of the best lines to turn men and women down when they came on to her.

"Oh, come on," Sabryn said with a roll of her eyes. "You guys make it sound like I get asked out all the time."

Elias, Finn, and Carlyle replied in unison, "You do."

Bronwyn laughed out loud at the seriousness of their expressions versus Sabryn's dismayed one. Bronwyn also discovered that she enjoyed the food. She ate until she couldn't put another bite into her mouth.

"Where did you learn to cook?" she asked Carlyle.

He shifted his chair to the side, then leaned back and stretched out his legs as he looked at her. "When I was a lad, one of the cooks made the best pastries. She was French, and I'd wake up every morning smelling the fresh bread and sweets. I'd sneak down to steal some. She found me one morn, and after that, she always left a stash just for me. It wasn't long before I woke earlier and earlier to go down and watch her. Then, I asked if she'd show me how to bake. She did, and I even made some things myself. But I soon realized that my real love was food. Our cook saw that and went to my parents. My father wasn't thrilled, of course, but Mum convinced him it would keep me out of trouble. And it did. For a while," he finished with a wink.

"The meal was excellent," Bronwyn told him. "I hate cooking. I don't really like food."

Carlyle gasped at her. "How is that possible?"

She shrugged. "If I didn't have to eat, I wouldn't."

"Ugh. I wish I were like that," Sabryn replied with a twist of her lips. "I have such a sweet tooth."

Finn quirked a brow. "I thought it was bread you loved."

"It's both," Sabryn lamented with a dramatic eye roll.

Bronwyn joined in on the laughter. She looked around the table, noting the empty plates, the smiles, and the relaxed banter. Again and again, her gaze went to Elias, who sat on the other side of the table with the guys. Each time it did, she found him staring at her.

She was surprised to discover they had talked for almost two hours after the meal. But everything had to come to an end, and, unfortunately, the dinner did. With all five of them pitching in, they cleaned the kitchen quickly.

"We'll be in touch," Sabryn told Elias as they walked from the room.

Bronwyn followed at the rear of the group as they made their way to the front door. She stood off to the side as Carlyle, Sabryn, and Finn put on their coats. Bronwyn was sad to see them go. She'd been having such a good time that she wanted them to remain, to keep the merriment going for another hour —or forever.

She had thought she was fine on her own. And she had been —sort of. The dinner and the people who took part had helped her in ways she hadn't realized she needed. For the first time ever, Bronwyn felt a part of something.

Sabryn turned to her. "There's an envelope of cash for Elias's stay. It should get him through the week. If you require more, let him know."

Bronwyn nodded, unsure how to reply. Then, the trio was gone, leaving her and Elias alone. The silence was deafening.

"Are you sure about this? About me staying?" he asked.

She wasn't, but there was no going back now. She met his gaze and decided to be brutally honest. "Not really. I'm used to being on my own. Are you sure about staying with a *drough*? One who does blood magic?"

"Truthfully, I'm no'."

"Fair enough. Thank you for being candid."

He nodded once. "What I am sure of is that we need each other right now. I never got a chance to thank you for earlier." He glanced at the door. "When my friends came and told me about the..."

"Murder," she supplied after he trailed off.

His gaze went distant. "It felt like I was drowning."

"I know the feeling well."

His attention snapped back to her. "Your touch saved me. I doona make light of that. It's the truth."

The intensity of his look and the depth of emotion in his voice was like a current moving between them. She couldn't have looked away if she wanted. A man she didn't know, someone who came from a vastly different life than hers, keenly understood what it was to be submerged in an onslaught of events that seemed intent on destroying someone.

"Thank you."

A shiver went through her at his whispered words.

CHAPTER SIXTEEN

Elias flipped the burner phone Carlyle had picked up for him—along with some clothes—over and over in his hand as he stared at the fire. His thoughts were on the enigmatic woman sitting on the sofa bed across from him, but he couldn't continue staring at her without it becoming awkward. He had done enough of that at dinner.

The healing spell hadn't just worked. It had brought a bloom of life back to Bronwyn's cheeks. Seeing her smile and laugh during the meal had been like a sucker punch to his gut. Her natural beauty was stunning, but she was breathtaking when she smiled. It lit her hazel eyes in a way that was indescribable.

It was good that he'd been sitting on the other side of the table because he wasn't sure he would've been able to keep his hands off her. It had been like that ever since she had reached out for him earlier.

That moment had connected them forever. And the bond

would always be there, no matter how many miles separated them.

While his mind turned everything over and over, Bronwyn sat with her laptop, clicking away at the keys. He didn't know what she was doing, but he wanted to ask. A comfortable silence had settled between them after the Knights departed. He yearned to call his sisters and assure them that he wasn't a killer. He wanted to contact Rhona, but he wasn't entirely sure she wouldn't tell Frasier where he was. More than anything, Elias longed to find Sydney and force him to admit they had dumped the body at Elias's.

But he did none of those things.

Still, it made him wonder how Sydney had learned where he lived. Did the wanker have friends on Skye? Elias had been away for a long while, but he didn't think anyone would give up his rental address to strangers. That took his thoughts back to someone helping Sydney. But who?

Elias's gaze swung to Bronwyn. Curiosity finally got the best of him. "You're verra focused on the computer."

She looked up, her gaze clashing with his. He saw the hesitancy there, as if she couldn't decide whether to answer. "I'm working."

"Oh?" Now, he was even more intrigued. "Do you mind if I ask what you're working on?"

Another hesitation. Finally, she answered, "A design."

"You're a graphic artist?"

She shrugged slightly. "Aye."

"That's impressive. May I see?"

Bronwyn bit her lower lip. Then she turned the laptop around. Elias scooted to the edge of his cushion and leaned forward to see the screen. His eyes moved over the design, taking in the flourishes and the embracing couple.

"It's a cover," she told him. "For a romance novel."

He didn't know much about covers, but he liked her work. "Wow. That's amazing. Do you do many?"

"It's my first," she admitted. "I've always wanted to design them."

He shot her a grin. "I like it."

"It isn't finished. I just started, actually."

"I'd like to see it when you're done."

She looked away quickly as if his words surprised her. "Sure."

"Can you show me some of your other designs?"

She flipped the laptop back to her and punched a few keys before showing him the screen once more. It scrolled on its own, displaying a myriad of designs from restaurant napkins to pub coasters to store signage and social media graphics.

"You have incredible talent," he said.

He saw a ghost of a grin on her face as she settled the computer to face her once more. "Thanks. I enjoy it, and it brings in money. I have return clients, which is always good. And I can work from home."

"Do you get a lot of work for places on Skye?"

Her grin vanished instantly. "My work is contracted all over the world. Being based online allows me to find interested parties that know nothing about my personal life."

Elias blew out a breath and sat back in the chair. "I'm sorry you've had such a hard time of it here, lass."

"Everyone has problems." She held his gaze. "Including you."

"Are you referring to my father dying, or recent events?"

"Both," she replied.

Elias nodded and scratched his temple. "Just when I thought things with my family had been fixed… I doona know why George accused me, but we're going to figure it out. As for this most recent event, I'll clear my name."

"It must be nice to have friends like yours."

He smiled as he thought about the Knights. "We've been through a lot together, that's for sure. You've no' met our fifth member. Sabertooth is a white hat hacker. In other words, he does ethical work. I know without a doubt that each of them has my back, and they know I have theirs."

"I can't imagine how that feels."

No, he doubted she could. Yet he knew few could have withstood the onslaught of hatred doled out to them the way Bronwyn had. "Our shared history has banded the Knights together."

"The Knights?" she asked.

"It's what we call ourselves."

"Rescuing damsels in distress?" she asked with a slight grin.

Elias chuckled. "Something like that." He rubbed his thumb over the edge of the chair's arm. "Each of us lost someone close. All of them were murdered Druids. We've been searching for those responsible."

"Have you had any success?"

"We've helped a lot of people, but as far as finding the one who put a price on Druids' heads? No' yet."

Her brow furrowed. "You think someone put a price on our heads?"

"Figuratively speaking. It's a theory, at least."

"That's…frightening."

He nodded. "Aye, it is. We're sorting through a few leads. Or we were until all my shite." He shrugged one shoulder. "We'll stop the murders. One way or another."

"That's why you're so upset you've been blamed for them."

"Aye. Though anyone would be shaken to be called a murderer when they're innocent."

"True. Tell me more about the Knights. I get the feeling Sabryn is the leader."

Elias usually wasn't keen on talking about his friends, but he wanted her to know everything. Though he wasn't quite sure why as yet. "She is that. She's the one who put the group together. Our funds come from her and Carlyle, but we've been paid for some jobs."

Bronwyn's brows drew together into a frown as she tilted her head. "So, people know about the Knights? Do you have a website or something?"

"Nothing like that, lass. There are places online that Druids can go to interact with other Druids."

"Couldn't someone lie and *say* they were a Druid to get in?"

He nodded, grinning. "Aye. And at first, some did. But we're resourceful. In order to enter any of the chat rooms, you have to do a spell."

"Through the computer?" she asked, her eyes wide. "That works?"

"It does. Of course, that doesna mean that a Druid can no' have non-Druids sitting beside them at the time, but only so much can be done by no' meeting in person."

"Are there any of those?"

He enjoyed her interest. Like her, he'd been raised on Skye and was used to the isle's traditions. Things were vastly different in other parts of the world. "There are. More than most people know. Would you like the link to a chat room?"

She started to reply, but then her expression closed off. "I imagine they're for *mies* only."

"Some are, but I've encountered *droughs*."

"Is that why you aren't afraid to be around me?"

Elias crossed his ankle over his knee. "Things here on Skye are usually one way or the other. Black or white. This or that. There is rarely anything in between, which goes against the natural order of things. Nothing is black or white. Good or bad. I've known some good people who do terrible things and vice versa. You're labeled as a *drough* here," he began.

"Because I am," she replied.

He shrugged. "Be that as it may, you've shown me nothing but kindness. You allowed me to remain, offered comfort at one of the worst times in my life, and opened your home to my friends. If I listened to others, I would think you were the worst person to walk the Earth, not worthy of my spit if you were on fire. That isna how I operate, lass."

"You can say that without knowing me?"

"I can say that because it's been my job to learn people by watching them. Actions speak a lot louder than words."

She drew in a deep breath and slowly released it before softly closing the laptop. "I think you've guessed why I use blood magic, but it's to shield the house. It's a large residence, and it takes tremendous magic to keep the spell in place."

"Do you know what blood magic will do to you?"

"I do," she answered.

Elias linked his hands over his stomach. "Is it to guard against Sydney?"

"Sydney Russell. Aye."

"You could ask for help. Rhona would come."

"Maybe, but I can't involve her. I can't involve anyone. Not even you."

He twisted his lips. "It's a little late for that."

"It isn't. If you're here when Sydney returns, I ask that you stay out of it."

"I'm no' sure I can," he told her honestly. "It isna in my nature."

She swallowed and glanced at her hands before looking back at him. "I'm asking as your host."

"What does he want from you?"

"He wants my cousin's location."

"Why?"

"Beth has something he wants."

That certainly didn't sit well with Elias. "And what's that?"

"Her ability. Sydney has a personality that draws others to him, especially Druids. Once he discovers your specialty, he decides whether he can use it or not. If your magical ability can help in whatever illegal and dangerous scheme he's come up with, then he convinces you to join him."

Something about the way she talked told Elias that the bastard had also used her. It made him regret not ending Sydney's life the night before. Had he known all of this, he might have done just that.

"People rarely refuse Sydney," Bronwyn continued. "I was lured in by him a few years ago. He's attractive, and he uses that on women, but he isn't kind. I came across him during a time in my life when I wanted an escape. He found me in Inverness, and

I was looking for something crazy and dangerous. He fit the bill perfectly."

Elias remained perfectly still, waiting and hoping for Bronwyn to continue.

She picked at a nail. "It was fun for a while, but all that ended when an elderly woman was killed. She lived alone in the house we'd broken into to steal something Sydney had his sights set on. I don't even remember what it was. She heard us and came out of her room, demanding we leave. When Sydney shoved her aside as if she were nothing, her small, frail frame tumbled down the stairs, and something snapped inside me. I took a cold, hard look at what I'd become and what I had helped him to do."

"Is that when you left him?"

She shook her head and looked away. "I tried, but Sydney seemed to know what I planned. He found ways to stop me. Threats without actually being threats, if you know what I mean."

"Unfortunately, I know exactly what you mean." And it infuriated Elias.

"I found myself in a situation I couldn't get out of. It wasn't just Sydney watching me, but all the others, too. I couldn't remember a time when I'd felt so scared. I didn't know what they would do to me if I tried to leave, and I didn't want to find out. I took the only option I had left. I reached out to my father." She paused and drew in a shaky breath.

Elias wanted to sit beside her, to reach for her hand as she had done for him. But he remained in his seat. He, better than most, knew all about violent loss. He wouldn't push Bronwyn to tell him something she wasn't ready to share.

Hazel eyes lifted to his. "I left Skye and this house because of him. I wanted him to suffer as I'd suffered since Mum's death. That sounds so childish."

"We can no' help how we feel, lass."

She kept picking at her nail as her gaze dropped to her lap. "After Mum, Dad became a ghost of the man he'd once been. He drank heavily, and there were nights I heard him crying. My parents were madly devoted to each other. The kind of love you always hear about but never actually think is real."

Elias knew it was real. He'd seen it with his sister and Scott.

"Dad blamed himself for Mum's suicide. I kept telling him that it wasn't his fault, but he wouldn't listen to me. He didn't know how to go on without her. I took care of him, did everything a child could do. I thought that would pull him out of it, but it didn't. I got in trouble at school, but that didn't do anything either. I ignored him, I berated him, I yelled at him. Nothing worked. I was losing him."

Like she had lost her mum. Elias briefly squeezed his eyes closed, his heart hurting for what she had endured, and all of it alone.

"I couldn't stay and watch it happen to another of my parents," she stated as she looked at him. "So, I left. I didn't think he'd notice, but after a few days of no one to cook his meals or make him get out of bed, he did. That was when he started calling. I ignored those and the dozens that followed. It wasn't until I got his voicemail that said he had hired a private investigator to find me that I sent him a text and told him I was fine, but that if I wanted to talk to him, I'd let him know. He continued calling once a week, but I never answered."

"Until you contacted him."

She nodded, the despair on her face heart-wrenching. "I did. And it got him killed."

Elias sat forward, anger simmering below the surface. "What happened?"

"Sydney happened. I thought I had been discreet, but someone must have known something. I snuck out before dawn, left everything, and just ran. Once I knew I hadn't been followed, I told Dad to meet me in an alley far from Sydney. But Sydney's gang hadn't followed me. They trailed my father. I spotted Dad. He held his arms out to me, a bright smile on his face, and that's when I saw Sydney behind Dad."

Elias fisted his hands. He knew what was coming.

Bronwyn swiped at her eye. "I didn't even have time to reach him. I didn't get to apologize for what I'd done or tell him how much I loved him. Sydney took his life in an instant. By the time I reached Dad, he was gone."

Aye. Elias should've made Sydney pay when he'd had the chance. But he would have a second opportunity. He'd make sure of it.

"I…" Bronwyn sniffed and drew in a shaky breath. "Let's just say the tethers of fear that had held me were broken. I turned my fury on Sydney. I didn't care if anyone saw us. I attacked. He didn't expect it. It was just Sydney and two others. I don't remember what I did. I was so furious that I lashed out. Whatever happened, they left me alone. I contacted the authorities, who came immediately. They ruled Dad's death as natural, said he had a heart attack. I couldn't prove otherwise, so I let it be. I alerted the police to Sydney and his group. They went looking for Sydney, which gave me the time I needed to get out of Inverness and bring my father home to be buried next to

Mum." She licked her lips. "Sydney always retaliates, so I waited for just that to happen. Days turned to weeks and then months. I thought he had forgotten about me. But I was wrong."

"Is that when you became *drough*?"

She slowly shook her head as she met his gaze. "I believed I could handle Sydney myself. I was ready for it. I didn't become *drough* until he turned his attention on Beth."

CHAPTER SEVENTEEN

Bronwyn didn't know why she had told Elias her story. She hadn't meant to, but the words had flowed. And once she began, she couldn't seem to stop. He listened raptly, taking in every word. For the first time in her life, she felt truly heard. As if he understood the complex emotions that'd led to her decisions.

She trusted him even when he said he didn't judge her for turning *drough*. That, in itself, boggled her mind. Yet she saw the acceptance in his eyes. The Knights had been the same.

Bronwyn was used to the hate and revulsion people hurled her way. She had grown accustomed to the disgust and animosity on their faces. She had been prepared for that. When anyone treated her with compassion, humanely, it rocked her to her very foundation.

Perhaps that was why she found herself spilling her secrets. Well, at least one of them.

The empathy, the kindness in Elias's gaze was almost too

much. Vitriol and contempt couldn't penetrate her armor. But respect and understanding brought her to her knees.

"Is Beth safe?" Elias asked.

Bronwyn nodded. "Absolutely."

"You seem certain of that."

"I am."

One side of his mouth curved upward in a crooked smile. "Good." He slowly sat back and stretched his legs, crossing his ankles. "If you doona mind me asking, why a *drough*? Why no' go to someone for help?"

"I did go to someone. Dad died because of me. I couldn't let anyone else lose their life because of my bad choices."

"Aye," he said softly. "I ken, lass."

She shifted beneath the weight of his gaze. "It wasn't an easy choice by any means. Beth is all the family I have left. I'll do whatever is necessary to protect her."

"You've already done it."

The graveness of his words struck Bronwyn. "You speak of the blood magic."

"You're a Skye Druid. You know our teachings the same as I do."

She linked her fingers together on her lap. "Blood magic is the most forbidden magic there is for a Druid. Even for a *drough*."

"The results are quick and powerful." Elias paused. "But the consequences of using it are always the same—death."

"As I said, I will do whatever I need to do to protect my cousin. Even if that means giving up my life."

"I doona disagree that Beth needs protection, but there are other ways to stop Sydney."

Bronwyn stood from the sofa bed and moved before the hearth for warmth, and maybe to be closer to Elias. She kept her gaze on the fire. "I tried speaking to the police I knew were Druids in Inverness. They wouldn't help me because of Sydney. They feared him. I didn't bother with any non-Druid police."

"Because magic was used," Elias said from behind her.

The erratic dance of the flames was comforting. Her gaze lingered on them even as her mind shuffled through memories better left forgotten. "Once I returned to Skye and prepared to bury my father, I was hit by the state of the manor. I'd only been gone a year, but the estate was a mess." She wrapped her arms around herself, feeling a coldness within her that had nothing to do with the weather. "When I saw everything…I lost it. Call it a mental break, an emotional breakdown, or both, but I sank deep into a place that I didn't think I could ever come back from."

"But you did. You're standing here now."

"I am. Because the blame for the state of the house and Dad's death is on me."

The chair creaked as Elias stood. "No' just you."

She felt him behind her. Close enough to touch. She almost leaned back against him. It had been so long since anyone had comforted her that she suddenly and desperately needed it, craved it. But she had stood too long on her own. Besides, Elias was a good man. She wouldn't pull him down with her.

"Was Beth here to help?"

That yanked Bronwyn from her thoughts. She briefly squeezed her eyes closed at the mention of her cousin. "She came to the funeral and stayed for about a month. She listened to me vent about Sydney and everything he had done. Her situation is my fault, as well."

She turned to face Elias then and saw how close he had gotten to her. His gaze captured hers, ensnaring her utterly. Completely. She should end the story there and keep the rest of it to herself. He didn't need to know all the dirty details.

"Nay, lass," he whispered as he gently removed a strand of hair from her lashes.

That simple gesture battered her walls. Tears gathered in her eyes, but she refused to let them fall. If she cracked now, she'd crumble. And that simply wasn't an option. "Beth is six years my junior. She has always been a free spirit, the kind of person who only sees the good in others. I poured my heart out to her knowing that."

"Because you needed someone," Elias said.

"Beth is a fixer. She wants to repair the problems of those she loves. When I thought she'd returned home, she actually went to Inverness to seek out Sydney and convince him to leave me alone for good. It worked. Sydney forgot about me and turned his full attention on her. When she phoned and told me, I was beside myself. I begged her to come back. I told her I needed help and made up all kinds of lies. I even demanded she return, but she got caught up in Sydney's world. Just as I once had."

Elias didn't look away, didn't react. He stood as strong and unmovable as a mountain. "What happened?"

"I thought about going to Rhona, but she was involved with important issues. And it couldn't wait. That was when I..."

"Did the ceremony."

She nodded. "It's simple to become *drough*. Perhaps a little too easy. Afterward, I headed to Inverness. I debated whether to confront Sydney, but he's rarely alone. He keeps the most powerful of his Druids around him, especially when he leaves his flat. I would have gone up against any of them. I wanted retribution, but I couldn't kill the others—and I would have. There was so much rage within me. So, I watched his flat. I saw Sydney and Beth together. I saw how he held her, looked at her. I saw the love in Beth's eyes. Seeing my cousin involved with such a vile man made me sick."

Someone she had slept with for months. But Bronwyn couldn't think about that now. She moved her gaze away, but almost immediately looked into Elias's bright blue eyes again. She was drawn to him, pulled by some unseen force.

"And then?" Elias urged.

"It took weeks before I saw my opportunity present itself when Beth was alone. I confronted her. She told me I didn't know the real Sydney. I realized arguing with her would be pointless, so I asked her to return to Skye with me. She wouldn't leave. She brushed off my words and went back to him. I got another chance a week later. Still, she ignored me. I knew I had one more opportunity. When it came, I didn't give her a choice."

Elias's eyes widened a fraction. "What did you do?"

"I took her away. She needed distance to see who Sydney really was, to know the monster he hid from everyone."

"Did it work?"

Bronwyn wanted to lie to him, to let Elias think she was a good person despite being *drough*. But she couldn't. "Nay."

He searched her eyes, a small frown puckering his brow. "She obviously didna return to Sydney. Where is she now?"

"When I came home, I knew Sydney would come here looking for Beth. As you've pointed out, the Druid community is disconnected, divided. Scattered. So many have no idea they even hold magic, much less how to use it. But Druids who know who they are, somehow know about those of us on Skye. Sydney was enamored with everything having to do with our culture here. He asked endless questions about how we were taught magic, our hierarchy, and how our leaders were chosen. He was, in a word, obsessed. Sydney has connections everywhere. He learned who I was before I had a chance to tell him. I had to prepare for his arrival. Being *drough* gave me more power, but it wasn't enough. That was when I turned to the blood magic to strengthen the manor's defenses."

Elias's throat bobbed as he swallowed. "How long ago was that?"

"Two months." She knew why he asked. Druids rarely lived past a year once they turned to blood magic. The more taboo magic a Druid used, the faster they died.

"You're trapped in this house, though. As beautiful as it is, it's still a prison," he argued.

She tried to keep her mouth shut, to hold that remaining secret, but her lips parted on their own, and the words spilled out. "I'm not just protecting myself."

Elias blinked in confusion. Then his face smoothed as the truth came to him. "Beth's here."

"Aye."

His brows snapped together. "I looked through the manor."

"You could pry up every board, and you still wouldn't find her."

His gaze sharpened, interest clear in his eyes. "You've hidden her."

"I have."

"Will you show me?"

She knew she shouldn't. Bronwyn didn't understand this

sudden need to share everything with a man she barely knew, but he had come to her aid twice. He and his friends had saved her life. For the first time in years, she wasn't alone.

And it felt so good.

Whether he stayed or left would be up to Elias. Bronwyn motioned him to follow as she stepped out of the parlor. He pulled the door closed behind him, his gaze meeting hers. He fell into step beside her as they walked the corridor to the staircase.

He remained at her side as they climbed to the second floor. Bronwyn fought against the chill as she turned to the left and meandered down the hallway until she reached the second to last door on the right. She had put off coming up here for too long. Maybe it was fitting that Elias was with her.

She faced the door and put one hand on the knob before turning it slowly. A click echoed through the quiet of the house. She pushed the door. It swung wide, revealing a normal bedchamber with covered furniture.

Bronwyn felt the tingle of her magic at the doorway. She surreptitiously glanced at Elias, who stood behind her and slightly to the right. Magic sizzled beneath her skin and pooled in her palms. The heady feel of it made her sway. From her earliest memories, magic had always been there, like a comforting friend.

She lifted her hand and placed her open palm against the invisible layer of enchantment that stood at the threshold. Bronwyn closed her eyes, soaking in the rapture of the magic. It flooded her, swirled through and around her, before caressing her.

"*Nochd,* reveal."

Then she opened her eyes.

CHAPTER EIGHTEEN

Elias's breath caught when the air became charged. His skin tingled, the hairs on his arms standing on end. His eyes couldn't make out the magic, but he experienced the sheer potency of Bronwyn's power crackling around him.

It was tantalizing, captivating.

Seductive.

His body responded instantly. He didn't fight the rising tide of desire that assailed him. Instead, he embraced it. His blood sang through him, hot and eager. His balls tightened. His cock hardened. Elias fisted his hands from the onslaught of need so intense it was inescapable.

His gaze slid to Bronwyn. She stood with her eyes open and her lips parted. Her pleasure was made evident by her shallow breaths. He'd been around formidable Druids before, but never someone who had such command, such authority. The wanton desire that flooded him threatened to rob him of thought.

A strange vibration began when she uttered the Gaelic

command. He stood in shock as the air at the doorway began to flicker and then swirl. And at the center of it, Bronwyn's hand. Elias couldn't look away from the wide branches of the vortex. The current began leisurely but soon increased in speed until the sections merged and it became one spinning maelstrom.

Bronwyn dropped her hand to her side. The opening was no bigger than her palm, but he was able to see into the center of the quagmire. It was no longer the bedroom from before. He couldn't clearly make out what was there, but he knew he was looking at someplace different.

The gap began to widen, bit by bit. As it did, the vortex started to slow. Elias felt Bronwyn's gaze on him, but he couldn't look away from what was happening. He'd never seen anything like it before. Finally, the spinning halted, taking with it the unfathomable desire and leaving an empty doorway.

All thoughts of pleasure were shoved aside when his gaze landed on a platform draped in purple fabric so dark it was nearly black. On it lay a woman with dark hair who appeared to be sleeping. The air around her was gray, the vaporous atmosphere thick as it coiled and curled as if alive.

"My secret," Bronwyn said.

It took him a second to find his voice. "Where is she?"

Instead of answering, Bronwyn raised her hand once more. "*Falach*, conceal."

Everything he'd just witnessed reversed until he once more looked into the empty bedroom, causing him to battle between shock and the raging hunger to claim Bronwyn's body with his. Elias stepped forward and put his hand through the opening, but he felt nothing. The charge around him vanished, and with it the sultry magic that had held him captive.

He turned to Bronwyn, only to find the space empty. He whipped his head around and saw her retreating back. "Wait."

She halted but didn't turn.

"What did I just see?" he asked as he glanced once more into the bedroom before starting toward her.

"My ability."

She said it with such desolation that he said nothing more until he reached her. Elias moved in front of her to see her face. She met his gaze, but she didn't have the same openness as before. Her walls had gone back up. He wanted to touch her, but he feared if he did, he would want more—or worse, she would wrench away from him. He didn't know what would be worse at the moment. So, he forced his desire to the side. "Thank you."

She jerked in surprise, confusion marring her features. "What?"

"Thank you for showing me. It'll stay between us."

Bronwyn eyed him suspiciously. "Even from the Knights?"

"We doona tell each other everything. We all have our secrets. You have my word. I know that may no' mean much to you, but I'll hold to it."

She swallowed, looking uncertain and vulnerable. "I don't know why I told you any of this. I certainly don't know why I showed you Beth."

He could see her bewilderment. For the second time, he fought not to reach for her, to offer comfort…maybe more. The attraction was becoming harder to ignore even before her magic had turned him on. "Your secrets are safe with me."

She observed him for a full minute before sighing, her shoulders drooping in acceptance. "Agreed. Anything we tell the other stays between us."

"Aye." He glanced over her head to the bedroom. "Between us."

Bronwyn tucked her hair behind an ear. "What you saw was me opening the curtain between dimensions."

"Bloody hell," he murmured, his brain hardly able to register what she'd said.

A fleeting smile pulled at her lips. "I've gotten used to it. I forget that it's shocking to others."

"It's astonishing, astounding, fucking incredible. I'm sure there are other words, but that's all I have right now." He ran a hand over his face, more flabbergasted by the second. "You can penetrate the veil between dimensions. That takes unimaginable power."

She nodded. "It does."

He watched her for a moment as things began to click into place. "And I'm guessing even more to keep Beth there."

"Aye. A lot."

"Is she injured?"

Bronwyn shook her head. "Think of it as resting."

Elias was missing something. He was sure of it. But what he'd just seen boggled his mind. He needed time to think. It would come to him later. "If you can open dimensions, why use blood magic? Sydney would never be able to find her."

Bronwyn glanced over her shoulder at the open door. "I don't trust that. If Sydney can't get into the manor, then it doesn't matter if he gets a hold of me. He can do anything he wants to me, but I wouldn't be in the house and be tempted to do what he wants."

"Makes sense, I suppose. What happens when…?" He couldn't even finish the sentence.

"What happens when the price for using the blood magic demands its due? Or if Sydney kills me?" She shrugged and walked around him toward the stairs. "I've made sure Beth will be released."

"Let me help."

"Nay," she stated firmly.

Elias caught up with her in a few strides. "You doona have to do this alone."

"You know why I won't take your help. Why I won't take anyone's."

"You're risking a lot."

"As much as I want to end Sydney, I'm not a killer. I couldn't do it in Inverness before I welcomed the darkness in the ceremony to become *drough*. It doesn't have control of me."

She didn't add *yet*, but it remained unsaid. They both knew it.

"What I can do is protect Beth and the house," Bronwyn finished.

Elias knew all about sacrifices to protect one's family. He'd done it for years. "At the cost of your life?"

"If I'd never been selfish and self-centered, I wouldn't have left my father. I certainly wouldn't have taken up with Sydney. Then Dad wouldn't have been killed, and Beth wouldn't have been sucked into Sydney's world. So, aye, I'm willing to pay the price."

"There's no use looking back on things like that. Trust me."

She walked around him once more and ascended the stairs. "Looking back is all I can do. There is no future for me."

He didn't point out that she'd made sure of that by using blood magic. That would be rubbing salt in the wound. Elias hurried down the stairs and moved in front of her again. She came to a halt, her irritation clear as she glared at him.

"Go to Rhona. Explain everything. She and Balladyn can help," Elias begged.

Bronwyn quirked a brow. "Really? That's what you think I should do?"

He hesitated at the sound of her voice pitched higher and the fact that she feigned her enthusiasm. "Aye."

"In other words, I should go running to someone else every time there's a problem?"

"That's no' what I said," he began.

"And perhaps you should take your own advice. I don't see you contacting Rhona," she quickly said over him.

Damn if she didn't have him there. Elias watched her walk around him a final time. He followed her slowly. He knew there was no saving Bronwyn, but that didn't mean he didn't want to try.

She could tell him to stay out of her business all she wanted. He would even allow her to believe he did just that. But he wouldn't stand idly by and watch someone attack her. Because Sydney would return. And the next time he came, he'd likely bring more Druids with him.

They hadn't expected him the first time. No doubt the group would be more aware of their surroundings the next go-round. It wouldn't do them any good when it came to the Knights. They had perfected their approach. One way or another, Elias would make sure Sydney Russell never bothered Bronwyn or Beth again.

As for Beth and the blood magic…he didn't know what to do. But he knew someone who may.

He paused when he reached the bottom stair. The click of the parlor door behind Bronwyn told him he was alone. He sat on the riser and pulled out his mobile. Each of the Knights had memorized the other's contact information, so there was no need to program them in.

Elias put in Sabertooth's address and wrote the email asking for anything on the use of blood magic, as well as any reversals. Within seconds of hitting send, Sabertooth replied with: ON IT.

Next, Elias called Sabryn. He put the phone to his ear and got to his feet to walk outside into the garden.

"Is everything still kosher?" she asked in greeting.

Elias thought of what he'd just learned. It was far from all right, but he kept that to himself. "It is. Just checking in."

"Well, your name is on everyone's lips."

"Bloody hell. I need to contact my sisters."

Sabryn made a sound in the back of her throat. "You can't."

"I have to get some kind of message to them."

"I figured you'd say that. Saber says he has an idea."

That perked Elias up. "What's that?"

"He's going to hack into their computers and leave a message. By the time he's finished, it'll be routed through so many countries the authorities will never be able to trace it back to him or us."

Elias paused beside a tomato plant. "Anything I send Elodie and Edie will make it back to the police."

"Yep."

"I'll keep it brief."

"Good." Sabryn paused. "How are things at the manor, really?"

He picked a dead leaf off a plant. "She's a graphic designer."

"Interesting. But not what I was referring to."

"I know what you want to know. What I can tell you is that she uses the blood magic to protect the house."

Sabryn issued a loud sigh through the phone. "We figured that."

"I'm confirming it."

"You learned something else."

He'd learned a lot, actually. "I promised it would stay between Bronwyn and me."

"Anything that puts you in danger? Besides the fact she's a *drough* who uses blood magic?"

For some reason, Sabryn's words angered him. "You met her. You sat and talked to her for some time. If you had any doubts, you would've left immediately."

"Yes, I would've."

Elias frowned at the way she softened her words. "What are you playing at, Sabryn?"

"I'm not blind, idiot. I saw the way you looked at her. More importantly, I saw how she reached for you when you had that meltdown."

"It wasn't a meltdown."

"It was damn fucking close. Don't forget, I know you, Elias. Each of the Knights does. We all saw the way you clung to her—and how you looked at her. I love you like a brother, but you have a savior complex. I'll tell you again, as I've told you for years, you were a kid, one who had been physically and verbally abused by his father. You watched that same man attack your mother and then Elodie."

"And I didn't do a goddamn thing," he bit out. "My baby sister did. If not for her, we'd likely all be dead."

Sabryn sighed again, louder this time. "I wish I was there so I could punch you. Then, of course, I'd have to hug you. The past is the past. Your family is whole once more. Be happy about that."

Elias glanced toward the loch, thinking about Bronwyn and her family. "I wish I could."

"You can't save everyone."

"I need to save her."

"If anyone can, it's you. But even this one is out of your hands, E. She used blood magic," she said sadly.

Elias looked at the ground, hating that Sabryn was right.

"Do me a favor, will you?"

He could never refuse her anything. "What's that?"

"Don't fall for her. Bronwyn is pretty, but her time is limited. You've suffered enough."

"So has she."

"Maybe. I know your story. I know you deserve to find happiness, but you won't allow yourself to do it. Women flock to you, Elias, but you find one excuse or another to leave them behind. I fear this time you've chosen one because you know she's going to be the one doing the leaving."

Was that what he did? He didn't know anymore. He had thought he'd found his footing, but he was falling through an abyss of terror with no end in sight.

"If they pin these murders on me..." he began.

"Don't," Sabryn stated furiously.

He ignored her and kept going. "If they do, promise me you and the lads will leave and continue what we've been working toward."

"Kiss my ass, you ungrateful shithead," Sabryn retorted icily.

"We're a fucking family, in case you needed a reminder. We're not leaving you anywhere. Get used to it. Do you understand?"

It was his turn to sigh. "Aye. I doona like it, though."

"I don't care," she said tersely. Then her voice softened. "And, by the way, we love you. So don't be an idiot."

CHAPTER NINETEEN

"You know what to do."

Kirsi's eyes snapped open. She looked around the co-op, grateful there were no customers. She rubbed her tired eyes and rose from the chair, trying to wake herself. She had slept little the past few nights because of dreams that faded as soon as she came awake.

She might not recall what they were, but they left residual feelings behind that set her on edge. Dismay. Disquiet. Distress.

Dread.

The harder she tried to remember the details, the faster they faded. It was like attempting to catch smoke. She was restless and agitated. She wasn't known for snapping at people, but that was all she had been doing lately.

Thankfully, it was time to lock up the shop. Kirsi went through the motions as she mulled over the latest events on Skye. She'd been shocked when the news broke about the police looking for Elias MacLean, who had just returned to Skye. And he'd asked her about Bronwyn. At the time, she hadn't realized it was him.

The rumors swirling said that Elias was the one responsible for the Druid murders on Skye, but that couldn't be true. She knew for a fact that Elias hadn't gotten to the isle until after the last Druid was murdered. Edie had been overjoyed about her brother's return and had told everyone.

Yet the authorities must know something Kirsi didn't. Besides, her intuition wasn't the greatest. She had only left Skye for a few trips with her family before her mother got sick. It was difficult to base her conclusions on the things she read and saw on TV. She had no practical experience with anyone but those she'd been around her entire life, and tourists who barely left a mark.

Real-world experience. That was what she needed.

She flipped off the lights and locked the shop doors. Kirsi pocketed the keys and started her short walk home. She checked her phone and saw a text from Ben, her ex-boyfriend, who was still trying to get back together with her. She ignored it as she had all the others.

Kirsi put away her phone and looked up at the night sky. The day had been clear and beautiful, but the clouds had rolled in a few hours ago. Every once in a while, moonlight would peek through the dense clouds. She spotted the luminescent glow as it backlit a cloud.

Thin, wispy vapors that hung near the treetops stretched out like fingers before curling in on themselves and elongating outward again. Almost as if someone were beckoning her. It was a ridiculous, fanciful thought. She might be a Druid, but she had no discernable abilities other than the fact that she could do magic. Why would anyone want her?

Her gaze lowered as her thoughts turned back to the dreams. Whenever she thought of them, she saw ghost-like figures in her mind, but when she focused on the faces or anything that would show them clearly, they vanished.

She entered her parents' house, where she still lived, and hung up her coat on a peg near the door. The kitchen lights were off, but the undercabinet LED strip lights she'd gotten her mother for her birthday were on. Kirsi smiled as she stood and stared at them. She'd known they would look amazing.

"Mum. Dad. I'm home," she called.

She doubted her mother could hear her over the television, and no doubt her father was in his office with his nose buried in some book about moths—his latest obsession. Kirsi hunted through the cupboards for something to eat, but nothing sounded good. In the end, she settled for herbal tea to help her sleep.

She sank into a kitchen chair and closed her eyes as she yawned. Just a few years ago she had stayed up all hours of the night running around with her friends, existing on four hours of sleep. And she'd been fine. Was there some unwritten rule that people's bodies changed once they hit the twenty-five-year mark? Because it sure felt like it. She didn't want to think about what she'd be like at thirty. Or thirty-five.

Oddly, however, she couldn't imagine herself past thirty.

She forced open her eyes long enough to drink some tea. It was good. So much better than the herbal brews sold in the stores. Then again, this tea had been made by a Druid. Ariah's special blends were unique. The woman could make a fortune from them if she wanted, but she was content selling small batches to visitors and locals, with exclusive fusions just for Druids.

The one Kirsi had chosen was a bedtime tea mixture sold at the co-op. It wasn't the first time she had used this blend. It'd worked before, and she was counting on it working again. If it didn't, then she planned to pay Ariah a visit and see about getting something more specialized. Perhaps a type that could sharpen her dreams so she knew why they kept returning and what they tried to tell her.

She propped her elbow on the table and leaned her head against her hand as she allowed her tired eyes to close for just a few seconds.

"You know what to do."

Kirsi jerked awake and tipped to the side, catching herself just before she fell. The voice had been so clear—like it was right beside her.

"Everything all right, sweetheart?"

Her head swung around to see her father's outline in the doorway. He stepped forward into the light. His brown eyes studied her closely. He ran a hand over his beard and quirked a bushy eyebrow.

"Did you hear something?" she asked.

He pulled a face. "You mean other than your mum's show she turns up too loud?"

"I heard that," her mother said from the other room.

Her dad grinned and pulled out the chair across from her. "What's going on? You look exhausted."

"I am."

"Is it Ben? He came by here and left those," her father said, nodding to the left.

Kirsi followed his gaze and saw the bouquet. "I don't know how many times I have to tell him that it's over for good."

"He's no' willing to give up. Some might consider that a good sign."

"Some, but not me."

"Nay," her father said with a chuckle. "You've always known what you wanted. I take that to mean Ben isna the one keeping you from sleep."

Kirsi shook her head. "Nay, it isn't him. I…" She paused and pressed her lips together. "I keep having these dreams."

"About?"

Before she could answer, her mother rolled into the kitchen in her wheelchair and asked, "What's going on, pet?"

Kirsi shook her head and shrugged. "I don't know what the dreams are. It's been two nights of them on repeat. I sense it's the same dream, but I don't know for sure because I can't remember them. As soon as I wake, they're gone."

Her parents exchanged a look. The two had always been close. Even after her mother's diagnosis of muscular dystrophy, which might have torn other couples apart, they remained devoted. They weren't perfect by any means, but they had always been there for her. She told them everything, sharing things her friends would never speak about to their parents. But that was the kind of household she had grown up in, and she loved it.

"What? Do you know something?" Kirsi asked as she looked between them.

Her mother shook her head, her gray-streaked light auburn hair kept in a pixie style. Pale green eyes the same shade as Kirsi's stared back at her. "There are a lot of strange things happening on Skye of late, pet."

"There's been a change," her father said. "A shift in the magic around here. It began with Corann's death."

"Not to say that Rhona isn't doing a good job," her mother hastened to add.

Her dad quickly nodded. "Right. Right. Rhona was the correct choice. Corann knew that."

"But?" Kirsi pressed when her parents paused.

Her mother folded her hands in her lap. "The big battle recently, the Reapers showing themselves, the forging of friendships with the Fae once more, the mist, and…the murders. Something isn't right."

"It's evil," her father stated.

"Everyone now claims Elias MacLean is responsible." Her mother shrugged. "That family has suffered like few others have."

Kirsi finished off her tea. "Do you really think Elias killed those people?"

"No one could've imagined that Emily MacLean would kill her husband," her dad replied.

Her mother snorted. "If Emily did it, there was a reason."

"*If?*" Kirsi asked.

Her father swiped his hand through the air. "You were young and doona remember, but a lot of that didna make sense. It all happened hurriedly, and Corann was quick to move forward after speaking with Emily. Your mum's right, though. Something happened that the family didna want to get out."

"And now the son is being accused." Her mother's lips twisted. "I knew Emily well. She was a sweet soul who loved her children beyond reason. I can't imagine how she'll react when she hears about Elias. And with Elodie finally back on Skye…" Her mother grunted, shaking her head.

Her father patted Kirsi's folded hands. "If the dreams return tonight, and you still can no' see them clearly, we'll take the next step."

"Thanks. I think I'm turning in." She rose, kissed both of them, and put her cup in the sink before walking to her bedroom.

Kirsi closed the door and kicked off her shoes before falling face-first onto the bed. She grabbed one of the faux fur pillows and hugged it to her as she rolled onto her back. She had hung pink lights around her room, casting the space in a subtle glow. Her bedroom was her sanctuary, her refuge. As she stared at the lights, her eyes began to lose focus, and her lids became heavy. She closed them and was almost immediately asleep.

"You know what to do."

Kirsi was in that space between sleep and dreaming. The voice was strong, distinctive. Feminine. It came from all around her. She tried to open her eyes to see something.

"Forget about seeing. You know what to do."

But she didn't.

"Yes, Kirsi, you do. You always have. Now is the time. Look deep within yourself. You know what to do."

Who was this person talking to her?

"One who is reaching across time and space. Lower your walls."

What walls? She was trying to understand, to see.

"You don't need to see anything. That's why the dreams are eluding you. Stop looking and feel."

Kirsi tried to do as the voice asked, but she wasn't sure what to even attempt.

"The time is coming. You need to be ready. You know what to do."

"I don't!" Kirsi yelled.

"You always have—in this life, and the hundreds before. Lower your walls. The time is coming. You must *be ready. Just remember, you know what to do."*

Kirsi's eyes flew open, her heart pounding in her chest. This time, she remembered *every word.*

Ferne sucked in a much-needed breath and yanked the blindfold from her eyes. She shivered despite the heat of the fire where she sat before the hearth. Rain beat a steady tempo against the windows, but she barely heard it. Her thoughts were elsewhere.

She had finally reached Kirsi. It had taken her far longer than it should have, but the Druid was exceptionally strong. Kirsi had no idea of her power yet. It was by happenstance that Ferne had stumbled upon her to begin with.

And if she did, then so could the evil that continued to grow on Skye.

Ferne had no interest in going to the infamous isle. Her family had been driven from it generations ago, and none of them had stepped foot on Skye since. It was why she had reached out the way she had to Kirsi.

All Ferne could do now was watch and wait to see if the

young Druid figured things out. Rhona needed to be warned. All the Druids on Skye—*mie* and *drough* alike—needed to prepare.

How the largest group of Druids in the world didn't realize what had happened boggled her mind. The fact that they didn't know told Ferne just how critical things were.

She rose on shaky legs and walked around her small flat, pulling the sheets from all reflective surfaces. By the time she reached the kitchen, she could barely stand. It took great effort for her to open the fridge and get out the container of orange juice. She drank it straight from the carton, liquid seeping from the sides of her mouth and running down her face.

Ferne gulped down several swallows before lowering the jug to the nearby table. She half-sank, half-fell into one of the chairs. She then kicked the fridge door closed and leaned her head back. It had been some time since she had used so much magic at once. But it had been imperative.

After so many failed attempts to connect with Kirsi, Ferne knew her time was running out. Yet, even now, she wasn't sure that what she had done would be enough. Her gaze landed on her mobile. It wouldn't be hard to find Rhona's number and call her. It was a last resort. Unfortunately, they were nearing that point.

She wiped her mouth with the back of her hand and drank more orange juice. The sugar helped her recover her strength. She wouldn't be fully back to normal for another thirty minutes or so, but at least she hadn't passed out.

The dull headache that always followed such use of magic began. She reached across the table for the bottle of ibuprofen and took three pills. Her eyes drifted shut. She didn't know how long she hovered there before a loud banging startled her.

Her brother's angry voice reached her through the door. "Open the fucking door, Ferne."

She pushed to her feet and walked the short distance to the front of the house on semi-solid legs. After unlocking the three bolts and lowering the wards, she opened the door.

Mason's stormy gray eyes met hers and, somehow, grew even angrier. He stepped into the flat and closed the door behind him. He gently took her face in his hands, turning her head one way and then the other. He must not have liked what he saw because his lips pinched. "Goddamn it. What have you done?"

"What had to be done."

"I felt your magic across London. The others will have, too."

She lifted her chin defiantly. "Then let them come for me."

His nostrils flared as he released her. "They're already on their way."

CHAPTER TWENTY

Bronwyn could feel Elias in the house. His presence was everywhere. Somehow, he filled the manor in a way that no one ever had. It was distracting, disturbing. Downright off-putting.

Yet her thoughts drifted to the magnetism she felt between them. The primal attraction that went deeper than anything she'd experienced before. The longer he was around, the stronger she felt it, like weighty bonds. Those ties weren't heavy. No, they were light as a feather, but as strong as the mighty mountains of Skye. And as bottomless as the sea.

Elias filled her every thought no matter where in the house he went. She could feel him, like a pulse. And when he was near, the desire was so absolute, so momentous, that she wondered how she hadn't given in to the yearning, the bone-deep ache to feel his body against hers. It would be good between them. Great, even. She knew it with a certainty that alarmed her.

Bronwyn slammed her laptop closed and shoved the computer off her lap. She had tried, unsuccessfully, to work for hours. Everything she did to the cover was wrong. She'd spent more time deleting work than actually creating it.

And she blamed Elias.

That wasn't exactly fair. He hadn't forced her to spill her secrets. The blame rested entirely on her shoulders. What had she been thinking telling him *everything*? She'd thought she would see revulsion in his eyes. Maybe even disgust. That might have helped combat the overwhelming, uncontrollable desire she felt in his presence.

Instead, there had been empathy and understanding. What was she supposed to do with that? She should've been appreciative, but she had lashed out. Because she didn't trust anyone who didn't see her as the horrible person she knew she was.

Bronwyn surged to her feet and walked the parlor, hoping to rid herself of the pent-up energy and the advancing, fervent longing that had been building since her encounter with Elias at the co-op.

The strings of some melody reached her through the closed parlor door. She didn't know what Elias was doing. She tried not to care, but she was as successful at that as she was at ignoring the ache inside her that only he could quench. He hadn't returned to the parlor after their quarrel. At first, she'd been happy that he'd left her alone. But as the hours stretched, she wondered what he was doing—and thinking.

Did he stare at the wall, fantasizing as she did? Did he close his eyes and wonder what it would feel like to kiss her as she longed to do? Did his skin tingle then heat when he imagined holding her as she did him?

Bronwyn had seen the desire in his eyes. It had been

impossible to miss. She wanted to be strong enough to keep him at arm's length. This was the worst time for him to come into her life. He kept talking about helping her, and oh, how she wished he could. But it wasn't possible. She had accepted her fate the moment she'd first done blood magic.

Not once had she even entertained the thought of someone affecting her as Elias did. If she had, would she still have done the blood magic? Bronwyn looked up and thought of her cousin. The answer was yes. She owed her entire family a great debt. She was the cause of…everything.

The last thing she deserved was someone like Elias. It was a cruel, brutal deed by Fate to tease her so unbearably with a handsome man who had such a pure soul. He was better off far, far away from her.

Bronwyn yanked open the door and stalked into the hallway to listen for him. The music came from the back of the house, and somehow, she wasn't surprised to find Elias in the kitchen. He sang along to an upbeat song as he moved between the stove and the table, where he chopped garlic and onions.

Whatever he was cooking smelled delicious. Her irritation soared when her stomach growled. She didn't want to desire Elias. She certainly didn't want to like him. She still didn't understand what had made her agree to let him stay at the manor, but to open herself up to him in a way she had never done with *anyone*? Not even Beth?

Simply put, he had the means to end everything she was doing with one word to Rhona. Blood magic wasn't tolerated. It didn't matter the reason it was used. But more than that, she didn't want to make his already complicated life more problematic by knowing her.

"Hey," Elias said when he noticed her. He turned down the music, his gaze searching. "Was that too loud?"

She shook her head.

He studied her for a lengthy moment. "Hungry?"

She should make him leave. She should say that he was no longer welcome. The house would ensure he was gone. "I am."

"It'll be done shortly." Elias moved back to the stove and stirred whatever was in the pan.

Bronwyn's gaze moved to his tee, the long sleeves pushed to his elbows. She took in the muscles of his forearms that bunched and flexed before letting her eyes rake over his broad shoulders. Sizzling, wanton desire hummed through her. She struggled to bring air into her lungs as she imagined those amazing arms gathering her against him before he lifted her onto the counter, spread her legs, and pressed himself against her.

Her lips parted on a shaky breath as wetness flooded her panties. She wanted to run back to the parlor and forget about Elias and his sinfully sexy voice and eyes that saw to her soul. She'd gotten really good at keeping her walls up and everyone out. He made her reconsider things, yearn and wish for things she couldn't have—not in this life. Not after everything.

"Everything all right?" he asked.

Bronwyn nodded and forced herself to walk to the cupboards. She got out plates and utensils while trying not to stare at Elias. She'd thought she knew what kind of man he was when he'd helped her against Sydney. Then, she'd thought she knew who he was when the Knights came for him. He had upended all of that by his reaction to learning her secrets. Which begged the question: What kind of man was he to willingly stay with someone like…her?

Thanks to Sydney, she knew what wickedness looked like, and Elias was the opposite of that. While she might not be the best at reading people, the greatest actor in the world couldn't have pulled off Elias's shock at learning that he was wanted for murder. He hadn't taken that man's life, though she had no way to prove it. The person she'd look at was Sydney, because it sounded exactly like something the arsehole would do.

As Elias moved around the kitchen, focused on cooking, she thought back to the day so many years earlier when she had fallen. She and every other female in school had had a crush on Elias. It didn't matter that he was older. He had been one of those people who just had something special about them, a kind of spark that was impossible to resist. It wasn't only his good looks, it was his smile and innate goodness.

That embarrassing morning had begun like any other. Her dad had dropped her off at school because her mum hadn't left the bed in days. Bronwyn had spotted Elias instantly as if someone had told her exactly where to look. He was surrounded by friends and girls who sought his attention.

Bronwyn had drunk in everything about him, from the blue jean jacket he wore over the white shirt to the way he shoved his hands through his dark blond hair. Her dad had been speaking the entire time, but she hadn't paid attention. How could she when she was so focused on Elias?

Once she got out of the car and started toward the school entrance, Bronwyn realized that she had to walk past Sarah and the popular kids. She had once yearned to be in that group—or any faction if she were honest. She just wanted to fit in, and where else other than among her community should she have been welcomed? But she had never found a place. She'd once heard someone say there was something odd about her. She didn't know what that was, but others *still* recognized it—whatever it was.

She'd had no choice but to walk past Sarah that morning, but Bronwyn didn't look at the pretty, popular girl. Her dad had told her not to engage Sarah and that things would settle between them eventually. So, that's what Bronwyn did.

When Sarah called out to her, Bronwyn ignored her. That enraged Sarah. The next thing Bronwyn knew, the ground rushed up to meet her. She let go of her books in an attempt to break her fall. Bronwyn just managed to keep her face from slamming into the concrete sidewalk. The wet ground littered with leaves stung her palms and knees, but it was the sound of laughter from everyone that made tears prick her eyes.

Just as suddenly as the laughter began, it halted. That was when Bronwyn saw the boots in front of her. She lifted her head, her heart stopping in shock as Elias lowered to his haunches. His bright blue eyes searched her face. Then, he shot her a quick smile.

He held out his hand, and Bronwyn's brain froze. She wondered if all of it was a dream, but her body moved of its own accord, and the feel of Elias's strong, steady fingers closing around hers as he helped her to her feet was a balm to her bruised ego. She couldn't stop staring as he gathered her books and straightened to tower over her. His lips curved into a smile as he handed the books to her before picking leaves from her hair.

Every hurt she had vanished. Elias had noticed her. *Her!* Odd, outsider Bronwyn.

Elias had said nothing that day. He hadn't needed to. She'd seen the kindness in his eyes.

Something she had never forgotten.

Was that why she'd reached for him, offering comfort when he needed it the most? Could that be the reason she allowed him to remain at the house?

"Bronwyn?"

She blinked, focusing on his face that now wore a frown as he stood across the table. "Aye?"

"Are you all right? You looked far away."

"Just thinking." She glanced around and realized the food had already been set on the plates.

Elias pulled out his chair and sat. "I hope you like stir-fry."

"It smells delicious," she replied as she lowered herself into a chair, still caught up in the feelings from long ago that now mixed with the current ones. Her palm tingled with the memory of his hand against hers.

They ate in silence for several minutes. Bronwyn felt his gaze on her, but she didn't look at him. Her brain told her he would be safer anywhere but at the manor, but her heart urged her to let Elias stay. And her body, well, it also advocated for him to remain.

Bronwyn shifted in her seat uncomfortably. She hoped Elias couldn't tell what she was thinking. It seemed as if it were written all over her face. "I'm not used to anyone being in the house," she blurted out.

His fork paused on the way to his mouth. He lowered it and looked into her eyes. "The manor is large enough that I can make sure you don't see or hear me if that's what you wish."

That wasn't what she'd meant. Or had it been? Dammit! Why was she so confused? She wanted to feel his hand against hers again. She wanted to know the taste of his lips, the feel of his hard body, but she knew it was reckless and stupid. Anyone near her when things imploded would likely be taken out with her. Elias deserved so much more than what she could offer.

He cleared his throat, his gaze briefly lowering to the table. "About earlier," he began.

"Don't. Whatever you want to say, don't." She was hanging on by a thread, and if he said the right thing, she was doomed. It was better if he didn't say anything at all. She moved her attention to her plate, unable to meet his probing scrutiny any longer.

"Bronwyn, look at me."

His voice was soft and deep, a plea in every syllable. Did he have any idea what he did to her? He dredged up that long-buried hunger, the cavernous, aching loneliness to be accepted by someone. She had looked for it in all the wrong places. She had even believed she'd found it with Sydney. But it was there, in Elias's eyes—if she dared but look. But she didn't, she *couldn't*.

"Please," he implored.

Damn him for the hold he seemed to have over her. The walls she'd crafted didn't stand a chance against him. Neither, it seemed, did her willpower. She lifted her gaze to his. The instant she looked into his bright blue eyes, she was ensnared, entangled.

What was it about Elias that made her feel as close to being safe as she ever had? There was an openness about him that compelled her to share more of herself. But most of all was the attraction. The wanton, primal need to claim him and be claimed by him in turn. It had been there from the instant she'd seen him at the co-op, and it continued to flourish exponentially, culminating upstairs when she used her magic.

If only she had found him instead of Sydney. Her life would

be so different. But it hadn't been Elias, and wishing it had been didn't undo her horrendous decisions.

"I understand why you've retreated to the manor," Elias said. "I get why you keep everyone away. I also understand why you believe you deserve the cruelty you receive from others. I want to help you. Let me help," he beseeched. "I willna let you down."

Bronwyn wanted to wrap her arms around him and flee the manor at the same time. She did neither. Instead, she did her best to strengthen her walls against the bright flame that was Elias. "You can't help me. No one can."

"Then let me be your friend. We could both use one of those right now."

She wanted to refuse him, but he had asked for the one thing she couldn't deny. Because she desperately wanted a friend. Even as she started to agree, she was reminded of those closest to her she had lost because of her decisions. "You deserve a better fate than what you'd get being my friend."

"I disagree," he stated calmly as if expecting that answer.

She pushed her half-eaten plate away. "You think you know me, but you don't."

"I'm trying to know you. I *want* to know you." His brows snapped together. "Why is that so difficult for you to accept?"

Bronwyn pushed the chair back as she got to her feet. "Because I know who I am. I know what's coming. And I know that anyone near me will suffer the same fate. I don't want that for you."

He got to his feet and leaned his hands on the table, never breaking eye contact. "Then you doona have any idea of who I am or what the Knights and I are capable of."

"Why haven't you asked how Beth got here?" she demanded.

Elias blinked, quickly hiding his flash of surprise. "What?"

"Why haven't you asked me how Beth got here?" she repeated. Bronwyn was shaking, hating herself for what she was about to do. But if anyone could blow up a potential friendship—or more—it was her.

He slowly straightened. "Because it doesna matter."

"Oh, but it does. You want to know me? Then let me tell you the type of person I am. When I finally got to talk to Beth, she laughed off my fears. She told me I was deluded and that she loved Sydney. They were to be married, you see. As she turned to walk away, I knocked her out. It took some doing getting her into my car, but I did it. I drove straight to Skye. She started to wake when I was dragging her into the manor, so I knocked her out again. You see, Elias, I'm the kind of woman who kidnaps her cousin forcefully and puts her between dimensions against her will."

CHAPTER TWENTY-ONE

Elias had guessed about Beth when Bronwyn hadn't given him details for how she'd gotten to the manor. He hadn't asked questions because he hadn't *wanted* specifics. Now, he stared at Bronwyn, unsure how to respond. He knew she was trying to shock him, attempting to repulse him so he'd leave.

What he saw was a woman who had hurt for so long she'd lashed out to protect herself so no one could injure her again. He wanted to walk around the table, drag her into his arms, and shelter her from anyone and anything who dared to do her harm. She had stood on her own for so long. Her strength, the way she endured alone against the world, battling anyone and anything that rose against her, made him admire her even more.

Only someone who had felt the lash of injustice and the cruelty of the world could see it in another. And he saw it clearly in the woman standing before him, daring him with her mesmerizing hazel eyes to turn on her and go back on everything he had said. It was what she wanted, what she expected.

And he was going to prove her wrong.

"Nothing to say to that?" Bronwyn demanded with one brow arched.

To a passerby, she looked wholly capable of doing anything. No doubt she could—and would. While he doubted she'd call him a friend, she had bared her secrets to him. He saw the cracks and chinks in her carefully placed armor as well as the trepidation that remained as her constant companion. She did a valiant job of hiding all of it, at least to those who didn't bother to look too closely.

With her wounded soul and raw, festering emotional scars, the woman before him needed a friend. Someone who would stand with her no matter what. Someone who wouldn't let her down. Someone who loved and accepted every bit of who she was.

His heart hurt for the anguish she couldn't hide from him. As much as he wanted to protect Bronwyn, she didn't need that. She was too strong and independent. No, what she needed was someone to stand with her, beside her. Someone she could lean on and trust.

"I guessed," he finally answered.

That wasn't what she wanted to hear. Her hazel eyes narrowed dangerously, the copper becoming darker. "You guessed?"

"I'm no' excusing your kidnapping, but I know you thought you did the right thing."

"I did the *only* thing I could. You don't have a clue who Sydney is or what he's capable of. He turned my sweet, innocent cousin into someone I didn't know. He twisted her."

The anger in her voice didn't stir his. He recognized that

Bronwyn was looking for a fight, but he wouldn't give her one. Too many had formed their own opinions and didn't mind spilling their vitriol when it came to her.

Bronwyn shook her head as she snorted and looked him up and down with disgust. "Can't you see what I am? Or do you fear saying anything because of what I might do to you?"

"I doona fear you, lass. You've a lot of pent-up anger inside you. Years' worth is my guess. The people on Skye, your people, *our* people, turned against you. No one bothered to ask what happened to you or your father. No one offered to help."

Bronwyn tried to maintain her anger as she looked away, but not before he saw the torment in her eyes. He fisted his hands, hands that wanted so badly to hold her, to comfort her. To tell her he understood. Because he did. Probably better than anyone.

"Don't," she said, her voice, barely above a whisper, cracking slightly. "Don't you dare make it out as if I did the right thing. We both know I didn't."

"I'm sure some would happily condemn you. Some would praise your actions. The simple truth is that sometimes it isna between right and wrong when we're faced with a decision. I've found it's more like deciding between bad or worse. We make the best choices we can in the moment."

Her head swiveled back to him. She regarded him with clear eyes devoid of feeling. He was careful not to show her pity. He suspected that was the last emotion she would welcome.

"There's still time to fix things," he told her.

One brow quirked as she tilted her head to the side. "Is there? What would you suggest?"

Her soft voice didn't fool him. She still sought a fight, still needed to lash out. "Release Beth."

"So she can return to Sydney?"

"We'll talk to her first. Perhaps we can convince her what kind of man he is."

"And if we can't?"

Elias shrugged. "We keep trying."

"All the while keeping her against her will. How is that different than what I've done?"

It wasn't. Fuck. "Then we let her go."

"I see." Bronwyn's smile was forced and held no humor. "Shall I tell you what she confided that caused me to take such drastic measures? One of the Druids in Sydney's crowd worked at an assisted living facility for the elderly. The Stewart bloodline has always gifted us with a magical ability. Beth was no different. She can get into someone's mind, though she had to be touching them to do it. She had gotten a job at the residence home, and they were planning to get certain individuals to sign over their money, lands, and property to Sydney in new wills. Those people would then die a short while later—in a way that looked natural when it was anything but—before their families could discover what happened."

"Bloody hell," he murmured.

"Beth was on her way to that job when I confronted her."

Elias ran a hand over his face as he wondered what kind of actions he would've taken in Bronwyn's place. "If Beth was so integral to the plan, Sydney must have been searching for her."

"I had time to get back here and get her set up while he searched the city, but he came to Skye almost immediately. I convinced him that I hadn't spoken to her since the funeral. He bought it, barely, but I knew he'd return."

"You shared your story with me for a reason. Because you trust me."

She grabbed her plate and brought it to the sink without responding.

He followed her movements as she shifted about the kitchen cleaning. "You're no' alone anymore."

"I've been alone from the moment of my birth," she replied.

He took his plate and walked to the sink, stopping beside her. "You're no' alone now."

She stopped what she was doing and looked at him. "I told you so you'd understand exactly what was going on here. Because I want to ensure you leave and forget this noble idea you have of helping me."

"Liar."

Her eyes flared at his comment. "Excuse me?"

"You told me because you wanted to share it. You needed to unburden yourself. And because you knew I'd understand."

"You flatter yourself," she bit out.

Elias shook his head. "You know I'm right."

She faced him, fury burning so brightly in her eyes that they turned gold. "You're certainly full of yourself. I think it's time you left."

"I remember, you know," he said, ignoring her. "It was autumn. It had rained during the night. I stood with some friends as you walked to the school. I saw the group of girls talking about you, pointing and giggling. One of them tripped you. I have a particular hatred for bullies. I've been on the receiving end myself. I remember the way you looked at me when I helped you to your feet. I've never seen eyes like yours before—or since. I intended to give the girls a piece of my mind, but my anger melted away when I touched you. The same way you steadied me the other morning."

Elias couldn't look away from her. Those stunning eyes of hers shifted colors right before him. The green became more dominant now as her breathing changed, becoming harsher, quicker. His gaze dropped to her mouth as her lips parted. She leaned toward him. Their fingers brushed once. He craved to feel her against him, and it was everything he could do not to reach for her and bring her softness against him. To drown in her tumultuous eyes.

His body flared to life, throbbing with a hunger only she could slake. The desire was thick, scalding him as it rushed through his veins. Blood rushed to his cock, hardening him nearly to the point of pain. He was past the point of needing Bronwyn. She was the very air he breathed, the light that gave him life.

She turned away from him and rested her hands on the counter. "Thank you for dinner. I can clean by myself."

And with that, he was summarily dismissed.

Elias stood there for another handful of seconds, trying to rein in the desire that threatened to consume him. Finally, he took a step back. Because to be so close to her was to invite madness. He glanced around the kitchen, trying to find a reason to stay. Unfortunately, there wasn't one. He strode out of the room, the swinging door thumping behind him as he alternated between anger and disbelief. She wanted him. There was no denying what he saw. Why then had she turned away? But he knew. Just as he knew why she tried to repulse him so he'd leave.

Once in the corridor, he halted. Nothing about the evening had gone as he'd hoped, but he and Bronwyn had made progress.

Whether he'd gotten through to her at all remained to be seen. She was stubborn, but more than that, she guarded herself prudently. She had lost so much, and she refused to open herself to more. He understood that because for a very long time, he had done the same.

The mobile phone in his pocket vibrated. He pulled it out and saw the text from Sabertooth.

MESSAGES SENT TO BOTH SISTERS.

Elias sighed. At least his siblings knew he was okay for the moment. He still wanted to talk to them, but that would have to wait. He started toward the parlor when he drew up once more. That was Bronwyn's room. He needed to give her some space. While he'd prefer to sleep in the same room, it was enough for now that they were in the same house.

He looked up. There were rooms aplenty, but they would be far from Bronwyn. Even if he offered to keep the fire lit in a bedroom for her, he didn't think she'd take him up on that offer. Which meant he would stay on the ground floor with her.

Elias considered his many options and decided on the library. It was across the corridor but still close enough to Bronwyn. Plus, he'd always had a love for being surrounded by books. Many of them were gone, but he was sure he could find something that interested him in the long hours that awaited him.

He walked to the library door and opened it. The drapes were tightly closed, but the fire Sabryn had created earlier still raged, shedding a warm glow on the room. He removed the sheets from the furniture and piled them in a corner, wincing only slightly from the pain in his ribs. They felt better since the chant they'd used on Bronwyn. He wondered if it was powerful enough to have also begun healing in him. If he ever got the chance to ask a MacLeod Druid, he would.

The sofa didn't convert to a bed, but it wouldn't be the first time he'd slept on a couch that was too small to accommodate his height. At least he could lay flat. Mostly. His feet would have to rest over the arm, but it was better than sitting in a chair and waking up with another crick in his neck.

"Scott!" Elodie called.

He raced into the room. "What is it?"

She glanced at him and motioned to her mobile screen. "An email from Elias."

"Really? Filip and I have had no luck finding his vehicle on Skye. Is he still here?"

Elodie handed her phone to him and anxiously waited for him to read it. She was tapping her toe impatiently by the time he looked up. "Well?" she asked.

"He's taking a chance in corresponding," Scott said carefully.

Elodie blew out a breath and fought for calm. "He wanted to let me know he's safe."

"Let's hope he was smart about keeping his location secret. The authorities will try to trace this."

She accepted her phone back. "How are you coming along with talking to George?"

"She's not responding to texts or answering my calls. I know she isna happy about my and Filip's decision to remain on Skye, but this is a bit much."

"She needs to get over it. Filip was born here, and you and I are together now. Can't she see that?"

"George is…"

Elodie snorted. "Resentful? Bitter? Unable to let go?"

"Sadly, I'm seeing all of those things that I didna before. I did get ahold of Willa."

Scott's sister and father still lived in Edinburgh and were a part of the Druid Others there. "And?"

"George has already alerted everyone about Filip and me. She didna come right out and tell them to ignore us, but she made it clear we were no longer welcome among them."

"As I said, resentful and bitter. What about your dad and Willa? How are they being treated?"

"Willa said things were different. That people went out of their way *not* to talk about me or Filip. She intentionally brought me up in a conversation, and the Druids walked away."

Elodie was flabbergasted. "Wow. Tell me she and your dad are coming here."

"Willa is a city lass, through and through. She willna willingly leave Edinburgh. Same with Dad. At least with them staying, we have some idea of what's going on."

"True, but be aware that George knows that, too. She could use it to her advantage."

Scott grinned. "Then she really doesna know my family."

"Aye," Elodie said, thinking about her siblings. "I think it's time I did something."

"Like what?" Scott asked, alarm in his voice.

She pulled him down for a kiss. "First stop, a visit to my sister. After that, I'd like to have a little chat with George on my own."

"I wouldna suggest that."

"Too bad," Elodie said with a wink.

The longer they were on Skye, the more worried Nikolai became. He didn't sense anything wrong on the isle, but Esther did. And if his mate was upset, then he was, as well. The problem was he didn't know how to help.

"Stop staring," she told him as they walked the Fairy Pools.

"I can no' help it. You willna tell me what to do."

Esther sighed and turned to face him. "I can't tell you what I don't know, honey. You really don't feel anything?"

He opened himself up and expanded his senses. "I feel the magic of the realm, as I always do. It is still strongest on Dreagan, but Skye has a significant amount. It doesna feel any different than it has before."

"Ugh," Esther said and closed her eyes. "That doesn't make sense."

Nikolai moved up beside his mate. He took her fisted hands in his and waited until she looked at him. "I doona sense anything wrong with the magic, but that doesna mean there isna something wrong."

"You're a Dragon King. You and yours have been safeguarding Earth since the beginning of time. If you don't feel anything, then there isn't anything to worry about."

He shook his head and tugged her coat tighter when he saw her shiver. The Fairy Pools were gorgeous at any time of year, but the biting cold made things uncomfortable for Esther. "You're the TruthSeeker for the Druids, my love. Those abilities brought you to Skye, home of the largest gathering of Druids on the planet. Doona discount that."

"If I could just understand what's wrong..."

"The fact that you know something is amiss is enough for me. We're no' going anywhere until we sort things out. Perhaps now is the time to seek out Rhona."

Esther sighed but shook her head. "Not yet. Give me a little more time."

CHAPTER TWENTY-TWO

Rhona had never been so furious in her life. After the agreed-upon time and date of the meeting with George, the Druid had texted thirty minutes after they were to meet and canceled.

She was done playing nice.

"This could go badly," Balladyn warned.

Rhona cut him a look. "She decided that when she refused to speak to me."

"Agreed. I just want to point out the obvious."

"You have. Now, let's go."

His red eyes met hers before he teleported them to the hallway outside a room at the B&B. As soon as they arrived, Balladyn released her and raised his veil that would keep him invisible from everyone except Reapers. But Rhona knew he was there.

She rapped on the door and heard movement from within. Footsteps sounded as they drew near. But the door didn't open.

From the other side, George asked, "Who is it?"

"Rhona. You've put off our meeting long enough. Open the door."

"I don't think that's a good idea."

"I don't care. You don't come into someone's territory and ignore their repeated attempts to have a discussion."

George barked a laugh. "This isn't the Middle Ages, Rhona. Another may have chosen you to lead, but that doesn't mean I have to recognize your station."

"And that, right there, proves why you wouldn't get the same respect from others."

"You Skye Druids have been too isolated all these generations. You have no idea how the outside world works. Perhaps it's time someone showed you exactly what has happened."

Rhona turned her head toward Balladyn and nodded. In the next instant, they were inside George's room. Once Balladyn released her, Rhona said, "I know exactly what's going on."

George spun around so quickly she tripped over her feet and fell against the door. Her deep brown eyes widened in fright, but anger soon took over. She sneered at Rhona. "Of course, you'd use your Reaper lover to get into a place you aren't welcome."

Rhona let her gaze run over George's dark skin and tight corkscrew curls that formed an afro. "I'm finished being polite. I'm done trying to do this on your terms. You've come to Skye and accused a Skye Druid of murder to everyone except me."

"Why should I have spoken to you?" George asked as she raked her gaze over Rhona. "Just so you can shove it under the rug and pretend it never happened?"

"Why should I believe you? For all I know, you have a

grievance against Elias. Maybe this is your way of getting revenge."

George pushed away from the door and glared. "I have proof."

"So I've heard."

"You don't scare me. Neither does your pet Reaper hiding here somewhere. If I'm killed, others will come and continue shouting Elias's guilt."

Rhona crossed her arms over her chest. "In other words, you won't rest until he's charged."

"That's right."

"Surely, you're aware that several Druids were killed here recently. Elias wasn't anywhere near Skye. That wasn't him."

George shrugged indifferently. "I'm sorry for the deaths, but I'm more concerned with those in my city."

"*Your* city? Interesting you should say that. What about all the Druid deaths elsewhere around the world." Rhona tried not to gloat when surprise flickered across George's face. "There's more going on than you know."

"You won't change my mind about Elias. He was seen."

"Edinburgh is a major city. I've been there plenty of times myself. Just because someone is in the city at the same time as a death doesn't mean they killed the person."

George opened the door. "We're done."

Rhona walked to the threshold before pausing and meeting George's gaze. "We're not even close to being finished. I will get to the bottom of things. I hope for everyone's sake that you aren't here under false pretenses. I won't take kindly to that."

The instant Rhona entered the hallway, the door slammed

shut behind her. She met Balladyn's gaze as he dropped his veil. "Well?"

"I think we need to do some investigating."

"We need to find Elias."

Balladyn's lips twisted. "Aye. That, too."

It wasn't Elias's words that Bronwyn thought about as she put away the leftovers and cleaned. No, it was the way her body had moved to his, how she yearned to have his lips pressed against hers. How she hungered to know what he felt like moving inside her, his length filling her over and over.

She had come so close to kissing him. So very close to giving in and letting desire win. Even now as she dried her hands and replaced the towel, she wondered what a kiss from him would be like. Would he tease and tempt? Maybe he would ravage and plunder. However he kissed, she knew he would do it with complete fervor.

Bronwyn wiped the counters and table before putting the containers of food into the fridge. She walked from the kitchen, wondering where her boldness had gone. She hadn't found it until she reached Inverness. Once she discovered it, it was as if the world had opened to her, presenting endless possibilities within reach. All she had to do was go for them.

It felt as if the universe were doing the same to her now by putting Elias not just in her path but also her home. Tempting her with opportunities, with rewards that would be worth everything.

If only she had made different choices. Then she wouldn't hesitate to show Elias how much she wanted him. She had glimpsed the heat flaring in his bright blue eyes, the unmistakable passion that promised untold pleasure. But she had stopped him with her words. Because she was a coward. She feared what would come of giving herself to a man like Elias.

Maybe that was for the best. Why get a taste for something that wouldn't be hers for long? If Sydney didn't kill her, then she would die soon enough from using blood magic. Her days were numbered either way she looked at it. And that was what soured her. Because being near Elias brought up all the things she had dreamed about and longed for as a young lass.

There wasn't a girl around who hadn't coveted Elias. She had watched him from afar at school as he moved from girl to girl. His relationships never lasted longer than a week or two. Then, one day, he was gone. Not that she blamed him. After her mother died, she had wanted to leave, too.

Bronwyn meandered through the manor with no particular destination in mind. So many rooms lay dormant, almost as if they were waiting for the next generation to bring the entire house back to life. She had wanted it to be her, but sadly, it wouldn't be.

She moved from dark room to dark room through the sprawling manor, but she wasn't thinking about her family or the house. Her thoughts remained on Elias. She wondered where he had gone when he left Skye. She wished she would've paid more attention to the outside world instead of the shite storm of her life during that time. Everyone knew about the death of Elias's father by his mother's hand because it was in the paper and on everyone's lips, but she hadn't listened to the gossip. Though whether she liked it or not, the blathers usually had more knowledge than the paper. Elias didn't speak of his parents. She had lost both of hers, but not at the same time as he had. Though Elias's mother wasn't deceased.

The Skye Druids might be powerful and well-known in the Druid world, but they didn't live normal lives. It wasn't just the magic they possessed that changed things. Sometimes, it was their abilities. Other times, it was that they couldn't find their place in a world that couldn't understand them. But usually it was because the very land they were bound to turned against them.

Bronwyn spotted the light beneath the library door. She walked to it and leaned an ear against it, listening. When she didn't hear anything, she knocked.

"Come in," Elias called.

She opened the door but didn't cross the threshold. Her gaze landed on Elias unfolding his tall frame from the sofa as he stood to face her. She took in the fire and the removal of the sheets from the furniture.

"I figured you'd enjoy your space without me in it," he said.

Her eyes jerked to him. She had said something about that, hadn't she? This would be better. She was sure she wouldn't be able to sleep in the same room as him anyway. "There are numerous rooms."

"I'm fine here."

She glanced at the sofa. "I'm not sure how comfortable that will be."

He shrugged, a crooked smile on his face. "I've slept on much worse."

"I'll get a pillow and blankets."

She left before he could refuse. In no time, she returned. Elias stood just outside the library door. When he took the items, their hands brushed. A shock went through her, and it was everything she could do not to throw her arms around him.

"Thank you," he said.

Bronwyn hastily pulled her arms against herself, even as her blood heated at the small touch. She thought again of kissing him, glancing at his mouth before looking away. She wanted to say something, but she didn't know what. Finally, she turned to leave.

"Goodnight," he called after her. "I'll be close if you need anything."

She raised her hand in acknowledgement. "'Night," she said and hurried into the parlor.

Bronwyn leaned against the door as she closed it. Had his words been true at dinner? She had expected a certain reaction from him, and when he hadn't given it, she'd lashed out. Mainly because she had prepared for him to be sickened—not sympathetic.

He was right about one thing, though. She had shared her story because she was lonely. And because she'd wanted to see his reaction. What she learned was that Elias was as perplexing and unflappable now as his younger self. More so, actually. He had clearly seen much in his travels, and the bond he shared with the Knights was the kind she had always dreamed of.

His tragedy had set him on a path that gave him purpose.

Hers had led to the downfall of the Stewarts—all by her hand.

"Sorry, Mum and Dad," she murmured.

She wondered if she would be buried in the family plot next

to her parents. Or would her fellow Druids discard her body like rubbish. If Elias was around, she suspected he would see her properly buried. But she hoped he cleared his name and left soon.

He, out of everyone, deserved to be free of the tangles she had put herself in. And if she had her way, he would be. Though it would be hard to send him away. She enjoyed everything about him—his conversation, the way he looked at her, and even his cooking.

A momentary lapse of madness had caused her to agree to him staying at the manor. The money had been too hard to pass up, but she had forgotten the main reason she remained alone—Sydney. And the wanker would be back.

He always got what he wanted, and right now, his focus was on her. Sydney didn't know the meaning of giving up. No matter how long it took, he would come for her again and again. Even with her blood magic, the house would only be able to withstand so much. It was a solid structure that had stood guard over plenty of Stewarts before her. She put the manor at risk by being here, and that was wrong.

Bronwyn rubbed her hand across the wall. "I'll keep you safe," she told the house. "Somehow, some way, I'll make sure you aren't harmed."

That left her one option: She had to kill Sydney.

It was the only way he'd leave her alone for good.

But if she did, she'd become the thing everyone on Skye already assumed she was. Evil. On top of that, the Ancients would immediately strip her of her magic. But at least Beth and the house would be safe.

That was worth the cost of her soul.

CHAPTER TWENTY-THREE

The vibration of his mobile on the table pulled Elias from sleep. He was instantly awake as he sat up. Only the Knights had his number, and if they were contacting him in the middle of the night, that meant an emergency.

The screen lit up as he lifted the phone. There, he saw the message from Finn's contact:

You've got company!

Elias yanked on jeans and a sweatshirt before stuffing his feet in boots. He quietly exited the library and made his way to the dark, unused dining room. There, he sidled up to a window and, careful not to move the curtains, peered through the slit. He looked at the sky, thinking the mist had returned, but movement on the ground caught his attention. He let out a curse when he spotted Sydney.

Elias spun around and hurried to the parlor. The door swung open silently. His gaze immediately went to the sofa bed, where he found Bronwyn sleeping soundly beneath a pile of blankets.

He strode over, stopping when he stood at her side. Elias gently put one hand over Bronwyn's mouth.

Her eyes flew open. He put a finger to his lips to urge her silence. Then he motioned for her to rise. Elias went to the doorway as she threw off the covers and found her boots, tugging on a sweater over the tank she wore with her pajama bottoms. He stood half in the parlor and half in the corridor, listening to see if anyone approached the front door.

A hand on his arm pulled his attention away. He met Bronwyn's gaze before he motioned for her to follow him. He took her to the window where he had seen Sydney. It was all he could do not to yank the curtains open and get a better view of the property to see what Sydney and his friends were about.

Several tense minutes passed before Bronwyn stepped away from the window. Her head turned to him. "Do you know what they're doing here?" she whispered.

Elias shook his head. "I think we should wait it out and see what they plan. They've no' come to the door yet."

Since Bronwyn had all but locked herself in the manor, he thought she would agree with him. When she said nothing, an uneasy feeling filled him. He caught a look of determination in her gaze that made his blood run cold.

He took hold of her arm when she moved to turn away. "What are you planning?" he demanded.

"He will keep returning until I take action."

"We doona have a plan. We need a strategy before we face him."

Bronwyn carefully pulled her arm from his hand. "There is no *we*, Elias. I made that clear. It was the stipulation of you staying. This fight is mine."

"So, what?" he said, then winced when he heard his voice raising. He lowered back to a whisper and continued. "You're going to leave the safety of the house and face Sydney and his three friends? Alone?"

"I was always going to face him on my own."

That couldn't happen. The cold hand of panic wrapped around Elias and squeezed so tightly he couldn't breathe. "That's suicide."

"I'm strong enough to take him."

Elias ran a hand through his hair. "Need I remind you that your magic is locked up in this house and with Beth? I see you touch the banister each time you pass it. It's done casually, but I know that's magic moving from you into the house."

"So?" she asked, lifting her chin.

It was a move he was coming to recognize as pure brashness, something Bronwyn fell back on when she didn't see another way. He drew in a breath and admonished himself to remain composed. If he allowed his anger and frustration to show, Bronwyn would likely shut down—and shut him out even more than she already had.

"You're really going to wager your life, Beth's life, and the manor on a single battle with someone who has proven to use underhanded tactics?"

"I'm not above using those same devices myself."

Elias shook his head. "How many battles have you been involved in?"

"That doesn't matter."

"It does," he insisted, then had to lower his voice again.

Bronwyn dropped her gaze for a heartbeat before looking at him. "I know what I have to do. I've always known, but I didn't want to admit it. Putting it off is only delaying the inevitable."

"You're going to kill him." Elias didn't know why he hadn't realized that sooner. Maybe it was because he was trying to put death and murder as far from his thoughts as possible that he hadn't reached the same conclusion. If she turned to that side of her *drough* magic, the darkness would take her. He could very well lose her forever.

"It's the only way."

Her simple statement was like a punch to the gut. "The Knights are out there," he said, moving to prevent her from leaving. "They're the ones who alerted me that we had visitors. Let us help you. We would outnumber them."

Bronwyn put a hand on his chest, the heat of her burning through his sweatshirt and skin, straight to his heart. It was only the second time she had willingly touched him. He hadn't realized how much he had wanted it, *needed* it, until that moment.

"You're a good man, Elias. But you can't save everyone."

"I can damn well try."

She flashed a sad smile. "You've been there for me three times in my life. We both knew how all of this would end. I chose this. And I'm going to face what's coming. I had a chance to end Sydney's life in Inverness, and I couldn't do it."

"Because you are no' a killer."

"It's the only resolution to this situation. I have the means to do it now."

His heart skipped a beat at the implications. "The darkness will—"

"Take me," she said before he could. "I know."

"Call Rhona. Please," he begged.

Bronwyn dropped her hand. "I've already told you, this is my mess. I'm going to clean it up. No one else will be hurt because of me."

"Contact her, or I will." The threat was out of Elias's mouth before he could think twice.

All the warmth left Bronwyn's gaze. "Don't make me regret granting you sanctuary. You contact her, and you'll be turning yourself in."

"Then so be it. I'd rather that than watch you be taken by the darkness."

Her nostrils flared as fury rolled off her. She took a half-step toward him. "You think so little of my abilities, then? I've kept the darkness at bay."

"Killing someone invites it in. You're a *drough*, which means you've already invited it. You'd be allowing it to take you."

Need I remind you that I'm a *drough* who has turned to blood magic."

"As if I could forget," he retorted, letting his anger show. His phone vibrated. Elias yanked it out and read the text. "They're gone."

"For now. Sydney will return. You're only here because I allowed it. You know what's going on because I've shared it. Don't mistake that to mean you have a right to interfere."

He watched her walk around him, and Elias turned with her. "Right, because God forbid you actually *feel* something for someone."

That halted her in her tracks. She whirled around to face him and stalked back to where he stood. "You know a small fraction of my life. You don't know *me*."

"Oh, I know you better than you think."

They were nose to nose now, tension sparking in the room. And God help him, but all he wanted to do was press his lips to hers. Taste her, take her.

Claim her.

His gaze dropped to her mouth, and his anger switched to white-hot passion in a heartbeat. He looked into her eyes and saw her desire reflected at him. But they'd been here before, dancing close to the flames but never plunging into them.

Suddenly, her lips were on his. Elias wound his arms around her and pulled her flush against his body. He groaned at her sweet taste, her soft curves. He forgot Sydney, the Knights, the threat, and their fight. All that mattered was her—and the raw, unadulterated need that surrounded them.

He'd never felt this heat, this longing before. No one had ever moved him as Bronwyn did. He was in too deep, in way over his head. Because he knew that what he felt, what had driven him to her, was something special.

Her hands tangled in his hair as the kiss deepened, intensified. All the hunger, all the longing he'd tried to ignore rose to the surface. He rocked his aching cock against her, and his desire doubled when she moaned in response. He didn't just want Bronwyn, he craved her, yearned for her. He needed to be inside her, to have their bodies joined in a dance as old as time.

He slid his hands over her round bottom and lower to her thighs. Then he straightened, lifting her as he did. She wrapped her legs around his waist. He carried her the short distance to the dining table and lowered her. She arched her back, pulling him close. He followed her, consumed by the fire surging through him.

His kiss was everything. Bronwyn was lost the instant her lips met Elias's. The blaze of passion, the unmistakable heat between them was all-consuming. Pleasure skidded along her skin, sparking each nerve ending until her entire body hummed with a need only he could quench.

She moaned when he ground his arousal against her center, teasing her with what was to come. Being touched, being *seen* had brought her back into the land of the living. Whenever she tried to retreat, Elias was there, coaxing her back out.

Her head fell to the side as his lips trailed down her neck. He tugged at the neckline of her sweater to expose more skin. Yes! That was what she needed. His skin against hers. She slid her hands beneath his sweatshirt and flattened her palms against his abdomen. His stomach quivered at her touch, his muscles contracting.

She shoved the sweatshirt upward. Elias yanked off the top before claiming her mouth once more. She could get lost in his kiss. She tasted his insatiable hunger, felt his ravenous desire. Drank in his yearning. She couldn't get enough of him. In his hands, she felt alive for the first time in her life.

Their tongues tangled while her hands explored his incredible body. Thick, broad shoulders. Muscular chest. Defined abs. She reached the waistband of his jeans and unbuttoned them. He sucked in a breath and stilled. She slid the zipper down slowly and reached inside his pants to cup him.

His groan, filled with pleasure and longing, brought a smile to her lips. Then his heat was gone as he yanked down his pants and underwear. She used the time to sit up and pull off her jumper and the tank beneath. She had been in a hurry, so she hadn't put on a bra.

"Fuck. You're the most beautiful thing I've ever seen," he murmured as he pulled her against him.

She gazed into his mesmerizing eyes and flattened her hands on his chest. Her eyes closed when he slid a hand between them and cupped her breast. The breath left her in a whoosh as he thumbed her nipple. The pleasure went straight to her center that throbbed with need as wetness flooded her.

"I need you inside me," she begged.

His lips skimmed her ear, his warm breath fanning her neck. He lowered her to her back and met her gaze. He didn't let her look away as he found the waist of her flannel pajama pants and tugged them down. She lifted her hips so he could remove the bottoms. Then he reached for her soaked panties.

She drank in the sight of him standing in the sliver of moonlight. His body was toned in a way that spoke of a lifetime of training. Her eyes lowered to his arousal. It jutted out between them, long and thick, begging for her attention.

Elias felt Bronwyn's eyes on his cock. It jumped in response, eager to slide inside her, but it would have to wait. He had other plans first.

He rested his hands on her bare legs and gently spread them. She grinned, desire in her eyes. His breath caught when he saw her spread on the table in the soft moonlight like a decadent enticement. With a hand on her thighs, he bent and placed a kiss on her stomach.

Her breath hitched, causing him to smile inwardly. Elias ran his hands upward to the flare of her hips and then the indent of her waist before finding her full breasts. She arched her back when he massaged the globes. He spent some time teasing her nipples. All the while, his tongue trailed along her stomach. He retraced a path to her thighs with his hands. Kneeling on the floor, he caressed close to her sex.

"Elias," she whispered in a breathy voice.

He smoothed his fingers over her trimmed curls, coming ever closer to her center. She shifted her hips, trying to reach him. He dodged her and kissed the inside of one thigh before moving to the other. He repeated the gesture, placing his lips closer to her center each time.

By the time his mouth hovered over her sex, her chest heaved with loud, ragged breaths.

CHAPTER TWENTY-FOUR

Elias would be the death of her.

But oh, what a beautiful death it would be.

Bronwyn's body vibrated with anticipation, with a longing so deep and penetrating it was like an awakening. As if her arousal had stirred her from a long, restless slumber, and Elias had removed the blinders from her eyes.

The instant his lips touched her center, her body went rigid, and her breath locked in her lungs. He ran his tongue along her sex, licking every part of her before swirling around her swollen, throbbing clit.

It had been so long since anyone had touched her that she came apart immediately. The intensity of the orgasm was such that it robbed her of voice and thought. It was the sensation of electrical currents shooting through her one after the last, coming so fast they were on top of each other. She drifted along tides of bliss that surged through her over and over again.

A lifetime must have passed when she sucked in a breath and

forced open her eyes, her lethargic body still rocked by pulses of aftershocks. Her gaze landed on Elias, who finished sliding a condom onto his engorged rod. Her sex throbbed at the thought of him inside her. She reached for him as he leaned one hand on the table near her head.

He looked at her, his eyes flashing with hunger. "You have no idea how sexy that was to watch."

She lifted her head in time to see him as he brought his cock to her entrance. He gently rubbed the head against her sensitive flesh, causing her to gasp at the feel of him. Then, he slowly pushed inside her.

Her head dropped back, and she dug her fingers into his arms as he pulled out and thrust deeper. Inch by inch, her body stretched to accept him. With one final push, he filled her completely.

She felt his muscles trembling beneath her hands. Bronwyn held his gaze as she undulated her hips. A muscle tensed in his neck.

"Doona," he bit out in a voice roughened with longing. "You'll finish me too soon."

Unable to help it, she grinned. She'd never had such sway over a man before. It felt wonderful knowing he held on by a thread just as she had moments before. She was glad she had given in to the temptation and kissed him.

The muscles beneath her palms bunched and moved as he began pumping his hips in long, slow strokes. She lost herself in the rhythm. She'd known he would feel amazing, and she had been right. Bronwyn wrapped her legs around his waist again, shifting herself, which allowed him to go deeper.

He increased his cadence little by little until their bodies slapped together, and a fine sheen of sweat covered their skin. He never stopped, didn't slow. It wasn't long before desire began to tighten low in her belly again—the familiar build of pressure that she eagerly reached for.

Paradise. Nirvana.

Complete and utter rapture.

That was what it was like being with Bronwyn. He'd never known anything so evocative, so incredible could transpire between two people. But, somehow, he'd found it with the most astonishing woman. He never wanted the night to end.

The more he gave, the more she returned. Pleasure flowed easily between them, arousing them and bringing them to new heights. His body had never known this kind of hedonism, never experienced such carnal ecstasy. He'd found his match in every way with Bronwyn.

He felt her legs tighten around him, saw her eyes drift shut, and heard her breathing become erratic. She was close to climaxing again. He leaned on one hand and splayed the other on her stomach. Then, he found her clit with his thumb, swirling around the tiny bud until he felt her begin to tremble.

Elias couldn't take his eyes off her as he continued thrusting deeper and harder. Her back arched, her mouth opening on a silent scream as her body jerked and stiffened. He bit his tongue to keep from crying out when he felt the slick walls of her sex clenching around him, sending him spiraling into a climax.

He thrust one final time, his muscles locked as his cock

throbbed, and wavelike spasms moved through his rod as his seed spilled from him. The euphoria was so intense that it felt as if he were floating, unattached to his body or the Earth. *Le petite mort*, the little death.

Elias had had bad sex. He'd had good sex. He'd even had great sex.

He'd never had mind-blowing, life-altering sex until tonight.

It took everything he had not to collapse on Bronwyn. He found her eyes still closed, but she held on to him still as if he were the only thing that kept her rooted. He understood that all too well.

Finally, her eyes opened. A stunning shade of copper and gold that met his. Her kiss-swollen lips curved into a grin that matched the satiated look on her face—one he also wore.

"Fuck, woman. I have no words," he told her.

Her smile widened. "It was pretty incredible."

He stiffened, moaning when he felt her clench around him again. His breath came out in a hiss of pleasure before he rocked his hips. "I'm no' nearly finished with you."

"I was hoping you'd say that."

"How about somewhere more…comfortable?"

She laughed, the sound so surprising that he could only stare in wonder. "I never thought I'd say I like this dining table, but I think it did well."

He grinned and wished again that he had the power to halt time so they could stay in this moment for eternity. That way, the outside world and all the problems that came with it could never touch them.

Elias slowly pulled out of her. "I need to take care of this."

Bronwyn sat up, and he saw chills pebble her skin. "I'll meet you in the parlor."

He stepped back and grabbed his clothes as he headed to the bathroom. Once he'd disposed of the used condom, he hurried to Bronwyn's room. He welcomed the warmth that awaited him. Elias was about to suggest they check on what Sydney had been up to when his gaze landed on the bed.

All thought fled as he stared at Bronwyn's naked body under the glow of the fire. Before his very eyes, her nipples hardened. Her lips parted, and her eyes filled with longing. His balls tightened as hunger surged anew. He tossed aside his clothes and climbed onto the bed, reaching for her.

She came into his arms willingly, their limbs tangling as their lips met. To his surprise, she pushed him onto his back and straddled him. She moaned as she rocked her hips, the sound as sexy as it was hedonistic. He palmed her breasts, glorying in the weight that filled his hands. She dropped her head back, her short, brunette locks falling aside as he teased her nipples. She moaned again, the sound going straight to his cock.

Their first coupling had been quick. He wanted to take his time now and savor each moment, heightening their need until they were drunk with it. Elias sat up and wrapped his lips around one turgid peak. He flicked his tongue around it before suckling.

Bronwyn cried out and rotated her hips. He could feel how wet she was against him, and it urged him on. He moved to her other breast and spent his time teasing her. It was Bronwyn who took his head and lifted it to kiss him.

Once more, she pushed him onto his back. His eyes closed when she kissed down his neck and across his chest, briefly pausing to flick her tongue over his nipples. She continued moving down his stomach as she settled between his legs. Only then did she wrap her fingers around his cock.

Elias fisted his hands in the blanket as hers slowly moved up and down his hardened length. She placed tiny kisses along his inner thighs and on his balls, but never his staff.

It was frustrating—and erotic as hell.

His attention moved between her mouth so near him and the way her hands stroked him, particularly how she spent time running her thumb over the head of his cock. His need built at such a rapid rate that it took all his effort to remain still and not reach out to plunge inside her.

Her hands stroked him as no other ever had. She knew just where to touch, just how to caress to bring him exquisite pleasure.

Then he felt her breath on his arousal. His body shuddered, impatiently awaiting the feel of her mouth on him. He opened his eyes to discover her watching him. She shot him a sexy grin before parting her lips and taking him into her mouth.

Elias's hips came off the bed as he bit back a shout. His cock throbbed, heat rushing to the head.

Bronwyn was awed at how Elias responded to her touch. She took him deep and felt him swell in her mouth. He had given her so much pleasure earlier that she wanted to return the favor.

She used both hands, along with her mouth, as she moved up and down his length. He whispered her name in a raw voice filled with need that made her shiver.

"I'm about to come," he warned.

That was just what she wanted. She redoubled her efforts, and a heartbeat later, she swallowed the first mouthful of his seed. She only raised her head when she'd drained every drop from him.

"Lass," he murmured in a deep voice roughened with pleasure.

"That was for earlier."

Suddenly, she was on her back, and he was between her legs.

"My turn," he said.

Bronwyn was powerless to do anything the moment his mouth was on her. She basked in the feeling of his tongue circling her clit. Then he slid a finger inside her. She rocked her hips forward, her eyes drifting shut as heat engulfed her.

A second finger soon joined the first. He was relentless in his attention. Her eyes flew open when he found her G-spot and began stroking it masterfully. Her body tingled, and her blood ran like liquid fire in her veins.

All that mattered was Elias.

The pleasure was even more intense, as if their joining had only strengthened what they had. The way her body opened for him, sought him, was exhilarating and frightening. But it was the mounting need for him, and him alone, that gave her pause.

She forgot it in the next second as an earth-shattering orgasm shot through her, sweeping her away on a journey of ecstasy and decadence that she knew she would never recover from.

When Bronwyn finally came to again, she was curled against Elias's side, her head on his chest. One of his legs rested between hers.

"Welcome back," he said and kissed her forehead.

"If you keep that up, we'll never leave the bed."

He chuckled. "I'm in agreement. I can no' remember ever been so satiated."

Her eyes drifted closed as he stroked his hand up and down her back. There was something she needed to remember to do, but her brain couldn't think clearly at the moment. Sleep called to her, and she fell under quickly.

Sometime in the night, Elias's lips on her neck and the feel of his arousal against her back woke her.

"I need you again," he whispered.

With just those words, her sex throbbed, and she felt wetness between her legs. "I'm yours," she answered.

He moved her to her hands and knees and slowly entered her from behind. The moment he began to plunge into her, she felt him graze her G-spot. Her fingers dug into the mattress as she met his thrusts, their breaths coming harsher, faster.

CHAPTER TWENTY-FIVE

The warm body pressed against him caused Elias to wake with a contented smile. He opened his eyes to find Bronwyn curled around him, an arm draped across his chest. Memories of their incredible night filled his head.

The new day, however, wouldn't change the problems that plagued them. That didn't mean he would let those issues ruin things. Bronwyn was…he couldn't find the right words. She was extraordinary. Being with her had been life-changing. And if the way she'd reacted to him was any indication, she felt the same.

Elias wasn't a stranger to having women in his bed. But it was odd to have someone there that he never wanted to leave. The emotions he experienced left him dazed and euphoric. He wasn't sure he could name any of the other feelings. Though he could say without a doubt they were things he had never faced before.

He contemplated waking Bronwyn for another round of sex with the arrival of dawn, but since he'd roused her twice in the night, he decided to let her sleep. Gently, he turned her over and extracted himself from the bed. He couldn't stop grinning as he dressed to make tea.

It wasn't until he reached for his mobile that he realized it wasn't in his pocket. He searched the parlor, but the phone was nowhere to be found. Elias put on his socks and quietly slipped out of the room. His next logical stop was the dining room. Sure enough, he found it under the table. It must have fallen out when he undressed.

He paused beside the table, grinning as he recalled their wild night. Damn. Bronwyn was all fire and passion. The room would always be special to him because it was there that they had ignited.

His mobile buzzing drew his attention. He glanced down to see over twenty texts and five missed calls.

"Shite," he murmured and quickly answered the call.

"Where the fucking hell have you been?" Carlyle bellowed.

Elias grimaced and walked to the kitchen. "I was sleeping."

"You're not a light sleeper, mate. I was about to bust down the bloody door," Carlyle growled.

"Sorry. Bronwyn and I…we were…"

"Yeah, yeah. I get it." Carlyle sighed loudly. "Next time, answer your fucking mobile."

Elias winced at the annoyance in his friend's voice. "I didna know it had fallen out of my pocket."

"It isn't like you to think with your dick."

"You're right. It willna happen again. Tell me what's going on."

Carlyle blew out a breath. "First, don't let Bronwyn out back."

"Out back?" Elias frowned as he looked out the kitchen window, but he didn't see anything. "Why?"

"Your visitors decided to take their anger out on the chickens. There's not much left of the birds, I'm afraid."

Elias closed his eyes, sickened. "Fuck."

"That isn't all. They stayed on the estate for most of the night. We thought they left, but they only turned their attention from the manor."

That caught Elias's interest. He opened his eyes and set about heating the water and getting out cups. "That bothers me more than I care to admit. What were they after?"

"We couldn't determine. Sabryn is following them to see where they go on Skye. She also intends to get some pictures so Saber can get details on them. Finn and I shadowed them around the estate to determine their intentions. If I hadn't seen them attack the chickens, I'd say they were just exploring."

"They were up to something," Elias stated.

Carlyle grunted. "Agreed. Wish I could say what it was, though. What do you think Bronwyn will do?"

"She wanted to go out and meet them last night. To fight them on her own."

"She seems like a smart woman. Why would she do that?"

The electric kettle beeped. He poured water over the tea bags in the mugs. "To kill him."

"But...wouldn't the Ancients take away her magic? That's what happens to you Skye Druids, right?"

"Aye." Elias squeezed the bridge of his nose with this thumb and forefinger. "She thinks it's the only way."

The rustling of foliage came through the phone. "Please tell me you told her we were here to help."

"You know I did. She doesna want our assistance. She keeps saying that this is her problem and she needs to clean it up herself. I then threatened to notify Rhona."

Carlyle made a sound. "That would bring things down upon you, old boy."

"I know, but I can no' let her die."

"She's a *drough*, E."

"With her magic wrapped up in the manor."

Carlyle was silent for a moment. "That should still leave her plenty to protect herself."

"It doesna."

"What aren't you telling us?"

Elias took a deep breath and released it. "Trust me when I say she's risking too much by facing that group on her own."

"I don't like this. Any of it." Carlyle blew out a breath. "Bloody hell. Alert Bronwyn about her chickens. We'll be back in touch after Sabryn returns. Finn is getting a few hours of sleep before he relieves me here."

"Talk then." Elias disconnected the call.

He pocketed his mobile and began looking through the windows until he found one that gave him a clear view of the chicken coop. Blood and feathers were everywhere.

"What are you up to, Sydney?" he murmured.

Elias removed the tea bags and added honey to Bronwyn's cup before bringing both to the parlor. She still slept soundly. He eyed the visible expanse of her back as she lay on her stomach. He hated to wake her, but she would have to face what had happened sooner or later. Elias set the cups down, climbed into bed, then smoothed aside her hair and kissed the back of her neck.

Bronwyn sighed softly. She rolled onto her back and smiled sleepily with her eyes still closed. "What time is it?" she asked with a yawn.

"Just after dawn."

"Already?" she asked, a frown wrinkling her brow.

He chuckled. "I should apologize for keeping you up throughout the night, wringing orgasm after orgasm from you, but I'm no' the least bit sorry."

Her eyes opened as she grinned. "I'm not either."

"I brought you tea."

"Hm. Just what I need."

Elias turned to get the mugs. He handed Bronwyn hers after she tucked the blanket under her arms and sat up. "I already added honey."

She quirked a brow. "How do you know how much I like?"

"You like it sweet. I watched you fill the entire teaspoon that first morning."

She chuckled before taking a sip. "Very observant of you."

"I even swirled the honey as you did."

Bronwyn drew up her legs. "Mum used to do that. She'd spell names or make designs. The first time I tried it, I got honey everywhere but in my tea."

"I can imagine."

"Mum and I used to have competitions for what we could make dribbling the honey. She always said I won, but I think most parents do that."

Elias leaned against the pillows that he stacked against the back of the sofa. "I know my mum would've. It's just the type of woman she was."

"I don't think I ever told you how sorry I was about what happened to your family."

He shrugged, not wanting to discuss that now—or ever. "We're oblivious to how horrible life can be when we're children. We only see the possibilities, the fun. And the good in everyone. No one prepares you for the reality. It just happens, and most times in the ghastliest of ways."

"But to have your father murdered…" she began.

"Doona," he said more harshly than intended. Elias briefly closed his eyes and shook his head. "I'm sorry. I didna mean that."

"You did," she said gently. "It's okay, though."

Elias looked into his cup before taking a drink. "What happened to my father was…" Fuck. Could he say it? It had taken him years before he shared anything with the Knights.

"You don't have to say anything," Bronwyn told him.

He met her hazel gaze and decided to offer as much of the truth as he could give her. "Doona mourn my father. I never have."

Bronwyn searched his gaze. "I see."

"I doona like to talk about him."

"I'll never ask anything about him again," she said with a firm nod, her eyes soft with understanding.

Elias blew out a breath. If that wasn't difficult enough, he now had to tell her the rest. "However, there is something you need to know."

"What's that?" she asked and drank her tea.

"Sydney left a message."

Bronwyn's entire demeanor changed. Her walls shot back into place at the reminder of her nemesis. "What message?"

"He slaughtered the chickens."

Fury glittered in her eyes. "He took his anger out on defenseless fowl? How…petty of him."

"Sydney and his people walked the estate for most of the night. Carlyle said it didna appear as if they were looking for anything."

"Oh, he was. Never doubt that," she stated tersely.

Elias hated that their morning was now spoiled, but it had been inevitable. No amount of wishing could erase their troubles. Neither would hiding. He needed to face the police. "Sabryn is following them. She'll discover where they're staying and if they're speaking to anyone on the isle. She and the lads will be by later."

"I need to see the damage Sydney caused," Bronwyn said as she threw back the covers and stood.

Elias didn't stop her. Bronwyn was strong and independent. She didn't need saving. She needed someone to stand beside her. He wanted to be that person. Before last night, he was sure she'd never allow such a thing. Now, he thought things might be tipped in his favor a wee bit.

As long as he didn't fuck things up.

Bronwyn stood naked before the fire, unaware of his thoughts. She stared into the flames as she drank her tea. "The amount of animosity I have for Sydney scares me. I want him dead. Maybe being *drough* has begun to eat away at any good that might still be inside me."

Elias slid from the bed and set aside his cup before coming up behind her. He rested his hands on her shoulders and moved until his body was pressed to hers. "Hate is just another emotion. Everyone feels it. It doesna matter if they're *mie* or *drough*. You have every right to whatever you're feeling. He killed your father and was party to killing others."

"I can feel the loathing consuming me. It's like a swirling, black pit in my stomach, and every time I think of Sydney, it grows."

"Doona push your emotions away, but doona let them rule you either. Acknowledge them and why you feel the way you do. The feelings will pass. They always do."

She didn't respond, instead seemingly becoming lost in her thoughts. Elias wanted to ask what she was thinking, but he could guess that it involved Sydney. Elias was all too familiar with the past controlling people's decisions. He still struggled with that.

"How about I make us some breakfast while you shower?" he offered.

Bronwyn nodded absently. He glanced at the bed, lamenting the rising sun. Then he dropped his hands from her and walked from the parlor. He made his way to the kitchen and stared at the stove for a moment. When he heard the downstairs shower turn on, he shook himself and set about making their meal.

CHAPTER TWENTY-SIX

Bronwyn didn't wait until after breakfast to see what Sydney had done to her chickens. She went outside as soon as she was showered and dressed. A light rain misted over her as she stood huddled in her coat against the cold, wet air, surveying the savagery before her.

The four chickens she had raised from hatchlings had been eviscerated. It was the only word for what she observed. It took a special kind of beast to kill an animal in such a way. The smiley face painted in blood on the coop itself turned her stomach.

Yet Sydney hadn't stopped with mutilating the fowl. He'd turned his wrath on her vegetable garden, as well. Pots had been overturned, plants ripped apart, and any vegetables stomped on.

Movement drew her attention. She glanced over to see Elias walking up. He held an umbrella and covered both of them with it.

"I'm sorry," Elias said. "We can get this cleaned up quickly. We might even be able to save a plant or two."

Bronwyn felt dead inside, which was strange after coming alive in Elias's arms the night before. "This is what Sydney does. He destroys things, but his speciality is people. He gets pleasure from the pain of others."

"He can be stopped."

"And he will be." She faced Elias. "By me."

His lips pressed together as he turned to her. "There's no shame in accepting help."

"It's not shame that keeps me from accepting. It's facts and knowledge. I know Sydney. You don't. I refuse any help because I don't want anyone else affected by the viciousness that is Sydney. I brought him into my life. Me."

"But he isna alone. He has friends."

Bronwyn knew it was pointless to continue the discussion. "I've said all I'm going to say on the matter. If you cannot or will not abide by my decision, then you need to leave."

"Can you no' see that I'm trying to help?"

She saw the hurt in his eyes, but she wouldn't waver from this. She couldn't. If she could do one thing right, it would be keeping Elias and the Knights safe. "You want to save everyone, Elias. That's admirable. But the truth is, you can't. No matter how hard you try, you'll fail. The one person you should be focusing on is yourself."

"Excuse me?" His tone was soft, belying the flash of anger on his face.

"I freely admit that I'm holding on to the past. I know it isn't healthy, but I have things to atone for. More than you can possibly imagine. You can fool those who aren't from Skye, but you can't fool me."

A muscle ticked in his jaw. "You say that because I doona wish to speak of my father."

"It was the rage you couldn't hide when speaking of him. The difference between us is that I'm aware of my feelings regarding Beth, Sydney, and my parents' deaths. You're hiding yours."

"You speak freely for someone who has hidden away from the world."

She had struck a nerve. Maybe he needed that. What she knew was that he had to leave Carwood. If he remained, he and the Knights could be killed. She'd never survive if that happened. He was the closest thing she had to a friend, and they had crossed into lovers. Bronwyn wanted to say that was a mistake, but she couldn't. Because it had felt too damn good.

He was, without a doubt, the only good decision she'd made.

"You have family," she told him. "You have the Knights. Use all of them to help you. Go to Rhona. As you said, she'll help. You have a network of people who will stand beside you."

The rain began to pelt faster against the umbrella. His bright blue eyes held hers. "You could have that, too."

"You know things are different for *droughs*."

"I'll stand beside you."

She looked away. He had no idea how hard this was for her. She'd had the best night of her life, and now she had to end things before she didn't have the strength to let him go. "You can remain at the manor until you and your friends sort out a plan today."

"Today?" he asked, shock making his jaw go slack. "You want me out today?"

No. She wanted him to stay forever. "Aye," she said and walked back into the house alone.

She stopped at the table in the kitchen and looked at the cold eggs and bacon. Though she didn't want to eat, she knew she had to keep up her strength. Bronwyn ate standing up, shoveling it into her mouth as quickly as she could chew and swallow. She felt a modicum of relaxation when she heard the shower turn on. Even the house seemed sad.

If Bronwyn had learned one thing from the previous night, it was that she could've had something truly wonderful with Elias. Waking up with him had been one of the best things to ever happen to her. Her thoughts had been on Elias and the way she felt with him.

But Sydney had intruded, as he always did. She had forgotten about him while in Elias's arms. In the dark of the night, she had built hopes and dreams without meaning to, but they had been made of wishes and smoke that'd vanished with the sunrise. And it was so painful she could barely keep it contained. She wanted to double over and keen about all the anger and agony that forever seemed a part of her life.

Sydney's message was clear: Anyone with her would be killed like the chickens. It was tempting to take Elias's offer, but she kept seeing her father's death playing over and over in her head. She couldn't carry anyone else's demise. Especially not someone like Elias, who felt a driving need to put his neck out for others.

She couldn't tell him how much she cared, how much he meant to her because he'd never leave. That was just the type of man he was. So, she did the only thing she could—she was brutally, heartlessly honest. The misery and visceral torment she saw reflected in his eyes had nearly brought her to her knees. But she was trying to keep him alive. She clung to that. She'd made bad decisions time and again, especially when it involved Sydney. This was one she could proudly say was a good choice.

For Elias.

For what could've been…

Bronwyn was in the middle of cleaning the kitchen when the shower cut off. She listened to see if Elias would search her out. As she hung up the hand towel, the bathroom door creaked as it opened. She heard the soft tread of feet as he moved away. A few moments later, she picked up the sound of a door opening and closing.

It was what she wanted. She'd known it would hurt to cut him out of her life, but that didn't mean it was easy. The only thing that kept her on her current path was that people could say that she hadn't taken others down with her when they looked at her life and talked about her poor choices.

Bronwyn made herself more tea, determined to put Elias out of her mind. She wanted to finish her project today. Sydney would likely be back later tonight, and she hoped the author would approve the cover before then. That meant she had to get to work immediately.

Cup in hand, Bronwyn returned to the parlor. She made the bed, trying not to think about Elias lying next to her on it—or the pleasure they'd found in each other's arms. Then she sat in the chair and reached for her laptop. She opened it and took a sip of tea.

"Now, then," she said, rubbing her hands together. "Let's get to work."

London

Ferne didn't look away from the group of Druids. They liked to think of themselves as elders, but the name she preferred to call them wasn't so benevolent. They got their positions not by the strength of their magic or even their wisdom but by bribes and enticements—the very things that'd gotten them kicked off Skye. It seemed corruption wasn't so easily shaken.

She compared her people driven from Skye to the way England had pushed out the Puritans. And just like the Puritans had once they reached America, they governed with an iron fist and little to no mercy. It was on the tip of Ferne's tongue to say exactly that to the assembly before her. It wasn't as if remaining silent would grant her any reprieve. She knew what was coming.

And she welcomed it.

She didn't worry for Mason. Her brother could handle himself. He always had.

"Ferne Crawford." A deep, male voice rang out, belonging to the middle and eldest of the Druids. Isaac reminded her of a young Christopher Lee. He even had that same booming voice, but that was because he had been in the theatre and loved to mimic others.

The five stood in shadows with spotlights directed at their faces—it would've been a marvelous look for the stage. The first time she had stood before them thus, she had been summarily frightened and duly chastised by the end of the dressing down. But she was used to their theatrics—and she hated them for it.

"You know our rules," Isaac stated.

Same old Isaac. "Times have changed."

Behind her, she heard Mason grumble under his breath. Her brother meant well, but things were at a crossroads. She could no longer stand aside and watch things unfold.

Isaac's eyes narrowed on her, his glare intense and frightening. "You don't make the rules, girl."

"I've tried to tell all of you for months now that something is developing on Skye."

"We don't care about the isle or the Druids there," Isaac clipped out harshly.

Ferne gave him a glare of her own. "Well, you should. What's happening there won't stay there. It *will* reach us."

"I'll hear no more of that talk!" Isaac bellowed, his voice bouncing around until her ears hurt.

Ferne probably shouldn't be elated at causing Isaac to lose his temper, but she was. She'd hated them for so long, but she had done what they wanted of her. She couldn't do that anymore. Lives were at stake. "If you don't listen to me, Druids will die."

"Is that a threat?" Isaac asked, his voice low and threaded with danger.

She shook her head. "It's a fact."

"I warned you what would happen if you broke our rules again. We've been more than lenient with you because of your family. No longer will you have the protection of our faction. Henceforth, you are stripped of your standing and cast out of the London Druids—and the city. You have twenty-four hours to leave before we hunt you down and exact our vengeance."

Even though Ferne had expected the verdict, it was still difficult to take. Strong hands took her arms and turned her away. She heard Mason's voice, but the blood rushed too loudly in her ears for her to make out his words clearly.

The world blurred and people and faces vanished as she fought to put one foot in front of the other as Mason led her out of the building. Then she was in a car. The rev of the engine as the vehicle shot forward knocked her head back against the seat and cleared her vision and hearing.

"Bloody wankers. Every fucking one of them," Mason ground out.

Ferne swallowed. "I knew this would be my fate."

Mason glanced at her, his stormy gray eyes clouded with concern in the bright morning light. "I'm sorry, sis."

"Don't be." She looked forward and forced her fingers to uncurl and lay flat on her lap. "The threat I've felt has grown significantly. It will come to London. It'll sweep over the entire world unless something is done."

"And you're sure about the girl on Skye?"

"Kirsi? I am. I broke through to her, Mas, but I don't know that it was enough."

The car slowed as he came to a red light. His head swiveled to her. "Please tell me you aren't going to do what I think you are."

"I don't have a choice." She met his gaze. He'd always been there for her. A rock that never shuddered. He deserved a better sister than her, someone who caused problem after problem. "Besides, I don't have a home in London anymore."

"You've always preferred the country house. Go there for a bit."

She wanted to refuse, but the two of them were all they had left. Their parents had died in a plane crash five years before.

Mason inherited the family title and estates, as well as their mother's leadership position in the London Druids.

"Please," he urged.

Ferne had never been able to refuse her brother anything. They might have fought wildly as children, but they were extremely close now. Tragedy did that to people. "For a little while."

"That's all I ask," he said as he pressed the accelerator and continued driving.

As he talked about hiring movers for her things, she was already planning on reaching across the distance to Kirsi.

Pounding on the door interrupted Bronwyn's work. She irritably glanced at the clock on the laptop, thinking it had only been a few moments, to see it had actually been three hours. She moved the computer aside and got to her feet.

Elias stood in the hallway when she approached. He didn't look her way, and that hurt, but it didn't change her mind about things. She opened the door to Sabryn, Carlyle, and Finn.

"We bring news," Sabryn said.

Bronwyn stepped aside. "Come in."

The three filed into the manor. Before she could say anything, Elias motioned for them to follow him into the library. Bronwyn watched them. She thought about joining but decided it would be better if she didn't, even if they were talking about Sydney.

"You're not coming?"

She turned at the distinguished voice and found Carlyle standing in the open doorway to the library. Bronwyn looked past him to see Elias observing the exchange. "I assumed the four of you wished to talk."

"We do," Carlyle replied. "But this involves you since what we have to say is about Sydney and his associates. Come," Carlyle beckoned.

Bronwyn thought about the cover she was near to completing. If she was going to face Sydney alone, it would behoove her to have all the information she could. She nodded and walked past Carlyle into the warmth of the library.

The room had been one of her favorites as a child. The array of books that lay within reach, each offering a different adventure, the large, stained-glass windows, and the comfort of one of the oversize chairs had been her best friends. She wasn't sure when the room had lost its luster. Or perhaps she was the one who had changed. Either way, she missed the security the room had given her.

Bronwyn sank into one of the chairs she had once curled up in to read and folded her hands in her lap. Sabryn and Finn claimed the sofa while Carlyle stood sentry at the hearth, and Elias leaned against a wall far from her.

"First, we want to say how sorry we are about the chickens," Sabryn said.

Bronwyn inclined her head. "Truth be told, I should've expected it out of Sydney."

"Do you need help cleaning things up?" Finn asked.

Before Bronwyn could answer, Elias said, "I've already done it."

Her gaze jerked to him. She hadn't realized he had gone

outside. Then again, she had buried herself in work so she didn't have to think about the horrid scene. "Thank you," she told him.

Elias shrugged as if it meant nothing when, in fact, it did.

Three pairs of eyes watched them closely. Bronwyn got the feeling the trio had deciphered the tension between them without needing to be told specifics. She met Sabryn's gaze and waited.

"Do you know what Sydney was looking for on the estate?" Sabryn asked her.

Bronwyn shook her head. "The estate is comprised of about twenty-six acres of land. There is an old hunting cabin, but there isn't anything left other than the chimney and one stone wall."

"What about entrances to the estate?" Carlyle asked.

Bronwyn thought about that, digging through memories. "My great-grandparents once ran sheep. There are most likely gates along some fences to herd the animals from one field to another."

Finn rested his arm along the back of the couch. "I've been thinking about that. Sydney and his acquaintances never split up while Carlyle and I trailed them. They didn't appear to look for anything, but he seemed to know exactly where they were headed."

"And where was that?" Elias asked.

Sabryn turned her head to him. "Where you left your car."

"We'd moved it already, though," Carlyle added.

Bronwyn didn't like any of this. "That means Sydney knows who Elias is."

"That was our thought, as well," Sabryn replied. "And I think I know who told him."

Elias pushed away from the wall. His hands were in his

pockets, and he stood as still as a statue, his irritation palpable. "Who?"

"George," Finn replied.

Bronwyn was so taken aback that her mouth fell open.

Sabryn nodded as she looked between Elias and Bronwyn. "I followed the group to a café, where they split up. The woman and one of the men headed to the police station, while Sydney and the third man visited none other than Georgina Miller."

"Bloody hell," Elias murmured.

Sabryn licked her lips. "It gets worse. Saber got into the CCTV at the police station again."

"And?" Elias urged when she paused.

Sabryn sighed loudly. "All recording devices were shut off prior to the duo issuing statements."

"Fuck me." Elias angrily raked a hand through his hair.

Finn nodded. "That's exactly what I said."

Carlyle scratched his jaw. "We might not know what was said to the authorities or Georgina, but we didn't come here empty-handed. Saber was able to identify Sydney's friends from the pictures Sabryn got."

"Lucy Smith, Thomas Carter, and Jacob MacAfee," Sabryn said as she turned to Bronwyn. "Do you know any of them?"

Bronwyn shook her head. "Sorry, I don't. It's been years since I left Sydney."

"We know their names and faces now," Finn said. "So, how are we going to fight these arses?"

Elias met Bronwyn's gaze. "We're no'."

Once more, every eye was on her. Bronwyn looked at each of them. "He's right. I've made my stance clear. This is my problem. I caused this, and I'm going to clean it up myself."

"Well, that's all fine and dandy," Finn stated as he sat forward, "but you've forgotten one thing."

She frowned. "What's that?"

Carlyle crossed his arms over his chest. "They involved us the moment they targeted Elias. We can work together, or we'll go after Sydney without you."

CHAPTER TWENTY-SEVEN

Elias couldn't take his eyes off Bronwyn. She sat still as stone, the passion he'd witnessed and felt last night tightly leashed. But he knew the real her. The unconventional, independent beauty who bewitched completely. She hid her emotions well but not so thoroughly that he couldn't tell she was chafing at the facts set before her.

"You're not leaving me much choice," Bronwyn replied icily.

Carlyle nodded once. "We're like that sometimes. Shall we begin planning?"

Sabryn held up a hand to Carlyle and looked at Bronwyn. "I understand how you feel. Sydney came with numbers to intimidate you."

"It's his way. He's never alone. Ever. He doesn't like doing the dirty work himself," Bronwyn added.

Sabryn's lips twisted. "That's good information to know. My point is, he's down one man. You're up four. That puts us at an advantage. He knows Elias is helping you, but he doesn't know about the rest of us."

"I can't wait to see the surprise on his face," Finn said as he rubbed his hands together eagerly.

Carlyle caught Bronwyn's gaze. "You have to admit this is good for you."

Elias saw the varied emotions cross Bronwyn's face from anger to agitation to unease. He knew the reasons she wanted to battle Sydney alone, and while Elias might commend her for such ideas, it would cost her in the end—be it her life or her magic.

Bronwyn lowered her gaze to the floor, choosing not to reply to Carlyle. Elias felt the scrutiny of his friends. He looked at them and shrugged. He had nothing to add. He'd said everything he had to say last night and this morning to absolutely no effect.

Sabryn cleared her throat as she locked her eyes on Bronwyn. "If we're going to succeed, then we need to know everything."

Bronwyn's gaze slowly lifted to meet Sabryn's before she cocked a dark brow. "And by *everything*, you mean?"

"We need to know the full extent of your *drough* magic as well as how you're using blood magic."

"That doesn't concern you."

Elias stepped forward, the need to defend Bronwyn rising swiftly, sharply. "I know the use of her blood magic, and it doesna concern us."

"I disagree," Carlyle replied.

Elias shrugged, fighting irritation. He had to remind himself that these were his friends, his family. They only wanted to help. But when it came to Bronwyn, rational thought went out the door. "I doona care. If it would put any of you in danger, I'd tell you, but it doesna."

"But you know how she uses it?" Finn asked.

Elias nodded once. He felt Bronwyn's eyes on him, but he didn't look at her. Her earlier words had cut him to the quick, and he wasn't over that yet.

"Well," Sabryn said as she shot him a confused look, "we trust you, E. If you say we don't need to worry about any repercussions stemming from Bronwyn's use of blood magic, then we'll accept that."

"Will we?" Carlyle asked curtly as he faced Elias.

Finn got to his feet. "Our brother is asking us to take his word. I don't have a problem with that. Neither do you. Do you, *Carlyle?*"

It was a tense moment before Carlyle finally turned away, grumbling, "No problem at all."

Elias breathed a sigh of relief that Carlyle backed down. His friend might not be pleased, but he'd never hold a grudge. That allowed Elias's thoughts to turn to Bronwyn. He'd wanted to help her from the beginning, but he hadn't wanted her to be pushed into agreeing. He should be pleased with the outcome, but he wasn't.

"So, regarding the planning," Finn said as he resumed his seat. "I suspect Sydney and his crew will surround the manor."

Elias thought about that. "If they do, they'll leave large spaces open between them."

"If Sydney doesn't bring in more people," Bronwyn replied.

Sabryn's brows snapped together. "Shit. We need to prepare for that."

"I don't know. He seemed too confident last night," Carlyle added. "He believes he's only going up against two people."

Bronwyn shot to her feet suddenly, her eyes focused on one of the stained-glass windows. "Unless he has taken action to ensure I'm alone."

That's when Elias heard the crunch of gravel of an approaching vehicle. He looked at his friends. "Where's your car?"

"Hidden half a mile to the north," Sabryn said.

Finn put a hand on the arm of the sofa and launched himself over the side. "We were careful in case of just such an event."

But Carlyle had already beaten Finn to the entrance. A heartbeat later, he said, "It's the police."

Elias shared a look with Finn and Sabryn. In unison, they said, "George."

Carlyle strode back in. "Where are the secret tunnels in the manor?"

"There aren't any," Bronwyn answered.

"There has to be," Carlyle stated firmly.

Elias slid his gaze to Bronwyn because he knew what she was thinking. "Nay."

"It's the only way," she told him.

Carlyle looked between them. "Every bloody house like this has hiding compartments. Where are they?"

"Follow me," Bronwyn said as she hurried from the room.

Elias brought up the rear as everyone raced up the stairs. They had just reached the second floor when someone pounded on the door. He paused and looked below. "We're no' going to have time."

"They can't get in unless I give permission," Bronwyn said, out of breath as she ran.

She skidded to a halt in front of the second to the last door on the right and yanked it open. Bronwyn didn't look at anyone as she put her hand out and said, "*Nochd*, reveal."

Elias glanced at his friends, watching their varying expressions as the air began to twist and turn and the hole opened between the dimensions.

"Get in," Bronwyn demanded before the gap had expanded all the way.

Elias didn't hesitate to jump through. Sabryn was next, then Finn. Carlyle met Bronwyn's gaze for a heartbeat before joining the rest of them. Bronwyn's eyes then slid to Elias. He wanted to reassure her, but he didn't get the chance as she closed the hole.

"Okay. What the fek?" Finn demanded.

Elias turned to his friends, who stood looking at the prone, sleeping form of Beth. "That's Bronwyn's cousin, Beth. She's who Sydney is searching for."

"I assume Bronwyn is going to release us?" Carlyle asked.

Elias blew out a breath. "Of course."

"You say that, but I'm not sure I believe it."

"Enough," Sabryn hissed angrily and walked a few steps away.

She turned her head as if listening. As Elias grew quiet, he picked up the sounds of footsteps descending the stairs, mingled with loud, persistent pounding on the door. Suddenly, the banging stopped.

"What can I do for you, DI Frasier?" he heard Bronwyn ask.

Within moments, Finn and Carlyle had moved next to him and Sabryn.

"We've been knocking for some time," Frasier replied.

Bronwyn's voice was calm as she said, "It's a rather large house. I was upstairs."

"Are you alone?" Frasier demanded.

Elias grinned when Bronwyn answered, "Nay. I'm here with you and the twelve police officers behind you."

"You know what I mean," Frasier snapped. There was a pause before he continued. "I have a warrant to search your house."

Sabryn turned her head to Elias. "It'll look odd if she doesn't allow them inside."

"She will," he told his friend in a soft voice.

Sure enough, they heard Bronwyn say, "Help yourself, but I'd appreciate it if you didn't leave a mess."

Just in case those in the house could hear them, the Knights remained quiet and still as they listened to the stomping of feet as police fanned throughout the house. Doors were thrown open one by one. Elias whirled around when the door to their room swung inward. They couldn't see anyone, only shadows, but they could hear everything clearly.

The sounds were magnified between dimensions. Thankfully, the person searching left the room quickly. It was a long time before the noise of the police died down, leaving only Bronwyn with Frasier.

"I take it you didn't find what you were looking for," Bronwyn said.

Frasier's voice sounded weary and on edge. "Where is he?"

"Who?"

"Elias MacLean."

"I have no idea."

Frasier sighed loudly. "Look, Bronwyn, do yourself a favor and tell me where he is."

"I just told you, I don't know. You've searched the entire manor. If he was here, you would've found him."

"I can get a warrant for the grounds."

"I have nothing to hide. I don't know who told you that Mr. MacLean was here, but they sent you on a wild goose chase."

Frasier went silent for a moment. "I hope, for your sake, that you've no' gotten mixed up with him."

"I assure you, I can handle my affairs. If you're finished, it's time you left," Bronwyn replied.

It wasn't long after that Elias heard the front door close.

Carlyle then turned to Elias. "Exactly where are we?"

"Between dimensions."

Finn's face was pale as he spun toward him. "You're joking."

Elias shook his head.

"This is what Bronwyn uses the blood magic for?" Sabryn said.

Elias twisted his lips ruefully. "Actually, this was always her magic. Becoming *drough* allowed it to strengthen."

"We've seen *drough* use the surge of power for many things," Finn said. "Never something like this."

Carlyle nodded slowly as he faced Beth. "I think I understand why Bronwyn didn't want to tell us."

Their discussion was interrupted by air that began to swirl. Elias moved to the doorway. As soon as the gap widened, his gaze landed on Bronwyn.

CHAPTER TWENTY-EIGHT

Elodie was pissed. Every time she attempted to talk to George, the woman managed to find a way to get out of it. It was becoming ridiculous. As well as obvious that George had no intention of speaking with her.

Worse was her sister. Edie seemed distracted and easily angered of late.

"Are you okay?" Elodie asked from across the breakfast table at her sister's.

Edie forcibly set down her gin and tonic. "That's the third time you've asked me that in the last ten minutes."

Edie might have requested the lunch date last week, but from the moment she'd arrived, Elodie got the feeling that her sister didn't want her here. Something was going on with Edie, but Elodie couldn't pry it out of her. The chasm between them seemed to be widening instead of narrowing, and Elodie was at a loss for what to do.

"I keep asking because it's obvious something *is* wrong," Elodie replied.

Edie sighed dramatically. "Just because I'm not in a good mood doesn't mean anything is wrong. People have bad days."

"You haven't been yourself these past few days."

"How would you know who I am? You only just reentered my life. You didn't care for the fifteen years before this."

Ouch. That was brutal, but it was also true. Elodie tried a different approach. "I realize we haven't been a close family, but things have changed."

"Aye, apparently, they have," Edie mumbled under her breath before reaching for her drink.

Now it was Elodie's turn to stare angrily. "If you have something to say, say it, Edie."

"Fine, I will." Her sister sat up in her chair and parted her lips, but she didn't speak.

Elodie leaned her forearms on the table, concern replacing her ire. "I can't take back the past and my actions, but I want to move forward to a different place. You're my sister. You can tell me anything."

"Can I?"

"Of course."

"Do you share everything with me?"

Elodie reached across the short distance and covered her sister's hand. "Other than the specifics of my sex life, aye," she said with a grin.

Instead of reassuring Edie, it only seemed to anger her.

"Don't," Edie stated and leaned back, pulling her hand from Elodie's. "I'm the one who has held this family together. I'm the one who went to visit Mum. I'm the one who kept in contact with you and Elias. Neither of you did any of that."

So *this* was what was wrong. Elodie licked her lips and nodded in agreement. "I know. You've always been good at things like that. My life was a mess, Edie. You know that."

Edie's blue eyes were hard and cold as she stared. "And now it isn't?"

"It's better."

"Why?"

Elodie hesitated. She couldn't tell Edie the truth because her sister wouldn't understand what had transpired between her, Elias, and their parents. It was better if Edie never knew the horrors of that day. If Elodie could save her sister from that, then she considered it a win. "Scott," she finally answered. "Having you and Elias in my life again."

"Even with Elias wanted for murder?"

Elodie was fast losing patience. How she wished Elias was here to help her handle whatever was going on with Edie. "I don't believe our brother killed anyone. I know you don't either."

"Do you?" Edie asked and looked away. "I don't know him anymore. I don't think I ever did."

Elodie struggled for a response as Edie rose and poured herself another gin and tonic. Elodie had no idea if this was normal for her sister, and that was on Elodie because she didn't spend as much time with Edie as she probably should.

"How are my niece and nephew?" Elodie asked, changing the subject.

A smile played on Edie's lips as she leaned a hand on the kitchen island. "Busy with school and friends. They're always going. It's a good thing I'm able to drive them everywhere. Their schedules are very busy."

"If you ever need help, let me know."

Edie's gaze was soft and kind when she looked at Elodie. "Thank you. I'll do that."

"And Trevor? How is he?"

Edie's lips pinched for an instant. "Working."

Uh-oh. That didn't sound good. "Why don't the two of you plan a date night soon? Scott and I will watch the kids. Better yet, take a weekend. That way, I can have the kiddos all to myself for a wee bit," she offered.

Edie nodded, her interest seemingly piqued. "That sounds like a good plan. Let me talk to Trevor. He's been working entirely too much lately. I think that's why we got into an argument this morning."

Ah. So that was the problem. The few times Elodie had been around her brother-in-law, he couldn't keep his hands off Edie. The love they shared was apparent to anyone who looked.

"It's easy to get caught up in work," Elodie said. "A weekend away, where the two of you can reconnect sounds like exactly what you need."

Edie returned to the table and sank heavily in the chair. "Maybe. I'm just so angry all the time lately. I bit his head off this morning because he had to cancel our lunch yesterday and tomorrow. To top it off, there was a last-minute meeting he had to take in Oban today that goes into tomorrow, which means he's away tonight."

"Come have dinner with Scott and me."

Edie shook her head. "Thanks, but no. I've already planned to get pizza. I need to sort myself out before Trevor comes home.

Even the kids pointed out how I'm always snapping at them lately. Things just seem…off…and I don't know why."

"So much has changed," Elodie said. "I returned to Skye and fell in love with Scott, Druids were murdered, and Elias came home. That's a lot, sis. For anyone. Even you, Wonder Woman."

That caused Edie to chuckle. "I'm far from Wonder Woman."

"You say you don't work, but you handle eight different rental houses and all the issues that go with them while taking care of two kids, your home, and your husband. Aye. You're definitely Wonder Woman in my book."

Edie laughed, a slight blush filling her cheeks. "Stop."

With the mood lightened, Edie turned the conversation to the kids for a bit. It was only after they ate their grilled chicken salads that Elodie decided to bring up George.

"You're doing that thing," Edie said.

Elodie swallowed as she frowned. "What thing?"

"That thing with your eyes where you try to watch me covertly while determining when it's the right time to ask me something. You've done it since we were kids."

"Thanks for telling me." Elodie wiped her mouth with her napkin. "I've been trying to talk to George for days about Elias, but she won't talk to me."

Edie shrugged as she lowered her fork. "I don't think I'd want to talk to the family of the man I was accusing of murder."

"I want to know why she thinks Elias did it. Don't you?"

"If she had proof, the police would've already arrested him."

Elodie rolled her eyes. "George should've gone to the Edinburgh police, but she didn't. Why? That concerns me. Why come to Skye and make those claims?"

"The one thing I know about Elias is that he's resourceful. He always has been. If he's innocent—"

"*If?*" Elodie repeated, shocked that her sister would even suggest that.

"—he'll prove it."

But Elodie couldn't let it go. "You got the same email I did from Elias. He's innocent."

"They why run?"

"Because he's being framed!" Elodie hadn't meant to yell, but she didn't think she needed to spell this out to her sister, of all people.

Edie dabbed at the corners of her mouth. "We don't know the facts of the case. We don't know the evidence."

"We know our brother."

"Do you, though? Do you *know* Elias? Do you know who his friends are? What about his favorite food? What about the name of the company he works for? Because I don't know any of that."

Elodie blew out a breath. "He's our brother."

"That doesn't make him innocent."

"I may not know the answers to your questions, but I know Elias has a good heart. He was here for me when I needed him."

Edie's gaze intensified. "Oh? And what did you need him for?"

Damn. She'd nearly said too much. Thankfully, Elodie had something to fall back on. "I told you the mist came for me and Scott. It nearly killed us both."

"Aye, and how Elias happened to arrive at the right time to help."

"That's right."

Edie tossed down her napkin and got to her feet. "I've been battling a headache. I need to lie down before I get the kids."

"Let me help you clean up then," Elodie offered.

"Thanks, but I'll be fine."

Elodie had never been ushered out of her sister's house before. As she drove back to the cottage, she thought over the conversation. Something had upset Edie, and Elodie was beginning to think it was Elias. Or was it her, and Edie couldn't say, so she blamed it on their brother?

As Elodie drove past the police station, she spotted Theo Frasier climbing out of his vehicle. She pulled into the lot and rolled down her window as she stopped the car near him.

"Hey, Theo."

He looked drained as he stuffed his hands into his coat to brace against the wind. "What can I do for you?"

"I wondered if I could come inside and have you show me the evidence you have against my brother."

He looked away, shaking his head. "I can no' share anything in an ongoing investigation."

"Elias isn't a killer," she insisted.

Theo briefly closed his eyes. "Right now, I just want to talk to him. Let him know that, please."

"He said it wasn't him."

Theo's dark eyes jerked to her, narrowing slightly. "When did he say that?"

"In an email."

"When were you going to tell me about that?"

She clenched the steering wheel anxiously. "I just did."

"Bloody hell, Elodie," he said, half-turning away. He swung his head to her. "I need to see it. Immediately."

She pulled out her mobile and opened her inbox. Then she handed the device to Theo. "There it is."

He read the short email twice and then sent it to himself. He handed the mobile back as a smattering of rain pelted him. "We will find him. I'd hate to charge you with obstructing an investigation."

"I gave you the email," she reminded him.

His lips flattened. "So you did. Doona wait next time you hear from him."

"You have to think it odd that George came here accusing Elias."

Theo ran a hand over his mouth wearily. "I think a lot is odd right now. Please convince your brother to talk to me."

"He's not talking because he doesn't think anyone will listen to him. At least that's my thought."

"Get him to come in, Elodie. Please."

Theo turned and walked away. She watched him for a moment before she rolled up the window. As her wipers cleared the windscreen, she saw a man and a woman sitting in a car, watching her. Something about them made a chill run down her spine.

Elodie hadn't been to Hell and back to lose her family now. She'd do whatever she had to in order to prove her brother's innocence.

CHAPTER TWENTY-NINE

So much had changed. Bronwyn wasn't sure how she felt about it. She couldn't say she had gotten used to being alone because did one ever really get used to that? But she had accepted it.

Then, before she knew it, Elias was in her life, and she was spilling all her secrets. She still couldn't understand why she had done that. Perhaps, subconsciously, she had known there was something between them, something that went deeper than just physical attraction. Or she could just be bullshitting herself about that reasoning. She really couldn't tell anymore.

Because she had put Elias and the other Knights in the space between dimensions without hesitation. Maybe she had lost her mind. That sounded plausible. If she had gone daft, how would she know? She had been alone. Now, with others around, it was finally coming to light. It was the only explanation.

"Bloody hell," Finn said, his eyes wide with awe as he walked back into their dimension. "That was…"

Carlyle quirked a brow in a very British-aristocrat way as he paused beside her. "You've left him speechless. I didn't think it could happen."

"Damn, girl," Sabryn replied. "That was amazing. You could've warned us you had that kind of power."

All Bronwyn could do was look at them in confusion. No one mentioned Beth. Yet. The questions were coming. She knew it.

Elias was the last to exit. He said nothing, but he didn't need to. It was all in his eyes. The way the bright blue depths studied her, silently questioning. She hadn't wanted to fight with him. She had only done what she thought she needed to do—and it had all been for nothing. It seemed the Knights weren't going anywhere.

She had to admit she felt a measure of relief knowing she wouldn't have to face Sydney alone. Her father hadn't been prepared for the encounter. But the Knights were another matter entirely. If she didn't have to end Sydney's life, at least she had saved herself from that.

But was it fair to put that in the hands of others? None of those around her deserved to have that smear on their souls. They were good people. She, on the other hand, hadn't just turned to the dark side to become *drough*, she had also crossed into the realm of the forbidden with blood magic. Nothing could save her now.

Not even Elias's soul-stirring kisses.

He linked his pinky with hers. "Thank you."

She nodded, unable to find her voice. Bronwyn turned her head away and closed the portal. Her gaze locked on Beth as the opening shrank until it was gone—along with her cousin.

"Carlyle, keys," Finn called. "We need to move your vehicle before Frasier and his people find it."

There was a jingle, and Bronwyn saw Carlyle toss the keys to Finn, who sprinted downstairs and then out of the house. With nothing else to do, Bronwyn faced the remaining three.

"We heard everything," Carlyle explained.

Elias nodded. "Everything was amplified. We couldna see who was in the room with us, but we saw shadows."

"We kept quiet and still, just in case," Sabryn added.

Bronwyn was shocked. "I didn't know any of that."

"You've never put yourself between dimensions?" Carlyle asked.

Bronwyn repressed a shudder. "Once. To put Beth inside."

"Why no' other times?" Elias asked.

Bronwyn shrugged. "I don't like it there. It's too…unnatural."

Carlyle grunted in response.

"Have you gone to other dimensions?"

Her gaze shifted to Sabryn, who had posed the query. "Why would I?"

"To escape," Sabryn replied.

Bronwyn pushed down the anger that threatened to swallow her. "There is no escape from life. My mother used to push me relentlessly to be powerful enough to open a gateway big enough for her to escape through. Those were her exact words. Escape. From me, from Dad. I refused to do it because I wanted her to stay and get better. To go to the doctors and discover what was wrong. Dad would find her a doctor, and they would prescribe medicine to help with her depression and anxiety. She would improve for a little while, then everything would start again. Until…"

She faltered, thinking about that day.

Elias's pinky tightened on hers. She looked at him and remembered how safe and treasured she had felt in his arms.

"It's okay," he told her.

Bronwyn knew it wasn't. It hadn't been for a long time. "Mum died because of me."

Elias shook his head. His voice was barely above a whisper when he said, "Nay, lass."

"She begged me to help her that day. She pleaded and yelled and cried. She gripped my arms so tightly she left bruises. She kept saying she had to leave. Dad was away on business. She'd let the few servants we had leave early so it was just the two of us here. She kept telling me I didn't understand. That the only way she'd get better was if she escaped. I was angry and overwhelmed and scared. I told her I'd never use my magic for such a purpose. I told her she needed to stay with Dad and me." Bronwyn drew in a breath. "That night, she walked into the loch and drowned."

The compassion in Elias's eyes was her undoing. For the first time in years, Bronwyn felt tears threatening when she thought of her mother. Her mum had done the best she could with her mental issues. Maybe she and her father should've done more to get her Mum to take the meds.

Bronwyn sniffed, realizing then that others were with her. She glanced at Carlyle and Sabryn. "I only use my power as a last resort."

"I understand," Sabryn said. "It was insensitive of me to say anything."

Bronwyn flashed her a quick smile. "You had no way of knowing. Can we talk about something else, though? Please?"

"What did you get from Frasier?" Elias asked. "How did he act?"

Bronwyn was grateful for the change of subject. "He suspects that I'm hiding something, which, of course, I am. He's tenacious. He won't give up easily."

"Then we need to settle things quickly with Sydney," Carlyle replied.

Elias grunted. "My thoughts exactly."

"We also don't know when Frasier will return to search the estate," Bronwyn cautioned.

Sabryn shrugged. "I don't think it matters at this point."

"Nay, she has a point," Elias said. "Sydney sent his people to the police for a reason. He knows I'm here, but if they doona find me, then—"

"Frasier suspects Bronwyn is hiding you," Carlyle finished.

Elias nodded. "Precisely. That means Sydney knows there's a good chance she's hiding Beth, too."

"Okay. I buy all of that. How does George factor in?" Sabryn asked.

Bronwyn shoved a lock of hair out of her face. "They're working together. George wants Elias, and Sydney wants me."

"Then we'd better prepare for George joining the battle," Sabryn replied.

Carlyle crossed his arms over his chest, a slight frown lining his face. "I don't think George will do that. She hasn't shifted her focus from her original objective. If anything, I think she's giving Sydney information."

"For what purpose?" Bronwyn asked. "I might not have met

George, but I know people like her. She won't give up something important unless she gets something in return."

Elias blew out a breath. "Sydney must have agreed to hand me over to her."

"Or to the police," Carlyle added.

Sabryn rolled her eyes. "We've faced tougher adversaries than George or Sydney. So what if they've teamed up? We're the Knights." Her gaze slid to Bronwyn. "With a portal-opening Druid. We've got this."

"Then let's get to formulating how we're going to do it. Finn will return shortly, and we need to fill in Saber," Carlyle said.

Sabryn and Carlyle turned together and made their way down the hall as they talked. Bronwyn couldn't help but notice that she and Elias still had their fingers linked. She started walking, and he fell into step beside her.

"I'm verra sorry you went through that with your mum. Alone, at that."

Bronwyn shrugged. "It wasn't something we broadcasted. Dad was devastated and blamed himself. But we both knew it was my fault."

"Nay, lass. Your mum was hurting. She wanted it to end, and she found a way. It had nothing to do with you."

Their steps slowed, putting more distance between them and the others. "She would still be alive if I'd helped her."

"You doona know that. She thought by going somewhere else the pain would cease. The truth is, there were two ways she could've helped herself. By taking the meds and by taking her life. She chose the latter."

"I hated her for so long for leaving us and leaving Dad in such a state."

"You lost two parents in one day."

She turned her head to Elias. "So did you."

His bright blue eyes briefly met hers. He turned away, shoving his hand through his dark blond locks that had fallen across his forehead. "It's difficult to bear."

"You handled it better than I did."

He snorted as they began descending the stairs. "That's up for debate."

"You made something of your life. I've done nothing but make one horrible decision after another. So, yeah, you did better than me."

He grasped her arm and drew her to a halt as they reached the landing before the final flight. "You were right earlier. About what you said regarding my father and me."

"I had no right to speak like that."

"But it was true," he insisted. His hand slowly slid down her arm until their fingers entwined. "I needed to hear that."

She pressed her lips together, feeling that same pull from the night before. Like an electrical current that moved between them, tugging them together as if they were magnets.

"Mum didna kill my dad," Elias suddenly said.

Bronwyn blinked, unsure if she'd heard correctly. "What?"

"Dad physically and verbally abused Mum for their entire marriage. He had begun to beat me, trying to teach me what a real man was supposed to be."

Bronwyn clung to his hand, feeling anger rolling off him with every word. She couldn't imagine what Elias and his mother had endured at the hands of his father.

"As far as I know, he didna hurt Edie or Elodie. Mum didna know about him hitting me until shortly before his death. I tried to keep it from her because I knew she already had enough to deal with. But she came home and found us one day. That was when she decided to leave him." Elias swallowed, pain flashing across his face. "She told him that morning. He became enraged and wouldna accept her decision. Edie was outside. Elodie and I heard the crashes in our parents' room. I told her no' to go in, but she didna listen. That was the morning she saw our father for the monster he truly was."

Bronwyn fought against the surge of tears, overwhelmed by emotions for Elias and his family.

He paused and took a deep breath. "Elodie saw him trying to strangle Mum. Elodie went after him, and he hit her. I can still hear it. The violence in his hand as he backhanded my baby sister. Then he turned on me. No' with his fists but with his mockery. I stood there, trying to figure out how to get all three of us out of the house and away from him, then he began hitting me. I tried to block the strikes, but he was so big.

"I heard Mum crying, screaming at my dad to leave me alone. I knew Elodie was hurt and watching everything. And I… I lost it. I doona remember calling to my magic, but suddenly it was there. I used it to throw him away from me. He hated that we had magic and he didna, and it felt good to hurt him as he had us." Elias shook his head. "And that scared me as nothing else could. But I liked how it felt to hit him."

A tear fell from Bronwyn's eyes. She tried to hold them back, but she couldn't. She was in that room with Elias, witness to the horror, the absolute carnage that had befallen them. She *felt* his anguish, his suffering.

And his fury.

But Elias wasn't finished. "If he had been livid before, he got enraged then. I doona know where the knife came from, but suddenly it was in his hand. Elodie rushed to me. We both thought Dad was coming to take my life. Instead, he went to Mum. Before I even knew what was happening, Elodie's magic erupted from her hands. It grabbed him and lifted him into the air as he pleaded with her to stop. Then his body turned in on itself until he was just…gone."

Bronwyn could only stare at him, surprise, sorrow, and rage warring within her for what had happened. She wanted to say something, but everything that came to mind didn't hold the amount of empathy or compassion she felt.

"Elodie went into meltdown after that. She was so afraid of the power of her magic that she wouldna stop screaming or crying," Elias said as his gaze briefly skated away. "Mum jumped into action. She wanted to save Edie from the truth, while helping us at the same time. She offered to take Elodie's magic, and her memories of what'd happened with it. Elodie agreed."

"Oh, my God," Bronwyn whispered.

He nodded slowly. "Once Mum bound Elodie's magic, and her memories were gone, she finally stopped screaming. Even to this day, I often wake to the sound of those screams. It fell to me then to keep my sisters safe and ensure Elodie never learned what she had done."

"And your mum confessed to the murder."

"Aye. I left Skye soon after because I'd have ended up saying or doing something that would have brought Elodie's memories back, and that was a truth she couldna handle."

Bronwyn swallowed, putting her hand on his chest. She needed to touch him, to offer whatever comfort he'd take. And to try to take away some of his pain. "I'm so sorry."

A muscle jumped in his jaw, his eyes filled with anguish and torment that ran deep. Bronwyn wrapped her arms around him. The way he held her tightly as if she were the only thing keeping him going caused another tear to fall down her cheek.

They stayed wrapped together for a long time. She had known by his earlier comments that he didn't care for his father, but she'd never imagined anything so horrid. No one had, apparently, because there had never been any gossip. And if someone had seen something, it would've made the rounds on Skye.

"No one should suffer like that," Bronwyn said. "You lost everything. Your childhood, your family, and your home."

He drew in a deep breath that expanded his shoulders. Then he released it slowly. "I had to protect my sisters."

"But you returned."

"Because Elodie did," he explained as he leaned back, but he didn't release her. He gently caressed his fingers down the side of her face. "She moved into our parents' cottage and, eventually, went into their bedroom. The very thing I stayed away to prevent happened. All her memories returned, and with them, her magic."

"Bloody hell." Bronwyn couldn't imagine how it felt not to have magic but then to regain such memories on top of that? "How is she doing now?"

Elias shrugged half-heartedly. "Remarkably well, thankfully. She was able to face things. I think, in part, because she has someone with her. Scott is a good man, even if George sent him to the isle."

Bronwyn blew out a breath, her frustration clear. "Seems like

George has her fingers in a lot of pies. What did she want with Elodie?"

"She wanted her to join the Druid Others."

"You've got to be kidding," Bronwyn said, utterly floored by the statement.

Elias shook his head. "Elodie refused, and to make things worse, Scott and Filip Gordon decided to remain on Skye."

"I had heard that Filip was back. George can't be happy about any of that. Do you think that's why she's targeting you?"

"I doona know, but I aim to find out."

CHAPTER THIRTY

If there was ever a time of true gratification, of absolute contentment, it had finally come to Kerry. And it was all because of the Ancients. It was difficult to keep the knowledge inside her as she sat in the pub, her gaze moving from tourists to the locals she had once called friends—friends who hadn't hesitated to seek her guidance.

Even with the power she now wielded, she couldn't release the grudge against Rhona and every Druid in her zone. They looked down on her now as if she were less than.

As if she were *lacking*.

They were the deficient ones, and she would soon pass judgment on each and every one of them. The Ancients had spent an eternity watching the Druids muck things up, time and again. The reckoning was nearly upon them. And it would begin on Skye.

Kerry thought it fitting since the seat of the Druids had begun here. It'd commenced on the isle eons ago, and it would begin here once more, washing away the old and purging the ground of everything stale and archaic.

A whisper behind Kerry caught her attention. Her ears pricked at the mention of Bronwyn Stewart. There were few Druids on Skye who didn't gossip about the young *drough*. They knew nothing about her. Not even why she had chosen to become *drough*. To them, she had written herself off. She, like Kerry, had been left wanting. Found *lacking*.

Perhaps that was how Kerry's interest in her had begun. It didn't take much digging to discover that Bronwyn had lived a very short brutal life by losing both her parents. But there was more to the story if Bronwyn had sought out the additional power that came with being a *drough*.

The Druids had failed Bronwyn—specifically Rhona.

Kerry was mildly surprised that Bronwyn wasn't on the Ancients' list to be removed. Obviously, they knew something about the young Druid that could benefit the new regime. And if the Ancients approved of her, then Kerry was delighted to welcome Bronwyn.

Kerry focused on the conversation behind her. She didn't need to turn around to recognize the voices of Florence and Martha, both middle-aged busybodies who spent more time gossiping than anything else.

"I heard DI Frasier went to Carwood to search the manor for Elias MacLean," Martha said.

Florence sighed longingly. "Theo is one handsome man. If I were younger…" she said wistfully.

"Enough, Florence. Stop mooning over someone you can't have. You're not young, and he wouldn't give you the time of day," Martha snapped.

Florence huffed. Her voice was stiff when she said, "There's been talk about Elias at Carwood for a couple of days now."

"Well, if he was there, Frasier would've brought him in."

"Martha, please," Florence said drolly. "You're forgetting that Bronwyn is *drough*."

It was Martha's turn to huff. "I'm not a nitwit. Everyone knows she's *drough*, but that doesn't necessarily mean she does evil things."

"Of course, it does. That's why *droughs* are considered evil." The snort that followed was filled with disdain.

"I saw Bronwyn a week before last. She didn't look like she'd done evil."

"What's evil look like, Martha?" Florence retorted. "I'd like to know."

There was silence. Kerry grinned because she knew they looked her way. She turned in her chair to face them and smiled. The two blanched and hurriedly looked away. Unable to help herself, Kerry rose, her knees creaking from age and extra weight, and walked the short distance to their table.

"Hello, ladies," she said. Florence wouldn't meet her gaze, but Martha did. Kerry sank onto one of the empty chairs. "I couldn't help but overhear your...we'll call it a conversation. As a matter of fact, the entire pub heard it."

As if to see if she were right, the two women looked around. Florence's cheeks bloomed bright with color while Martha suddenly found her empty teacup interesting.

"You two seem awfully interested in Elias and Bronwyn," Kerry continued.

Martha quickly said, "Elias is the killer."

"Is he?" Kerry asked. "Who told you that?"

Martha jerked her gaze to Florence. Kerry turned her attention on the woman.

Florence shot a dark look toward Martha before clearing her throat. "The woman from Edinburgh is staying at my B&B. I… hear things."

"You mean you eavesdrop," Kerry stated.

"N-no, not at all."

Kerry cut her hand through the air. "I don't care about that. This woman? Who is she?"

"Georgina Miller, but she goes by George. She's here to make sure Elias is arrested for the murders committed in Edinburgh."

Kerry leaned back slowly. "Is she now?"

Florence nodded, her unease vanishing as her eyes glittered at the idea of sharing gossip. "George claims that Elias didn't just kill people in the city but here, as well. Now that the police have found a dead body at Elias's place, we know he's the one murdering people."

"Do you?" Kerry had kept up with the news on Skye, but she hadn't known about George. Perhaps it was time to make the woman's acquaintance. Especially if it would remove Elias as the Ancients wanted.

"George isn't the only newcomer," Martha whispered conspiratorially, leaning forward. "There's a man."

Florence kicked Martha beneath the table.

"What?" Martha asked wide-eyed.

Kerry quirked a brow and waited for one of them to explain.

Florence sighed loudly. "His name is Sydney Russell. He's Bronwyn's ex, who then moved on to her cousin, Beth. Apparently, Beth has been missing for weeks. Sydney believes Bronwyn is responsible somehow. He's here to find Beth."

"He and his four friends," Martha said with a firm nod.

Kerry rose to her feet. "You two have been very helpful. Thank you."

As she walked to her table, Kerry's mind whirled with the new information. She paid for her meal and left. It was time to talk to the Ancients.

Elias tried to pay attention as everyone batted around ideas while he paced the library, but he couldn't stop thinking about Bronwyn. He was glad he'd shared with her what'd happened with his father. It hadn't been easy, but he'd known she would understand. And he'd been right. He didn't necessarily feel lighter for sharing his past, but the hatred didn't seem to feel as cloying.

His thoughts kept tripping on something Bronwyn had said about not escaping life. She hadn't meant the words for him, but there was no denying they had struck a nerve. Because he'd been trying to escape for as long as he could remember.

He'd run from Skye and everything that'd happened with his father, and he'd kept his sisters at arm's length because he hadn't wanted to face the past. Now, he had hidden instead of facing things because he was being framed. All he'd been doing was running. He'd made an art form of it. Oh, he spun things to make himself feel better, said the Knights needed him and they couldn't do a mission without him. That he couldn't take a day or week to see his family.

Now that past had caught up with him whether he wanted it to or not. It was time to stop running, stop hiding.

"I'm going to talk to Frasier," he announced.

The conversation halted as four pairs of eyes swung to him.

"Um, excuse me?" Carlyle asked from his position at one end of the sofa.

Finn, who sat in a chair, shook his head. "Have you taken leave of your senses? I don't think that's wise."

Elias held up his hand to quiet any more remarks. "The longer I hide, the worse it makes me look."

"While I understand what you're saying, I don't think now's a good time." Sabryn scooted to the edge of the sofa cushion.

Elias faced the group. "Frasier will return. We all know this. It doesna matter if George or Sydney told him something or if Frasier figured things out on his own, but he will keep coming to the manor until he finds me."

"If you're dead set on this, then at least allow my solicitor to join you," Carlyle told him.

Finn sat forward, his brows furrowed. "Of course, he will. Elias would be stupid to go without one, and he isn't dumb. Well, on most days, he isn't. I'm not sure about today."

"Why now?" Bronwyn asked.

Elias swallowed and swung his eyes to where she sat in the other chair. He wished they were alone. He wanted to kiss her again, hold her, feel himself inside her. He wanted to hear her scream in pleasure. Simply put, he ached for her. Even when they were arguing, he couldn't get enough of her.

They'd both experienced heartache and pain that few could understand. He hadn't grasped the truth of his life until he met her. He'd been reckless and rash for so long, uncaring if he lived or died. He knew his sisters were fine and his mother would get her life back. So, he helped everyone else when he should've aided himself and his family through the trauma they still didn't talk about.

"There's no escaping life."

Something flashed in Bronwyn's eyes. "I didn't direct those words at you."

He twisted his lips and shrugged. "I know, but it fits. I can no' keep running. It makes me look guilty when I'm anything but."

"Sydney is trying to frame you," Sabryn added. "And I can almost guarantee he did that to help solidify George's allegations."

Elias scraped a hand down his face. Fuck, he was tired. He wished this was all a dream and he would wake in Bronwyn's arms. "I'm going to have to prove my innocence."

"That might be harder than you think." Carlyle squeezed the bridge of his nose with his thumb and forefinger as he leaned forward on the sofa. "It won't matter how good my solicitor is if the job done to frame you is good enough."

Finn jumped up and sliced both arms through the air. "This is fekking stupid. Stop talking like that, Elias. We need you for this battle."

"I want to be here for it, but we need a plan B in case something goes sideways," Elias said.

Bronwyn crossed one leg over the other. "Like if Sydney waits days to attack as he has in the past."

"Then we don't allow him that option," Sabryn said.

Elias frowned as he looked her way. "What are you thinking?"

"We talk to him," Sabryn replied.

"No. Nope. No way," Finn stated, raking his hands through

his dark hair in agitation. "What's wrong with everyone? Are Bronwyn and I the only sane ones?"

Carlyle shot him a peeved look. "Excuse me? I'm here, too."

Finn rolled his eyes in response.

"But Finn isn't wrong," Carlyle said as he looked between Sabryn and Elias. "Sabryn, you can't show yourself to Sydney or any of his people. We need to have that advantage. And, Elias… seriously, mate, we're counting on you for our numbers."

Sabryn shifted sideways to look at Carlyle. "If we want to take care of Sydney quickly, then someone needs to alert him."

"I'll do it," Bronwyn said. Before Elias could reply, she looked at him and added, "And I don't have to leave the manor to do it. I'll text him."

Finn flipped his hand toward Bronwyn. "See? Sane."

"How do you know he'll come?" Elias asked, ignoring Finn.

Bronwyn glanced up at the ceiling. "He wants to know about Beth. I'll consent to give him that information if he agrees to leave me alone."

"He might demand to know it over text," Sabryn said.

Finn shrugged one shoulder. "That's easy to work around. Bronwyn can tell him he needs to come here."

"He'll know it's a trap," Carlyle pointed out.

Elias rubbed his hands over his face. "It doesna matter what we do, he'll know it's a ruse."

"Unless I agree to meet him somewhere," Bronwyn said.

Elias jerked his head up. "Nay. The house protects you."

"I told you from the beginning that I was prepared to end this however I could. I thought I'd be doing it alone, but I have help." She cut her eyes to Carlyle. "Even if I was coerced."

Carlyle winked at her. "You'll thank me later."

"Besides," Bronwyn continued, "I won't allow Sydney inside the manor. I was always going to have to leave the safety of my home."

Finn crossed his arms over his chest. "Where's the best place for a battle on the estate? Somewhere we could see them coming but would also hide us."

"I know just the place. It's about five miles out," Bronwyn said.

Sabryn slapped her hands on her legs. "All right. Then we need to talk about how we're going to approach this. Bronwyn, you'll need to be visible so Sydney can see you."

"I'll be with her," Elias said. "He knows I'm here. If I'm no' with Bronwyn, he'll suspect something."

He met Bronwyn's gaze. She nodded, her lips softening.

CHAPTER THIRTY-ONE

Kirsi stood outside at one of Skye's various scenic overlooks, gazing out at the sea, her thoughts a jumbled mix of indecision and uncertainty. There was no denying the voice she'd heard—or its instructions. She had no idea who the woman was, why she had contacted Kirsi, or if she could even be trusted. No matter how Kirsi looked at it, she didn't have a clear idea of what she was supposed to do. But the one thing that had been unmistakable in all of it was the warning and distress in the woman's voice, in each syllable of every word.

That was what kept running through Kirsi's mind.

She and her parents had gone over the dream for hours. She believed they would be able to help her unravel the tangle of emotions and theories. Instead, they'd piled more on her to consider. Like it might not have been a dream at all. Hence, why she stood out in the misty weather. As if the answer would spring up from the water.

Kirsi turned on her heel and made her way to her car. She

climbed inside and started the engine. The blast of warm air thawed her chilled face. She rubbed her hands together in an effort to get her blood flowing. Then she put the vehicle into reverse and pulled onto the road. There was one person she needed to speak with.

It didn't take too long to reach the cottage. Kirsi had never ventured to Rhona's house on her own before. Even though Rhona should be aware of what had happened to her, Kirsi hesitated. The five deputies, each with a section of Skye, were there so the people went to them instead of Rhona. Kirsi had considered going to Violet first. She adored the older Druid, but her gut kept urging her to see Rhona.

"It's now or never," Kirsi told herself as she climbed out of her car.

Large drops of rain pelted her before she reached the small porch. Kirsi drew in a deep, steadying breath and knocked. She steeled herself, waiting for the door to open, but the seconds lengthened with no response.

Kirsi's shoulders sagged. Rhona wasn't home. She'd have to come back. She retraced her steps to her vehicle and had just opened the door when she heard her name. Kirsi's head swung back to the cottage to see Rhona standing in the doorway.

"Come in," Rhona beckoned with a welcoming smile.

Kirsi glanced at the sky and the angry gray clouds churning above her before dashing back to the porch. "I'm sorry to bother you, but there's something you need to know."

"Then I'll make us some tea."

Rhona closed the door behind Kirsi and watched her for a moment. Kirsi was only a handful of years younger, but Rhona didn't know her that well. The woman had always been quiet and reserved. She was also extremely well-liked on the isle.

Rhona motioned for Kirsi to follow her to the kitchen. There, she filled a kettle with water and set it on a lit burner of the stove. Then, she turned to face the Druid. It was hard to miss Kirsi's nervousness. Rhona smiled, hoping to ease her. "Sit, please."

"Thanks." Kirsi removed her coat and hung it on the back of the chair before lowering herself.

Rhona wanted to urge the Druid to get to things, but she kept silent. Kirsi would talk when she was ready. Besides, the morning had been chaotic. Balladyn was off on Reaper business, and some Druids had gone to her deputies with more than normal concerns. Yet all of that fell away as she stared at Kirsi's pinched lips and the panic in her pale green eyes.

"I," Kirsi began, only to pause and clear her throat. "I know I should've gone to Violet first."

"You're here now. Tell me," Rhona urged patiently.

Kirsi placed her hands on the table and met Rhona's gaze. "Someone spoke to me. Through a dream. Well, my parents don't think it was a dream, but I don't know what else to call it."

Druids could do all sorts of amazing things. Rhona didn't know of anyone on Skye who had the ability, but that wasn't to say they hadn't kept it a secret. Or it could be someone elsewhere in the world. She prepared herself in case this was another oddity to put with the other unusual and worrying things. "What did they say?"

"She kept repeating that I knew what to do."

"She?" Rhona asked, her brows raised.

Kirsi nodded. "It was a woman. She sounded British, but I can't be certain. I mean,"—she paused again—"I could hear her clearly, but her voice was slightly distorted."

"Okay. Go on."

"She told me she was reaching across time and space to contact me."

The kettle began to whistle. Rhona removed it from the stove, cut off the burner, and got out cups and tea bags. Then she poured the water over the tea and set the cups on the table. Rhona lowered herself onto a chair across from Kirsi. "What else happened?"

"I think she's been trying to reach me for a few days. I haven't been able to sleep well, and I kept waking up from dreams that I couldn't remember but seemed important. Then, it was clear. I didn't *see* anything, but I heard her as distinctly as I hear you now." She fiddled with her hands. "The voice told me that I know what to do and that I always have—in this life and hundreds before it. She said I need to look deep within myself and lower my walls. I was also told that I don't need to see anything. That I need to feel instead. That the time is coming, and I need to be ready."

Rhona didn't like the churning in her stomach. The voice had been a warning to Kirsi, which could be taken as a good sign. The fact that there had to be a warning at all is what concerned her. "But the voice didn't say *what* was coming?"

Kirsi shook her head.

Rhona wrapped her cold hands around the mug to warm them. "Do *you* know what's coming?"

Kirsi's brow furrowed deeply as she shook her head again. "Do you know what the woman was talking about?"

Rhona didn't answer as she removed her tea bag and rose to throw it away, doing the same with Kirsi's. Once she had taken her seat again, she said, "I don't. Not yet. I only know things aren't right on Skye."

"Did the Fae Others do something? Maybe that's what this is about."

"They've been defeated and are gone for good. I'm not saying they didn't do something, but I'm looking at every possibility."

Kirsi took a drink of tea and lowered the cup. "The woman sounded frightened. For herself. And for us."

There was much Rhona couldn't tell Kirsi, at least not yet. The last thing she wanted was to send the isle into a panic, and that was exactly what would happen if word got out about everything she was dealing with. For the moment, it was just her and the deputies who were gradually unraveling the facts coming to light.

"I came to you because I feel this…need…to do something," Kirsi said. "But I don't know what to do."

Rhona twisted her lips. "I feel that way most times. I'm glad you came to me. If you hear more, will you let me know?"

"Absolutely."

"Also," Rhona said hesitantly, "have you heard from anyone that their magic isn't working?"

Kirsi's hand holding the tea stopped halfway to her mouth. "What?"

"Word spreads quickly, so I'm sure you'll hear it soon enough, but I would appreciate it if you didn't say anything."

"I promise."

Rhona played with the handle of the mug. "A wind talker has been unable to hear the wind for over a week now. He isn't the only one. A water dancer and a tree whisperer are having the same issues with the water and trees."

"I've not heard anything like that. Is their magic gone?"

"They still have their powers, but they're unable to communicate as they used to with the elements. It isn't affecting everyone. Just a few." But that number was growing, and that concerned Rhona the most.

Was the Skye Druids' magic waning as some feared? Or was something else at work here? Rhona had to find answers soon.

"What about the mist?" Kirsi asked.

Rhona drank before answering. "What about it?"

"It isn't gone, is it?"

"Why do you ask that?"

Kirsi shrugged. "A hunch. No one has seen anything since the last murder, but mist doesn't kill on its own."

"Nay, it doesn't."

"Do you know who's controlling it?"

"Not yet." But she would find out if it was the last thing she did. Her Druids were being killed on her watch. That was unacceptable.

Kirsi pressed her lips together for a heartbeat. "I want to help. I *have* to help."

Rhona almost refused the offer, but then remembered the connection Kirsi and her family had to the rest of the isle. "All right. Here's what I need from you."

It had taken Kerry some time to lower her plump, old frame to the floor. Her bones had creaked and popped the entire time, and she was concerned that she might not be able to get back up without help. But she'd worry about that later.

She sat cross-legged in a circle of candles, then closed her eyes and whispered, "Ancients, please hear my call."

It was rare for her to reach out to them since they'd first contacted her. She never wanted to overstep because they could take away her power as easily as they had granted it. They didn't speak to her regularly. Sometimes, it was several times a day. Other times, days passed before she heard from them. But she knew they were there, waiting to implement the next step of their plan.

"*It isn't time to release the mist again yet,*" the Ancient said.

"I will wait for your word on that. I wish to speak about Bronwyn Stewart."

There was a lengthy pause. "*Go on.*"

"Her family can trace their roots back to the original Druids who settled on Skye. The power in that family is immense."

"*Her name isn't on the list of those needing to be removed. You know that.*"

"I think she could be an asset to the Druids' new direction."

"*She uses blood magic. She won't be alive for long.*"

So that was why Bronwyn hadn't been on the list. "But think of what she could do for us while she lives."

The Ancient made a sound. "*She's been targeted by someone.*"

"I know. I want to intervene, to take Bronwyn's side. She'll be a valuable asset."

"*And you want our permission?*"

Kerry swallowed. "Others on Skye are disrupting your plans. Are they our allies or enemies?"

"You speak of the seer from Edinburgh, and the male from Inverness."

"Aye."

The Ancients went silent. It stretched so long that Kerry thought they had left. She was about to end the session when the voice rang out.

"Do what you will with the male. You'd best hurry, though. Their battle will commence soon."

With that, a gust of wind extinguished the candles. Kerry opened her eyes. The Ancients hadn't stated whether George and Sydney were enemies, but they hadn't said the two weren't, either. Yet she had permission to take a stand against Sydney.

Kerry uncrossed her legs and moved onto her hands and knees. She crawled to a nearby chair and used it to get to her feet. When she straightened, she wore a smile because she knew exactly what she would do to Sydney. By helping Bronwyn, Kerry would gain an ally.

She hadn't known about Bronwyn's use of blood magic, but that didn't change her mind about the young Druid. If anything, it confirmed what she'd known about the Stewart family. The Ancients had the power to do whatever they wanted. They could save her life if they deemed Bronwyn acceptable to the cause.

Kerry walked to the door and put on her coat. She buttoned it before wrapping the scarf around her neck and tugging the beanie onto her head. Last were her gloves. Then she was out the door to her car.

The battle brewing between Sydney and Bronwyn was about to boil over, and Kerry would have a front-row seat.

CHAPTER THIRTY-TWO

Bronwyn sent the text. She hated contacting Sydney in any way, but this could end it all. Just as she expected, he replied promptly. He'd tried to suggest a different location, but she refused. She told him if he wanted Beth, he had to meet her on the estate. Sydney caved after that. Everything was set.

Just as everyone knew it was a trap.

She hoped they could outwit Sydney. He always thought he was the smartest person around. It was time for his particular kind of malice to be over. Sydney's death might not come with the dawn, but she hoped he was beaten soundly enough for him to change his ways. It was a futile hope, but one she clung to—because she didn't want any of them to take his life.

In the short time she'd been around the Knights, she'd seen their tight bond and the love they shared. They were a family. One that called each other on their bullshit but loved unconditionally. They were good people who did great deeds.

She wanted this with Sydney to end. She was ready for it.

Past ready, actually. Or so she thought. As the time drew near to facing off against the man who had murdered her father, Bronwyn's nervousness grew. She remembered the hate that had consumed her when she opened the door and saw Sydney standing there. She wasn't sure what she would've done if she hadn't been taken from the house. The darkness had surged inside her, growing her anger until it was all she saw. If she gave in to the darkness being a *drough* gave her, if she allowed the bitterness and contempt to consume her, she would become someone else—someone Elias wouldn't want.

In the hours since the planning of the battle in the library, everyone had separated. Each of the Knights readied for that evening, including Elias. Bronwyn used the time to complete her first cover design. As she stared at the project, she hoped she got the chance to create many more. It was hands down the most difficult thing she had ever done, but at the same time, it was the most exciting, the most exhilarating. And the thought that she might see it on the shelves in a bookstore was beyond thrilling.

If she lived through the night.

Bronwyn tried not to think about that. She sent off the cover to the author and closed the laptop. Her nerves were stretched taut. She stood and looked around the parlor, recalling a time when the room had been alive with people and merriment, the lights glittering during a party, or the walls decked out for the Christmas season.

Her house. Her *home*.

There was a good chance she wouldn't walk back through the door once she left. She headed to the nearest wall and put her hand on it. Her magic passed from her palm into the wood, to the very foundation of the manor.

She gazed lovingly at the walls. "You've sheltered me against the elements, the outside world, and those who would do me harm. You watched over me like a silent sentry, offering comfort in my darkest days. You deserve better than what I've done to you. If I don't make it out of this battle, grant Elias and the Knights refuge, guarding them as you have me all these years. One day soon, there will be laughter and joy filling you again. You've served my family for generations as a grand manor and a home. For that, I thank you from the bottom of my heart."

There was no answer, at least not in words. The house was relaxed, welcoming. It had heard her. Bronwyn let her hand slide down the wall to her side. She then walked out of the parlor and ascended the stairs to the second floor. As she made her way down the hall to Beth's room, she was surprised to find Finn there. He glanced at her as she approached, but he said nothing as he continued staring at the closed door.

"You have a skill I didn't know was possible," he said without looking at her.

"I doubt I'm the only one who can open a portal between dimensions. If I'd had a choice, I'd much rather communicate with fire or wind. This is…not beneficial."

"Your gift is fekking terrifying."

She turned her head to him and studied him as regret filled her. "You're frightened of me."

"Nay." He released a breath and looked at her. "I'm scared of what's on the other side."

"I don't understand."

"When we were in that place…" he began.

"I call it the In-between."

"The In-between. Aye." Finn glanced at the closed door

again. "At first, we were focused on listening to you and Frasier. That's when I saw it."

Her brows snapped together at his words. "Saw what?"

"Movement. Like a shadow out of the corner of my eye. Then I searched for it. And found it. There was no shape that I could make out, but it was huge. Tall, wide. Just…big. It was on the other side, the other dimension."

Bronwyn faced him, her blood running cold. She had stood in the In-between with Beth before, and she'd never seen anything. But she hadn't been looking, either. It'd never dawned on her that something might realize she or Beth were there.

Bloody hell. Beth.

"I disregarded it, thinking it was the police from our side. Then one came in the room." Finn's throat bobbed as he swallowed. "We couldn't see her, but we knew where she was. I looked back at the shadow. It had stopped moving, and though I can't explain it, I knew it was focused on me." He ran a hand down his face lined with apprehension. "I've encountered a lot of bad people in my life. The truly malicious ones, those wicked to their core, have a hollowness about them. That's what the shadow felt like. There's something evil there, Bronwyn, and there's only a thin veil separating it from Beth."

Bronwyn found herself looking at the door as she thought of her cousin. Did she pull her out now? She couldn't fight Beth and Sydney because she knew Beth would be furious. She had to make a decision. She just hoped it was the right one.

"This shite with Sydney ends tonight. One way or another. If I'm killed, I've ensured the portal will automatically open for Beth. She should awaken and get out on her own, but just in case," she said as her gaze slid back to him.

Finn nodded. "One of us will be here for her."

"Thank you. And if we defeat Sydney, well, I intended to release my cousin anyway. It's time for Beth to wake and live her life. She'll never forgive me for what I've done, and I don't think I should be absolved. If we succeed, it'll be enough that I've saved her from a horrible life with him."

"There's a reason you have your ability, you know," Finn said.

She frowned as she cocked her head. "It's come in handy to hide Beth as well as all of you, but I can't imagine why else I'd need it."

"To hinder something from crossing into our dimension."

Bronwyn clenched her heads as dread thrummed through her. "If it were easy to move from one plane to another, individuals would do it all the time."

"It might not be easy for us, but we don't know about other worlds. You might have woken something without even being aware of it."

He had a point. One she had never considered. Bronwyn assumed that nothing could harm Beth in the In-between. What if she *had* woken something? What if she'd put their world in danger? Beth in danger. The thought left her shaken.

Finn held her gaze. "I'm sure I'm being overly concerned. Beth has been in there for weeks. A few more hours can't hurt."

"Right," Bronwyn said, but she didn't sound convinced, even to her own ears.

Finn took one final look at the door and walked away, but his words stayed with Bronwyn long after he was gone. She debated whether to open the portal and retrieve Beth right then. She even contemplated going into the In-between with her cousin to see if she sensed the shadow Finn spoke about.

In the end, she did nothing.

"There you are."

She jerked at the sound of Elias's voice, her heart in her throat. Bronwyn put a hand on her chest and bent over at the waist. "Bloody hell. You scared the shite out of me."

"I'm sorry," Elias said as he put a hand on her back. "I thought you would've heard my approach."

She straightened. "I was thinking."

He turned her toward him, worry filling his eyes. "About?"

"Did you…see…anything when I hid you from Frasier?" she asked hesitantly.

Elias contemplated her words before shaking his head. "Nay. I heard things, but I didna see anyone. Why?"

"Finn did." She explained what Finn had told her.

Elias leaned a shoulder against the wall and whistled low. "Damn. I wish he would've pointed it out."

"I've never seen anything, but then I've never looked. What if I've put everyone in danger?"

He pushed away from the wall and took her hands in his. "We can inspect things right now if you'd like."

"I wish I could, but I need to save my magic. I've already opened the portal twice today. It takes a lot to do that."

"All this will be over soon. Sydney will be handled, and we can get Beth out," Elias assured her.

Bronwyn nodded woodenly. She clung to his words, praying they were true. But she couldn't stop thinking about Beth and the shadow. If she didn't talk about something else, she'd give in and open the gateway regardless of what it might do to her. "I finished the cover."

"Aye?" Elias asked with a grin. "Congratulations."

"You can say that after the author approves it. I'm hoping she'll only want minor changes."

Elias glanced at their hands. "Sabryn and Finn left a few moments ago to get in place at the locations Sydney could enter the estate. We should leave soon, but I wanted a wee bit of time with you."

She understood because there were things she needed to say, too. "I need to apologize for this morning."

"Nay," he said with a shake of his head. "I knew better than to push, but I did it anyway."

She smiled as she gazed into his bright blue eyes. Bronwyn reached up and moved aside the lock of hair that continued to fall onto his forehead. "Perhaps I should've pulled you into a bedroom and enjoyed your body instead of working on the cover."

"There's always later tonight," he said as he pulled her closer until their bodies touched.

"I want you to know that if something happens to me—"

"Doona," he stated, his voice deep with emotion.

She put a hand on his chest and felt the beat of his heart. "Let me say this, please."

Elias relented with flattened lips and a slight nod of his head.

"You and the Knights will be able to come and go in the manor. Everything is in order if I should die. I saw to that when I became *drough* and used blood magic. The house and estate pass to the next relative, which is Beth. My will is under my mattress."

"Nothing will happen," Elias stated.

"You need to know. Just in case."

His arms tightened around her. "We're good at what we do. Trust me."

"I do," she said as she wound her arms around his neck. It was Sydney she didn't trust.

Elias's lips softened. "There's something I need to say to you, too."

"Oh?" Her heart began to race.

"Aye," he murmured as his head lowered and his lips brushed hers. "You're in my blood now, Bronwyn. There will never be another for me, lass."

He didn't give her a chance to reply as he captured her mouth in a scorching kiss that stole her breath and weakened her knees. Her breasts swelled, and her sex clenched greedily for him.

Elias spun them until he pressed her between him and the wall. The feeling of his arousal made her moan as she recalled how he felt moving inside her, thick and hard. Her fingers dug into his neck while she rocked against him. She was on fire for his touch, and his alone.

He tore his mouth from hers and pressed his forehead against hers. His voice was roughened by desire when he said, "Och, lass. I want you."

She took his hand and led him down the hall to her bedroom. She pulled him inside and closed the door behind them. Then she wrenched off her boots and jeans as she made her way to the bed. She managed to get one leg free of the denim before Elias hauled her against him. His eyes burned with a need that matched hers.

He kissed her, then palmed her hips and spun her around. Bronwyn grabbed the footboard as one of his large hands moved around to the front of her. She gasped when his soft fingers slid through her curls and teased her tender flesh. His finger entered her, sliding deep.

"You're so wet," he whispered.

She pushed her hips back, seeking more of him. Elias chuckled and moved his finger, slick with her juices, over her throbbing clit. She cried out as pleasure shot through her. The sound of a package crinkling reached her. He moved away to put on the condom. She bit her lip when she felt the head of his cock at her entrance. Then, with one thrust, he was inside her.

Elias leaned over her as he continued circling her clit with his finger. "I've never burned for anyone as I do you," he whispered hotly next to her ear. He pulled out and shoved himself deep again. "You're no' just in my blood, lass. You're in my heart. My verra soul."

With every sentence, he pulled out and drove deep as if punctuating his words. The fire between them, the need—and his declaration—had her trembling, right on the precipice of an orgasm.

She tried to find words to answer him, but she couldn't think clearly when her body teemed with the exquisite carnal pleasure he wrung from her effortlessly. Her knees began to shake as his finger moved faster around her clit, urging her toward climax.

Bronwyn clung to the footboard, her eyes closing as she gave in to the sensations coursing through her and reveled in the sounds of their bodies coming together.

"Elias," she whispered tightly.

"Aye, lass," he replied. "I'm nearly there."

She pressed her forehead to the wooden footboard as pleasure swept through her. She gasped when the first wild, hedonistic waves of pleasure rolled through her. Elias gripped her hips with both hands and thrust hard and fast until he let out a guttural sound and buried himself so deeply he touched her womb. She could feel him pulsing within her, and in response, her body clenched around him firmly.

The harsh sounds of their breathing filled the room.

Bronwyn shoved her hair out of the way to look at Elias over her shoulder. His chest heaved as he grinned. He pulled out and turned her around. She cupped his face. "You're in my blood, too. My heart. My soul."

CHAPTER THIRTY-THREE

Elias's heart missed a beat. He searched Bronwyn's hazel eyes, finding truth to her words. He parted his lips, ready to say the words he had already all but said, when Carlyle's voice rang out from the hall, calling their names.

"We'll be right there!" Bronwyn shouted in reply.

She gave him a long, tender kiss before pulling away to dress. Elias wanted to reach for her, to return them to where they had been before being rudely interrupted. It wasn't his friend's fault, however. It was his. Three words. That was all he needed to say, but they stuck in his throat.

Bronwyn faced him and winked. She was already dressed. Her gaze lowered to his now flaccid cock and the condom that hung precariously from it. "The bathroom is through there," she told him and pointed to a door behind him.

She walked to him and pressed her lips to his again. Instinctively, his hands held her against him. Now. This was the time he could tell her. But when she leaned back and met his gaze, the words wouldn't come.

"Is everything okay?" she asked, a small frown wrinkling her brow.

Elias forced his hands to release her. He'd never told a woman that he loved them. He'd never pledged his heart to anyone. He'd never had a real relationship. He'd never wanted one. How could he after what'd happened with his dad? A part of him wasn't sure he was meant to love anyone. The other part of him, the side that churned with long-held anger and resentment was terrified that he'd become like his father.

He'd ignored that part of himself for so long. It had been easy since no one had ever made him think about a future. Then Bronwyn came into his life again. He didn't just want a relationship with her, he wanted it all. With her.

More than he'd ever wanted anything else in his life.

That was when memories of his father reared their ugly head. His dad's taunting words of how a real man should act seemed to reverberate through his mind in a never-ending toll.

"Elias?"

He pulled himself to the present and tucked a strand of her dark locks behind her ear. "I'm fine."

"I don't believe that."

"Elias!" Carlyle bellowed.

Elias sighed. "I will be. Promise," he told Bronwyn. "Let me clean up. I'll be right down."

She studied him for a moment longer before stepping back and letting her arms fall from him. "I'll go see Carlyle."

Elias forced a smile and turned on his heel as he made his way to the bathroom. He glanced over his shoulder when he heard the soft click of the door closing behind her. He braced his hands on the sink and shook his head. He'd thought he had banished his father from his mind years ago. It was just like the bastard to ruin things now when Elias had found something good, something meaningful.

He removed the condom and cleaned up before hurriedly dressing, all the while telling himself that it was a simple thing to declare his love to Bronwyn. Simple and easy. There was nothing standing in his way. Not the past, not a person, and certainly not irrational fears.

Elias started to leave when he drew up short. There was something he needed to do. He pulled his mobile from his pocket and dialed the number he had memorized in case of an emergency. It connected on the second ring.

"Rhona, it's Elias. I want you to know what's about to occur. No' because we can no' handle it, but you have a right to know who can be trusted and who can no'."

There was a beat of silence. Then she said, "Go on."

Elias took a deep breath. "I'm at Carwood Manor. I've been with Bronwyn since I helped her fend off an attack a few days ago."

"What?" Rhona asked in shock.

"The man's name is Sydney Russell. He's from Inverness. There isna time for specifics. Bronwyn got mixed up with him, and when her father tried to help her, Sydney killed him."

"Shite," Rhona whispered.

"Bronwyn's cousin became involved with Sydney, and Bronwyn took matters into her own hands."

"That's why she turned *drough*."

"Aye. It's also why she's used blood magic. That isna why I'm calling, though. Sydney is working with George to frame me. The man they found at my house was part of the group Sydney brought to Skye to attack Bronwyn. They were verra much alive when I left them."

Rhona's voice was fierce and steady when she asked, "When is this battle?"

"Tonight, on the estate. My team is helping Bronwyn, but I wanted you to know that once this is finished, I'm going to Frasier to make my statement and clear my name."

"We'll talk about that later," Rhona hurried to say. "I'm on my way."

"There's no need."

"There's every need," she said and hung up.

Elias pocketed his mobile and walked from the room. He found Bronwyn and Carlyle on the main floor. Bronwyn had just finished buttoning her coat when her head swung to him.

"You two had hours, and you chose now for a dalliance?" Carlyle snapped.

Elias shot him a flat look. "Does anyone actually say dalliance anymore?"

"Would you rather I say—?"

"All right, lads," Bronwyn said over him. She looked pointedly at Elias before sliding her gaze to Carlyle. "We apologize. There were things we needed to say, and we wanted to do it in private."

Carlyle wiggled his fingers as he pulled on his custom leather gloves. "There will be all the time in the world once we put Sydney and his associates in their places."

"About that," Bronwyn said.

Elias quirked a brow. "What's wrong?"

She licked her lips and played with her gloves. "I've been thinking. I know we agreed to capture them and turn them over to the authorities, but if, for some reason, things don't go according to plan, I'll be the one to take his life. My life is already forfeit with the blood magic."

"Absolutely no'," Elias and Carlyle said in unison.

Bronwyn lifted her chin and locked gazes with Elias. "You're already under suspicion for murder. I don't want any of this touching you."

"Agreed," Carlyle replied.

Elias turned his head to his friend. "Excuse me?"

Carlyle shrugged. "Sorry, mate, but Finn, Sabryn, and I already decided you won't be connected to any deaths for the time being."

"It isna going to matter. We're capturing them," Elias said to both Bronwyn and Carlyle.

Carlyle grinned. "Exactly."

"The plan is a good one. I was just overthinking it," Bronwyn said.

But they all knew the likelihood of things going according to plan was about a billion to one. The Knights were good, but no one was perfect. And Sydney had proven that he would stoop to new lows for what he wanted.

Carlyle tossed Elias his coat. Elias slipped it on. He left his head and hands bare since that was how he preferred to face his enemies. The three walked from the house. Bronwyn was the last to leave. She closed the door, put her hand on it, and bowed her head.

Elias spotted the blood on the wood. She met his gaze as she hastily pulled on her gloves. "What was that?"

Bronwyn looked away as she walked to her vehicle. "I made sure that if I should die, the blood magic will dissipate from the house."

Elias glanced at Carlyle, who shrugged, one brow raised. They climbed into Bronwyn's SUV and began the drive over rough terrain to the meeting spot. No one said anything as the vehicle bounced along. Elias thought about his father, who still had a hold of him.

He thought about his mother who had sacrificed everything for her children.

He thought about his sisters and how much time he had missed with them.

He thought about the friends who had become a second family to him and how they always had his back.

And he thought about Bronwyn.

He didn't know how much time he had with her, but he wouldn't waste a second of it. That only fueled the flames of anger at Sydney for putting her in the position she was in. And that, of course, caused Elias to wonder what might have happened between Bronwyn and him had he never left Skye. He could've been there for her so she wouldn't have felt as if turning *drough* and using blood magic were her only options.

But he couldn't change the past. What was done was done.

However, there was the present, and he and the other Knights could ensure that Sydney never bothered Bronwyn or Both again.

The SUV rocked to a halt. Bronwyn turned off the ignition and swiveled her head to him. Their eyes locked in the dim light of the interior. Their hands linked. Then there was movement from the back seat as Carlyle leaned forward and put his hand on theirs.

"Let's kick some ass," Carlyle said.

Bronwyn laughed, and Elias grinned. The three exited the vehicle. Elias slapped Carlyle on the back as he melded into the shadows. Elias walked around the front of the SUV to where Bronwyn waited. They stood in silence, each letting their eyes adjust to the darkness.

"I don't have a good feeling about this," Bronwyn whispered.

Elias leaned against the front of the vehicle. "I try no' to think about it. There are too many factors at play in any battle. You think you know what to expect, but there are always surprises. You heard us calling out different scenarios to prepare, but we couldna think of everything. No one is ever fully prepared. It's the ability to shift course quickly that is the answer."

"How many of these battles have you been in?"

"More than I like to admit." His breath billowed from his mouth in a white puff. "What you need to remember is that you're no' alone. We know what we're doing. Doona separate from us. We have each other's backs."

Bronwyn nodded. "Though I hate to admit it, I'm glad you're here."

"Me, too."

The night was cold and quiet. Elias had spent so much time in cities over the past years that he had forgotten how much he loved the peace of the countryside.

"Did you miss Skye?" Bronwyn asked.

He glanced over to find her gaze on him. "Nearly as much as I missed my family."

"Our community likes to talk about how much more powerful we are than other Druids, but have you noticed that we pay for it with unspeakable horrors? Look at what happened to your family. Mine. And there are others, I know it. They're just keeping things secret as we both did."

He nodded and saw her shiver. "You're probably right. Tragedy strikes everyone, but when you add magic into the mix, the stakes rise significantly."

"Sometimes I wonder if we should have magic. There was a point in history when Druids were revered and trusted. Now, we keep ourselves secret. We've gotten so good at hiding who we are that people with Druid heritage aren't even aware of it. Then there are those like Sydney who use their magic to harm others and expand their material things."

"It wouldna matter if Sydney did or didna have magic. He would always be the way he is."

"Maybe, but I know magic made it easier for him."

Elias scanned the open area and the tree line beyond. "Speaking of the wanker, he should be here by now."

Bronwyn pulled out her phone and looked at the time. "Any second now."

CHAPTER THIRTY-FOUR

Kerry had never minded the cold. In fact, she enjoyed it. While others huddled beneath blankets before a hearth, she stood in the moonlight. Of course, that had always been done in the privacy of her home.

Except for tonight as she waited for the upcoming showdown.

She parked as close to Carwood Manor as she dared. Her knees weren't what they used to be, which meant she couldn't walk long distances. The mist, however, was ever eager to do as she wanted. It had spread itself across the entire twenty-six-acre estate, waiting and watching.

While the mist was hers to control, it couldn't communicate with her. She solved that by telling it to look for Sydney Russell and his cohorts. Bronwyn would be wherever Sydney was. So, she waited and gazed at the millions of stars above.

Thick clouds that blocked out portions of the sky mingled with thin, delicate wisps that made the moon look milky as they slid past. The air was damp with the promise of rain. It was a beautiful night. Unfortunately, for some, it would end in their deaths. There was only one Kerry was intent on ensuring lived. Anyone else who got in her way would be dealt with swiftly.

The longer time dragged on without a word from the mist, the more concerned Kerry became. The battle was set for tonight. So where was Sydney?

She tapped her nail on the car and was about to call the mist when she spotted a tiny cloud of it speeding toward her. It coalesced into a writhing ball of moving vapors before stilling to hang in midair.

"Sydney has arrived?" she asked.

The mist moved up and down as if nodding.

"Good. Take me to him," she commanded.

The mist remained at the front of her vehicle. Once she was inside with the engine started, the mist moved away. She followed as it led her down the road and then onto the estate's main drive. Kerry turned off her headlights but left the fog lights on. It allowed her to see the mist but not alert others of her arrival.

Kerry drove down the long, winding drive at a slow pace until the mist veered off to the left. She continued following it until it stopped behind what had once been a large garden. The remnants of a tree, the thick, twisting branches of dead roses, and tall hedges hid her well enough as she parked.

She exited the vehicle and moved around the bushes to see the manor farther down the drive. Standing in front of the impressive house were four individuals attempting to get into the building.

Kerry started toward the manor while keeping to the

shadows. The four were intent on the house, though they scanned the area around them often enough that they were clearly worried about being discovered.

"Hurry the fuck up!" a man shouted. "Bronwyn will realize why I'm no' in the clearing soon."

So, that must be Sydney. Tall, thin, with a horrible haircut and dreadful taste in clothing. She didn't know what Bronwyn had seen in him, but that didn't matter. He wanted inside the manor. What could be within its grand walls that meant so much to him?

Kerry turned her head toward the mist. "Return to the others." Then she lifted her face to the sky. "Hear me, mist. Your master beckons you."

She sidled closer to the manor. The huge tree she hid behind would be the last bit of protection between her and the house. It was a good place to hide and wait for Bronwyn, because Kerry knew she would come.

The four attempted to break down the door. They tried to bust various windows. They even endeavored to pick the lock. But everything they did ended in defeat.

"Clever girl," Kerry murmured, impressed with Bronwyn.

"Something's wrong," Bronwyn murmured as the unease in the pit of her stomach intensified.

Elias nodded. "I agree. He's fifteen minutes late."

Bronwyn turned toward the manor as if something were pulling her attention there. "He wouldn't dare."

"Get in the vehicle," Elias urged as he gave her a small push.

Bronwyn didn't have to be told twice. She was inside with the engine started in seconds. As she floored the accelerator, something hit the side of the SUV. She slammed on the brakes, causing the vehicle to lunge forward. Then the back passenger door flew open, and Carlyle dove inside.

"Drive!" he bellowed.

Bronwyn stepped on the gas again as they sped off. "What about Finn and Sabryn?"

"They'll find their way to the manor," Elias said as he held on to the handle above his head.

Bronwyn shook her head. "I should've known he'd do something like this."

"He must know Beth is in the house," Carlyle said.

Elias grunted. "He suspects. What better way to find out than when no one is inside?"

"I should've known," she said again and drove faster.

"Careful!" Carlyle shouted as she jerked the wheel to miss a fallen tree.

Sydney had never hated someone as much as he did Bronwyn. She had been nothing but a bane to his existence since the beginning. He'd been fooled by her pretty face and adventurous spirit. He should've known that she would royally fuck up his life in every way possible.

But she wouldn't take Beth from him.

He knew how much Beth loved him. She would never have

willingly left, and nothing Bronwyn said could make him believe otherwise. He cared for Beth as much as a man like him could care about anything. But Beth's real appeal was her magic. With her by his side, he could acquire the things in his life that should've been his from the start. The only one standing in his way was Bronwyn.

"Break down the fucking door," Sydney ordered his crew.

Lucy stopped and glared at him. "What do you think we've been trying to do, Syd?"

"Oh, shut up and get back to it," he said, dismissing her.

Jacob bent over at the waist and rested his hands on his knees. "There's no way we're getting inside."

"There's always a way," Sydney replied.

Thomas glanced around. "It might go quicker if you helped instead of just issuing orders."

Sydney turned his head to Thomas. "If you want to return to Inverness alive, you'll keep your opinions to yourself." But the way Thomas continued fidgeting nervously caught his attention. "There's nothing out there."

"There is," Thomas insisted in an urgent whisper.

Sydney put his back to the manor and looked out at the landscape. The grounds could use a bit of work. Just like a woman to let things go. Proof that men were better at running estates—and the world.

"There's nothing out there," Sydney repeated.

About that time, he heard the revving of an engine approaching fast. He smiled and turned toward it. Bronwyn had finally realized where he was. He couldn't wait to get his hands on her. When he did, he was going to wrap his fingers around her neck and squeeze. Well, after he broke her body and spirit to get Beth's whereabouts. He would enjoy killing Bronwyn.

"There's the bastard," Elias said.

Bronwyn had spotted Sydney even before the headlights hit him. She gripped the steering wheel tightly. The hate inside her spun like a black ball of tar in her stomach, growing bigger and wider. As a *mie*, she would've been terrified of her overwhelming need to hurt Sydney.

As a *drough*, however, she looked forward to it.

Sydney had hurt countless people. He had killed her father. He had turned Beth into an uncaring arse. He had to pay.

And who better to collect payment than her?

Bronwyn slammed on the brakes when she reached the drive, causing the SUV to slide on the gravel and rock violently from side to side. "Carlyle, stay hidden," she ordered as she threw the vehicle into park and cut off the engine.

"Bronwyn," Elias called.

But she was done talking. She had dreaded this battle up until this moment. It had nothing to do with Sydney deceiving her again—she had expected that. The truth was, she had known she would embrace her role in doling out retribution. It was time for the nightmare that was Sydney Russell to end.

For good.

Bronwyn threw open the door and climbed out of the SUV, locking her gaze on Sydney as she walked to stand in front of the vehicle. Sydney wore his signature cocky smirk, the one that said he didn't know the meaning of failure. By the time she finished with him, he would. Because the woman he faced wasn't the same one who had run scared and devastated from Inverness. Grief, bitterness, and rage fueled her now. She was a storm he'd never see coming.

"Took you long enough," Sydney mocked.

Bronwyn's gaze cut to the left as Lucy and Thomas lined up with Sydney. Jacob was on his other side. The fury within urged her, *begged* her to kill them all right then. She could do it, too. All she had to do was release her magic.

Magic she had sought for just such an event. She had been afraid of the additional power, worried about how it would change her. She had even refused to use it for something as simple as fire because she told herself she needed to save it, to hold it until she needed it. It was laughable now that she embraced it fully. The potency of it, the utter dominance, was mindboggling.

The dozen different ways she could end the lives before her ran through her mind. She dismissed each of them because she wanted Sydney to suffer horribly, to scream in pain for hours while begging for her to end his life.

The creak of the passenger door broke into her thoughts. Bronwyn didn't need to look to know that Elias had shown himself. She didn't want him there to witness what she would become. There would be no coming back from the place she was going. She should've known that from the beginning, but she'd gotten too caught up in the wonderful feelings Elias gave her.

In his arms, she'd forgotten the horrors of the past and the fact that she was a *drough*. Elias turned her mind away from the blood magic and the payment that loomed over her. She shouldn't have given in to the pleasure he roused or the temptation of a future that could never be hers. Yet she didn't regret a single second of it.

Elias might by the end of the night, though.

Bronwyn didn't look at him. There was no future with him. She'd known that from the beginning. She was the one who had been too weak to send him away, to ignore the passion that tempted her like nothing else. Just one more bad decision.

Sydney flashed white teeth. "I see you brought a friend again, Bron. I thought you might, which is why I brought my own."

The shape of a woman took form in the shadows at the side of the house. The figure never looked at Bronwyn. Instead, her eyes were locked on Elias, her hatred palpable. Bronwyn didn't need to ask to know it was George. They had expected her to be in attendance, and it only fanned Bronwyn's anger.

George stopped on the other side of Jacob, her hands in her pockets as if she didn't have a care in the world. "No more hiding, Elias. You're going to pay for your sins."

"You want justice for the murders," Elias told her. "I understand. But it wasna me."

George shrugged one shoulder. "You should've turned yourself in. You might have stood a chance in court, but you made it plain that you weren't going to play by the rules."

"Rules?" Bronwyn snapped at the newcomer. "You haven't been playing by the rules. Shall we discuss *your* sins, seer?"

George's dark eyes narrowed on her. "Tonight isn't about me."

"Oh, you ensured it was when you showed up," Bronwyn threatened.

George pulled her hands from her pockets and quirked a brow. "You don't scare me, *drough*."

"That's your second mistake," Bronwyn stated.

George snorted. "It's two against five. You're outnumbered. Give up while you still can."

"You might want to count again," Elias said.

Bronwyn heard movement behind her. A heartbeat later, the sound of the other door to the SUV opening filled the silence.

"That's five against five, in case you were wondering," Sabryn declared from somewhere behind Bronwyn.

Sydney's smile slipped a little. "You found more friends, Bron."

"How 'bout we shut up and get to this?" Jacob interjected.

Finn laughed. "Wait your turn. Your time is coming, mate."

"You know, Bron," Sydney said, contempt in his words and bearing as he took a step toward her, "you could've had it all, but you had to go and fuck everything up."

Bronwyn's magic pooled in her palms as the black ball of wrath intensified. She lifted her hands a second after Sydney, so she didn't block his magic completely. Enough of it slammed into her that she went down on one knee.

Chaos reigned all around her as magic flew from one side to the other, but she wasn't worried about anyone but the man who had murdered her father. Bronwyn got to her feet slowly, the magic coursing in her so fast it could barely be contained in her body. She saw Sydney's eyes widen a fraction before she sent a surge of magic toward him.

CHAPTER THIRTY-FIVE

Elias dug in his toes as he was shoved backward in the gravel. He fought for breath after the assault of George's magic. There was no mistaking the hatred in her eyes directed at him. He'd had enemies before, but no one that came close to her. What made it worse was that he was innocent. There was no talking to her, though. He accepted that.

The only way he would unravel the mayhem he was embroiled in was to first subdue George. Running from his issues had never solved anything. He should've realized that sooner. Now, look where it had gotten him.

Elias pulled back his right arm and shoved it forward, hurling magic at George. He didn't put his full force behind it because he didn't wish to kill her. She, however, had no such compunction. Just as his shot landed on her shoulder, his knee buckled from another strike.

He rolled to the side and came up on his knees before releasing a blast. George cried out as she spun backward. Elias used the opportunity to get to his feet and glance at the others. As usual, Finn had gotten close to his opponent while Carlyle kept his distance. Sabryn used varying tactics to keep her adversary guessing. And Bronwyn was holding her own.

Her anger concerned Elias, though.

He didn't get a chance to do more as his focus returned to George.

"Dammit!" Rhona shouted as she slammed her hand against the steering wheel while speeding along the roads as she raced to Carwood Manor.

This was one of those times when Balladyn's teleportation ability would've come in handy. She was wasting precious time driving when she could be defusing a volatile situation.

Or engaging in battle.

"Dammit!" she said again.

Every time she thought she was coming into her own as leader of the Skye Druids, something happened. How had Corann handled it? How had he known how to react and what to do? Rhona knew it would take time. Corann had been leader for hundreds of years. No one knew the exact age of the now-dead Druid, but it had been far longer than any human should live.

And no one had ever discovered how he had lived so long.

Rhona didn't care about that. She just wanted to be the kind of adviser Corann had been. People had trusted him, respected him. She was still trying to earn that among many of those in the community. What irritated her most, was had Elias not phoned her, she would never have known about Bronwyn's problems, the battle, or George's involvement.

The more Rhona discovered about Georgina Miller, the more unsettled she became. Something wasn't right about George—or her arrival on the island.

Rhona nearly missed a sharp curve. She jerked the wheel and slammed on the brakes, making her tires squeal as she fought to stay on the road. Her heart jumped into her throat and time slowed for a split second before she got her vehicle back under control. Balladyn's name was on the tip of her tongue.

She could call him. He'd come immediately, but despite being the Warden of Skye, he was, first and foremost, a Reaper, beholden to Death. It was only by Erith's goodwill that Balladyn was able to spend as much time with her on Skye as he did. Rhona couldn't call him back every time something upset her. She needed to be able to handle things herself. And she could only do that if she stood on her own.

Rhona spotted the entrance to the Stewart estate as she came even with it. She had to slam on her brakes again and wait until the car slid to a stop before throwing it into reverse and pressing the accelerator. Then she shoved the gear into drive and turned the wheel rapidly onto the gravel-lined driveway.

As she drove like a maniac toward the manor, she saw of a group of people attacking each other.

"Here we go," she murmured as she hurried toward them.

She could kill Sydney. Bronwyn knew that for a fact. It would only take one assault.

And little effort.

The additional power she'd received upon turning *drough* assured it was possible. It roiled within her, in turns urging and demanding her to give in to the darkness. She had fought it for weeks. Buried it, ignored it.

But she couldn't do that anymore.

It was too loud. Worse, it matched the wrath within her, blocking out everything but one person—Sydney.

She delivered strike after strike. None of them killing blows. Yet. Just enough to cause him pain and knock him around. She enjoyed his suffering, but it did little to erase the image of her father crying out from the blow of magic Sydney delivered. It didn't stop the memory of her dad collapsing to the ground, never to move again.

It didn't ease her pain of never speaking to her father again.

Yet Sydney wasn't to blame for everything. A great portion rested on her shoulders. Maybe that was why she wanted to hurt Sydney so desperately. Because she couldn't hurt herself.

Or perhaps she already had by using blood magic.

Bronwyn tried to drown out her thoughts as she advanced on Sydney, easily dodging his half-hearted shots of magic while trying to scramble away. She could take him down and end everything. Bronwyn reared back her hand.

She came to a sudden halt when something stirred in the air, something she recognized. Bronwyn lifted her face and looked upward to see the mist advancing and receding in rhythmic movements that she realized were in time with her heartbeat.

At almost the same instant, she knew that whoever

controlled the mist was here. Bronwyn looked toward the oak. She couldn't see the person, but they were there. Watching. She wanted to know who it was and what they wanted, but she had Sydney to deal with first.

The bounce of headlights then caught her attention. Bronwyn glanced from the approaching vehicle back to the mist. Its attention was no longer on her. Instead, it was directed at Sydney.

The mist gathered together tightly, almost like a snake coiling as it readied to strike. Bronwyn couldn't explain it, but she knew it was about to attack. She hadn't felt any danger when it had been fixated on her. Indeed, it had almost seemed as if it were there to…support her…if that was possible.

"Bronwyn!"

She heard the panic in Elias's voice, but she couldn't look at him. Her attention moved between the mist and Sydney. It was going to kill him. She knew it with the same certainty she knew she was past saving. With the same sureness that she knew she loved Elias.

Elias.

She didn't want him to see what she was now, what she had fought—and lost—against. Deep down, she knew she would embrace the darkness of being a *drough*. That was why she hadn't wanted anyone fighting alongside her. She'd lied to herself when she said she was strong enough to ignore the wickedness that came with becoming *drough*.

All this time, she had thought about how she would make Sydney suffer in the hopes it would ease the emptiness and grief that had been her constant companions since she'd lost her father. She *needed* Sydney to physically hurt.

But did she have to do it? The mist was here. It could take Sydney's life. She wouldn't lose her soul to the darkness. Though she might have already and simply wasn't aware of it. She couldn't give in to her animosity and wrath and come away unscathed.

She looked at Sydney. His confidence was shaken. He breathed hard and couldn't put weight on his left leg. He also favored his right arm. She glanced upward and watched as he lifted his gaze. A smile pulled at her lips when his eyes rounded in horror, and a new kind of fear took hold of him—the kind of fright that froze a person in place.

Bronwyn was there, watching, and yet she felt detached from it all. As if she were watching it in a dream. She spotted Sydney's chest heaving as his breaths came quickly. She noticed the dots of sweat on his brow and the way he trembled. He tried to run, only to trip over his feet and fall on his arse, his hands behind him.

Her eyes drifted upward as the mist grouped itself into the unmistakable form of a fist. This was it. This was how Sydney would die. She had prayed for his death. In the next heartbeat, Sydney would be dead. Her nightmare would be over.

But then a memory surfaced of Elias gazing at her with such love in his eyes that she felt safely cocooned in it. Love blossomed rapidly and pushed away the hate and anger, tamped down the blackness that tried to claim her.

"You have my heart. My soul."

Bronwyn's eyes swam with tears before one dropped onto her face. She didn't hesitate as she loosed a scream and used all her magic to open a portal between Sydney and the mist. The mist back peddled quickly to keep from being sucked in. Then it retreated—and came for her.

"Bronwyn!" Elias bellowed again as he watched the mist turn and attack her.

He watched her lift her hands in defense, but she was no match for it. It plowed into her, knocking her sideways into the house, causing the windows to rattle. Then she fell in a heap, unmoving. Elias forgot about everything but her. He tried to go to her, but George used his distraction to deliver a hit that landed him on his back, knocking the wind from him so he saw stars.

Elias fought the panic that set in when he couldn't catch his breath, even as he attempted to roll to the side. Pain radiated everywhere, but his only thought was Bronwyn. The woman he loved, the one he had promised to save.

A foot pushed against his chest and kept him on the ground. He blinked, willing the pain to retreat to a manageable level. He wheezed, dragging air into his starving lungs. And found himself looking up at George as she stood with one foot on him, triumph in her eyes.

"You will pay for what you've done," George said.

Elias glanced at Bronwyn. She hadn't stirred, and the mist continued moving around her as if it hadn't yet decided whether to kill her or not. He reached out a hand to Bronwyn, needing to touch her one last time. But she was too far away.

He groaned as George put weight on his chest and leaned

over him. The little air he had managed to drag in dissipated quickly. The aches of his body combined with that in his heart was too much. The edges of his vision darkened. He tried to pool his magic to dislodge George so he could get to Bronwyn. If he was going to die, he wanted to be beside her.

George's face filled his vision as she knocked his hand away. "Your days of killing are done, asshole."

One minute, George was there. The next, she was gone. Elias didn't look for her. He rolled onto his hands and knees, pulling in air. He crawled as fast as his broken body allowed over painful gravel and between his friends still in the throes of battle.

All to get to Bronwyn.

Elias kept one eye on the mist and the other on his woman as he crept ever closer. When he finally reached her, he gathered her in his arms and settled himself against the manor. Then he looked at the mist. It sat there as if it were a sentient being studying him. And he couldn't say for sure that it wasn't.

"She saved me."

Elias glanced where Sydney sat frozen to the side, his wild eyes locked on the mist.

"She saved me," Sydney said again, disbelief coloring his words.

Elias looked down at Bronwyn and smoothed the hair from her face. One side was dotted with blood from hitting the ground. He'd promised that the night would end in their victory. Defeat wasn't something he was accustomed to, and he didn't like it. Mostly because Bronwyn had been hurt. But if he had to die, doing it holding the woman he loved was a good way to go.

Elias glared at the mist. "What are you waiting for?"

The mist shifted, readying to strike. Elias held Bronwyn

tighter, and there, in that moment leading up to their deaths, he found the will to say the words he hadn't been able to earlier.

"I love you," he whispered as the mist dove for them.

Instead of pain or the emptiness of death, there was a loud boom as all the windows of the manor shattered outward.

CHAPTER THIRTY-SIX

Rhona covered her head with her arms and ducked into a tight ball, waiting to feel the rain of glass. But there was nothing. She chanced a glance up and gasped when she saw the shards circling the mist and refusing to allow it to get away.

"What the bloody hell is happening?" asked a man with an Irish accent.

Rhona slowly straightened. She couldn't believe what she was witnessing. Her gaze darted around to determine who was responsible for the glass, but everyone seemed to be as shocked as she. Elias was near the front door, slumped to the side with a motionless Bronwyn in his arms. Near them was a man on his side, curled in the fetal position. George had risen onto her elbow near the SUV, her eyes wide. The remaining four men and two women had paused in their fighting to stare at the glass and mist that seemed to be having a battle of their own.

If none of them manipulated the glass, then someone else

out there was. And quite possibly the person who commanded the mist, as well.

Rhona turned in a slow circle, her eyes searching the darkness and shadows for a figure or anything that could give her a clue. No matter how hard she looked, she didn't see anything.

"Incoming," warned a woman with an American accent.

Rhona whipped around in time to see the mist fight to expand, but the glass held it tightly, refusing to let it budge. The unmistakable soft clink of a lighter opening filled the silence before the rasping sound of a spark wheel igniting, and then the hiss of a flame as the light broke through the night.

She turned to see a man with auburn hair glance her way before whispering to the tiny flame. In an instant, a spark shot up and out, directly for the glass and mist, growing larger by the second.

Rhona was about to extinguish it when the American lifted her hand and said, "We're trying to get rid of the mist. Wait."

Rhona hesitated, hoping she had made the right choice. The flame reached the glass and mist, and as she watched, the glass separated just enough for the fire to slip between it and the mist. Within moments, the mist began burning off. Rhona's lips parted in astonishment as it struggled much as a person would to stay alive.

Then it was over. One moment, the night was lit by flame, and then it was a tiny spark. With the mist gone, the glass fell to the ground in a pile, and the fire returned to the lighter.

The scrape of gravel broke the silence. Rhona looked over to George and stalked to the seer. "I'd stay right there if I were you."

"Finn," the American called.

The dark-haired man nodded before moving away from the

unconscious guy at his feet to stand guard next to a woman while the American limped toward Elias and Bronwyn.

"You picked the wrong side, Rhona," George said.

Rhona cut her gaze back to the woman. "Your mistake was coming to Skye, thinking you had the run of the isle."

"He's breathing," the American woman shouted. "So is Bronwyn. But they're injured badly."

Rhona held up a hand when the fire walker started to move.

He flashed her a smile after putting away the lighter. Then he bowed his head in a gentlemanly manner. "I was hoping I'd get the pleasure. Carlyle Oliver, at your service," he said in a refined British accent. He nodded at the dark-haired man. "That's Finn O'Connor, and Sabryn Beaumont is with our friends."

So these were Elias's colleagues. The Knights. The others, then, were Sydney and his acquaintances.

"You can't hold us," George said with a smirk. "It isn't like we can go to jail."

Rhona quirked a brow. "Who says you can't be detained?"

A small frown formed on George's forehead. "No police, not even the Druids here, would hold any of us."

"In case you've forgotten, you're on the Isle of Skye," Rhona said.

"And what's that supposed to mean?" George demanded.

Rhona smiled. "It means we have our own kind of punishment for Druids."

Kerry seethed. She fumed.

She almost walked from her hiding place and showed everyone there just what happened to those who fought against her and the Ancients, but she managed to hold herself back. Much more needed to be done before she could put everyone in their place. She wouldn't be the one to disrupt the Ancients' plans.

Even if she wanted to show the others what she was capable of.

Especially Rhona. She would pay for disgracing Kerry. Then there was Bronwyn. Of all people, Kerry had been so sure of where Bronwyn stood. She had seen the darkness take the *drough* that night. There was no way Bronwyn should've come back from that.

How had Kerry gotten it wrong? But she wasn't giving up on the Druid yet. The darkness was within Bronwyn, and it always would be. Kerry had been awed by the sheer strength of Bronwyn's magic. But that was what happened when a family could trace their heritage to one of the first Druids.

The Ancients needed those like Bronwyn. And she would make an adequate assistant when the time came. Kerry just needed time to work on her. As much as the young Druid had angered her by protecting Sydney, Kerry had learned to play the long game as the Ancients did. Small losses were nothing. It was the bigger battles that mattered.

She slipped back into the shadows and returned to her car while the others were occupied with the wounded and securing the prisoners. She knew exactly where Rhona would take them because *she* had been housed in the ancient Druid prison within the Red Cuillin.

Elias clawed through the layers of consciousness, his anxiety high. He was worried about something. No, he needed to get to some*one*.

Bronwyn.

"She's safe. Relax," someone said softly.

It took a moment to recognize Sabryn's voice. Elias forced open his eyes to find his friend sitting beside him. She wore a weary smile. Her right arm was in a sling, and she had cuts along her neck.

Elias shifted and immediately regretted it as pain shot through him. He grunted and closed his eyes as he fought a wave of nausea.

"Yeah. I'd stay still," Sabryn advised gently.

"Where am I?" he bit out.

"The manor."

"Did we…did we win?" he asked and opened his eyes again. Her deep blue gaze met his. "We did, indeed."

Elias searched the library for Bronwyn. "Where is she?"

Sabryn's gaze skated away as she pushed to her feet and faced the hearth, careful to keep her weight on one foot, signaling another injury to her leg. "She's in the parlor."

"What are you no' telling me?" he demanded.

Sabryn turned to face him. "She's not woken, Elias. We can't find any injury that would keep her unconscious. We all saw her hit her head…"

"And it's her second head injury," he finished. Elias gritted his teeth and used his hands to help him sit up. The room spun, but he fought against it.

"About bloody time," Carlyle said as he strode into the room. He rounded the sofa and stopped. "You had us worried."

Elias took in the black eye and giant bruise along the left side of Carlyle's face. "What are everyone's injuries?"

"Don't worry about that," Sabryn said.

Elias just stared at her.

Carlyle blew out a breath and moved to the chair, slowly sinking into it. "Our fearless leader there has a dislocated shoulder and a fractured kneecap. Finn has a broken wrist, two broken fingers, and bruised ribs. I also have some damaged ribs, along with the loveliness you see on my face."

"And you?" Sabryn asked.

Elias blew out a breath. "Everything hurts. No' sure I could pinpoint exact things right now." All he wanted to do was sleep for a year. He was physically and emotionally spent. He fought to pull up his last thoughts. "The mist was coming for Bronwyn and me. What happened?"

"The manor's windows shattered," Sabryn said. "Every damn one of them. The glass contained the mist."

"Who thought of that?" he asked.

Carlyle shrugged and then winced. "It wasn't us. I thought it was Rhona, but she said it wasn't her."

Rhona. That was right. She had been there. "Where is she?"

"The house wouldn't let her inside. She called a few of her people, and they took George, Sydney, and the rest away," Sabryn explained.

Elias was having a hard time keeping his thoughts in line between his pain and his worry about Bronwyn. It took great effort for him to move first one leg and then the other to place his feet on the floor. "If none of us caused the glass to break, then who did? Bronwyn was out cold, so I know it wasna her."

Carlyle exchanged a look with Sabryn. "We've been talking about that. I think it was the manor."

Elias turned his head toward the open windows hidden by the closed curtains. "Bronwyn used blood magic on the house. It has protected her. But for it to respond on its own?"

"It's something to consider."

"Like the manor acted on its own? Like it was sentient?" Elias asked, his brows raised.

Carlyle's face pinched in pain as he shifted in the chair. "I find it hard to believe myself, but it makes sense. We may never know. It isn't as if we can ask the house."

Elias steeled himself before he scooted to the edge of the cushion. He fought another debilitating wave of pain.

"You shouldn't be sitting up, much less standing," Sabryn scolded as she put a hand on his shoulder to steady him.

He looked up at her. "I have to see Bronwyn."

Instead of fighting him, Sabryn nodded slowly. "We'll help."

"You'll do no such thing," Elias told her. "Your knee, remember?"

Carlyle grunted loudly as he stood—and promptly fell back down. "Bloody hell, that hurts," he said between clenched teeth, his face pale. He found his feet on the second attempt and faced Elias. "I'll help."

"And chance us both falling?" Elias asked, somehow managing to find a grin.

Carlyle laughed before his face contorted in pain. "You're an asshole for doing that."

"No' my fault you laughed."

A fine sheet of sweat covered Elias by the time he got to his feet. He didn't know if anything was broken because everything hurt.

"I want it noted that it's a mistake for you to move," Carlyle said.

Elias nodded. "Noted."

He used furniture and walls to steady himself as he agonizingly made his way to the door. He glanced into the hallway and saw the distance he had to walk without something to hold on to.

"Bet I'm looking good right about now," Carlyle replied from behind him.

Elias chuckled. "I stand a better chance alone. I doona have to look at you to know you're swaying."

"You're both swaying, idiots," Sabryn stated.

A knock on the door had all three of them turning their heads toward it. Sabryn moved around Elias and limped to the entry. She opened it a crack to peer outside. Then she pushed the door wide. Elias spotted Rhona with Balladyn beside her.

"I'm hoping you can allow us inside," Rhona said to him.

Elias shrugged. "We can try. You and Balladyn are welcome."

Rhona tentatively put a foot out and was allowed entry. She walked in with Balladyn on her heels. "It looks like you all need some assistance."

"Perhaps you can talk him into returning to the library," Carlyle said.

Elias shook his head. "I have to get to Bronwyn."

"Then let me help," Balladyn said as he moved toward him.

Elias took the Reaper's hand, and when he blinked, he stood

beside Bronwyn's sofa bed in the parlor. She lay so still that he had to touch her to make sure she was still alive. Bending caused him pain, and he would've toppled over had Balladyn not caught him.

"Looks like we need healers," Rhona said as she entered the parlor.

Elias tried to nod, but the room went black.

CHAPTER THIRTY-SEVEN

"You should've called for me."

Rhona stood at the manor's door and waited for the healers to arrive. She glanced at Balladyn. It was the fifth time he'd made such a comment. He had been less than thrilled when he learned what she had faced alone. Even though she'd tried to tell him that she had to do things on her own, his protective nature wouldn't let it go.

"I'm fine," she told him.

His red eyes didn't move from her face. "I don't question your abilities, love. I just don't like you standing on your own when you don't have to."

She reached over and took his hands as she faced him. "There will be times I have to when you're doing your Reaper duties. We both knew that."

"I do," he said tightly. "That was before all of this went down."

She squeezed his hand as she heard the approaching cars.

"Thanks for repairing the windows. That will save Bronwyn a hefty sum."

"I'll feel better once I know who caused the windows to shatter."

Rhona let her eyes move around the manor's large entrance hall. "Sabryn thinks it was the house."

"It would be highly unusual. Then again, the Stewarts have lived in the manor for generations. You said it was built by Druids, which means magic has been in it from its very foundation."

She frowned. "And Bronwyn used blood magic on the manor."

"You'll get details when Bronwyn wakes."

"Let's hope the manor allows the healers inside." Rhona opened the door as four Druids stepped out of their vehicles.

Just as she feared, the house wouldn't allow them in. She had to call for Carlyle, who allowed them entrance. Rhona led the Druids into the parlor, where Bronwyn and Elias lay together on the bed.

"Let's see to these two first," she told the healers. "Then we'll focus on the rest."

Sabryn shook her head. "I know how much magic it takes to heal someone. Bronwyn and Elias are more important. My injuries will heal in time."

"So will mine," Finn stated.

Carlyle bowed his head. "What they said."

Rhona met Sabryn's gaze. She liked the leader of the Knights. They were an unlikely team, but they worked well as a unit. She suspected they had similar traumas that'd brought them together. Elias was loyal to them, and they to him.

Rhona wasn't a healer, but she would add her magic to theirs. The five of them moved to Elias's side of the bed and linked hands. She cast a look at Balladyn, who winked at her before she closed her eyes. Her magic rushed through her, answering her call. She joined in the ancient chant of the healers.

The magic that filled the room made her body tingle with awareness. Chills raced over her skin, and the hairs along her arms stood on end. For just a moment, she could've sworn she heard the drumbeat of the Ancients. Or maybe it was her imagination.

Rhona's breath locked in her lungs when she felt magic coming from beneath her. The only other magic besides hers she had felt was Balladyn's, but this was unmistakable. It wasn't Reaper or even Druid magic. It was stronger, brighter. It cut through her with dazzling intensity, and in its wake, she felt a connection to Skye that she'd never had before.

She focused on it, strengthening the bond that she innately knew was important. The magic suffused her in a blanket of warmth and peace. And, somehow, she understood that the isle had acknowledged her as the leader of the Skye Druids.

The quiet stillness, the serene tranquility that saturated Rhona was unlike anything she had ever experienced. She knew the potency of Balladyn's Reaper magic. She knew the strength of hers. And the combination was one that had never occurred before, leaving its own kind of sway.

But this, the pure magic of the earth that came directly from Skye was something else entirely. It may have taken her a while to accept the position Corann had given her, but it wasn't until now that it felt as if she were supposed to be here.

Rhona tried to hold on to the magic as it began to wane. She wasn't ready for it to leave, but she couldn't hold it any more than she could stop the tides. As it slipped away, an image of Corann standing at the Fairy Pools filled her mind. She had often found him there. The place was magic. Not because it had been how the Fae had come to the isle, but because the magic was more potent there.

She'd only had to visit the pools, just as Corann had, to feel the rush of magic again.

Rhona realized the chanting had stopped. She opened her eyes to find Balladyn in front of her, his face lined with apprehension as he held her hands.

"Where did you go?" he whispered.

She smiled, remembering. "I'll tell you all about it later."

Rhona glanced to the side to see Elias sitting up, his hand gripping Bronwyn's as he stared at her in earnest. Rhona's eyes then moved to Bronwyn, who still hadn't woken. Rhona turned to find Finn and Sabryn fully healed. Carlyle walked into the parlor with bruises still on his face.

"Ah. You're back with us," he said. "I've seen the healers out. Lovely people who don't like being told that I'll be fine without them."

Finn rolled his eyes. "They still checked him out before they relented."

"We were getting concerned about you," Sabryn said.

Rhona shook her head. "I was fine. Promise. When do they expect Bronwyn to wake?"

"They don't know why she hasn't," Balladyn told her. "They healed the concussion as well as the fracture in her hip."

"She should be awake," Elias said.

Rhona swung her gaze to him. "She will. Give her time.

While we wait, tell me everything. I need to know about George and Sydney, as well as Bronwyn's use of blood magic. I'm also extremely curious about what she opened to stop the mist."

"Aye. I've an interest in that, as well," Balladyn said.

Elias's bright blue gaze moved between them. "Bronwyn can open portals between dimensions."

"We stood in it for a short while," Sabryn added.

Carlyle nodded. "That was where we were when DI Frasier searched the manor for Elias."

"We weren't alone in there," Finn said.

Rhona's gaze jerked to the Irishman. "What do you mean?"

"I saw a shadow on the other side. It seemed to know we were there."

"Bronwyn plans to remove Beth as soon as she wakes," Elias said.

It was just one surprise after another. Rhona raised her brows. "I'm sorry, but did you say Beth is in there?"

Elias swallowed and glanced at his hand holding Bronwyn's. "You want to know everything. I'll tell you."

For the next thirty-two minutes, Rhona and Balladyn listened as Elias and his friends detailed it all. When they finished, Rhona sank into a chair in disbelief. She could hardly wrap her head around learning about Robert Stewart's murder. She hated that Bronwyn had felt she couldn't turn to anyone in her time of need.

"We'll sort things out with Bronwyn when she wakes," Rhona said. "For now, I'd like to focus on George and the proof she has on you."

Carlyle snorted. "There's no proof. Elias didn't murder anyone."

"We, ah, have someone getting into the police computers," Sabryn said. "The fifth member of the Knights is an internet expert known as Sabertooth."

"That's his real name?" Balladyn asked, his face creased with distaste.

Finn smiled. "It's his hacker name. No one goes by their real names in his line of work."

"He's our eyes and ears in places we can't go," Sabryn continued. "We keep things as legal as we can, but sometimes the rules have to be bent a little. As is the case with Elias."

Rhona nodded in agreement. "Theo is a good police officer. He's just doing his job, and I understand why he couldn't share anything with me. However, I want to know what proof George gave them."

"We're still waiting on that," Carlyle replied.

Elias blew out a breath. "I should've talked to Frasier the first time he asked. I never should've run, hoping I had time to clear my name. All it did was bring George and Sydney into each other's orbits."

"It's done. Let it go," Sabryn told him. "We need to move forward, and we can now. We'll clear your name."

Balladyn leaned against the side of the overstuffed chair Rhona sat in. "It appears someone wants Elias out of the way. We need to know if its George or someone else."

"There are a couple of people we can ask," Rhona said as she turned her head to look at him.

"By the way, where are George and the others?" Elias inquired.

"They're—" Rhona began when the fire in the hearth

suddenly fluttered as if a gust of wind had come through the chimney.

On the heels of that was the sound of a door slamming upstairs.

No one said a word. The atmosphere of the house had changed, moving from friendly and welcoming to what Rhona could only describe as troubled and agitated.

"Bronwyn?" Elias asked.

Rhona's head swiveled to the bed to find the Druid's eyes open. Bronwyn sat up and swung her legs over the bed. As she stood, her eyes lifted to the ceiling.

"All of you need to leave. Now," Bronwyn demanded.

Elias got to his feet and never took his eyes off her. "I'm no' going anywhere."

The house gave a loud moan.

Rhona frowned when she saw Bronwyn's face drain of color. Rhona got to her feet. "What's going on?"

"A problem I need to fix." Bronwyn looked at Rhona. "You don't want to be here." She then looked at the others. "None of you do."

Finn scrubbed a hand over his jaw. "It's that shadow I saw, isn't it?"

"Maybe." Bronwyn shook her head. "The house is warning me. Something is trying to come through."

Rhona got to her feet and looked at Balladyn. He gave a nod without her having to say anything. She should have known that he would always stand by her side no matter what she faced. "You don't have to do this by yourself, Bronwyn."

"She isna doing this alone," Elias replied.

Sabryn shrugged, her lips twisting. "The Knights have never turned away from a challenge."

"Count me in," Carlyle said.

Finn glanced at the ground. "Bugger it. I'm not going to run from a fekking shadow."

The sound of boards creaking as if something were bending them reverberated through the manor.

Bronwyn ran from the room.

CHAPTER THIRTY-EIGHT

Ice-cold dread filled Bronwyn's veins as she raced up the stairs as fast as her legs would carry her. The chilling voice that had whispered in her ear, "*It's coming!*" had jarred her awake. She'd been in the most amazing dream that'd begun with her parents before shifting to glimpses of life with Elias—one that even included children. She hadn't wanted to wake. Had actively fought against it because she knew what reality awaited her.

The house that had kept her safe and accepted her blood magic had gone above and beyond to warn her of the impending disaster. Bronwyn didn't have time to convince everyone to leave, and she knew Elias wouldn't go no matter what. She was grateful for his support, but she also feared what could happen to him and the others.

She tripped on a stair. Before she fell, strong hands grabbed her.

"I've got you," Elias said.

She looked at him. There was no panic in his eyes. Instead,

he showed her a calm, unruffled composure that bolstered her courage. Bronwyn squeezed his hand before continuing to the room.

They halted before the door, chests heaving from the exertion. Bronwyn concentrated on the entrance as the others filled the hallway. Everything looked normal, but she knew it wasn't. She walked to the door and tried to open it, but it wouldn't budge. She then placed her hand on it before snatching it away quickly at the emotion she sensed.

"The house is scared," she said.

Bronwyn licked her lips and prepared herself as she returned her hand to the wood. She closed her eyes and soothed her racing heart. Then she allowed warm feelings of love and gratitude to move from her into the house. Several long moments passed before the house gave a slight shudder and settled more peacefully. The distress was still there, but it wasn't as severe.

"I'll fix this," Bronwyn promised the manor.

Just as she was about to pull her hand away, images of the windows shattering and how the slivers had contained the mist flashed in her head. The house was showing her how it had protected her and her friends.

Tears prickled her eyes. "You've always protected me. Let me do that for you now."

When Bronwyn opened her eyes, she took a deep breath and let her hand skim down the wood to the handle. She gave the house another moment, and then she turned the knob and opened the door. This time, it swung open easily.

She had made so many mistakes during her grief and rage, things she would never have done otherwise. But that was what happened when a person sank into such despair. It didn't excuse her actions, though. Payment would come in the form of her death.

But that wouldn't happen today.

Bronwyn extended her arm before her, palm out, and said, "*Nochd*, reveal."

Her heart thudded as she watched the swirls of air begin thickening to become visible before moving as the vortex opened. Her eyes were locked on the maelstrom. It was so beautiful, and she had mistakenly believed that she had found a safe place for her cousin—a family member she had kidnapped. Someone she had made sure escaped the world when she hadn't given her mother the same opportunity. It didn't matter the reasons Bronwyn had helped Beth. It had been wrong on every level.

As the gap widened, Elias came up beside her and took her free hand. She linked her fingers with his. Until that moment, she hadn't realized how much she needed him and his strength. Just knowing he was there gave her the courage to face whatever was to come.

Before the breach filled the doorway, Bronwyn released Elias's hand and stepped over to the other side. She rushed to Beth and tried to lift her. Elias gently moved her aside and gathered her cousin in his arms. Bronwyn began turning when she saw the shadow. She did a double-take, her heart in her throat. It was enormous. She couldn't make out the shape, but she didn't need to. She knew whatever it was meant them harm.

It pressed against the thin veil that separated them, stretching it. She saw the outline of large talons as it tried to break through.

"Bronwyn!" Elias shouted.

She ran back through the opening. Bronwyn quickly lifted her hand and bellowed, "*Falach*, conceal!"

The vortex began to close. Her eyes were locked on the shadow that fought to get through its side to them. She didn't take her eyes off it until the fissure was finally closed. Then she leaned against the wall and rested her forehead on it in relief. A smile pulled at her lips when she felt the house return to its happy state.

Bronwyn straightened and turned toward the others. Elias met her gaze, wearing a smile of his own. They had done it.

"I have so many questions," Rhona said.

Sabryn chuckled. "I did, too."

"I've never seen anything like that," Balladyn said, his forehead creased in a frown as he stared into the room. "I didn't know anything like that was possible."

Carlyle cleared his throat. "What about Sleeping Beauty here?"

As if on cue, Beth moaned.

Bronwyn went into the bedroom and yanked the sheet covering the bed. "Place her here. She'll wake in a bit."

Elias gently laid Beth on the mattress and stepped away. Within moments, she put a hand to her head as her eyelashes fluttered open. She looked around groggily until her eyes landed on Bronwyn.

"Hey," Bronwyn said with a smile.

Beth sat up and glared coldly. "What did you do? Why am I here instead of Inverness?"

"I can explain," Bronwyn began.

"You damn well better," Beth stated as she swung her legs over the bed.

Elias said, "Give Bronwyn time to talk."

"Who the hell are you?" Beth demanded. She shook her head and threw out her arms in defeat. "You know what? I don't even care. I'm going back to Sydney."

"You can go back to Inverness," Rhona said. "Going back to Sydney will be another matter."

Beth's head snapped to the doorway where Rhona stood before she made her way to the Druid leader and pointed a finger at Bronwyn. "Do you know what she did? She hit me over the head in Inverness and brought me here. That's kidnapping."

"It is," Rhona said with a nod.

Beth made a sound. "What are you going to do about it?"

"Please, let me explain," Bronwyn tried again.

Beth crossed her arms over her chest and glared, but her attention was on Rhona. "Why did you say I can't return to Sydney?"

"Because he suffered a mental break. He's being looked after at a hospital now," Rhona answered.

Bronwyn looked at Elias, who shrugged as if he, too, had just learned that information.

"Excuse me?" Beth asked in a voice that said she didn't believe a word of it.

Rhona gave her a small smile. "I'll be happy to take you there. You see, a lot has happened while you've been here. Especially last night."

"Exactly how long have I been here?" Beth demanded as she looked at Bronwyn.

This was the part Bronwyn had been dreading. "Um…weeks."

"You're lying."

There was no outrage, no demands for reasons why, just a certainty that she was untruthful.

Bronwyn took a step toward her cousin. "I'm telling the truth. I know you'll hate me for what I've done, but I did it all for you. Sydney planned to use your magic for—"

"I know exactly why Sydney wanted me," Beth interrupted.

Bronwyn paused as surprise went through her. She was seeing her cousin with new eyes, and she didn't know what to think about what she saw. "You knew?"

"Yes," Beth replied.

Bronwyn was at a loss. Beth had always been so innocent, so trusting. What had happened to change her? But Bronwyn knew the answer. Sydney had happened. He'd sunk the claws of his wickedness into her. Gone was the sweet cousin Bronwyn had known. In her place was a cold woman who held no warmth.

"Well?" Beth prompted. "What else do you have to tell me?"

Bronwyn swallowed, the sound loud even to her ears. "Sydney came for you."

"He better have." Beth smiled then. "We love each other."

"And the fact that he killed my dad?"

Beth shrugged. "Sydney said it was an accident and that you overreacted. It happened because he defended himself against your attack, and Uncle Robert got in the way."

It felt as if someone had punched her in the stomach. Bronwyn gasped for breath, her fist on her chest as she bent over. Elias put a hand on her back. She was screaming inwardly, but outwardly, she managed to remain calm.

She looked at Beth. "You were here for the funeral. I told you everything."

"You did. Then I heard Sydney's side." Beth shrugged as if that said it all.

Bronwyn was drowning. She couldn't pull air into her lungs. She had known Beth would be angry, but Bronwyn hadn't been prepared for this reaction. This was something altogether different.

"You're my cousin," Bronwyn said.

Beth shot her a flat look. "And Sydney is the man I love. Are you telling me not to believe him?"

"That's exactly what's she's telling you," Elias stated angrily.

Bronwyn straightened and grasped his hand, needing him more than ever. "Beth, I'm not lying. I was there. Dad was as close to me as you are now. I never used my magic. I never attacked Sydney. He was the one who struck first, the blow directed at Dad."

"Then why didn't you go to the police in Inverness?" Beth demanded. Then pointed to Rhona. "Why didn't you tell her?"

A tear escaped, and Bronwyn hastily swiped it away. "Sydney hurts people, Beth. That's why I left."

Beth barked a laugh. "Oh, that's rich. He never wanted you. Sydney told me he tried to get you to leave several times. He was *relieved* when you were finally gone."

The room began to spin. Bronwyn clung to Elias. Was Beth right? Was that what had happened, and she misremembered? Bronwyn shook her head. No! She wouldn't be told that her memories were fiction. She knew they weren't. She had lived every painful second of it.

She dragged air into her starved lungs, and the room righted itself. She knew what was true and what wasn't. That was all she needed. It wasn't up to her to convince anyone else of that.

"You're wrong," Bronwyn replied. "About all of it."

Beth snorted loudly as she rolled her eyes. "I'm going to find Sydney, and we'll be back to settle this."

Tears stung Bronwyn's eyes, her heart splitting in two as she said, "Sydney isn't welcome here, and as long as you feel the way you do, neither are you."

A slow smile spread over Beth's face. "We'll see about that."

Beth then shouldered her way through the crowd at the door and stalked away.

The tears Bronwyn had been holding back coursed down her face. Elias pulled her into his arms and held her as she buried her face against his neck and cried for her many bad decisions, for the mess she'd made of her life, and for losing the only family she had left.

"She'll come to see the truth," Elias whispered in her ear.

She wanted to believe him, but she'd never seen Beth act like that before. Her cousin was different, and it had happened long before Bronwyn had brought her back to Carwood. Maybe she had always been like that, and Bronwyn hadn't seen it before. Or perhaps it was all Sydney's influence. Either way, Bronwyn suspected she was seeing a side of Beth that would likely never change.

It was a long while before Bronwyn's tears dried up. When she leaned back to look at Elias, he gently wiped the wetness from her face before kissing her forehead. The others had gone, leaving the two of them alone.

"Thank you for being here," she told him. "I don't know if I would've survived this without you."

His crooked smile melted her heart. "You would've. You're one of the strongest women I've ever known. There's nothing you can no' do all on your own. It's a privilege to be beside you. One I doona take lightly."

"Even though I'm *drough*?"

He looped his arms behind her. "Aye."

Bronwyn swallowed and glanced at his chest. "I felt the darkness inside me when I faced Sydney," she admitted. "I felt it, and…I embraced it. I let it take me."

"I know," he said solemnly.

She frowned up at him. "What?"

"I saw the change in you. I tried to get to you."

"I wanted to kill Sydney. I heard you shout my name, but…"

"You didna harm him," Elias said softly.

She swallowed, shrugging. "I thought about it."

"Thinking and doing are two different things."

"Maybe."

He gave her another crooked smile. "Trust me, I'm right."

She couldn't return the grin. "It was you who made me change my mind about hurting Sydney."

"Good." His bright blue eyes filled with warmth.

"I stopped this time. I might not in the future."

"We'll face that if the time comes. Right now, you need to think about how you overcame that darkness."

She nodded. "You're right." Then she frowned as she sorted through her memories. "I remember stopping the mist, and I remember it attacking me." Bronwyn pulled out of his arms. "We need to find the others. There are things I need to tell everyone."

Elias took her hand, and they walked downstairs together. They found the others in the library. The conversation ceased when they walked in.

"I tried to drive Beth somewhere, but she wasn't interested," Sabryn announced.

Bronwyn smiled gratefully. "Thank you. I, um, I need to tell all of you a few things. First, the person who controls the mist was here."

"What?" several asked in unison.

Bronwyn's gaze moved to Rhona, whose interest had sharpened. "I couldn't see them, but they weren't far. They hid behind a tree. While I have no proof other than a feeling, I think the mist was there to help me.

"I second that," Elias said. "We all saw it. It could've attacked any of us at any time, but its focus was Sydney."

Bronwyn moved to the fire, trying to thaw the coldness that had settled around her since Beth's hateful words. "I…was going to let it kill Sydney," she admitted softly. She closed her eyes and shook her head, shame filling her. "I wanted his death, but I feared doing it myself."

"But you didn't let it kill him," Carlyle said.

She opened her eyes and looked at the Englishman. He gave her a nod. Bronwyn blinked rapidly to stop the tears. She took a deep breath and slid her gaze to Elias. "Then I thought of you. Of…us. As I told you upstairs, it shoved aside the darkness within me and cleared my head. That was when I stopped the mist."

"And the mist attacked you," Elias said.

Sabryn frowned. "It didn't kill Bronwyn, though."

"There must be a reason for that," Balladyn said.

Bronwyn grew uneasy at the Reaper's words because they were true. Why hadn't the mist taken her life? She had felt its anger.

"We still don't know who shattered the windows," Finn said into the silence.

Bronwyn cleared her throat. "Actually, we do. The house showed me all of it upstairs. It was the manor who took the initiative and protected us."

"It protected *you*," Elias said.

Rhona nodded. "I agree. The connection you have to the house is something I've not see before. We're glad it stepped in. Otherwise, none of us would be here now."

"Bloody hell," Finn replied in a hoarse tone. "The manor."

Bronwyn watched as everyone looked around them as if seeing Carwood for the first time. She smiled as she sensed their appreciation and gratitude, and she knew the house did, too.

"So, what now?" Sabryn asked. "Sydney seems to be taken care of. What about George?"

Rhona sighed. "There are few Skye Druids who might remember that we have a prison of sorts. It's deep within the Red Cuillin. I recently had to make use of it for a short while, and I was tempted to transport the group who attacked tonight."

"Tempted?" Carlyle said, one brow raised. "I take that to mean you didn't?"

"I did not. Times have changed, and while it might have been acceptable to put Druids away before, I'm not inclined to do that without good cause," Rhona said.

Elias jerked back as if struck and angrily asked, "And them attacking us wasn't a good cause?"

Bronwyn had to agree with him. If anyone should be locked away, it was the five they had battled earlier. But she was a blood magic practitioner, and she thought it better to keep her mouth closed for the time being.

"If you didn't take them to your prison, then where are they?" Finn asked.

Rhona turned her head to Bronwyn. "I didn't lie to Beth. Something in Sydney's mind broke at the sight of the mist. He's in a psychiatric hospital under observation to determine the extent of the damage to his mind. I'm not sure he'll ever get out."

"That means Beth and I are free of him." Bronwyn sighed in relief. She might have done irreparable damage to her relationship with her cousin, but at least Beth wouldn't be under Sydney's influence any longer.

Sabryn tucked her hair behind an ear. "And the others?"

Rhona hesitated a moment. "They're with Theo at the police station where various charges are pending."

"Then nothing is finished." Finn shoved to his feet and sighed loudly. "Elias is still being looked at for murder."

Elias nodded slowly. "I'm going to talk to Frasier today. It's time."

"You won't be going alone," Sabryn said.

Carlyle stretched his legs out. "No, he will not."

"That's probably a good idea," Balladyn told them. "You all can account for Elias during the time that George is claiming he killed."

Finn rocked back on his heels. "Gladly. Except none of us were with him the night Sydney's man was killed."

"We'll figure something out," Sabryn stated.

Rhona's green gaze moved to Bronwyn. "I'd like a private word, please."

"Nay," Elias stated.

Bronwyn gave him a quick smile. "It's okay. I was expecting this."

"I wasna," he replied.

She walked to him and took his hands in hers. "Go talk to Frasier. We'll meet back here."

He searched her face before nodding once. "There are things we need to discuss."

"There are," she agreed.

Elias leaned down and pressed his lips to hers in a soft, lingering kiss. "You're no' alone," he whispered.

"I know," she said as she squeezed his hand.

CHAPTER THIRTY-NINE

Bronwyn wasn't prepared to find herself taken from the manor to Rhona's house in a split second. Yet that's exactly what had happened. She looked around the homey cottage and immediately missed the manor. She had agreed to the discussion at Rhona's, and there was no going back on that now.

"Tea?"

Bronwyn turned her head to see Rhona walking toward the kitchen. "I'm fine, thanks."

There was no sight of Balladyn now. Bronwyn wasn't sure how that made her feel. She drew in a shaky breath.

"I wish you felt you could've come to me," Rhona said, her back to Bronwyn as she filled the electric kettle with water.

Bronwyn clasped her hands together to keep them from shaking. She had much to answer for. Turning *drough*, using blood magic, not reporting her father's murder, and kidnapping and imprisoning Beth. The outcome couldn't be good, no matter how she looked at it.

"If it makes you feel better, I wouldn't have gone to Corann, either," Bronwyn told her.

Rhona turned the kettle on. As the water heated, she crossed her arms over her chest and faced Bronwyn. "I have to admit it does—a little. Our community has survived all these thousands of years because of the structure we have in place. I used to balk at it, but I see the sense in it now." She paused and reached for a mug. "I'm still learning. Corann never prepared me for any of this. I had no idea he wanted me to take his place. I'm sure he thought he had many years before his time was finished."

"But here you are."

Rhona grinned. "But here I am. I don't know the right answers. I have to follow my instincts and fall back on the things we're taught. The deputies handle the majority of the issues. The larger things fall to me."

"Like someone becoming *drough*."

"Like that. Elias explained a lot to me. I wish it had come from you, though."

Bronwyn lowered her gaze to the floor for a heartbeat. "There are many things I wish I could take back, but what's done is done. I could attempt to explain my emotions and what drove me to choose the paths I did, but you wouldn't understand because you haven't been in my shoes."

"You're right. The most I could do is empathize. Which I have." Rhona motioned to the table. "Sit, please."

Bronwyn took the chair as the kettle signaled it was ready with a beep. Rhona gathered loose-leaf tea in a holder and placed it in a mug before pouring water over it.

"Ariah makes the best teas. This one helps ease anxiety. I find that it helps. If you want to try it," Rhona said as she set the cup in front of Bronwyn.

She inhaled and caught the scents of lemon balm and ginger. Bronwyn wrapped her hands around the mug and sighed as heat seeped into her skin. She hadn't realized she had been shaking until that moment.

Rhona sat opposite her and folded her arms on the table. "The community's treatment of you has been abysmal. As you know, you aren't the only *drough* on Skye. Every leader of our people has made the decision to welcome *any* Druid who vows not to do evil."

Bronwyn stared into the mug, watching the steam rise in wispy curls. This was it. This was what she had dreaded since deciding to seek out the extra power of being a *drough*. She would have to leave Skye, leave the manor. "I understand."

"Understand what, exactly?"

Bronwyn looked up to find a frown of confusion on Rhona's face. "I understand that you want me to leave Skye."

"This is your home. Your family's seat is Carwood Manor. There have been generations of Stewarts since the time of the very first Druids on Skye. You're not going anywhere unless you decide that for yourself."

Bronwyn could only shake her head in bewilderment. "But...I thought..."

"I can see how you would think that." Rhona compressed her lips. "You felt the darkness."

"I didn't just feel it. I welcomed it."

"As you explained earlier. However, you didn't give in to it."

"You have no idea how close I came."

Rhona smiled sadly. "The difference is that you chose not to."

"What if I'm not that strong again?"

"That is something each of us faces every day of our lives. I suspect it will be more difficult for you since you are *drough*, but I don't doubt you can handle it. You faced the man who took your father's life. Honestly, I'm not sure I could've turned the darkness away if I had been in your place. You worry about what you'll do in the future, but I suspect you'll be just fine."

Bronwyn wished she had Rhona's conviction. She had never felt such anger before, but really, her anger had been directed at herself—because everything that happened began with her.

Rhona reached across the table and took out the tea. She set it in the sink before returning with a spoon and honey. Bronwyn accepted them, filled the spoon, and then let the sweetener dribble into the tea, writing Elias's name. She hoped he was faring well.

"What I brought you here to discuss was the use of blood magic," Rhona said.

Bronwyn stirred the tea, using the time to brace herself before taking a drink. It was smooth and delicious, the flavors blending so well that neither overtook the other. She drank more before setting the mug down and meeting Rhona's gaze. "What's the punishment for using it?"

"You know the punishment, and it's handed down by something mightier than anyone on this planet."

Bronwyn nodded. "My death."

"We know very little about blood magic or its uses. As you know, we're never taught anything about it other than not to do it because it results in the person's death. How did you know about it? More importantly, I'm curious what it felt like becoming *drough*."

Bronwyn leaned back in the chair but kept her hands around the mug. It was the first time anyone had asked her those questions. Elias accepted her for who she was, but she suspected she would tell him every detail later.

She was impressed at how Rhona handled the situations around her and was surprised by the queries. Just as she was about to begin, Rhona held up a hand.

"One other question. What was the ceremony? How did you even know what to do?"

"When I was in Inverness, Sydney showed me a book. I know it was stolen because he crowed about that. In the tome were various ways to become *drough*."

"Various?" Rhona asked, her eyes wide. "I thought there was only one ceremony."

"You mean the one where the Druid promises their soul to the Devil?"

Rhona nodded. "That one."

"There are others. I studied the book. So many things in there are never taught. I understand why children aren't told about blood magic or becoming *drough*, but eventually, they should be. They need to understand every aspect of being a Druid. The good. The bad. And the ugly."

Rhona's face was lined with thought. "I believe you have a valid point."

"Though there are different ceremonies for those who choose the path of a *drough*, they all result in the same ending."

"That of darkness entering your magic."

Bronwyn nodded. "Exactly. It's what gives a Druid added power. And it's heady." She paused and licked her lips. "Have you ever felt an electrical current?"

"Aye."

"It's very similar to the instant rush of additional magic. I felt like I could've walked on water, that there wasn't anything I couldn't do. The blast waned, of course, but anytime I turned to my magic, it flooded me twice as powerfully as when I was *mie*." The smile faded from her lips. "However, with that surplus came the darkness. I didn't notice it at first, which allowed me to naïvely believe I could control it. It was always there, waiting for when I'd give in to my anger about Sydney."

Rhona listened intently. "What did it do?"

"It wasn't pushy. Nay, it was tempting, seductive. It said the things that fed my fury—and itself. Yet I still thought I'd be in control when Sydney showed up. I feared the only way I could stop him was to end his life. And if I did that, then it would be like I *had* given my soul to the Devil."

"Which is what it wants."

Bronwyn released a long breath. "Aye. The darkness won't stop until it achieves that. I saw the different ceremonies and believed I could skirt that. It's a trap a Druid doesn't realize they're in until the darkness has them."

"We're a community on Skye. No one, absolutely *no one*, should ever feel that alone. I'm sorry you believed you didn't have anyone to turn to."

Bronwyn drank more of the tea. Then tension inside her had begun to ease from her muscles. She stopped shaking, but the anxiety hadn't left her completely. "A lot of things change when you become *drough*. Things I never knew. You hear about Druids turning to the dark for the power, and I certainly got that. And it makes it easier to take revenge. It's what I craved when I faced Sydney and contemplated his death."

"No one could blame you for that. I certainly don't," Rhona said.

"I blame myself."

"Forgiving ourselves is sometimes the hardest thing we'll ever do."

Bronwyn smiled wryly. "No truer words have ever been spoken." She took a breath and slowly released it. "You also wanted to know about blood magic. I learned about that in the book, too. The writer explained the ease of using it. And it *is* very easy. It's only ever whispered about, so I expected there to be some kind of ritual or ceremony."

"There isn't?" Rhona asked in shock.

Bronwyn shook her head. "It's merely a matter of using your blood with magic. My family has always used wards to protect the house from evil, curses, and the like. I added my blood to that magic and a chant to refuse entry to anyone unless I granted it."

"I gather you then gave that power to Elias and the Knights?"

"Aye. In case something happened to me."

Rhona sat back in her chair. "Thank you for sharing that information. I don't suppose you still have the book?"

"It was one of Sydney's prized possessions. I have no idea where it is now."

"Pity. But you remember what was in it?"

"I do. Would you like me to share it with you?"

Rhona's shoulders lifted as she inhaled. "Actually, I had another thought. How do you feel about teaching us? Starting with the adults. Then we could figure out how young we think the Druids should be before we impart such information. It's time to stop whispering about things and fearing them. It's time to bring things out into the open."

"You know by doing that there will be *mies* who become *drough*."

"That happens anyway." She motioned to Bronwyn. "Case in point."

Bronwyn wrinkled her nose. "True. What about the fact that my days are numbered?"

"That is something for you to consider. Do you know how long you have?"

"Not really. I used blood magic sparingly, but I'm not sure that matters."

Rhona's lips curved into a smile. "Then you have a lot to think on. Regardless, I'll be implementing some changes immediately."

When Bronwyn looked down into the mug, she was surprised to see that she had drunk it all. She did have things to think about, but right now, her mind was focused on one person —Elias.

Rhona stood. "I'm sure you'd like to see Elias."

"I would," Bronwyn said with a smile.

Balladyn suddenly appeared out of nowhere. He held out his arm. "I'll take you."

CHAPTER FORTY

Elias sat in DI Theo Frasier's office, drumming his fingers on the desk as he waited for Theo to return. Elias didn't know how Saber had pulled it off, but he'd sent a video to Frasier that showed Sydney and his gang pulling into Elias's drive and throwing a dead body out of their vehicle before speeding away.

It had completely slipped Elias's mind that there might be cameras outside the house if he had found them within. Maybe he could've avoided this fiasco if he'd thought of that sooner.

The door to Frasier's office opened, and he entered. He tossed a file onto his desk as he sank into his chair with a sigh. Then he looked at Elias. And simply sat there.

"Well?" Elias asked, brows raised.

Frasier leaned back in his chair and linked his hands over his stomach. "Forensics has reviewed the camera footage from the home you're leasing, and they say it's no' been tampered with."

Elias held back a snippy response. That wouldn't benefit him right now. "I told you I didna kill anyone."

"It would've been better had you come in earlier with that evidence."

"With George telling anyone and everyone that I'm a murderer? Who would've believed me?"

"Me," Frasier snapped as he sat forward. "Because it's my job to follow the evidence, no matter where it leads."

Elias nodded. "I know that. Only, her accusations were stirring up everyone. The next thing I knew, there was a dead body in my drive."

"We're handling the individuals involved. We've located the vehicle and processed the prints inside, which just happen to match the three individuals Rhona brought to us. The fourth, it seems, is in a psychiatric hospital, yelling about mist coming for him." Frasier paused and glanced out the windows of his office before lowering his voice. "You're all lucky it didna kill you."

Elias blew out a breath. "We're verra aware of that. Bronwyn thinks the one controlling it was there."

"You mean one of those I locked away?" he asked with a frown.

Elias shook his head. "Someone else."

"Bloody hell. Please tell me she saw a face or something identifiable."

"Sorry. She didna."

Frasier beat his fist once on the desk. "Fuck. I thought we were done with that."

"I wish I could say we were. It's still around, so everyone needs to be vigilant. What about George? What's going to happen to her?"

"She's being charged with filing a false report and perverting the course of justice."

Elias felt some relief about that. "What about the accusations against me for the murders in Edinburgh?"

"That's out of my jurisdiction. I know she went to the authorities in Edinburgh. Has anyone contacted you?"

He shook his head. "I didna even know about any of it until she came here."

Frasier ran a hand down his face and leaned back in the chair once more. "I'll see what I can find out. George has made some enemies on Skye, no' the least of which is Rhona. However, she did make some friends."

"In other words, people who are demanding my head."

"In a manner of speaking." Frasier blew out a breath. "The coroner has ruled the death of the man found at your home as natural."

Elias was taken aback. "Natural?"

"Heart attack, it appears."

Elias remembered that Bronwyn's father had died of something similar—though it had come from Sydney, which meant there was nothing natural about it.

"You're no longer a suspect in the murder here. I can no' say the same for anywhere else," Frasier said, breaking into Elias's thoughts.

He rubbed his hands on his thighs. "I'm no' a murderer."

"Let's keep it that way, shall we?" Frasier stood and extended his hand.

Elias rose and shook it, a weight falling from him that he never thought to dislodge.

"Your family and friends are waiting in the lobby," Frasier told him.

Elias smiled and walked from the office a free man. He

wouldn't have been able to say that if it hadn't been for the Knights, who had ensured he was proven innocent. When he exited the station's locked door and entered the lobby, Elodie was the first to fly into his arms. He held her, more grateful than ever to have his family back.

"Are you really free?" she asked as she stepped back.

He nodded and looked at Edie. "It seems the security camera outside showed everything."

"I should've thought of that," Edie said with a frown. "I'm sorry, Elias. I've had so much on my mind that I didn't think about it."

He waved away her words. "None of us did. It all came out in the end."

"It's time to celebrate," Finn said as he clapped his hands together once and rubbed them vigorously.

Carlyle nodded. "I second that. We've earned it."

Scott put an arm around Elodie and grinned. "We didna doubt you for a moment, Elias."

"We can talk at the pub. I need a drink or three," Sabryn said.

Edie's face wrinkled. "I can't, guys. Sorry."

"Just one drink," Elodie begged.

Edie shook her head. "I've got an appointment I can't miss. I'll be there in spirit."

Elias pulled Edie against him for a hug. He kissed the side of her face. "How about dinner on Thursday? I miss my niece and nephew."

"I'll make it happen." Edie rubbed her hands up and down his arms as she leaned back. "I'm glad you're free. Have fun tonight."

Elias watched her hurry from the station.

"Something isn't right at her house," Elodie whispered as she leaned close.

Elias's brows drew together as he looked at her. "What do you mean?"

"I'll explain later. Right now, we're celebrating."

"Finally," Finn stated and turned to walk out.

When he got to the door, Elias heard him greet someone, but Scott was talking, so Elias didn't hear who it was. It wasn't until Sabryn walked out and Carlyle stepped aside that Elias got a look.

"Bronwyn," he said as a smile pulled at his lips.

She returned his grin. He closed the distance between them in a few strides and wound his arms around her. She felt so good against him. He closed his eyes, grateful for how everything had turned out.

Then he kissed her. A long, slow kiss filled with all the love and hunger he possessed for her. He no longer wanted to go for that drink. He wanted to return to Carwood with Bronwyn so he could tell her how he felt. And make love to her all night.

The catcalls had him and Bronwyn giggling, which ended the kiss. He gazed down at her and sighed, his heart fuller than it had ever been.

"I hear you're no longer a suspect," Bronwyn said.

He moved aside a lock of her beautiful, brunette tresses. "Aye."

"We're going to celebrate," Carlyle said.

Elias lifted his head to tell them he had changed his mind when Bronwyn put a finger over his mouth.

"Nay," she said with a smile. "We're going. We can talk later."

Scott chuckled. "I like her."

Elodie playfully slapped his chest. "Behave. Hey, Bronwyn. Let me introduce you to Scott."

"The guy who stole her heart," Scott said as he winked at Elodie.

Bronwyn smiled as she nodded at Scott. "I think she might have been the one to steal yours."

"She most definitely did."

Finn yelled from outside the open door. "Can we go now? I'm freezing my bollocks off."

"Aye, let's go," Elias said as he and Bronwyn walked hand in hand from the station.

The cloud over him wasn't completely lifted. It was still possible that the authorities in Edinburgh would come for him, but if and when they did, he'd face it head-on. He didn't have anything to hide. He wasn't the murderer George sought, and he could prove it if it came down to it.

He hadn't just exonerated himself from a murder on Skye. He had also faced his past in many ways. His anger toward his father would probably come up unexpectedly, but he wouldn't ignore it any longer. Nor would he run from things anymore.

Because he had something to hold on to—Bronwyn.

Even though he knew their time was short, he planned to savor every second they had. Because his other option was not having her in his life, and he simply couldn't handle that.

The celebration at the pub was loud, the conversation abundant, and the laughter boisterous. Drinks flowed, toasts were given, and memories made. He was surrounded by his closest friends, family—minus Edie and her crew—and the love of his life.

Yet he was more than ready to call it a night after a few hours. He sighed in contentment when he and Bronwyn finally returned to the manor.

She leaned against the closed door. "It's good to be home. I wasn't sure I'd get to return here."

"You thought Rhona would ask you to leave?"

Bronwyn nodded. "I did."

"How did that conversation go?"

"Good. Different than I thought."

Bronwyn took him into the library and explained her conversation with Rhona, and Elias was just as surprised.

"What are you going to do?" he asked when she finished.

She tucked her legs against her on the sofa and leaned into his side. "I think it's a great idea to teach the Druids more than we know. I have two concerns, though. One is that I don't have the book as proof. They'll have to take my word for things, and we both know how I've been treated."

"You have a point. Perhaps we can search Sydney's things for the tome."

"Maybe. But that brings me to my second issue." She looked up at him.

Elias saw her worried expression and knew immediately what bothered her. "You're thinking about how much time you have left."

"I am. It's hard not to, after all." She looked toward the fire and shrugged. "I want to teach what I've learned. I want others to know that being *drough* doesn't necessarily make someone evil."

He squeezed her against him. "I agree."

"But there's one thing I want more than that." Her hazel eyes reflected the dancing flames in the hearth. "I want you."

"You have me."

She shook her head and shifted to the other side, pulling away from him. "But we won't have a future. Not the kind I want or that you deserve."

"I doona care if I get one hour, one year, or a lifetime. The fact that I'll be with you is enough."

"Users of blood magic have violent deaths, Elias. I don't want you to witness what's coming for me."

"And I doona want to be anywhere else but beside you. I…" The words clogged in his throat again. He shoved aside his worry about becoming his father and focused on the man he was. Then he faced her and swallowed. "I love you."

As soon as the words were out, he smiled, relief rushing through him. Nothing had ever sounded so right. He had no idea why those words had been so hard to say, but now that he had said them when she could hear it, he would never hesitate again.

"I love your stubbornness and your strength. I love how you dribble honey into your tea. I love the way your eyes change color with your emotions. I love that you never give half measures on anything. I love that you follow your heart no matter where it might lead you." He smiled. "I love that you talk to the house and that it somehow communicates with you and protects you. I love that you'll move Heaven and Earth for those you care about."

Tears welled in her eyes before dropping onto her cheeks. "Stop. Please," she whispered.

He shook his head and moved closer. "I can no'. You said I

had your heart and soul. I know the feeling of your love, Bronwyn. It's bright and warm and all-encompassing. I found myself again. With you."

She wiped at her face and sniffed as she glanced away. "Those are beautiful words. The kind a woman longs to hear."

"I mean every one of them." He took her hand and rubbed his thumb across her skin. "Look me in the eye and tell me you doona love me."

"I cannot," she said as more tears fell.

Elias wiped them away. "Everyone and everything dies. It is the cycle of life. I'd rather spend what time we have enjoying each other than worrying about when and how one of us will go. That would be squandering the gift we've been given. What we have, this love between us, is special."

She dashed her tears away with her free hand and sniffed. "When I was unconscious, I dreamed of us and our future. I dreamed of our children."

Elias smiled. "Sounds like a verra nice dream."

"It was amazing. Then I woke to reality, still craving that which will never be in my grasp."

"I'm here now. I'm yours."

She turned to him. "You have no idea how much I yearn to take everything you're offering."

"You already have. You felt the same things between us that I did. I told you that you are no' alone anymore, and I meant that. If you're hesitating because you worry for me, doona. I've made my decision. I willna change my mind. I'm no' going anywhere."

Her face crumpled as her shoulders shook. She covered her face with her hands and sobbed. Elias sat frozen, unsure what he had done to cause such suffering—and wondering how the hell to fix it. He looked around helplessly.

Suddenly, Bronwyn threw her arms around him, her body colliding with his and sending him backward onto the cushions. He held her with a grin as she kissed along his neck and cheek until she reached his mouth.

Then she lifted her head and smiled through her tears. "I love you. I love you. I love you."

"Och, lass," he murmured. "You scared me."

"I don't want you to go anywhere, but I needed to know that you understand what's coming."

He smoothed her hair from her face and felt his eyes blur with unshed tears. "I'll say it every day we're together. I doona want to be anywhere but with you. My heart. My soul."

"My heart," she whispered and gave him a soft kiss. "My soul," she said and kissed him again, this time letting her lips linger.

Elias deepened the kiss as desire shot through him. He held Bronwyn tightly and heard her answering moan when he ground his arousal against her. As they gave in to desire, he could've sworn he heard the manor sigh with happiness.

EPILOGUE

A week later…

It was the smell of delicious food that pulled her away from her computer. She closed the laptop and set it aside, her gaze roaming the parlor. She'd moved her things into the master bedroom, where Elias had added his. The sofa bed was tucked away now, and the parlor was as it should be once more.

A lot had changed in a week. Every day was a different adventure with Elias. His interest in the manor had sent them exploring every part of it, opening rooms long shut and finding furniture that had been stored from generations before. They had begun to put the house back as it had once been.

They'd even found some old family portraits that had been tucked away. Once the walls were newly painted, they would hang them. In addition to her ancestral finds, there were new items, including a beautiful vase that was a gift from Carlyle. Not to be outdone, Finn gave them a box of books, some first editions to add to the semi-bare library.

Then there was the shipment of silver that graced the dining room. It wasn't until Sabryn arrived that they learned Sabertooth had tracked it down. And she didn't come empty-handed, either. She had used Saber to locate the buyers of two paintings as well as the blue and white ginger jars that had been Bronwyn's mum's favorites.

With the house now open, cleaned, and slowly being repaired, the structure had a new lightness about it. Though it might have to do with the laughter that was an everyday occurrence between Elias and her.

A sound at the door drew Bronwyn's attention. She grinned when she found Elias leaning against the doorframe, smiling at her. He straightened and made his way to her as she stood.

"You looked deep in thought," he said as he approached.

She twisted her lips as she wound her arms around his neck at the same time he wrapped her in an embrace. "I was thinking about all the work we've done to the manor."

"There will be more soon. I've got some savings set aside that we can use."

Bronwyn grinned. He'd already offered twice, and while she wanted the house restored, she didn't want to use all of his money. "I told you I'd think about it. I got some good news today."

"Oh?" he asked, his brows raised in interest.

"The romance author I just finished the cover for has booked me for two more."

Elias's face split into a wide grin. "I never had any doubt."

Bronwyn pressed her lips together, barely able to contain her excitement. "There's more."

"Doona keep me waiting," he said as he squeezed her.

"When she revealed the cover on social media, some authors asked who had designed it. She gave them my information, and I just finished booking two of them with a third possible."

Elias's eyes widened as he grinned. "Oh, baby. That's wonderful news."

"I just sent off the invoices for the deposits. Which means I'm booked for the next two months."

He lifted her and twirled her around. "I never had any doubt. I'm so proud of you."

"If this keeps up, I can use the funds to repair the manor." She wanted to get it back to its former glory before she died. Though Bronwyn tried not to think about that day too much.

Elias gave her a quick kiss. "How do you feel?"

Something in his eyes caught her attention. "Fine. Why? You're looking at me funny."

"I had a dream last night."

It was her turn to nudge him. "About what?"

"The house." He glanced to the side, a slight frown marring his forehead. "I saw you using blood magic."

She didn't like to be reminded of it, but what was done was done. There was no changing it. "Because I did," Bronwyn replied, some of her joy dissipating.

Elias caught her gaze and smiled. "Aye. It was exactly like the first time I saw you doing it, the night Sydney attacked. Except I didna walk away this time. It was as if I were being shown something. The wood absorbed the blood."

"The magic is absorbed, but not the blood. I've seen traces of it after I've used it."

"I did, too. When you used it on the front door the night of the battle, did you wipe away the blood?"

She shook her head. "I thought you must have."

"I asked the Knights, Rhona, Balladyn, and the healers who were here. None of them saw any blood on the door."

Bronwyn frowned as she thought back to that night. "Sydney and his gang were here. They must have done it. They tried to get into the house while we were away."

"That's what I thought, too. But I doona think that's what happened."

"What *do* you think occurred?"

"The house." Elias shrugged. "The manor did more than protect us from the mist that night. In the dream, I saw us, both of us together in old age, surrounded by kids and grandkids."

Bronwyn smoothed her hands through his hair. "I had that same dream when I was unconscious."

"I think the manor is trying to tell us something, love. I think it's trying to let us know that you willna die from using blood magic."

"That…that isn't possible." She stepped back and put her hand on her forehead. "I admit, the house is special, but it can't stop something like that."

"Just like it can no' protect others from a killing mist?" Elias asked pointedly. He shrugged. "The manor was built with magic on an isle that is known for its magic. I think anything is possible."

Bronwyn didn't want to hope for the impossible.

Elias reached for her, drawing her back into his arms. "The house showed you how it stopped the mist. If anyone can get an answer from it, it's you. So, ask it."

Her heart thudded against her ribs as she slowly walked from Elias to the nearest wall and put her hand on it. She took a deep breath and released it as she closed her eyes. "Is what Elias said possible? After everything I've done?"

Nothing happened for several moments. Just as Bronwyn was about to drop her hand, a rush of love poured through her palm and into her body. Images suddenly flashed in her mind of the times she had done blood magic, each time the house absorbing the blood minutes afterward, taking the dangerous magic into its very foundation and then releasing it into the ground.

As the images faded, another emotion coursed through her, this one she knew well thanks to Elias—safety.

"Thank you," Bronwyn whispered as she opened her eyes and turned to Elias.

He wiped away her tears as he searched her face.

She nodded. "It somehow took it all, including the negativity from doing blood magic, into itself and cycled it into the ground where the magic of the isle cleansed it. The house told me I was safe."

Elias enfolded her against his chest as they both absorbed the new information and what it meant for them.

"Oh, for Pete's sake," Finn said as he came into the room and immediately stopped at the sight of them. "Tell me there will be a day I walk into a room and you two aren't locked in each other's arms."

She and Elias laughed as they turned to Finn.

The Irishman grinned as he looked between them. "Carlyle has announced that the meal is ready. You know how he is about eating when he says. You've got just enough time to enjoy it before you're off to teach the Druids, Bronwyn."

"Then we'd better not keep Carlyle waiting," Elias said as they left the parlor hand in hand.

It had become a weekly event for the Knights to dine at the manor. She and Elias had even offered them rooms while they remained on Skye. Nothing had been decided yet, but Bronwyn suspected the trio would be staying with them soon.

When she walked into the kitchen, Bronwyn was reminded of the first time she had come into the room with the Knights. She hadn't had any idea then how much her life would change with their arrival, but she wouldn't change a single minute of it.

Not only had she found the love of her life, but thanks to Rhona, she now taught the Druids everything she'd learned about *droughs* and blood magic—though she still hoped to claim Sydney's book. Her career taking off was the cherry on top. After all the heartache and loneliness, she had the family she'd always longed for, as well as a purpose she hadn't had before.

Bronwyn sat at the table in the middle of the kitchen, smiling as Carlyle and Finn bickered playfully. The informal dinners were her favorites. She'd survived the darkest time of her life, and though there would inevitably be other highs and lows, she wouldn't face them alone. Elias would always be there, as would the Knights.

And the manor.

She couldn't ask for more than that.

Inverness…

Beth opened the door to Sydney's flat and walked inside. The hospital hadn't allowed her to see him, despite multiple attempts. They claimed that he was too fragile at the moment. She wouldn't give up, though. Sydney didn't belong there, and she would get him out.

Until then, she had other things to focus on. Like getting revenge against Bronwyn. Her cousin should never have interfered in things.

Beth walked through the flat to the bedroom. She squatted and flipped back the rug before running her fingers over the wooden slats until she felt one move. She pressed the corner of it until it popped up. Beth moved it aside and put her hand into the dark space in the floor. Her fingers searched until they bumped against it.

There was a smile on her face as she pulled up the item and set it down. She carefully unfolded the oilcloth around it until she looked down at Sydney's most prized possession. The title of the book had long since faded, but it didn't need one. Its pages contained a plethora of information about the Druids—and it was how Beth had discovered her calling.

"You messed with the wrong Druid, Bronwyn," Beth said as she brought the book to her chest and hugged it.

Edie stared at Linda while fighting to remain calm. It wasn't the assistant's fault that Trevor had forgotten their lunch date and hadn't called. Edie felt every eye in the office on her. There was an undercurrent that hadn't been there before, almost as if they knew something she didn't.

She chided herself. Her mind had been going to dark places for some time now. It caused quarrels with Trevor and arguments with the children—and Edie always came out the loser. No matter how certain she was of whatever led to the fights, the kids and Trevor showed her that was wrong. From texts she was sure she had never received—and somehow missed when she checked her mobile—to practices she hadn't known about only to be shown the sheet that was posted on the fridge, nothing seemed to be going right for her.

"Thanks, Linda," Edie said and turned to leave.

"I'll tell Trevor you stopped by," the woman called after Edie.

Edie didn't acknowledge her as she left the building and got into her car. She sat there for a few moments, trying to collect herself and calm the anger that seemed to build with each day.

She was tired of the constant rows with her husband. Though she wanted to call him right then and demand to know what had happened, she stopped herself. If she did that, it would only lead to another massive argument and put more strain on their previously solid marriage.

Instead, Edie started the car and backed out. She would give herself the time it took to drive home before she texted Trevor. Yes, texting would be better. She could craft her words carefully and make sure not to come off as angry as she was.

She got three miles away when her mobile rang. Trevor's name flashed on the large screen in the car's center dash. A part of her warned her not to answer, but she accepted the call anyway.

"Hey," she said in greeting.

There was a beat of silence, and then he said, "Hey."

His voice was tight, clipped. The way it got when he was pissed. "Bad day at work?"

A sigh came through the phone. "The worst."

"I was just at the office."

"I know."

She tightened her hand on the steering wheel and decided to pull over to have this conversation. "Linda call you?"

"Aye."

Edie pulled into a nearby carpark and took the vehicle out of gear. "Why are you mad at me?"

"You made a scene. At my work."

She closed her eyes and tried to count to ten. She got to three. "You forgot our lunch date. I went to the office to get you. Yes, I was irked that you weren't there, but I didn't make any kind of scene. I calmly walked out."

"Linda said you were unkind to her."

"What?!" Edie yelled. "How many times have you complained to me about her? You know she exaggerates everything."

"I'd rather not have my staff gossiping about my wife," he snapped.

Edie swallowed her next words. They would've only propelled the argument, and she didn't want that. "Are we still meeting for lunch?"

"I think it better that we doona. I'll see you tonight. And, Edie? I hope whatever is going on with you stops soon. It's disrupting the family."

He ended the call before she could respond.

Edie yanked on the steering wheel and let out a scream of rage.

Kerry watched Edie as she made her way to her vehicle. The Druid looked like she was having a meltdown. Kerry was interested in what could bring on that kind of rage. She smiled as she climbed into her car.

She knew just where she could get that kind of gossip—and use it to her advantage.

Derbyshire, England…

Mason accompanied the movers out of the house and closed the door behind them. He stood with his hand against the entry and sighed before turning his head to the side. Ferne hadn't been herself since leaving London. He knew that she was only at the country house because he'd asked it of her.

The elders of the London Druids demanded one thing from him, and his sister needed another. He'd been walking a tightrope since their parents' deaths. Soon, he would have to pick a side. There really wasn't a choice in his mind. Family came before anything. What the elders had done to Ferne was beyond the pale.

But he had to stay there for a little longer. He had to know if their parents' plane crash had been the accident everyone claimed —or if there was more, sinister actions behind it.

He turned to the morning room and spotted Billings, the butler, out of the corner of his eye. Mason turned to the man, who stood waiting. Billings had been with the family for over twenty years. His brown hair was always neatly trimmed with gray at his temples. His dark eyes saw everything, always anticipating what anyone in the family might need. Mason had only survived the first few months after his parents' funerals because of Billings and the other household staff.

"Tea, my lord?" Billings asked.

Mason shook his head. "Not now. Though I'm sure I'll need something stronger when I'm done."

"I'll have it waiting," Billings announced and turned on his heel to walk away.

Mason ran a hand over his jaw and strode to the morning room doors. They opened without a sound. As he stepped inside, he spotted Ferne standing at one of the large windows with her arms wrapped around herself and her gaze toward the elaborate gardens. But he knew she wasn't looking at the flowers. Ferne's thoughts were on Skye and the Druids there.

"I'm not some delicate flower that will wilt," she said. Her black hair was pulled into a haphazard high ponytail with the ends brushing her shoulders.

He smiled. "One day you'll have to tell me how you know when I walk into a room."

"That's my secret," she said, a smile in her voice.

Mason walked to stand beside her and clasped his hands behind his back. They stood in silence for several minutes, each lost in thought. "How long are you staying?"

Her head swiveled to him. "How did you know?"

"The same way you know when I walk into a room." He met her green eyes and forced a smile. They both sported the dark hair and brown skin of their mixed heritage, the only difference was their eye color, with his being gray. "I don't like you going to Skye without me. If you could wait but—"

"I can't," she said over him.

He blew out a breath and faced her. "They're not going to welcome you, sis."

"I'll deal with that when I get there." She swallowed and glanced down. "You hate the London chapter as much as I do. Why do you stay? Because of Mum's position?"

He wanted to tell her everything, but he didn't have definitive proof yet. If Ferne discovered the information he had stumbled upon, she'd burn the entire London Druids to the ground. He planned to do just that, but he would be more meticulous about it.

Where Ferne allowed emotion to rule her, he had inherited his father's calculating mind. Mason wanted every one of the bastards responsible to know that he had uncovered their secret. Then, he would burn it all down.

Literally and figuratively.

But not yet. He had to know every last person who had been in on it. In order to do that, he needed proof. He was close, just not close enough.

"Mason?" Ferne called, her brows furrowed in concern.

"I'll tell you as soon as I can."

She searched his eyes. "Do I need to be worried?"

"Only as apprehensive as I am about you going to Skye."

"That isn't funny."

"I'm not jesting."

Ferne sighed and shook her head. "Then I'll stay. I can't lose you."

She was giving him what he wanted, but it didn't feel right. If Ferne didn't go, people's lives would be at stake. For him, it was just revenge. Plain and simple. And it might be better if his sister wasn't anywhere near him when it all went down. "You have to go. We both know that."

"I don't like that we're being pulled in different directions. Are you sure your business can't wait?"

"It's waited long enough."

Her gaze narrowed on him for tense moments before she nodded. "Promise you'll watch your back."

"Always. Promise you'll check in daily?"

"Promise."

He grinned, hating the way his lips protested the action. But he feared the London Druids more than he did those on Skye. Ferne would be safer there. "Let's get you packed."

Thank you for reading **SHOULDER THE SKYE!** I hope you loved Elias and Bronwyn's story as much as I loved writing it. Next in the Skye Druids series is HEART OF GLASS.

A desire that won't be denied.

BUY HEART OF GLASS NOW at
www.DonnaGrant.com

If you love the Skye Druid series, you'll love the next Dark
Universe book set in the Dragon Kings series, DRAGON
ARISEN…

You have to burn before you can rise.

BUY DRAGON ARISEN TODAY at
www.DonnaGrant.com

To find out when new books release
SIGN UP FOR MY NEWSLETTER today at
http://www.tinyurl.com/DonnaGrantNews.

Join my Facebook group, Donna Grant Groupies, for exclusive
giveaways and sneak peeks of future books.

Keep reading for an peek of HEART OF GLASS and a glimpse
at DRAGON ARISEN…

ensnaring his at the same time. With their enemies closing in, Alasdair will do anything to protect the woman he's destined to love.

If there's one thing Lotti knows, it's that she's a danger to others. She keeps her distance. Always. But all that changes when she lands in a difficult situation…with a gorgeous, seductive man. Every choice somehow leads her straight back to Alasdair. She can't ignore his sexual magnetism or the undeniable desire between them. Their journey unravels everything she knew about herself to reveal a carefully constructed fallacy. Yet, she discovers an inner strength she didn't know she had. But is her yearning for Alasdair worth the risk for them both?

BUY DRAGON ARISEN TODAY at
www.DonnaGrant.com

ABOUT THE AUTHOR

New York Times and *USA Today* bestselling author Donna Grant® has been praised for her "totally addictive" and "unique and sensual" stories.

She's written more than one hundred novels spanning multiple genres of romance including the bestselling Dragon Kings® series that features a thrilling combination of Druids, Fae, and immortal Highlanders who are dark, dangerous, and irresistible. She lives in Texas with her dog and a cat.

www.DonnaGrant.com
www.MotherofDragonsBooks.com

facebook.com/AuthorDonnaGrant
instagram.com/dgauthor
bookbub.com/authors/donna-grant
amazon.com/Donna-Grant/e/B00279DJGE
pinterest.com/donnagrant1

www.ingramcontent.com/pod-product-compliance
Lightning Source LLC
Chambersburg PA
CBHW011218190726
48287CB00008B/2659